**Also by Clarence E. Mulford from
Tom Doherty Associates**

Bar-20
Bar-20 Days
Bar-20 Three
Buck Peters, Ranchman
The Coming of Cassidy
The Coming of Cassidy and Bar-20 (omnibus)
Hopalong Cassidy
Hopalong Cassidy and Bar-20 Days (omnibus)
Johnny Nelson
The Man from Bar-20
Tex
Wild Western Days (omnibus)

The Man from Bar-20

◆

Johnny Nelson

◆

Clarence E. Mulford

A Tom Doherty Associates Book / New York

THE MAN FROM BAR-20 AND JOHNNY NELSON

The Man From Bar-20 was originally published in 1918. *Johnny Nelson* was originally published in 1920.

A Forge Book
Published by Tom Doherty Associates, LLC
175 Fifth Avenue
New York, NY 10010

www.tor-forge.com

Forge® is a registered trademark of Tom Doherty Associates, LLC.

ISBN 978-0-7653-7778-4

Forge books may be purchased for educational, business, or promotional use. For information on bulk purchases, please contact Macmillan Corporate and Premium Sales Department at 1-800-221-7945, extension 5442, or write specialmarkets@macmillan.com.

First Mass Market Edition: November 2014

Printed in the United States of America

0 9 8 7 6 5 4 3 2 1

Contents

The Man from Bar-20

◆

I

◆

A Stranger Comes to Hastings

A horseman rode slowly out of a draw and up a steep, lava-covered ridge, singing "The Cowboy's Lament," to the disgust of his horse, which suddenly arched its back and stopped the song in the twenty-ninth verse.

"Dearly Beloved," grinned the rider, after he had quelled the trouble, "yore protest is heeded. 'Th' Lament' ceases, instanter; an' while you crop some of that grass, I'll look around and observe th' scenery, which shore is scrambled. Now, them two buttes over there," leaning forward to look around a clump of brush, "if they ain't twins, I'll eat—"

He ducked and dismounted in one swift movement to the vengeful tune of a screaming bullet over his head, slapped the horse and jerked his rifle from its scabbard. As the horse leaped down the slope of the ridge there was no sign of any living thing to be seen on the trail. A bush rustled near the edge of a draw, a peeved voice softly cursed the cacti and Mexican locust; and a few minutes later the shadow of a black lava bowlder grew suddenly fatter on one side. The cause of this sudden shadow growth lay prone under the bulging side of the great rock, peering out intently between two large stones; and flaming curiosity consumed his soul. A stranger in a strange land, who rode innocently along a free trail and minded his own business, merited no such a welcome as this. His promptness of action and the blind luck in that bending forward at the right instant were all that saved his life; and his celerity of movement spoke well for his reflexes, for he had found himself fattening the shadow of the bowlder almost before he had fully realized the pressing need for it.

Minute after minute passed before his searching eyes detected anything concerned with the unpleasant episode, and then he sensed rather than saw a slight movement on the mottled, bowlder-strewn slope of a distant butte. A bush moved gently, and that was all.

To cross the intervening chaos of rocks and brush, pastures and draws would take him an hour if it were done as caution dictated, and by that time the chase would be useless. So he waited until the sun was two hours higher, pleasantly anticipating a stealthy reconnaissance by his unknown enemy to observe the dead. He had dropped into high grass and brush when he left the saddle and there was no way that the marked man could be certain of the results of his shot except by closer examination. But the man in ambush had no curiosity, to his target's regret; and the target, despairing of being honored by a visit, finally gave up the vigil. After a silent interval a soft whistle from a thicket, well back in a draw, caused the grazing horse to lift his head, throw its ears forward and walk sedately toward the sound.

"Dearly Beloved," said a low voice from the thicket, "come closer. That was a two-laigged skunk, an' his eyes are good. Likewise he is one plumb fine shot."

Ever since he had listened to the marriage ceremony which had subjugated his friend Hopalong for the rest of that man's natural life, the phrase "Dearly Beloved" had stuck in his memory; and in his use of it the words took the place of humorous profanity.

Mounting, he rode on again, but kept off all skylines, favored the rough going away from the trail, and passed to the eastward of all the obstructions he met; and his keen eyes darted from point to point unceasingly, not giving up their scrutiny of the surroundings until he saw in the distance a little town, which he knew was Hastings.

In the little cow-town of Hastings the afternoon sun drove the shadows of the few buildings farther afield and pitilessly searched out every defect in the cheap and hastily constructed frame buildings, showed the hair-line cracks in the few adobes, where an occasional frost worked insidious damage to the clay, and drew out sticky, pungent beads of rosin from the sun-bleached and checked pine boards of the two-story front of the one-story building owned and occupied by "Pop" Hayes, proprietor of one of the three saloons in the town. The two-story front of Pop's building displayed two windows painted on the warped boards too close to the upper edge, the panes a faded blue, where gummy pine knots had not stained them yellow; and they were framed by sashes of a hideous red.

Inside the building Pop dozed in his favorite position, his feet crossed on a shaky pine table and his chair tipped back against the wall. Slow hoof-beats, muffled by the sand, sounded outside, followed by the sudden, faint jingling of spurs, the sharp creak of saddle gear and the soft thud of feet on the ground. Pop's eyes opened and he blinked at the bright rectangle of sunny street framed by his doorway, where a man loomed up blackly, and slowly entered the room.

"Howd'y, Logan," grunted Pop, sighing. His feet scraped from the table and thumped solidly on the floor in time with the thud of the chair legs, and he slowly arose, yawning and sighing wearily while he waited to see which side of the room would be favored by the newcomer. Pop disliked being disturbed, for by nature he was one who craved rest, and he could only sleep all night and most of the day. Rubbing the sleep out of his eyes he yawned again and looked more closely at the stranger, a quick look of surprise flashing across his face. Blinking rapidly he looked again and muttered something to himself.

The newcomer turned his back to the bar, took two long steps and peered into the battered showcase on the other side of the room, where a miscellaneous collection of merchandise, flyspecked and dusty, lay piled up in cheerful disorder under the cracked and grimy glass. Staring up at him was a roughly scrawled warning, in faded ink on yellowed paper: "Lean on yourself." The collection showed Mexican holsters, army holsters, holsters with the Lone Star; straps, buckles, bone rings, star-headed tacks, spurs, buttons, needles, thread, knives; two heavy Colts revolvers, piles of cartridges in boxes, a pair of mother-of-pearl butt plates showing the head of a long-horned steer; pipes, tobacco of both kinds, dice, playing cards, harmonicas, cigars so dried out that they threatened to crumble at a touch; a patented gun-sight with Wild Bill Hickok's picture on the card which held it; oil, corkscrews, loose shot and bullets; empty shells, primers, reloading tools; bar lead, bullet molds—all crowded together as they had been left after many pawings-over. Pop was wont to fretfully damn the case and demand, peevishly, to know why "it" was always the very last thing he could find. Often, upon these occasions, he threatened to "get at it" the very first chance that he had; but his threats were harmless.

The stranger tapped on the glass. "Gimme that box of .45's," he remarked, pointing. "No, no; not that one. This *new* box. I'm shore particular about little things like that."

Pop reluctantly obeyed. "Why, just th' other day I found a box of ca'tridges I had for eleven years; an' they was better'n them that they sells nowadays. That's one thing that don't spoil." He looked up with shrewdly appraising eyes. "At fust glance I thought you was Logan. You shore looks a heap like him: dead image," he said.

"Yes? Dead image?" responded the stranger, his voice betraying nothing more than a polite, idle curiosity; but his mind flashed back to the trail. "Hum. He must have a lot of friends if he looks like me," he smiled quizzically.

Pop grinned: "Well, he's got some as is; an' some as ain't," he replied knowingly. "An' lemme tell you they both runs true to form. You don't have to copper no bets on either bunch, not a-tall."

"Sheriff, or marshal?" inquired the stranger, turning to the bar. "It's plenty hot an' dusty," he averred. "You have a life-saver with me."

"Might as well, I reckon," said Pop, shuffling across the room with a sudden show of animation, "though my life ain't exactly in danger. Nope; he ain't no sheriff, *or* marshall. We ain't got none, 'though I ain't sayin' we couldn't keep one tolerable busy while he lived. I've thought some of gettin' th' boys together to elect me sheriff; an' cussed if I wouldn't 'a' done it, too, if it wasn't for th' ridin'."

"Ridin'?" inquired the stranger with polite interest.

"It shakes a man up so; an' I allus feels sorry for th' hoss," explained the proprietor.

The stranger's facial training at the great American game was all that saved him from committing a breach of etiquette. "Huh! Reckon it does shake a man up," he admitted. "An' I never thought about th' cayuse; no, sir; not till this minute. Any ranches in this country?"

"Shore; lots of 'em. You lookin' for work?"

"Yes; I reckon so," answered the stranger.

"Well, if you don't look out sharp you'll shore find some."

"A man's got to eat more or less regular; an' cow-punchers ain't no exception," replied the stranger, his soft drawl in keeping with his slow, graceful movements.

Pop, shrewd reader of men that he was, suspected that neither of those characteristics was a true index to the man's real nature. There was an indefinable something which belied the smile—the eyes, perhaps, steel blue, un-wavering, inscrutable; or a latent incisiveness crouching just beyond reach; and there was a sureness and smoothness and minimum of effort in the movements which vaguely reminded Pop of a mountain lion he once had trailed and killed. He was in the presence of a dynamic personality which baffled and disturbed him; and the two plain, heavy Colts resting in open-top holsters, well down on the stranger's thighs, where his swinging hands brushed the well-worn butts, were signs which even the most stupid frontiersman could hardly overlook. Significant, too, was the fact that the holsters were securely tied by rawhide thongs, at their lower ends, to the leather chaps, this to hold them down when the guns were drawn out. To the initiated the signs proclaimed a gunman, a two-gun man, which was worse; and a red flag would have had no more meaning.

"Well," drawled Pop, smiling amiably, "as to work, I reckon you can find it if you knows it when you sees it; an' don't close yore eyes. I'll deal 'em face up, an' you can take yore choice," he offered, wiping his lips on the edge of the bar towel, both the action and the towel itself being

vociferously described by his saddle-sitting friends as af-
fections, for everybody knew that a sleeve or the back
of a hand was the natural thing. "Now, there's th' Circle S;
but I dunno as they needs any more men. They could get
along with less if them they has would work. Smith, of th'
Long T, over in th' southwest, could easy use more men;
but he's so close an' allfired penurious that I dunno as
he'd favor th' idear. He's a reg'lar genius for savin' money,
Smith is. He once saved a dollar out of three cents, an'
borrowed them of me to start with. Then there's th' CL,
over east in th' Deepwater Valley. You might get something there; an' Logan's a nice man to work for, for a few
days. He allus gives his men at least two hours sleep a night,
averagin' it up; but somehow they're real cheerful about it,
an' they all swears by him 'stead of at him. Reckon mebby
it's th' wages he pays. He's got th' best outfit of th' three.
But, lemme tell you, it's a right lively place, th' CL; an'
you don't have to copper *that,* neither. Th' cards is all spread
out in front of you—take yore choice an' foller yore nat'ral
bend."

"Logan," mused the stranger. "Didn't you say something
about him before?" he asked curiously.

"I did," grunted Pop. "You've got a mem'ry near as bad
as Ol' Hiram Jones. Hiram, he once—"

"I thought so," interposed the cow-puncher hastily.
"What kind of a ranch is th' CL?"

"Well, it was th' fust to locate in these parts, an' had its
pick; an', nat'rally, it picked th' valley of th' Deepwater.
Funny Logan ain't found no way to make th' river work;
it wouldn't have to sleep at all, 'cept once in a while in th'
winter, when it freezes over for a spell. It'd be a total loss
then; mebby that's why he ain't never tried.

"But takin' a second holt," he continued, frowning with
deep thought; "I dunno as I'd work for him, if I was you.

You looks too much like him; an' you got a long life of piety an' bad whiskey ahead of you, mebby. An', come to think of it, I dunno as I'd stay very long around these parts, neither; an' for th' same reason. Now you have a drink with me. It shore is th' hottest spring I've seen in fifty year," he remarked, thereby quoting himself for about that period of time. Each succeeding spring and summer was to him hotter than any which had gone before, which had moved Billy Atwood to remark that if Pop only lived long enough he would find hell a cool place, by comparison, when he eventually arrived there.

"Sic 'em, Towser!" shrilled a falsetto voice from somewhere. "I'll eat his black heart!" Then followed whistling, clucking, and a string of expletives classical in its completeness. "Andy wants a drink! Quick!"

A green object dropped past the stranger's face, thumped solidly on the pine bar, hooked a vicious-looking beak on the edge of the counter, and swore luridly as its crafty nip missed the stranger's thumb.

The puncher swiftly bent his sinewy forefinger, touched it with his thumb, and let it snap forward. The parrot got it on an eye and staggered, squawking a protest.

Pop was surprised and disappointed, for most strangers showed some signs of being startled, and often bought the drinks to further prove that the joke was on them. This capable young man carelessly dropped his great sombrero over Andrew Jackson and went right on talking as though nothing unusual had occurred. It appeared that the bird was also surprised and disappointed. The great hat heaved and rocked, bobbed forward, backward, and sideways, and then slid jerkily along the bar, its hidden locomotive force too deeply buried in thought and darkness to utter even a single curse. Reaching the edge of the bar the big hat pushed out over it, teetered a moment and then fell to the floor, where Andrew Jackson, recovering his breath and vocabulary at the same instant, filled the room with shrill and clamorous profanity.

The conversation finished to his satisfaction, the stranger glanced down at his boot, where the ruffled bird was delivering tentative frontal and flank attacks upon the glittering, sharp-toothed spur, whose revolving rowel had the better of the argument. Andrew sensed the movement, sidestepped clumsily and cocked an evil eye upward.

"You should 'a' taught him to swear in th' deaf an' dumb alphabet," commented the puncher, grinning at the bird's gravity. "Does he drink?" he asked.

"Try him, an' see," suggested Pop, chuckling. He reached for a bottle and clucked loudly.

Andrew shook himself energetically, and then proceeded to go up the puncher's chaps by making diligent use of beak and claws. Reaching the low-hung belt, he hooked his claws into it and then looked evilly and suspiciously at the strange, suddenly extended forefinger. Deciding to forego hostilities, he swung himself upon it and was slowly lifted up to the bar.

Pop was disappointed again, for it was the bird's invariable custom to deftly remove a portion of strange forefingers so trustingly offered. He could crack nuts in his crooked beak. Andy shook himself violently, craned his neck and hastened to bend it over the rim of the glass.

The stranger watched him in frank disgust and shrugged his shoulders eloquently. "So all you could teach him was vile cuss words an' to like whiskey, huh?" he muttered. "He's got less sense than I thought he had," he growled, and, turning abruptly, went swiftly out to his horse.

Pop stared after him angrily and slapped the bird savagely. Emptying the liquor upon the floor, he shuffled quickly to the door and shook his fist at the departing horseman.

"Don't you tell Logan that *I* sent you!" he shouted belligerently.

The stranger turned in his saddle, grinning cheerfully, and favored his late host with a well-known, two-handed nose signal. Then he slapped the black horse and shot down the street without another backward glance.

Pop, arms akimbo, watched him sweep out of sight around a bend.

"Huh!" he snorted. "Wonder what yo're doin' down here? Galivantin' around th' country, insultin' honest, hard-workin' folks, an' wearin' two guns, low down an' tied! I reckon when you learns th' lay of th' country, if you stays long enough, you'll wind up by joinin' that gang up in th' Twin Buttes country. I allus like to see triggers on six-shooters, *I* do." He had not noticed the triggers, but that was no bar to his healthy imagination. Shuffling back to his seat, he watched the indignant Andy pecking at a wet spot on the floor.

"So you didn't chaw his finger, huh?" he demanded, in open and frank admiration of the bird's astuteness. "Strikes me you got a hull lot of wisdom, my boy. Some folks says a bird ain't got no brains; but lemme tell you that you've got a danged good instinct."

II

♦

A Question of Identity

Meanwhile the stranger was loping steadily eastward, and he arrived at the corral of the CL ranch before sundown, nodding pleasantly to the man who emerged from it: "Howd'y," he said. "I'm lookin' for Logan."

The CL man casually let his right hand lay loosely near the butt of his Colt: "Howd'y," he nodded. "Yo're lookin' right at him."

"Do you need any more punchers?" asked the stranger.

"H'm," muttered the foreman. "Might use one. If it's you, we'll talk money on pay-day. I'll know more about you then."

A puncher, passing the corral, noticed the two guns, frowned slightly and entered the enclosure, and leaned alertly against the palisade, where a crack between two logs served him as a loophole.

The two-gun man laughed with genuine enjoyment at the foreman's way of hiring men. "That's fair," he replied; "but what's th' high an' low figgers? I like to know th' limit of any game I sets in."

Logan shrugged his shoulders. "Forty is th' lowest I'd offer a man; an' he wouldn't draw that more'n a month. Any man as ain't worth more is in our way. It's a waste of grub to feed him. Th' sky is th' high limit—but you've got to work like hell to pass th' clouds."

"I'm some balloon," laughed the stranger. "Where's the grub shack?"

"Hold on, young man! We ain't got that far, yet. Where

are you from, an' what have you been doin' with yore sweet young life?"

The stranger's face grew grave and his eyes narrowed a trifle.

"Some folks allow that's a leadin' question. It ain't polite."

"I allow that, too. An' I'm aimin' to make it a leadin' question, 'though I ain't lackin' in politeness, nor tryin' to rile you. You don't have to answer. Th' wide world, full of jobs, is all around you."

The newcomer regarded him calmly for a moment, and suddenly smiled.

"Yore gall is refreshin'," he grinned. "I'm from th' Bar-20, Texas. I'm five feet ten; weigh a hundred an' sixty; blue eyes, brown hair; single an' sober, now an' always. I writes left-handed; eat an' shoot with both; wears pants, smokes tobacco, an' I'm as handy a cow-puncher as ever threw a rope. Oh, yes; modesty is one of my glarin' faults; you might say my only glarin' fault. Some people call me 'Dearly Beloved'; others, other things; but I answer to any old handle at grub pile. My name is Johnny Nelson an' I never had no other, 'cept 'Kid,' to my friends. I'm thirty years old, minus some. An'—oh, yes; I'm from th' Tin Cup, Montanny. I get things twisted at times, an' this shore looks like one of 'em."

"Of course," grunted Logan, his eyes twinkling. "That's easy. Th' two ranches, bein' so close together, would bother a man. Sorta wander off one onto th' other, an' have to stop to think which one yo're workin' for. They should mark th' boundaries plainer—or put up a fence."

Johnny flushed. "I allus say Bar-20 when I speaks offhand an' have more on my mind than my hair. That man in th' corral divides my attention. He flusters me. You see, I was cussed near born on th' old Bar-20—worked there ever since I was a boy. That crack in th' wall is big enough for two men to use. Thank you, friend: you near scared me to death," he chuckled as the suspicious watcher emerged and started for the bunk-house.

"You look so much like th' boss, I couldn't help watchin' you," grinned the puncher over his shoulder.

Logan grunted something, and then nodded at the stranger.

"Cut it loose," he encouraged. "I don't get a chance like this every day, my observant friend. I allus reckoned I could cover ground purty well, but I'll be hanged if I can spread myself so I can work in Texas an' Montanny at th' same time. You got me beat from soda to hock. Yo're goin' to be a real valuable man, which I can see plain. Comin' down to cases, you ain't really a cow-puncher; yo're a whole cussed outfit, barin' th' chuck waggin an' th' cook. I have great hopes for you. Tell me about it."

Johnny swung a leg over the pommel and smiled down at the man who was grinning up at him.

"Of course," he replied, "it ain't none of yore business, which we both admits. We just can't do any business on any other understandin'. But I waives that: an' here goes.

"I worked with the Bar-20 till Buck went up to run th' Tin Cup. Cow-thieves kept him so busy that our new foreman went up to help him. He stayed there. Red got lonesome for Hoppy, and shore follered. Skinny was lost without th' pair of 'em, so he up an' follered Red. Lanky, missin' Skinny, got plumb restless an' takes th' trail a month later. Then a railroad crosses our ranch an' begins layin' out two towns, so Pete gets on his hind laigs, licks a section boss, an' chases after Lanky. I'm gettin' lonesomer and lonesomer all th' time, but I manages to stick on th' job by pullin' leather, because I was drawin' down a foreman's pay. That ranch had five foremen in three months; an' they was all good ones, 'cept, mebby, me. But when I saw barbed wire on th' sidin', fence posts along th' right of way, sheep on th' hills, an' plows plumb ruinin' good grass land, I hunts up that same section boss, licks him again in mem'ry of Pete, packed my war bag, an' loped north after Pete. Th' old ranch has gone plumb to hell!"

Logan, a scowl on his face, rubbed the butt of his Colt and swore softly. "It'll be that way all over th' range, some day. Go on."

"Well, up on th' Tin Cup, Buck got married. Hoppy had been before he left Texas. Tex Ewalt's gettin' th' disease now. He quit drinkin', card playin', an' most everything worth doin'. He ain't fit company for a sheep no more. Not knowing he was framin' up th' play, I loafed along an' didn't propose quick enough. That's once more he saved my life. Th' air's plumb full of matrimony on th' Tin Cup. There was two black-eyed sisters in Twin River—Lanky takes one an' Skinny th' other. They tossed for choice. Pete, who was matrimony galled, raised such a ruction at th' doin's that there just wasn't no livin' with him. His disposition was full of sand cracks, an' he'd ruther fight than eat. We pulled off a couple of hummers, me an' him.

"Every time I'd try to get some of my friends to go to town for a regular, old time, quiet evenin' I found I didn't have no friends left; an' th' wimmin all joined hands an' made me feel like a brand-blotter. I was awful popular, *I* was! Ever try to argue with a bunch of wimmin? It's like a dicky bird chirpin' in a cyclone; he can't even hear hisself!

"We had a cook once, on th' Bar-20, that would run an' grab a gun if he saw a coyote ten miles away. That's th' way they acted about me, all but Mary, who is Mrs. Hop-along. She had th' idea she could make me all over again; an' I wouldn't a-cared if she hadn't kept tryin' all th' time. At first all my ex-friends would sneak around an' sort of apologize to me for th' way their wives acted; an' then, damned if they didn't get to sidin' in with th' wives! Whether I wandered into sight th' wimmin would cluck to their worse halves, an' scold me like I was a chicken hawk. An' I had lots of advice, too. It was just like my shadow, only it worked nights, too. Nobody called me 'Kid' or 'Johnny' no more. Them days was past. I was *that* Johnny Nelson: know what I mean?

"Red did sneak off to town with me twice—an' drank ginger-ale, an' acted about as free an' happy as a calf with a red-hot old brandin' iron over his flank. He wouldn't play faro because he only had two dollars, an' reckoned he might need it for somethin' before payday come round again. That was on payday, too! An' that was Red, *Red Connors!* Great polecats! Why, there was a time when Red—oh, what's th' use!

"Hopalong—you call him that now when his wife's around!—he was something on some board, or something; an' he said he had to set a good example. Wouldn't even play penny ante! Think of it! There was a time when a camel, with all his stummicks, an' a Gatlin' gun on his back, couldn't a follered th' example *he* set. I was just as happy as a bobcat in a trap—an' about as peaceful. There wasn't nothin' I could do, if I stayed up there, but get married; an' that was like hangin' myself to keep from gettin' shot. Then, one day, Mrs. Hopalong caught me learnin' William, Junior, how to chew tobacco. As if a five-year-old kid hadn't ought to get some manly habits! An', say! You ought to see that kid! If he won't bust his daddy's records for hell raisin' I miss my guess; unless they plumb spoils him in th' bringin' up. Well, she caught me learnin' him; but like th' boundin' jack rabbit I'm hard to catch. An' here I am."

Logan's grin threatened his ears. "I'm glad of it," he laughed. "There's something in yore face I like—mebby it's th' tobacco. Thanks; I will; I'm all out of it right now. How did you come to pick us out to land on? Pop recommend us to you?"

"Now don't blame me for that," rejoined Johnny. "Anyhow, he took it back later. As to stoppin' in this country, th' idea suddenly whizzed my way at them twin buttes north of town. I like this range. Things sort of start themselves, an' there's music in th' air. It reminds me of th' Bar-20, in th' old days. A man won't grow lazy down here; he'll keep jumpin'. An' I found a trace of lead at that funny-lookin' ridge east of them freak buttes; but I couldn't find where it come from. If I had, I'd 'a' salted th' mine with a Sharp's Special. You see, I'm ambidextrous—ain't that a snorter of a word?—an' when I ain't punchin' cows with one hand, I'm prospectin' with th' other. Somebody down here is plumb careless with his gun—an' he's got a good gun, too. He's too cussed familiar on short acquaintance. But it's too bad I look like you, 'though that's why I'm offerin' you my valuable services."

"I reckon it's a cross I got to stagger under," replied Logan, the smile gone from his face; "but I'll try to live it down. An' somehow my trusting nature leans toward you, though it shouldn't. Yo're a two-gun man, which acts like yeast in th' suspicious mind. I've seen 'em before; an' you looks most disconcertin' capable. Then you says Bar-20, an' Hopalong, an' Red Connors, an' th' others. You talk like you knew 'em intimate. I've heard of 'em, all of 'em. Like th' moon, you shine in reflected light. I've heard of you, too; I'm surprised you ain't in jail. Now then: If you are *that* Johnny Nelson, of *that* outfit, an' you can prove it, I yearns to weep on yore bosom; if you ain't, then I'll weep on yore grave. Th' question of identity is a ticklish one. It makes me that nervous I want to look under th' bed. As a two-gun man, unknown, yo're about as welcome on this ranch, right now, as a hydrophoby skunk; but as Johnny Nelson, of that old Bar-20, yo're worth fifty a month to me, as a starter, with ten dollars extra for each six-gun. But I've just simply got to have proof about who you are, an' where you come from. Let's pause for an inspiration."

Johnny grinned. "I don't blame you; for I've had a sample of something already. An' I've got a tail holt on an inspiration. You hunt up that pen you've had since Adam was a boy; find th' ink that you put away last summer so you'd know where it was when you wanted it in a hurry; an' then, in thirty minutes' hard labor you'll have something like this:

"'Mr. William Cassidy, Senior, Tin Cup, Twin Rivers, Montanny: Dear Sir: A nice lookin' young man wants to take seventy dollars a month away from me, as a starter. His undershirt is red, with th' initials "WC" worked near th' top buttonhole in pretty blue silk thread. He wants Pete to send him that eight dollars that Pete borrowed to buy William, Junior, a .22 rifle to bust windows with. Tell Red his pants wear well. Does William, Junior, chew tobacco? He has been shot at already. What is this young man's name? Did he work on th' old Bar-20 with you? Yours truly, Logan.'

"Exhibit I: Th' red undershirt. Hoppy has even more of 'em than Buck, 'though Rose is comin' along fast. Mary branded 'em all so she could pick 'em out of th' wash. It helped me pick this one off th' clothesline, because me an' Hoppy wears th' same size. Exhibit 2: A scab on my off ear. William, Junior, was shootin' at a calf an' I stopped him. He's a spunky little cuss, all right; but they'll spoil him yet. An' Pete never did have any sense, anyhow. Th' poor kid is shootin' blanks now, an' blamin' it on th' gun. An' it was a mean trick, too. That hit about th' tobacco will get under Hoppy's scalp—he'll answer right quick. You might say to tell William, Junior, that I ain't forgot my promise, an' that I'll send him a shotgun just as soon as he gets big enough to tote it around."

"I'll shore send it," laughed Logan, whose imagination was running wild. "But outside of the identity you suits me right down to the ground. If Hopalong Cassidy says yo're all right I'll back you to my last dollar. You mentioned hearin' music in th' air. It was a tunin' up. Will you stay for th' dance?"

"Sweet bells of joy!" exclaimed Johnny, leaving the saddle as though shot out by a spring. "From wimmin', barb wire, sheep an' railroad towns, to this! I can go to town with th' boys once more! I can cuss out loud an' swagger around regardless! An' some mangey gent is careless with his gun! You can lose me just as easy as a cow can lose a tick. I feel right at home."

"All right, then. Strip off yore saddle and turn that fine cayuse loose," replied Logan, chuckling. He hoped that he might be able to coax the new man to swap horses. "Th' cook's callin' his hogs, so let's go feed."

III

♦

The Wisdom of the Frogs

For two weeks Johnny rode range with the outfit and got familiar with the ranch. There was one discovery which puzzled him and seemed to offer an explanation for the shot on the trail: He had found the ruins of a burned homestead on the northern end of the ranch and he guessed that it had been used by "nesters;" and the evicted squatters might have mistaken him for Logan. His thoughts constantly turned to the man who had shot at him, and to the country around Twin Buttes; and often he sat for minutes, stiffly erect in his saddle, staring at the two great buttes, eager to explore the country surrounding them and to pay his debt.

From where he rode, facing westward, he could see the Deepwater, cold at all seasons of the year. Flowing swiftly, it gurgled and swished around bowlders of lava and granite and could be forded in but one place in thirty miles, where it spread out over a rocky, submerged plateau on the trail between the CL and Hastings, and where it grew turbulent and frothy with wrath as it poured over the up-thrust ledges. Along its eastern bank lay the ranch, in the valley of the Deepwater, and beyond it a short distance stood the Barrier, following it mile after mile and curving as it curved.

The Barrier, well named, was a great ledge of limestone, up-flung like a wall, sheer, smooth and only occasionally broken by narrow crevices which ran far back and sloped gradually upward, rock-strewn, damp, cool, and wild. It stretched for miles to Johnny's right and left, a wall between the wild tumble of the buttes and the smooth, gently rolling, fertile plain, which, beginning at the river, swept far to the eastward behind him, where it eventually became lost in the desert wastes. On one side of the rampart lay the scurrying river and the valley of the Deepwater, rolling, sparsely timbered and heavily grassed, placid, peaceful, restful; on the other, seeming to leap against the horizon, lay the grandeur of chaos, wild and forbidding.

Highest above all that jagged western skyline, shouldering up above all other buttes and plateaus, Twin Buttes peremptorily challenged attention. Remarkably alike from all sides, when viewed from the CL ranch house they seemed to have been cast in the same mold; and the two towering, steep-sided masses with their different colored strata stood high above the Barrier and the chaos behind it like concrete examples of eternity.

Twin Buttes were the lords of their realm, and what a realm it was! Around them for miles great buttes rose solidly upward, naked on their abrupt sides except for an occasional, straggling bush or dwarfed pine or fir which here and there held precarious footholds in cracks and crevices or on the more secure placement of a ledge. Deep draws choked with brush lay between the more rolling hills along the eastern edge of the watershed where the Barrier stood on guard, and rich patches of heavy grass found the needed moisture in them. On the slopes of the hills were great forests of yellow pine, a straggling growth of fir crowning their tops. Farther west, where the massive buttes reared aloft, the deep canyons were of two kinds. The first, wide, with sloping banks of detritus, were covered with pine forests and torn with draws; the second, steep-walled, were great, narrow chasms of wind- and water-swept rock, bare and awe inspiring. They sloped upward to the backbone of the watershed and had humble beginnings in shallow, basin-like arroyos, which gradually became boxes in the rock formation as the level sloped downward.

But the chaos stopped at the Barrier, which marked the breaking of stratum upon stratum of the earth's crust. Ages ago there had been a mighty struggle here between titanic forces. To the west the earth's crust, battered into buttes, canyons, draws, and great plateaus, had held out with a granite stubbornness and strength, defying the seething powers below it; but the limestone and the sandstone, weaker brothers, betrayed by the treachery of the shales, had given under the great strain and parted. The western portion had held its own; but the eastern section had dropped down into the heaving turmoil and formed the floor of the valley of the Deepwater. And as if in compensation, the winds of the ages, still battling with the stubborn buttes, had robbed them of soil and deposited it in the valley.

One evening, when Johnny rode in for supper, Logan met him at the corral and held out his hand.

"Shake, Nelson," he smiled. "Crosby went to town today and brought me a letter from th' Tin Cup. After you have fed up, come around to my room an' see me. I want to hold a right lively pow-wow with you."

"Shore enough!" laughed Johnny, an expectant grin on his face. "Bet he laid me out from soda to hock, tail to bit, th' old pirate!"

"Well, you've got a terrible reputation, young man. Go an' feed."

Johnny was the first at the table that night, and the first away from it by a wide margin. Rolling a cigarette, he lit it and hastened to Logan's quarters, where he found the foreman contentedly smoking.

"Come in an' set down," invited the foreman. "We're

goin' to do a lot of talkin'; it's due to be a long session. There's th' letter."

Johnny read it:

"Mr. John C. Logan. Dear Sir: I take my pen in hand to answer your letter of recent date. Pete paid Red the 8 dollars to even up for the pants, but nobody paid me for the shirt. Ask him why he took the best one. William, Junior, hates tobacco. We was scared hed die. He swears most suspicious like Johnny Nelson. I hid the gun in the storeroom. It cost me $12 damages the first week, besides a calf. Can you use Pete Wilson? I'll pay 1/2 his wages the first 6 months. I'd ruther have boils than him. He's worse since Johnny left. Don't let Johnny come north again, and God have mercy on your soul. He's easy worth $70, if you are in trouble. If you ain't in trouble he'll get you there. Excuse pensil. Yours truly, Wm. Cassidy, Senior. P.S. His old job is waiting for him and he can have the shirt. It must be near wore out anyhow. Tell him it only costs 2 cents to write me a letter, but I bet hell freezes before I get one. William, Junior, raised the devil when he missed Johnny. Yes, he worked on the Bar-20. If he sends the kid a shotgun, I'll come down and bust his neck. Excuse pensil."

Johnny looked steadily out of the door, ashamed to let Logan see his face, for homesickness is no respecter of age. He gulped and felt like a sick calf. Logan smiled at him through the gloom and chuckled, and at the sound the puncher stiffened and turned around with a fine attempt at indifference.

The foreman nodded at the letter. "Keep it if you wants. They must be a purty fine bunch, them fellers. I never knowed any of 'em, but I've heard a lot about 'em. 'Youbet'

Somes used to drop in here once in a while, an' he knowed 'em all. I ain't seen Youbet for quite a spell now."

Johnny managed to relax his throat. "Finest outfit that ever wore pants," he blurted. "Youbet's dead. Went out fightin' seven sheep-herders in a saloon, but he got three of 'em. Hoppy met up with two of th' others th' next summer an' had words with 'em. Th' other two are still livin', I reckon." He thought for a moment and growled: "It's th' wimmin that done it. You wouldn't believe how that crowd has changed! Damn it, why can't a man keep his friends?"

The foreman puffed slowly and made no answer beyond a grunt of understanding. Johnny folded the letter carefully and put it in his pocket. "What's th' cow business comin' to, anyhow?" he demanded. "Wimmin, railroads, towns, sheep, wire—" he despaired of words and glared at the inoffensive corral.

"An' rustlers," added Logan.

"They're only an incident," retorted Johnny. "They can be licked, like a disease; but th' others—oh, what's th' use!"

"You're right," replied Logan; "but it's the rustlers that have got me worried. I ain't thinkin' about th' others very much, yet."

Johnny turned like a flash. He wanted action, action that would take his thoughts into other channels. The times were out of joint and he wanted something upon which to vent his spleen. He had been waiting for that word to come from Logan, waiting for days. And he had a score of his own to pay, as well.

"Rustlers!" he exulted. "I knowed it! I've knowed it for a week, an' I'm tired of ridin' around like a cussed fool. I know th' job *I* want! What about 'em?"

Logan closed the door by a push of his foot, refilled and lit his pipe, and for two hours the only light the room knew was the soft glow of the pipe and the firey ends of the puncher's cigarettes, while Logan unfolded his troubles to eager ears. The cook sang in the kitchen as he wrestled his dishes and pans, and then the noise died out. Laughter and words and the thumping of knuckles on a card table came from the bunkroom, and grew silent. A gray coyote slid around the corral, sniffing suspiciously, and at some faint noise faded into the twilight, and from a distant rise howled mournfully at the moon. From a little pond in the corral came the deep-throated warning of the frogs, endless, insistent, untiring: "Go 'round! Go 'round! Knee deep! Knee deep! Go 'round! Go 'round! Go 'round!"

The soft murmur of voices in the foreman's room suddenly ceased, and a chair scraped over the sandy floor. The door creaked a protest as it swung slowly inward and a gray shape suddenly took form against the darkness of the room, paused on the threshold and then Logan stepped out into the moonlight and knocked his pipe against his boot heel. A second figure emerged and joined him, tossing away a cigarette.

The foreman yawned and shook his head. "I didn't know how to get 'em, Nelson," he said again. "I wasn't satisfied to stop th' rustlin'. I wanted to wipe 'em out an' get back my cows; but I didn't have men enough to go about it right, an' that cussed Barrier spoiled every plan."

"Yes," said the puncher. "But it's funny that none of th' boys, watchin' nights, never got a sign of them fellers. They must be slick. Well, all right' there'll have to be another plan tried, an' that'll be *my* job. I told you that I found traces of lead over near Twin Buttes? Well, I'm goin' prospectin', an' try to earn that seventy dollars a month. Any time you see a green bush lyin' at th' foot of th' Barrier, just north of Little Canyon, keep th' boys from ridin' near there that same night. I may have some business there an' I shore don't want to be shot at when I can't shoot back. It's too cussed bad Hoppy an' Red are married."

Logan laughed: "Then don't you make that mistake some day! But what about that feller Pete Wilson that Cassidy wants to get rid of?"

"Don't you worry about me gettin' married!" snorted Johnny. "I saw too much of it. An' as for Pete, he's too happy wallerin' in his misery. Anyhow, he wouldn't leave Hoppy an' th' boys; an' they wouldn't let him go. You couldn't drag him off the Tin Cup with a rope. Then we've settled it, huh? I'm to leave you tomorrow, with hard words?"

"Hard words ain't necessary. I know every man that works for me an' they'll stick, an' keep their mouths shut. Now, I warn you again: I wouldn't give a dollar, Mex. for yore life if you go through with your scheme. An' it'll be more dangerous because you look like me, an' have worked for me. You can give it up right now an' not lose anythin' in my opinion. Think it over tonight."

Johnny laughed and shook his head.

"Well," said the foreman, "I'm lettin' you into a bad game, with th' cards stacked against you; but I'll come in after you when you say th' word; an' th' outfit'll be at my back."

"I know that," smiled Johnny. "I'll be under a handicap, keepin' under cover an' not doin' any shootin'; but if I make a gun-play they'll begin to do some figgerin'. Gosh, I'm sleepy. Reckon I'll hunt my bunk. Good night."

"No gun-play," growled Logan. "You know what I want. How many they are, where they round up my cows, an' when they will be makin' a raid, so I can get 'em red-handed. _We_'ll do the fightin'. Good night."

They shook hands and parted, Johnny entering the house, Logan wandering out to the corral, where he sat on a stump for an hour or more and slowly smoked his pipe. When he finally arose he found that it was out, and cold, much to his surprise.

"Go 'round! Go 'round!" said the pond. "Better go 'round! Go 'round!"

Logan turned and sighed with relief at a problem solved. "Yo're a right smart frog, Big Mouth," he grinned. "'Go 'round' is th' medicine; an' I've got th' doctor to shove it down their throats! There's a roundup due in th' Twin Buttes, an' it's started now."

IV

♦

A Feint

Pop Hayes sighed, raised his head and watched the door as hoof-beats outside ceased abruptly.

"Dearly Beloved!" said an indignant voice. "If you tries any more of yore tricks I'll gentle you with th' butt of a six-gun, you barrel-bellied cow! Oh, *that's* it, huh? I savvy. You yearns for that shade. Go to it, Pepper."

"'Dearly Beloved'!" snorted Pop in fine disgust. "You'd think it was a weddin' tower! Who th' devil ever heard a cayuse called any such a name as that?" he indignantly demanded of Andrew Jackson; but Andrew paid no attention to him. The bird's head was cocked on one side and he sidled deliberately toward the door.

A figure jumped backward past the door, followed by a pair of hoofs, which shot into sight and out again. Andy stopped short and craned his neck, his beady eyes glittering with quick suspicion.

"I can shore see where you an' me has an argument," said the voice outside. "If you make any more plays like that I'll just naturally kick yore ribs in. G'wan, now; I ain't got no sugar, you old fool!" And the smiling two-gun man stepped into the room, with a wary and affectionate backward glance. "Hello, Pop!" he grinned. "You old Piute, you owes me a drink!"

"Like hell I do!" retorted Pop with no politeness, sitting up very straight in his chair.

"You shore do!" rejoined Johnny firmly. "Didn't you tell me that th' CL was a nice ranch to work for?"

"Yo're loco! I didn't say nothin' of th' kind!" snapped Pop indignantly. "I said they'd work you nigh to death; *that's* what I said!"

"Oh; was that it?" asked Johnny dubiously. "I ain't nowise shore about it; but we'll let it go as it lays. Then I owe you a drink; so it's all th' same. Yo're a real prophet."

Pop hastily shuffled to his appointed place and performed the honors gracefully. "So you went an' got a job over there, huh?" he chuckled. "An' now yo're all through with 'em? Well, I *will* say that you stuck it out longer than some I knows of. Two weeks with Logan is a long time."

"It's so long that I've aged considerable," admitted Johnny, smiling foolishly. "But I'm cured. I'm cured of punchin' cows for anybody, for a while. Seems to me that all I've done, all my life, was to play guardian to fool cows. I've had enough for a while. Th' last two weeks plumb cured me of punchin'."

He looked down and saw Andy, feathers ruffled, squaring off for another go at the spur, stooped suddenly, scooped the squawking bird into his hand, tossed it into the air, caught it, and quickly shoved it headfirst into a pocket.

Andy swore and backed and wriggled, threatened to eat his black heart and to do other unkind and reprehensible things. Giving a desperate heave he plopped out of the pocket and struck the floor with a thud. Shaking himself, he screamed profane defiance at the world at large and then made his clumsy and comical way up the chaps and finally roosted on the butt of one of the six-guns, where he clucked loudly and whistled.

Johnny gave a peculiar whistle in reply, and almost instantly Pop let out a roar and jumped toward the door to drive back a black horse that was coming in.

"Get out of here!" he yelled pugnaciously. Pepper bared her teeth and slowly backed out again. Turning, Pop glared at the puncher. "Did you see that? Mebby Andy ain't th' only animal that drinks," he jabbed, remembering a former conversation.

Johnny laughed and scratched the bird, which stood first on one foot and then on the other, foolish with ecstatic joy.

Pop regarded the bird with surprise. "Well, if that don't beat all!" he marveled. "There ain't another man can do that, 'cept me, an' get off with a whole hand. Andy'll miss you, I reckon."

"He won't miss me much," responded Johnny, comfortably seating himself in Pop's private chair. "I ain't leavin' th' country."

"You won't have to. There's other ranches, where they treats punchers better'n cows. There's another chair, over there."

"No more ranches for me," replied Johnny, ignoring the hint. "I'm through punchin', I tell you. I'm goin' to play a while for a change."

"Gamblin's bad business," replied Pop, turning to get the cards.

"Mebby some gamblin' is; but there's some as ain't," grinned Johnny. "I ain't meanin' cards."

"Oh," said Pop, disappointed. "What you mean—shootin' craps?"

"Nope; I'm goin' prospectin'; an' if that ain't gamblin' then I never saw anythin' that was."

Pop straightened up and stared. "Prospectin'?" he demanded, incredulously. "Regular prospectin'? Well, I'll be cussed! If yo're goin' to do it around here, lemme tell you it won't be no gamble. It'll be a dead shore loss. A flea couldn't live on what you'll earn on that game in this country."

"Well, I ain't aimin' to support no flea, unless Andy leaves me one," laughed Johnny, again scratching the restless bird. "But I'm tired of cows, an' I might as well amuse myself prospectin' as any other way. I like this country an' I'm goin' to stay a while. Besides, when I was a kid I shore wanted to be a pirate; then when I got older I saw a prospector an' hankered to be one. I can't be a pirate, but I'm goin' to be a prospector. When my money is gone I'll guard cows again."

"Lord help us!" muttered Pop. "Yo're plumb loco."

"How can I be plumb an' loco at th' same time?"

"Andy!" snapped Pop. "Come away from there! Lord knows you ain't got no sense, but there ain't no use riskin' yore instinct!"

Johnny laughed. "Leavin' jokes aside, me an' Pepper are goin' off by ourselves an' poke around pannin' th' streams an' bustin' nuggets off th' rocks till we get a fortune or our grub runs out. We can have a good time, an'—hey! You got any fishhooks?"

"Fishhooks nothin'!" snorted Pop. "Lot of call *I* got for fishhooks. Why, I ain't heard th' word for ten years. Say!" he grinned sheepishly. "Mebby you'll get lonesome. Now, if we went off together, with some fishhooks—but, shucks! I can't leave this here business."

Johnny hid his relief. "That's th' worst of havin' a business. You certainly can't go off an' let everythin' go to smash."

"Cuss th' luck!" growled Pop. "Gosh, I'm all het up over it! I ain't done no fishin' since I was a kid, an' there must be lots of trout in these streams." Then he brightened a little. "But I dunno. You look too cussed much like Logan to be real comfortable company for *me*. I reckon I'll pay attention to business."

Johnny showed a little irritation. "There you go again! You do a lot of worryin' about my looks. If they don't suit you, start right in an' change 'em!"

"There *you* go!" snapped Pop disgustedly. "On th' prod th' first thing! You'd show more common sense if *you* did some of th' worryin'. But then, I reckon it'll be all right if you does yore prospectin' an' fishin' south of here."

"No, sir! I'm goin' to do it north of here, in th' Twin Buttes country."

Pop's expression baffled description, and his Adam's apple bobbed up and down like a monkey on a stick. "Good Lord! You stick to Devil's Gap, an' south of there!"

Johnny's eyes narrowed and he sat up very straight. "This is a free country an' I goes where I please. It's a habit of mine. I said north, an' that's where I'm goin'. I wasn't so set on it before; but now I'm as set as a Missouri mule."

Pop growled. "There ain't no chance of you havin' *my* company; an' you leave th' name an' address of yore next of kin before you starts."

Johnny laughed derisively. "I ain't worryin'. An' now let's figger out what a regular prospector needs. Bein' new at th' game I reckon I better get some advice. What I'm dubious about are th' proper things to pry th' nuggets loose with, an' hoist 'em on my cayuse," he grinned. "Ought to have a pick, shovel, gold pan for placer fussin'—'gold pan' sounds regular, don't it?—an' some sacks to tie it up in. A dozen'll do for a starter. I can allus come back for more."

"Or you can borrow a chuck waggin; that would be handy because it would make it easy to get yore body out, 'though I reckon they'll just bury you an' let it go that way."

"They? Meaning' who?"

"I ain't got a word to say."

"There's some consolation in that," jeered Johnny.

"Yo're a fool!" snorted Pop heatedly.

"An' so that's went an' follered me down here, too," sighed Johnny. "A man can't get away from some things. Well, let's get back on th' trail. All th' prospectors I ever saw wore cowhide boots, with low, flat heels. Somehow I can't see myself trampin' around with these I'm wearin'; an' they're too expensive to wear 'em out that way. What else? Need any blastin' powder?"

"Cussed if I wouldn't grub-stake you if you wasn't goin' up there," grinned Pop. "It takes a fool for luck; an' it'll be just like you to fall down a canyon an' butt th' dirt off'n a million dollar nugget. I got a notion to do it anyhow."

"You needn't get no notions!" retorted Johnny. "I'm goin' to hog it. Prospectors never get grubstaked unless they're busted; an' I ain't got there yet. Oh, yes; I got to get them fishhooks—you see, I ain't aimin' to cripple my back workin' hard *all* th' time. I'll fill a sack in th' mornin', eat my dinner an' rest all afternoon. Next day I'll fill another sack, an' so on. Now, what am I goin' to get for my outfit? I'll need a lot of things."

"Go see Charley James, acrost th' street. He keeps th' general store; an' he's got more trash than anybody I ever saw."

"Mebby he can tell me what I need," suggested Johnny, hopefully.

As Pop started to answer, the doorway darkened and a man stepped into the room. Pop's face paled and he swiftly moved to one side, out of range. The newcomer glanced at Johnny, swore under his breath and his hand streaked to his holster. It remained there, for he discovered that he was glaring squarely down a revolver barrel.

"Let loose of it!" snapped Johnny. "Now, then: What's eatin' you?"

"Why—why, I mistook you for somebody else!" muttered the other. "Comin' in from th' sunlight, sudden like, I couldn't see very well. My mistake, Stranger. What'll you have?"

Johnny grunted skeptically. "Yo're shore you can see all right now?"

"It's all right, Nelson," hastily interposed the anxious proprietor, nodding emphatic assurance. "It's all right!"

"My mistake, Mr. Nelson," smiled the stranger. "I shouldn't 'a' been so hasty—but I was fooled. Yore looks are shore misleadin'."

"They suits me. What's wrong about 'em?" demanded Johnny.

"There you go again!" snorted Pop in quick disgust. "A gent makes a mistake, says he didn't mean no harm in it, an' you goes on th' prod! Didn't I *tell* you that yore looks would get you into trouble? Didn't I?"

"Oh! Is *that* it?" He arose and slipped the gun back into its holster. "I'll take th' same, Stranger."

"Now yo're gettin' some sense," beamed Pop, smiling with relief. "Mr. Nelson, shake han's with Tom Quigley. Here's luck."

"Fill 'em again," grinned Johnny. "Not that I hankers for th' kind of liquor you sells, but because we has to do th' best we can with what's pervided."

"Pop's sellin' better liquor than he used to," smiled Quigley. "Am I to thank you for th' improvement?"

"I refuse to accept th' responsibility," laughed Johnny.

"Well, he had some waggin varnish last year, an' for a long time we was puzzled to know what he did with it. One day, somebody said his whiskey tasted like a pine knot: an' then we knew th' answer."

"You both can go to th' devil," grinned Pop.

"Aimin' to make a long stay with us, Mr. Nelson?" asked Quigley.

"That all depends on how soon I gets all th' gold out of this country."

"Ah! Prospectin'?"

"Startin' tomorrow, I am: if this varnish don't kill me."

"There ain't never been none found around here, 'though I never could understand why. There was a couple of prospectors here some years ago, an' they worked harder for nothin' than anybody I ever saw. They covered th' ground purty well, but they was broke about th' time they started south of town, an' had to clear out. They claimed there was pay dirt down there, but they couldn't get a grub-stake on th' strength of that, so they just had to quit."

"That's where it is if it's any place," said Pop hurriedly. "Th' river's workin' day an' night, pilin' it ag'in them rock ledges above th' ford; an' it's been doin' it since th' world began."

Johnny shook his head. "Mebby; but there ain't no way to get it, unless you can drain th' river. I want shallow water—little streams, where there's sand an' gravel bars an' flats. I'm aimin' to work north of here."

Quigley forced a smile and shook his head. "I'm fraid you'll waste yore time. I've been all through that section, in fact I live up there, an' some of my men have fooled around lookin' for color. There ain't a sign of it anywhere."

"Well, I'm aimin' to go back north when I get tired of prospectin'," replied Johnny, grinning cheerfully; "an' I figgers I can prospect around an' gradually work up that way, toward Hope. I'll drop in an' see you if I run acrost yore place. I reckon prospectin' is a lonesome game."

"Didn't you ever try it before?" asked Quigley in surprise.

"This is my first whirl at it," reluctantly admitted Johnny. "I'm a cow-puncher, got tired of th' north ranges an' drifted down here. An' I might 'a' stayed a cow-puncher, only I got a job on th' CL an' worked there for th' last two weeks; an' I got a-plenty. It soured me of punchin'. Outside of bein' cussed suspicious, that man Logan is loco. I don't mind bein' suspected a little at first; but I ain't goin' to work like a fool when there ain't no call for it. I might 'a' stuck it out, at that, only for a fool notion of his. That's where I cut loose."

Quigley looked curious. "New notion?"

"Yes," laughed Johnny contemptuously. "He got th' idea that th' night air, close to th' river, ain't healthy for th' cows! Told us to drive all of 'em back from th' river every evenin' before we rode in. I said as how we ought to blanket 'em, an' build fires under 'em. I reckon mebby I was a mite sarcastic, at that. Well, anyhow; we had an argument, an' I drew my pay an' quit."

Pop let out a howl. "Good Lord!" he snorted. "Evenin' air too wet for cows! Drive 'em back every night! An' lemme tell you that outfit's just foolish enough to do it, too. He-he-he!"

Quigley laughed, and then looked at the proprietor: "Pop, we ain't forgettin'. We both has bought, an' it usually goes th' rounds before it stops."

"Oh, I'll set 'em up," growled Pop.

"You ranchin', Mr. Quigley?" asked Johnny.

"Well, I am, an' I ain't," answered Quigley. "I'm farmin' an' ranchin' both, on a small scale. I got a few head, but not enough to give me much bother. We sort of let 'em look after themselves."

"Oh," said Johnny regretfully. "I thought mebby if I got tired of prospectin', an' short of cash, that I might get a job with you."

"I ain't got cows enough to keep me busy," explained Quigley. "We let 'em wander, an' get 'em as we need 'em. Well," he said, turning as if to leave, "I'm sorry about that fool break of mine, Mr. Nelson; an' to prove it I'm goin' to give you some real good advice: Keep away from th' Twin Buttes country. So long, boys."

Johnny looked after him, and then faced Pop, shrugging his shoulders. "I don't quite get th' drift of that," he said slowly; "but he ought to know th' country he lives in. I'll try Devil's Gap first; but I got a cussed strong notion not to!"

Pop sighed with relief. "Let's go over an' see what Charley's got for yore kit," he suggested.

Charley James was playing solitaire on a box laid across a nail keg and he smiled a welcome as they entered.

"Charley," said Pop. "This cow-puncher's aimin' to change his spots. He's a amatchure prospector an' wants us to pick out his outfit."

"I can believe that he's an amatchure if he's goin' to try it in this part of th' country," smiled Charley. "Nobody's ever tried it down here before."

Johnny was about to mention the two prospectors referred to by Mr. Quigley, but thought better of it.

"Oh, it's been tried," said Pop casually. "But they didn't stay long. What you got in that line, Charley?"

"I ain't shore; but first you want an axe. Come on; we'll saunter aroun' an' pick things out as they hit our eye. Here's th' axe—double bitted, six-pounder."

"Too big," chuckled Pop. "There ain't none of them there redwood trees out here; they're in Californy."

"Huh!" grunted Charley. "Mebbyso; but that's a good axe."

"Pop's right; it's too heavy," decided Johnny. "An' I don't want it double bitted because I may want to drive stakes with it."

"All right," said Charley, who had hoped to at last get rid of the big axe. "Here's a three-pounder—'Little Gem'—an' it shore is. All right; now for th' next article."

In half an hour the outfit was assembled and they were turning to leave the store when Johnny suddenly grabbed his companions. "What about some fishhooks?" he demanded anxiously.

Charley rubbed his head reflectively. "I think mebby I got some; don't remember throwin' 'em away. There was some with feathers, an' some without; plain hooks, an' flies. Brought 'em with me when I first came out here, an' never used 'em. Ought to have some line, too; an' a reel somewheres. I'll hunt 'em up an' put 'em with yore duffle. You can cut yoreself a pole. They'll be a little present from me."

"Thank you," beamed Johnny, and forthwith Pop dragged them to his place of business.

Johnny left the following morning, and one week later he returned, trudging along beside his loaded horse, and he was the owner of a generous amount of gold, the treasure of a "pocket" upon which he had blundered. He determined to keep this a secret, for if he let it be known that he had found "color," what excuse could he offer for leaving that field? It fit too well into his plans to be revealed.

Pop grinned a welcome: "Have any luck?"

"Fishin', yes," laughed Johnny. "Bet I moved ten acres of gravel. I wasted a week; now I'm goin' north."

Pop frowned. "I reckon you'll have yore own way; but put in yore time fishin' an' prospectin', an' mind yore own business."

"Shore," said Johnny. "Look here," unrolling a bundle and producing two of the gold sacks, which were heavy and bulging. Pop stared, speechless, until his new friend opened one of them and dumped four dressed trout on the bar.

"Slip 'em in a fryin' pan with some bacon," grinned Johnny.

"Get 'em in th' river?" demanded Pop incredulously.

"You know that draw runnin' east from th' Gap—th' one with them two dead pines leanin' against each other?"

"Yes; 'tain't more'n a mile from th' ford!"

"I found 'em up there, hidin' in a bush."

"Reckon you think that's funny," grunted Pop. "Why them's *brook* trout! I ain't had any since I was a boy. Th' devil with business! I'm goin' fishin' one day a week. Now where you goin'?"

"Got some for Charley," laughed Johnny from the door.

Charley looked up from his eternal solitaire: "Hello, Nelson!"

"Look what I got," exulted Johnny, extending the bag.

"God help us!" exclaimed Charley. "Did you—did you—"

"I did. Brook trout, Pop says. Prospectin' ain't nothin' compared to fishin'. Pop's goin' one day a week, an' after you eat these mebby you'll be with him."

"Pop can't put on no airs with me," chuckled Charley. "If he can afford to close up, so can I. But you shouldn't 'a' poked no bulgin' gold sack at me like that! It was a shock. Come on; let's take somethin' for it." He grabbed the fish and led the way across the street; and for the rest of the afternoon three happy men discussed prospecting and trout fishing, but the latter was by far the more important.

V

♦

Preparations

The next morning Johnny said good-by to Pop and walked by Pepper's side, watching the big pack on her back, while Pop, shaking his head, entered his place of business and forthwith began work on a crude sign which, one day a week, would hang on his locked front door.

Well to the north of Hastings, Johnny came to a brook flowing through a deep ravine, and, forsaking the trail, followed the little stream westward and evening found him encamped in a small clearing. He spent several days here, panning the stream and fishing during daylight, and scouting in his moccasins at night. He paid a visit to Little Canyon and explored the valley he was in, and at the head of the valley he found a deep-walled pasture above a short, narrow canyon. Deciding to erect a cabin at the canyon entrance as a monument to the innocence of his activities, he prospected a sand bar near by and rediscovered the gold which he had found at Devil's Gap, which served as an excellent excuse for locating there permanently; and after a week of hard work, the cabin became a reality.

His every movement had been made upon the supposition that he was being watched; and the supposition became a fact when he discovered boot-prints along the opposite bank of the creek. These promised him a trail by which he could easily locate the rustlers' ranch, and at daylight the next morning he was following them and finally reached a great ridge, which he ascended with caution.

Below him was a deep valley, through which a stream moved sluggishly, and at the upper end was a narrow canyon, not more than ten paces wide, through which the stream escaped from another valley above. Twin Buttes were several miles to the east of him, lying a mile or more north of the valley. He looked through the deep canyon and at the corner of a stone house at its other end, and as he watched he saw several men come into view. One of them motioned toward the south and paused to speak to his companions, whereupon Johnny wriggled down the slope and set out for his camp.

Back again in his own valley, he built a sapling fence across the little canyon, cut a pile of firewood near by, and then rode to Hastings, where he nearly gave Charley heart failure by displaying a pleasing amount of virgin gold. He did not see Pop because on the saloon door he found a sign reading: "Back at 4 P.M."

It was a very cheerful cow-puncher who rode to the new cabin that evening, for he was matching his wits against those of his natural enemies, he was playing a lone hand in his own way against odds, and the game was only beginning.

In perfect condition, virile, young, enduring, he had serene confidence in his ability to take care of himself. He admitted but one master in the art of gunplay, and that man had been his teacher and best friend for years. Even now Hopalong could beat him on the draw, but barely, and he could roll his two guns forward, backward and "mixed;" but he could shoot neither faster nor straighter than his pupil.

Johnny could not roll a gun because he never had tried very hard to master that most difficult of all gunplay, regarding it as an idle accomplishment, good only for exhibition purposes, and, while awe inspiring, Johnny had no yearning for it. He clove to strict utility and did not care to call attention to his wooden-handled, flare-butt Frontiers. There was no ornamentation on them, no ivory, inlay, or engraving. The only marks on their heavy, worn frames were a few dents. He had such a strong dislike for fancy guns that the sight of ivory grips made his lips curl, and such things as pearl handles filled him with grieving contempt for the owner.

He never mentioned his guns to any but his closest friends, and they were as unconscious a part of him as his arms or his legs. And it was his creed that no man but himself should touch them, his friends excepted. He wore them low because utility demanded it; and to so wear them, and to tie them down besides, was in itself a responsibility, for there were men who would not be satisfied with the quiet warning.

In other things, from routine ranch work to manhunting, from roping and riding to rifle shooting, the old outfit of the Bar-20 had been his teachers and they had taken him in hand at an early age. His rifle he had copied from Hopalong; but Red had taught him the use of it, and to his way of thinking Red Connors was without a peer in the use of the longer weapon.

Johnny was a genius with his six-guns, one of those few men produced in a generation; and he did not belong to the class of fancy gun-workers who shine at exhibitions and fall short when lead is flying and the nerves are sorely tried. He shot from his hips by instinct, and that is the real test of utility. Had he turned his talents to ends which lay outside the law he would have become the most dangerous and the most feared man in the cow-country.

John Logan awoke with a start, sat up suddenly in his bunk and grunted a profane query as his hand closed over his Colt.

"It's Nelson," softly said a voice from outside the window. "Don't make so much noise," it continued, as its owner dropped handful of pebbles on the ground. "I wanted you awake before I showed myself. Never like to walk into a man's room in th' dark, when he's asleep an' not expectin' visitors. 'Specially when he's worryin' about rustlers. It ain't allus healthy."

"All right," growled the foreman, "but you don't have to throw 'em; you can toss 'em, easy, from there. I've got a welt on my head as big as a chew of tobacco. I'm shore glad you couldn't find nothin' out there that was any bigger. You comin' in or am I comin' out?"

The door squeaked open and squeaked shut and then a chair squeaked.

"You got a musical room," observed Johnny, chuckling softly. "Yore bunk squeaked, too, when you sat up."

"It was a narrow squeak for you," grunted Logan, reluctantly putting down the Colt. "If I'd seen a head I'd 'a' let drive on suspicion. I was havin' a cussed bad dream an' was all het up. My cows was goin' up Little Canyon in whole herds an' I couldn't seem to stop 'em nohow."

"Keepin' my head out of trouble is my long suit," chuckled Johnny. "An' there ain't none of yore cows goin' up Little Canyon—not till I steal some of 'em. Been wonderin' where I was an' what I was doin'?"

"Not very much," answered the foreman. "Got a match? We been gettin' our mail reg'lar every week, an' th' boys allus drop in for a drink at Pop's; an they're good listeners. Say! What th' hell is this I hears about puttin' blankets on my cows an' shovin' 'em into th' river every night? Well, that can wait. You've shore made an impression on Ol' Pop Hayes. Th' old Piute can't talk about nothin' but you. Every time th' boys drop in there they get fed up on you. Of course they don't show much interest in yore doin's;

an' they don't have to. They says yo're a damned quitter, an' stuff like that, an' Pop gets riled up an' near scalps 'em. What you been doin' to get him so friendly? I never thought he'd be friendly, like that, to anythin' but a silver dollar."

"I don't know—just treat him decent," replied Johnny.

"Huh! I been treatin' him decent for ten years, an' he still thinks I'm some kind of an unknown animal. If he saw me dyin' in th' street he wouldn't drag me five feet, unless I was blockin' his door; but he's doin' a lot of worryin' about you, all right. What you been doin' besides courtin' Pop an' Andy Jackson, washin' gravel an' ketchin' fish?"

Johnny laughed. "I've been playin' cautious—an' right now I ain't shore that I've fooled 'em a whole lot. Here, lemme tell you th' thing—" and he explained his activities since leaving the CL.

At its conclusion Logan grunted. "You got nerve an' patience; an' mebby you got brains. If you can keep 'em from bein' shot out of yore head, you have. An' you say they ain't usin' Little Canyon? I know they ain't usin' it now; but was they?"

"Not since th' frost come out of th' ground," replied Johnny. "I can't tell you about what they *are* doin' because I'm just beginnin' to get close to 'em. Th' next time you see me I may know somethin'. Now you listen to me," and he gave the foreman certain instructions, which Logan repeated over after him. "Now, then: I want about sixty feet of rope strong enough to hold me, an' I want a short, straight iron."

"Come with me," ordered the foreman, slipping on his clothes; and in ten minutes they emerged from the blacksmith shop, which also was a storeroom, and Johnny carried a coil of old but strong rope and an iron bar.

"I never thought I'd be totin' a runnin' iron," he chuckled. "If my friends could only see me now! Johnny Nelson, cow-thief an' brand-blotter!"

"You needn't swell up," growled Logan. "You ain't th' only one in this country right now."

"Well," said Johnny, "go back an' finish yore dream—mebby you can find out how to make them cows come back through Little Canyon."

"Yo're goin' to do that," responded Logan; "an' *I'm* goin' to close that window in case *you* come back. I ain't forgot nothin' you said—an' if we don't see one of yore signs for a period of five days, we'll comb yore valley an' th' whole Twin Buttes country. So long!"

Johnny melted into the dark, a low whistle sounded and in a few minutes Logan heard the rhythmic drumming of hoofs, rapidly growing fainter.

VI

♦

A Moonlight Reconnaissance

The evening following his visit to the CL, Johnny went to bed early but not to sleep. For several hours he lay thinking and listening, and then he arose and put on his moccasins, threw on his shoulder Logan's rope, now knotted every foot of its length, slipped out of the cabin and was swallowed up in the darkness along the base of the rocky wall. To cover the few yards between the cabin and the narrow crevice took ten minutes, and to go softly up the crevice took twice as long.

Reaching the top he listened intently, and then moved

slowly and silently to a small clump of pines growing close to the rim of the steep wall enclosing the walled-in pasture, at a point where it was so sheer and smooth that he believed it would not be watched. Fastening one end of the rope to a tree, he lowered the rest of it over the wall and went down. Pausing again to listen, he made his way to a line of stones which lay across the creek, crossed with dry feet, and reached the northern wall of the pasture. This could be climbed at half a dozen places and he soon was up it and on his way north. After colliding with several bowlders and tripping twice he waited until the moon arose and then went on again at a creditable speed.

The crescent moon had risen well above the tops of Twin Buttes when a man in moccasins moved cautiously across a high plateau some miles north of Nelson's creek and finally dropped to all fours and proceeded much more slowly. From all fours to stomach was his next choice and he wriggled toward the edge of the plateau, pausing every foot or so to remove loose stones. These he put aside before going on again, for there is no telling where a rolling pebble will stop, or the noise it may make, when the edge of a mesa wall is but a few feet away. Coming to within an arm's length of the edge, he first made sure that the rim was solid rock and free from dirt and pebbles; and then, hitching forward slowly, he peered down into the deep valley.

Its immensity amazed him, for upon the occasion of his former reconnaissance he had viewed it from the outside; and as a picture of his own pasture flashed into his mind he snorted softly at the contrast, for where he had acres, this great "sink" had square miles. It was wider than his own was long, and it stretched away in the faint moonlight until its upper reaches were lost to his eyes. It was large enough to hold one great butte in its middle, and perhaps there were more; and from where he lay he judged the wall below him dropped straight down for three hundred feet.

"There ain't no line ridin' here, unless th' cows grow wings," he muttered.

To the south of him were four lighted windows near the forbidding blackness of the entrance canyon, and from their spacing he deduced two houses. And across from the windows he could make out a vague quadrangle, which experience told him was the horse corral. As if to confirm his judgment there came from it at that moment a shrill squeal and the sound of hoofs on wood, muffled by the distance. And from the corral extended a faint line which ran across the valley and became lost in the darkness near the opposite cliff. This he knew to be a fence.

"If this valley ends like it begins, three or four men can handle an awful lot of cows, 'cept at drive time," he soliloquized, and then listened intently to the sound of distant voices.

. . . . many happy hours away,
A sittin' an' singin' by a little cottage do-o-r,
Where lived my darlin' Nel-lie Gr-a-ay,

came floating faintly from far below him.

He peered in the direction of the singing and barely made out a moving blot well out in the valley. As it came steadily nearer, the blot resolved itself into several dots, and the chorus had greater volume. It appeared that the group was harmonizing.

"You'll be doin' somethin' more than sittin' an' singin' at yore little cottage door one of these days," grunted Johnny savagely. It was his rebuff to the thought which came to him of how long it had been since he had ruined the silence in company with his friends. "That first feller is purty good; but one of 'em shore warbles like a sick calf."

Several other dots arose suddenly from the earth and lumbered sleepily away as the horsemen approached them.

"There's some of Logan's cows, I reckon," grunted the watcher grimly. "Wish I could see better. I've got to do my prospectin' in daylight; an' I got to find some way to ride over here—waste too much time on foot."

More squealing came from the corral and grew in volume as other horses joined in it. From the noise it appeared to be turning into a free-for-all. A door in one of the distant houses suddenly opened and framed a rectangular patch of light, dull and yellow; and from it emerged a bright little light which swung in short, jerky arcs close to the ground and went rapidly toward the corral. Soon thereafter the squealing ceased and a moment later the little light went bobbing back again, blotted out in rhythmic dashes by the swinging legs beside it.

"Big Jerry fightin' again," laughed one of the horsemen during a pause in the singing. Johnny barely was able to hear him.

Oh my darlin' Nellie Gra-a-y, they have taken her awa-a-y;
An' I'll never see my darlin' any more—ANY MORE!

rumbled the harmonizers, bursting into a thundering perpetration on the repetition of the last two words.

"Th' farther off they get th' better they sound," growled Johnny as the harmonizers were swallowed up in the darkness near the opposite cliff. "They'd sound better at about ten miles."

Lying comfortably on his stomach, his head out over

the rim of the wall, he was lost in thought when a sudden, startled snort behind him nearly caused him to go over the edge. A contortionist hardly could have changed ends quicker than he did; he simply went up in the air and when he came down again he was on hands and knees, one foot where his head had been. But he did not stop there; indeed, he did not even pause there, for he kept on moving until he was on his feet, his knees bent and his head thrust forward, and each hand, without conscious direction, held a gun. And almost instantly they chocked back into the holsters.

A gray shape was backing slowly into the shadows of a bowlder, two green eyes boring through the gloom, and Johnny's hair became ambitious.

"I dassn't shoot, I dassn't run, an' I can't back up! All right; when in doubt try a bluff; but I shore hopes it's th' bluffin' kind!"

He emitted a throaty, ferocious snarl, dropped the tips of his fingers to the earth and started for the bowlder and the green eyes, on a series of back-humping, awkward jumps, like a weak-kneed calf cavorting playfully. Another snort, curious, incredulous, frightened, came from the bowlder and a great gray wolf backed off hastily, but with a hesitating uncertainty which was not as reassuring as might be hoped for.

Johnny let out another snarl, more terrifying than the first, humped his back energetically, waved his legs, and then with a low-toned but blood-curdling shriek, leaped at the wavering cow-killer. The gray silhouette lengthened and vanished, simply melting into the darkness as though it had urgent business elsewhere.

Johnny arose, a rock in his hand, and sighed with relief; and his ambitious hair settled back again into its accustomed place while the prickling along his spine died out.

"Holy smoke! What if it had been half-starved, or a grizzly! Blast you!" he growled, shaking a vengeful fist at the presumed locality of the wolf. "You just come snortin' around *my* valley! I'll shoot yore insides all over th' landscape!"

Hanging onto the rock, he readjusted his belts and went nearer the entrance canyon to get a closer view of the houses and surroundings. When again he looked over the edge of the precipice he was directly over the corral and across from the houses, which the rays of the moon, slanting through a break in the opposite cliff, now faintly revealed.

There were three houses and they were low, long and narrow, and built of stone, with the customary adobe roofs; and they were built in echelon, the three end walls appearing as one from the canyon. He nodded appreciatively, for it required no great imagination to see, in his mind's eye, the loopholes which undoubtedly ornamented that end of the houses. The narrow canyon, straight as an arrow and fully half a mile long, lay at almost perfect right angles to the three walls. A handful of determined men, cool and accurate, in those houses could hold the canyon against great odds while their food, water and ammunition held out. Moving his head, he caught a sudden glint, and peered intently to discover what had caused it. He moved again until he saw it the second time, and then he knew. A small trickle of water flowed from a spring back near the great wall, and it passed under one corner of each house.

"That's purty good!" he ejaculated in ungrudging admiration. He was something of a strategist himself and he was not slow to pay respect to the handiwork of genius when he saw it. "Built 'em like steps so as to cover th' canyon from all three houses; an' diverted that little stream so they could get water without showing themselves. No matter which side of them houses is rushed, there is allus three walls to face. Th' only weak spots are th' north an' south corners. If they ain't loopholed a good man could sneak right up to th' corner of th' end houses; but what he'd do after he got there, I don't know."

He studied the problem in silence and then nodded his head: "Huh! Them walls don't overhang, an' so they can't shoot down close to 'em. Mebby I've found th' weak spot—but I'll have to get a whole lot closer than I am now before I'm shore of it. An' that can wait."

He wriggled back from the wall and arose. "Seen all I can at night. Don't even know if these fellers *are* rustlin'. Bein' suspicious an' bein' shore ain't th' same. But th' next time I come up here I won't leave until I am shore, not if it takes all summer. Logan said to be shore to find out how many there are, their trail from his ranch an' th' place where they operates on th' CL. Says he's got to get 'em actually stealin' his cows on his ranch. Says he ain't got no friends out here and that th' other ranches acts like they was sort of on th' side of th' thieves. That's a hell of a note, that is! Buck, an' Hoppy, an' us: we never gave a whoop where we found rustlers if they had our cows; an' we never gave two whoops in hell what th' rest of th' country thought about it. Times have changed. Imagine us askin' anybody if we could shoot rustlers! Huh!"

He started back the way he had come up, and reached his own valley without incident; but when he wriggled toward the wall he was puzzled, and worried. There was the clump of pines up above him, ghostly in the faint moonlight; but he could see no rope. Thankful that he had been cautious in crossing the valley, he wriggled a little closer and then started back over his trail, recrossed the valley, climbed the other wall in the shelter offered by a crevice and slipped along the great ridge. All he cared about now was to get back into the cabin without being seen. All kinds of conjectures ran through his head concerning the absence of the rope, and while he thrashed them out he kept going ahead, careful to take full advantage of the wealth of cover at hand.

His senses were keyed to their highest pitch of efficiency and at times he concentrated on one of them at the expense of the others. While he used his eyes constantly, it was in his ears that he placed the most confidence. The man who does the moving about is at a disadvantage, which he keenly realized.

He did not mind so much being away from the cabin if he could make it appear to be innocent; and to that end he moved steadily toward the Hastings trail. His horse was not to be seen, and that worried him. It could have strayed, for he had neither picketed nor hobbled it, but he feared that it had not strayed.

Passing his old camp site he heard a noise, and flattened himself on the ground. It came again and from the edge of the clearing where he had spent his first few nights in the valley. Anyone foolish enough to make a noise, under the circumstances, was foolish enough to be stalked by any man who had good sense; and he proceeded to do the stalking.

It took him quite a while to get around back of the place where his tent had stood, but when he finally got there he was repaid for his time and trouble. It was not the direction from which he would be expected, if the rustlers' suspicions were aroused; and there was a certain twisting path through the brush which was devoid of twigs and sticks.

Foot by foot he crept forward until he could see the big bowlder in the clearing, and then he paused as the

sound was heard again, and he tried to classify it. A
twig snapped, and then another sound made him nod
quickly. It was a horse; that was certain; but could it be
Pepper? While he pondered and listened to the slow,
interrupted steps, a dark shape moved out from the
deep shadows of the trees, pricked its ears, stretched
out its head toward him, nickered softly and slowly
advanced.

He stared in amazement, for while it was Pepper, the
saddle was on her back; and when he had left the cabin
the saddle was inside. But, was it, though? In a moment
his mind had marshaled in review before him all his
acts of the previous day; all but one. Had he unsaddled
the horse when he had ridden back from the upper end
of his little valley? Of course he had; why should he
have neglected to do such a thing as that? But, perhaps
he hadn't. He swore under his breath and backed away,
for the horse was coming nearer all the time. It was his
saddle; he could tell that easily. And then all of his
doubts cleared in a flash. When he had ridden in from
the pasture he had started to remove the saddle, but
when he thought of his boiling pots he had pushed the
end of the cinch strap back under the little holding strap,
and he had not shoved it home. Right now that cinch end
should be sticking out in a loop. Craning his neck and
shifting silently he managed to see it; and a chuckle escaped from him. He whistled softly, so softly that anyone a hundred feet away could not have heard it; but the
horse heard it and nickered again. What fools these men
were! Did her master think that she had to hear a whistle
to know that he was about, when the wind was right and
he was so close?

Pepper was a well-trained, intelligent animal, and
Johnny knew it better than anyone else; and Pepper had a

strong aversion to strangers, which he also knew; and knowing that, he was instantly assured that there were no strangers in the immediate vicinity because Pepper was thoroughly at her ease. The black head thrust forward into his face and the bared teeth snapped at him, whereupon he playfully cuffed the velvety nozzle. Pepper forthwith swung her head suddenly and knocked off her master's hat, and pretended to be in a fine rage.

"You old coyote!" chuckled Johnny, cuffing her again. "Cussed if you ain't th' most no-account old fool I ever saw. But I ought to be kicked from here to Hastings an' back again for leavin' that saddle on you all afternoon an' night. Will some sugar square it? Hey! Get out of my pocket—it's in th' shack," he laughed. And there was a note in his laughter that a horse of Pepper's intelligence might easily understand.

Mounting, he rode across the clearing, and when he reached the water course he followed it to his cabin. Pepper had given him the card he needed now for, in the saddle and careless of being seen, which was his best play, dangerous as it might be, he was riding home from an evening spent in Hastings. As to answering any questions about the dangling rope, he either would inform the curious that it was none of their business, or lie; and whether the lie would be a humorous exaggeration which could not possibly be believed, or adroit, plausible, and convincing would be a matter of mood.

Whistling softly he rode across the little plateau, stripped the saddle from Pepper, who waited until he returned with some sugar, and lit the lantern. Pepper was not the only member of that partnership whose nose was useful; and the faint odor of a vile, frontier cigar had lingered after its possessor had departed.

"Huh! We must 'a' swapped ends tonight; but I'll bet

he's doin' more wonderin' than me. He thinks he's got a lead, findin' that rope. I know he didn't see me put it there, or go down it; an' I'll bet he don't know that I came back to it. He can watch an' be cussed."

VII

◆

A Council of War

Clearing away the breakfast pans the following morning, Johnny did some soliloquizing.

"This is a nice little shack, but I ain't stuck on it a whole lot. Now that I've built it, I've got to use it or tip off my hand; an' as long as I use it they know where to find me. I've got to come back to it. At th' worst I can hold it against them for five days; an' then th' outfit'll be up here an' drive 'em off. But if it comes to trouble they won't let me get to it; they'll pick me off when I'm outside. They're gettin' more suspicious all th' time, too, judgin' from that missin' rope an' th' smell of that cigar. Nope; I don't like this shack a little bit. An' some night when I'm sneakin' back to it, suppose one of 'em is in it, waitin' for me? That wouldn't be nice. First chance I get I'll tote my tarpaulin an' some supplies out of here an' cache 'em some place not too far away."

Going into the little valley he was greatly surprised to see the rope hanging as he had left it, but he did not give it a second glance, and acted as though he was ignorant that it had been removed. He busied himself carrying firewood from the pile and heaping it up in the center of a cleared space, ready to be lit later on, and then removed the two saplings which made the gate to his rough fence and swung them aside so that they formed a V-shaped approach to the opening. Having performed these mysterious rites he passed the cabin, climbed up the crevice, recovered the rope, and returned. Carrying it into the house he carelessly closed the door behind him, went swiftly to the loose log in the rear wall and removed the things he had hidden behind it, rolling them up in the tarpaulin. Then he picked ravelings from an empty salt sack, tied them together and rolled them in the dirt on the floor until they matched it in color. After filling the water pails and chopping some firewood he took the gold pan and his rod and sought the creek, where he spent the rest of the day working and fishing.

Darkness found his supper dishes washed and put away, and, kneeling by the door, he stretched a string of weak ravelings across the opening, six inches above the sill. Cord not only would have been too prominent, but too strong; a foot would break the ravelings and never feel the contact. Whistling to Pepper, he took his saddle and the tarpaulin, stepped high over the door sill and in a few minutes was riding down the valley. Just before he came to the Hastings trail he threw the tarpaulin far into the brush without slowing the horse, and then, crossing the trail, plunged into the sloping draw which eventually became Little Canyon.

Pepper gingerly picked her way down the rough canyon trail without any directions from her rider, crossed the level, bowlder-strewn flat to the river, and stopped at the water's edge.

The Deepwater gurgled and swished, cold, swift, deep, and black, and Johnny shivered in anticipation of the discomforts due to be his for the next few hours. Unbuckling his belts, he slung them around his neck, and in his hat he placed the contents of his pockets. Giving Pepper a friendly and encouraging slap, he urged her into the river, a task which she did not like; but she overcame her prejudices against ice water and plunged in, swimming with powerful strokes. Emerging on the other bank they cantered briskly to the faintly beaten trail where Billy Atwood spent so many hours, and along it until a small, isolated clump of trees loomed up. There was a stump among them and on this Johnny placed a stone. Then he waited, shivering, until the moon came up.

A black blot arose hastily from the earth and became a cow. Two more near it also arose, and the three lumbered off clumsily, driven in the right direction by a horse that knew her work. It was her firm belief that cows had been put on earth to be bossed by her, and no matter how quickly they swerved she was always at the right place at the right time and kept them going as her master wished. She neither hurried them too fast nor pressed them too closely, for she knew that when a range cow is pushed too hard it is likely to go "on the prod" and change instantly from an easy-going, docile victim to a stubborn, vicious quadruped with no sense whatever and a strong yearning to use its horns.

It did not take long to get six cows to the edge of the Deepwater; but it took two hours of careful but hard riding, perseverance and profuse profanity to get them into the water. It was no one-man job, and with a horse that had less training than Pepper it might have proved to be an impossibility; but at last one cow preferred the water to being made a fool of, and when it went in the others reluctantly followed. Scrambling out on the farther bank they doubtless were congratulating themselves upon having escaped a pest, when the pest itself emerged behind them and drove them slowly but steadily toward Little Canyon.

In it they went, and up it; and as they paused on the main trail to determine which way to go, the pest arrived and decided the question for them, drove them across it and into a small valley; and as day broke, six unhurried, placid cows wandered slowly into the crooked canyon and through the opening in the fence.

Having changed the brands from the original CL to an equally sprawling GB, he returned to the cabin, unsaddled, and entered, stepping high over the sill. No one was there and nothing had been disturbed, but when he looked for the thread he found it snapped and lying on the floor.

Starting a brisk fire he hung his wet clothes before it on crude tripods made of sticks, hastily ate a substantial breakfast, fastened the shutter of the window, hung the gold pan over the closed door to serve as an alarm if anyone should enter, and in a few minutes was asleep.

Across the creek, high up the great ridge, a man lay behind a bowlder, a rifle in his hands, and he kept close watch on the cabin. Waiting a reasonable length of time, he finally arose, waved his hand and settled down again, the rifle covering the cabin door. In the pasture another man emerged from a thicket and hurried toward the canyon, swearing softly when he saw the changed brands. It took no second sight to tell him what the original brand had been. Emerging from the canyon he paused, glanced up at his friend, who made a significant sign, debated something in his mind, and then, pulling out a notebook, scrawled something in it and tore out the page. Creeping softly he reached the cabin door, stuck the page on it and then hurried away to join his friend. They climbed the ridge and hastened northward, conversing with animation.

When they reached the canyon leading to their ranch a tall, rangy man advanced to meet them. "Well," he said, smiling: "what did you find out about the rope? An' what kept you so long?"

"We found out a-plenty," growled Ackerman angrily. "That feller ain't no prospector. I've said so all along. He don't know enough about prospectin' to earn a livin' on th' top of a pile of gold!"

His companion nodded quickly. "Jim's right; he's a rustler. Doin' it single-handed, on a small scale."

"*I* ain't nowise shore that rustlin' is his game, neither," said Ackerman. "If he is he's a new hand at it. I could re-brand them cows in just about half th' time it took him, an' do a better job. He's dangerous; an' he should 'a' been shot long before this. I can get him today," he urged.

"I don't doubt that; but I wouldn't do it," smiled Quigley. "An' I hope *yo're* shore he ain't Logan."

Jim swore. "Yes; but if he keeps on rustlin' he'll have Logan after him. An' that'll mean that we'll have to look sharp, an' mebby fight. You let me get him, Tom."

Quigley shook his head. "'Tain't necessary. All we got to do is let him know he ain't wanted. Steal his cows, burn his cabin; an' shoot near him a couple of times, until he realizes how easy we can shoot *through* him. But I ain't shore I want him drove away."

"Huh!" questioned Ackerman.

"Huh!" repeated Fleming foolishly.

"Well," drawled Quigley, "for one thing Logan's purty shore to begin missin' cows before long. What puzzles me is that he ain't missed 'em long ago. Then he'll begin watchin' his range nights."

"But he won't watch up there," interrupted Fleming. "He don't know about that ford."

"There's only two breaks in th' Barrier," continued Quigley, ignoring the interruption, "that are near Nelson's valley; an' they're th' first places Logan'll watch. They're

Big an' Little Canyons. Some fine night Nelson will get caught or followed. Bein' a stranger, an' once workin' for th' CL, Logan will think he's got th' rustlers. He'll find signs that'll make him look in Nelson's pasture—if they ain't there naturally we'll put 'em there. They'll find his cabin an' his rebranded herd. When they go back again they'll reckon that th' rustlin' is all over; an' we'll still be in th' game, lettin' up a little for a while, an' be better off than ever. Savvy my drift?"

Ackerman shook his head savagely. "With them six cows, an' Logan missin' hundreds?" he sarcastically demanded.

Quigley smiled patronizingly. "Findin' only a few won't mean nothin', except that he's driven off th' rest every time he has got a few together, an' sold 'em. Now if you was to take that notebook that's stickin' out of yore pocket, an' write in it some words an' figgers showin' that he's sold so many cows, an' what he got for 'em each time, it might help. We'll know when Logan's due, an' we can drop that book where he'll find it. You never want to kill anythin' till yo're shore it ain't goin' to be useful. There's one thing I'm set on: there ain't going to be no unnecessary killin'."

Ackerman laughed grimly. "Well, anyhow; I've started things. I left a note on his door tellin' him what to do."

"What did you write?" demanded Quigley.

Ackerman told him defiantly. "An' what's more," he added, "I'm goin' to do some potshootin' before long."

"Well," replied Quigley, "I'd rather drive him out, an' then watch him for a while. I ain't shore he can't be scared. Do you think he suspects he's bein' watched?"

"I don't think so," answered Fleming.

"I know he does!" snapped Ackerman. "Why does he paw around that gravel bed an' pertend that he's found gold in it? There ain't no gold there!"

Quigley laughed. "He found gold, all right. Charley James saw it: an' he got it right there. He wanted Charley to take it in pay. I don't doubt that you know somethin' about prospectin' but 'gold is where it's found.'"

Ackerman thrust his head forward. "Gold in that gravel! Hell!"

"Charley saw it," grunted Quigley.

"Charley be damned!" snorted Ackerman. He looked closely at Quigley and suddenly demanded: "What makes you so set ag'in us shootin' him?"

Quigley regarded him evenly. "There was a lot of talk, when Porter was found dead. I told you all at th' time. Four men have got curious, come up in these hills an' never went out again. Twin Buttes has a bad name; an' th' next dead man that's blamed on us is goin' to make a lot more talk an' may stir up trouble.

"Now then: Pop knows that Nelson's up here, an' that means that everybody knows it. He saw me reach for my gun, an' heard me tell him to keep out of here. An' let me tell you Pop knows more about us than he lets on; an' he's as venomous as a snake when he gets riled. An' he ain't th' only one that knows things.

"Now we'll add it up: If we can scare Nelson away, or discourage him, he'll quit of his own accord; an' he won't talk because he knows that somebody knows he's been rustlin'." He turned on his heel. "Am I plain enough?"

"Wait a minute," called Ackerman. "That feller has got me worried. Mebby it would be reckless to let him disappear up here; but suppose I go on a spree in town when he's there? It's easy to start a fight with a gun-man, because he's got to toe th' mark. I can do th' job open an' above board, an' make it natural; an' that will keep us clear."

"Jim," smiled Quigley, "I don't want to lose you; an' if you pick a square fight with that man, th' even break that you demand in yore personal quarrels, we *will* lose you. I looked down his gun, an' I tell you that I didn't see him move. He's a *gun* man!"

Ackerman laughed. "We won't say anythin' about *that*. But if he did get th' worst of it in an even break an' a personal quarrel, would it hurt us up here? That's all I want to know."

Quigley thought deeply, and made a slow and careful reply. "If it wasn't bungled I don't see how it could. You'd have to rile him subtle, make him declare war an' be th' injured party yoreself; an' you'd want witnesses. But don't you do it, Jim; not nohow. I got a feelin' that he's th' best man with a Colt in this section. Yo're a wizard with a six-gun; but you ain't good enough for him. When he's around yo're in th' little boy's class; an' I ain't meanin' no offense to you, neither."

Ackerman, hands on hips, stared at Quigley's back as he walked away. "Th' hell you say!" he snorted wrathfully. " 'Little boy's class,' huh?" He wheeled and turned a scowling face to his friend Fleming. "Did you hear that? I calls that rubbin' it in! I got a notion to take that feller's two guns away from him an' make Tom eat 'em! Damned if I don't, too. You ride to town with me an' I'll show you somethin' you won't never forget!"

It may not be out of place here to say that the time soon came when he did show Fleming something; and that Fleming never did forget it.

Mr. Quigley smiled grimly as he entered the house, for it was his opinion that Mr. Ackerman had no peer in his use and abuse of Mr. Colt's most famous invention. He hardly could ask Mr. Ackerman to sally forth and engage in a personal duel with a common enemy, for it would smack too much of asking a friend to do his fighting for him. He believed that leadership is best based when it rests upon the respect of those led. He had no doubt about the outcome of such a duel, for he implicitly believed that the stranger, despite his vaunting two guns, had as much chance against Mr. Ackerman's sleight-of-hand as an enraged rattler had against a cool and businesslike king snake. The appropriateness of the simile made him smile, because the rattler is heavily armed and calls attention to the fact, while the king snake is modest, unassuming, and sounds no war-cry. Two guns meant nothing to Mr. Quigley, because he knew that one was entirely sufficient in the hand of the right man.

He had carefully pointed out the way for Mr. Ackerman to proceed in such a situation, and then warned him in an irritating way not to go ahead. So now he sighed with relief at a problem solved, for his knowledge of Mr. Ackerman's character was based upon accurate observations extending over a long period of time.

VIII

♦

Fleming is Shown

Johnny got up at noon, and when he saw the sign on his door its single word "Vamoose" told him that the valley and the cabin were of no further use to him; that the time for subterfuge and acting a part was past. That the rustlers were not certain of his intentions was plain, for otherwise there would have been a bullet instead of a warning; and he was mildly surprised that they had not ambushed him to be on the safe side.

It now remained for him to open the war, and warn

them further; or to pretend to obey the mandate and seek new fields of observation. Pride and anger urged the former; common sense and craftiness, the latter; and since he had not accomplished his task he decided to swallow his anger and move. Had he been only what he pretended to be, Nelson's creek would have seen some stirring times. As a sop to his pride he printed a notice on a piece of Charley's wrapping paper and fastened it on the door. Its three, short words made a concise, blunt direction as to a certain journey, popularly supposed to be the more heavily traveled trail through the spirit world. Packing part of his belongings on Pepper, he found room to sit in the saddle, and started off for an afternoon in Hastings, after which he would return to the cabin to spend the night and to get the rest of his effects.

When he rode into town he laughed outright at the sign on Pop's door, and he laughed harder when he saw another on Charley's door; and leaving his things behind Pop's saloon, he pushed on to Devil's Gap. At the ford he met the two happy anglers returning and they paused in mid-stream to hold up their catch.

"You come back with us," grinned Pop. "We'll pool th' fish an' have a three-corner meal. Where was you goin'?"

"To find you," chuckled Johnny. "I'm surprised at th' way you both neglects business."

"Comin' from you that makes me laugh," snorted Pop.

Charley grinned. "Did you see that whoppin' big feller I got? Bet it'll go three pounds."

"Lucky if it's half that," grunted Pop. "If I'd 'a' got that one *I* had hold of, we'd 'a' had a three-pounder, or mebby a four-pounder."

Charley snorted. "Who ever heard of a four-pound brook trout? Been a brown, now, it might 'a' been that big."

"Why, I caught 'em up to eight pounds, back East, when I was a kid!" retorted Pop.

"Yo're a squaw's dog liar!" snapped Charley. "Eight-pound brook trout! You must 'a' snagged a turtle, or an old boot full of mud!"

"Bet you five dollars!" retorted Pop, bristling.

"How you goin' to prove it?" jeered Charley. "Call th' dead back to life to lie for you?"

"Reckon I can't prove it," regretted Pop. "But when a man hangs around with a liar he shore gets th' name, too."

"Nobody never called me a liar an' got off without a hidin'!" snapped Charley. "I may be sixty years old, but I can lick you an' yore whole fambly if you gets too smart!"

Pop drew rein, his chin whiskers bobbing up and down. "I'm older'n that myself; but I don't need no relations to help me lick you! Get off that hoss, if you dares!"

"Here! Here!" interposed Johnny. "What's th' use of you two old friends mussin' each other up? Come on! I'm in a hurry! I'm hungry!"

"I won't go a step till he says I ain't no liar!" snapped Charley.

"I won't go till he says I caught a eight-pound brook trout!"

"Mebby he did—how do *I* know what he did when he was a boy?" growled Charley, full of fight. "But I ain't no liar, an' that's that!"

"Who said you was, you old fool?" asked Pop heatedly.

"You did!"

"I didn't!"

"You did!"

"Yo're a liar!'

"Yo're another!"

"Get off that hoss!"

"You ain't off yore own yet!"

Johnny was holding his sides and Pop wheeled on him savagely. "What the hell *you* laughin' at?"

"That's what *I* want to know!" blazed Charley.

"Come on, Charley!" shouted Pop. "We'll eat them fish ourselves. It's a fine how-dy-do when age ain't respected no more. An' th' next time you goes around callin' folks liars," he said, shaking a trembling fist under Johnny's nose, "you needn't foller *us* to do it on!"

Down the trail they rode, angrily discussing Johnny, the times, and the manners of the younger generation.

When Johnny arrived at the saloon and tried the door he found it locked. He could hear footsteps inside and he stepped back, chuckling, to wait until Pop had forgiven him; but after a few minutes he gave it up and went around to try the window of a side room.

"What you think yo're doin'?" inquired a calm voice behind him.

He wheeled and saw a man regarding him with level gaze, and across the street was a second, who sat on one horse and held fast to another.

"Tryin' to get in for a treat," grinned Johnny, full of laughter. "Had a spat with Pop an' Charley, an' cussed if they ain't locked me out!"

The stranger showed no answering smile. "That so?" he sneered. "Reckon you better come along with me, 'round front, till I hears what Hayes has to say about it. *I* don't believe he's home."

Johnny's expression changed from a careless grin to an ominous frown. "If you do any walkin' you'll do it alone."

Several people had been drawn to the scene and took in the proceedings with eager eyes and ears, but were careful to keep to one side. Jim Ackerman had a reputation which made such a location very much a part of discretion; and the two-gun man had been well discussed by Pop.

"I finds you tryin' a man's window," said Ackerman.
"So I stopped to ask about it. As long as I've took this
much trouble I'll go through with it. You comin' peaceful, or must I drag you around?"

"Mebby that's a job you'd like to tackle?" replied Johnny.

"I'm aimin' to be peaceful," rejoined Ackerman, his
voice as smooth as oil; "but I allus aim to do what I say.
You comin' with me?"

"If yo're aimin' to be peaceful, yo're plumb cross-eyed,"
retorted Johnny, slouching away from the wall.

Quick steps sounded within the building and a frightened, high-pitched voice could be heard. "Couple of bob-
cats lookin' for holts," it said. "That feller Nelson is pickin'
on somebody else."

The window raised and Pop stuck his angry face out to
see what was going on; and his wrinkled countenance
paled suddenly when he saw Ackerman, and the look in
his eyes. He had a trout in one hand and a bloody knife in
the other, and both fell to the ground.

"Jumpin' mavericks!" he whispered. "It's Ackerman!
What's wrong, Jim?" he quavered.

"You saved us a walk," replied Ackerman, not taking
his eyes from the flushed face of his enemy. "I caught *him*
tryin' to open that window."

Charley thrust his head out as Pop replied. "We was
playin' a joke on him. It's all right, Jim. Much obliged for
yore unusual interest."

"Well, I'm glad of *that*," smiled Ackerman; "but he
looked *suspicious* an' I reckoned I ought to drag him around
an' show you what I *found* tryin' to bust in. But if you *say*
it's all right, why I reckon it *is!*"

"I reckon it ain't!" snapped Johnny, enraged at his hu-
miliating position and at the way Ackerman accented his
words. "An' if that itchin' *trigger*-finger of *yourn* wants to

get *busy* it has my permission," he mimicked. "Pop," he said, sharply, "who *is* this buzzard?"

"No need to get riled over a thing like that," faltered Pop.

"Shut yore trap!" snapped Charley, battle in his eyes. "That's Ackerman, relative of Quigley's; th' best six-gun man in th' country."

"Thanks," growled Johnny, staring through narrowed lids at Ackerman, who stood alert, his lips twitching with contempt. "When a dog pesters me I kick him; if he snaps at me I shoot him. I'm goin' to kick you to yore cayuse an' yore friend." He had been sliding forward while he spoke and now they stood face to face, an arm's length apart.

Ackerman suddenly made two lightning-like movements. His left hand leaped out to block his enemy's right in its draw, while his own right flashed down to his gun. As his fingers closed on the butt, Johnny's heavy Colt by some miracle of speed jabbed savagely into the pit of the scheming man's stomach with plenty of strength behind it, and Ackerman doubled up like a jackknife, his breath jolted out of him with a loud grunt. Johnny's right hand smacked sharply on his enemy's cheek, left vivid finger marks, which flashed white and then crimson, and continued on down; and when it stopped a plain, Frontier Colt peeked coyly from his hip at the surprised and chagrined gentleman across the street, who had been instructed to remain a noncombatant; and had no intention, whatsoever, of disobeying Ackerman's emphatic order. To reveal his status he quickly raised his hands and clasped them on the top of his hat, which is a more comfortable position than holding them stiffly aloft.

Ackerman was dazed and sick, for the solar plexus is a peculiarly sensitive spot, and his hands instinctively had forsaken offense and spasmodically leaped to the agonized nerve center.

"Turn around!" snapped Johnny viciously. "*Pronto!* There's dust on th' seat of yore pants."

Ackerman groaned and obeyed, and the hurtling impact of a boot drove him to his hands and knees.

"Get agoin'!" ordered Johnny, aflame with anger, slipping the right hand gun back into its holster and motioning with the other.

Ackerman, his eyes blazing, started on his humble journey, assisted frequently by the boot; and having crossed the street, he paused.

"Get up on that cayuse!" crisply ordered Johnny, making motions which increased the mounted man's uneasiness.

The further Ackerman had crawled the angrier he had become, and tears of rage streaked the dust on his face. At Johnny's last command and the kick which accompanied it, his good sense and all thought of safety left him. He arose with a spring, a berserker, trembling with rage, and reached for his gun with convulsive speed while looking into his enemy's weapon with unseeing eyes. There was a flash, a roar, and a cloud of smoke at Johnny's hip, and a glittering six-shooter sprang into the air, spinning rapidly. Ackerman did not feel the shock which numbed his hand, but leaped forward straight at his enemy's throat. Johnny swerved quickly and his right hand swung up in a short, vicious arc. Ackerman, too crazed to avoid it, took the blow on the point of his jaw and dropped like a stone.

Johnny stepped back and looked evilly at the man on the horse.

"Gimme yore gun, butt first. Thanks. You work for Quigley?"

The other nodded slowly.

"Friend of this hombre?"

"Yes; sort of."

"Then why didn't you cut in?"

"Why, I—I—" the other hesitated, and stopped.

"Spit it!"

"Well, I wasn't supposed to," coldly replied the horseman.

"Then it was talked over?"

"Not particular. Jim does his own fightin', hisself."

"Good thing for Jim, an' you, too," retorted Johnny. "When it's crowded I can't allus be polite. Who put that sign on my door?"

"What sign?"

"I'm askin' *you* questions!" snapped Johnny, his eyes blazing anew.

"Dunno nothin' about it," answered the other.

"I reckon yo're a practiced liar," retorted Johnny. "But it don't make no difference. I'm leavin' th' valley, for I can't fight pot-shooters an' do any work at th' same time. Quigley don't own this country, an' you tell him that while he's boss of that little valley, *I*'m boss in this town. If him or any of his men come to town while I'm here I'll shoot 'em down like I would a snake. That means one at a time or all together; an' if he don't believe me, you tell him I'll be here all day tomorrow. There ain't no bushes in town, an' none of yore gang can fight without 'em. Now you say to him that I don't want no remarks made about what I was doin' up there—you savvy that? If I hear of any I'll slip up there some night an' blow him all over his shirt. An' damn you, I mean it!"

Ackerman stirred and sat up, looking around in a dazed way. When his eyes fell on Johnny they lost their puzzled look and blazed again with rage. He reached swiftly to his holster, found it empty, and shrugged his shoulders.

Johnny regarded him coldly. "Get on that cayuse, an' start goin'. This town ain't big enough for both of us at once."

Ackerman silently obeyed, but his face was distorted with passion. When he had clawed himself into the saddle he looked down on the grim master of the situation.

"Words are foolish," he whispered. "We'll meet again!"

Johnny nodded. "I reckon so. Everybody plays their cards accordin' to their own judgment. Just now I got a high straight flush, so you hit th' trail, *pronto*!"

He stepped aside to get out of the dust-cloud which suddenly swirled around him, and watched it roll northward until the dim figures in it were lost to sight around a bend. The slouch went out of his bearing as he straightened up and slid his gun into its holster, and walking over to Ackerman's glittering six-shooter he picked it up and sneered at it.

"I ain't surprised," he laughed, eying the ivory handle and the ornate engraving. Wheeling abruptly he glanced carelessly at the grinning audience and strode to the door of Pop's saloon.

"I'll be damned!" sputtered Pop, his eyes still bulging.

"Reckon you will," laughed Johnny, "unless you mends yore sinful ways."

"What you been doin' make Jim Ackerman pick a fight with you?" demanded Pop, recovering his faculties and his curiosity at the same instant.

"Here's his gun; an' here's his friend's," said Johnny. "Keep 'em for 'em. They plumb went off without 'em."

Pop openly admired Ackerman's weapon. "Bet that cost a heap," he remarked. "Ain't she a beauty?" He rubbed energetically at a leaden splotch on the cylinder.

"It was in good company," replied Johnny.

"You got to look out for him," Pop warned. "He's a bad Injun." Then he grinned suddenly. "But he come damned near bein' a *good* Injun!"

"Hey!" called a peeved voice from within. "If you reckon I'm goin' to clean *all* these fish myself, you better copper yore bets." Footsteps approached the door and Charley roughly elbowed Pop aside. "That means you, too, Nelson," he growled. "What you mean, hangin' back at th' ford? Figger we'd have 'em all cleaned before you arrove? Well, if you aim to eat any of 'em, you grab holt of a knife an' get busy!" He shuffled back into the room again, muttering: "Cripes! I'm fish from my head to my heels an' bloody as a massacre. An' what's more, I ain't goin' to clean another damned one, not nohow!"

IX

◆

A Skirmish in the Night

Saying good night to his two friends, Johnny rode north along the trail, but he had not ridden more than half way to the mouth of his valley when he swung Pepper into an arroyo which he knew led to the south side of the butte behind his cabin. While heavily fringed with brush and trees it was open enough along the dry bed of the stream to permit him to push on at fair speed, and while there were rocks and bowlders in plenty, Pepper easily avoided them in the soft moonlight and went on with confidence. At last, reaching a fork, he chose the right-hand lead and pushed on more slowly for a few minutes, and then, picketing the horse, he slipped out of his chaps and boots and put on the pair of moccasins which had been hidden under the saddle flaps. Taking the rifle from the long scabbard, he slung it across his back and slipped noiselessly up the ravine.

Half an hour later he stopped suddenly and sniffed, and then glanced quickly around him. The smoke was very faint, but it was something to think about because it meant either men close at hand or a forest fire. Going on again, even more slowly, he began to take advantage of cover, and as he proceeded the smoke became steadily stronger. A sudden suspicion made him set his jaws, for he was going straight up wind and toward his cabin. Stopping a moment to consider, he turned sharply to his left and went on again, a Colt swinging loosely in his left hand. Anything close enough to be seen plainly would be near enough for the Colt, and in such poor light the six-shooter was more accurate in his hands than a rifle.

The only things about him which he could hear were the holsters, which rubbed very softly as he walked, but the sound would not carry for any distance. Having gone around the little valley near his cabin, he crawled along below the ragged skyline of the ridge and reached a point close to the cabin, when he suddenly dropped to his stomach and flattened himself to the earth.

Some restless, gambling soul could not do without a cigarette and he had detected its faint odor in time. Turning his head slowly, he sniffed deeply and swore under his breath, for he was going partly with the wind, which meant that the smoker must be somewhere behind him. Then a gentle breeze, creeping along the ridge in a back-draft, brought to him the strong and pungent odor of the fire; and he nodded in quick understanding.

The back-draft told him that the smoker was in front of

him and cleared up one danger; but it also had blotted out
the odor of the cigarette, and as he started forward again
he put his faith in his eyes and ears. Slowly he moved
along, a few feet at a time, and then he caught the brief and
fragrant odor again. Worming around a great, up-thrust
slab of lava he stopped suddenly and held his breath. A
speck of fire, faint through the clinging ashes, moved in a
swift, short arc, became brighter and moved back again,
a gleaming dot of red. He could see the hand and part of
the arm of the man who had just knocked the ashes from
a cigarette in a characteristic and thoughtless gesture. He
was sitting just around the corner of a huge bowlder not
far away, his back to it, and a dull gleam of reflected
moonlight revealed the end of his rifle.

From where he now lay Johnny could see the smolder-
ing ruins of his cabin, where the flames were low and the
flying sparks but few. A little current of air fanned the
ashes for a few minutes and sent the sparks swirling and
dancing, and the flickering, ghostly flames licking upward with renewed life. The increased light, fitful as it
had been, brought a smile to his face; for he had caught
sight of a pair of spurred boots projecting beyond a rock
not far from the glowing embers.

"Ah, th' devil!" muttered the man near him. "I'm goin'
home. He's scared out."

The speaker arose and stretched, and grumblingly leaned
over to pick up his sombrero, the moon lighting his hair;
and he suddenly crumpled forward and sprawled out without a groan as Johnny's Colt struck his head.

The owner of the spurred boots, down behind the rock
near the cabin, wriggled backward and looked up to see
what had made the noise, caught sight of a dim, ghostly
figure moving past a bowlder and called up to it.

"Come on, Ben; let's get goin'. Where's Fleming?"

"Thanks to my fool idea of strategy," said a peeved voice high above the cabin, "which I borrowed from our doughty friend, Mr. Ackerman, I'm up here, smoked up like a ham. I ain't stuck on this. Shootin' a good man from ambush never did set well on my stummick. Reckon Ben's asleep, like a reg'lar sentry; he didn't have th' cussed smoke to make things interestin' for him. Hey, Ben!" he called, wearily.

"No use yellin'," warned Spurred Boots earnestly. "He ain't asleep. I just saw him move. Up to some of his fool jokes, I reckon; an' it's a damned poor time to play 'em. I'm a little nervous, an' might shoot without askin' any questions. Comin' down?"

"Yo're just whistlin' I am," growled Fleming. "It's all fool nonsense, us three watchin' an' waitin' to shoot that feller. When he finds his shack burned an' his rustlin' business busted up, he'll move out without us pluggin' him. Damn it! Didn't he say he was done? But you just listen to th' mockin' bird: If there's any shootin' to be done, he'll do his little, two-handed share. I've been eddicated today; done had a superstition knocked sprawlin'. An' so did Jim get eddicated. He made his play for that feller's right hand, when damned if he ain't left-handed. It made Jim near sick; for a minute I was scared he'd lose his dinner. An' I allus believed left-handed men came in third by two lengths; but lawsy me! What? I'm insulted! I said lawsy."

"You shore can talk!" admired Spurred Boots. "Sometimes a cussed lot too much. What in blazes is Ben doin'?" he asked petulantly, stiffly arising and working his arms and legs.

"Fixin' to jump out on us from behind a rock, an' yell 'Boo!'" grunted Fleming. "Ben, he's an original feller; allus was, even as a kid. Damn these thorns." A thin stream of profanity came from the crevice and Fleming slid down the rest of the way and rolled out into the circle of illumination. "Just like water down a chute, or a merry-hearted bowlder down a hill. Roll, Jordan, roll. Was you askin' about Benjamin, th' catcher of lightning? Benjamin Franklin Gates, his name is; an' he's done gone home. He's a sensible feller, B.F.G. is; but only in spots, little spots, widely spaced."

"You talk as much as Jim Howard's wife," grumbled Spurred Boots. "Jim he said—"

"Of course he did! wasn't it awful?" interposed Fleming. "It was just like a man. But I think it was me that told you that story; so we'll let it keep its secret. As I was sayin', getting in my words edgeways like, but shore gettin' 'em in: Ben has pulled th' picket stake, an' like th' Arabs, done went."

"You mean Arapahoes."

"Did I? I allus call 'em that for short. Have mercy, Jehovah!"

"I saw him move just before I spoke," replied Spurred Boots positively. "But that was a long time ago, before th' deluge, of words," he jabbed ironically.

"Cease; spare thy whacks. An' where th' hell did you ever hear of th' deluge? Some Old Timer tell you about it?" responded Fleming. "I been seein' things, too. All kinds of things. Some had tails but no legs; some had legs but no tails; an' to make a short tale shorter, that was a ghost what you saw. A wild, woopin', woppin' ghost. Come on, Nat; let's flit."

"Then my ghost lit a cigarette a long time back," retorted Nat Harrison. "An' then it said 'flop.' Do they smoke cigarettes?" he demanded with great sarcasm.

"Some does; an' some smokes hops; an' some smokes dried loco weed," grinned Fleming. "That was a spark what you saw, an' th' musical flop was a trout fish turnin' cartwheels on th' water. One of them sparks plumb lit on th' back of my neck, an' I cussed near jumped over th' edge an' made a 'flop' of my own for myself. An' it's a blamed long walk home," he sighed.

"There's th' lightnin's play-fellow now! See him, up there?" demanded Harrison. "Must 'a' been off scoutin'. Hey, Ben! Wait for us—be right up."

Fleming glanced up as another vagrant breeze fanned the embers, and he forthwith did several things at once, and did them quite well. Sending Harrison plunging down behind a rock by one great shove, he jumped for another and fired as he moved. "Ben hell!" he shouted, firing again. "I've seen *that* hombre before today. Keep yore head down, an' get busy!"

Two alert and attentive young men gave keen scrutiny to the ridge and wondered what would happen next. Thirty minutes went by, and then Harrison rolled over and over, laughing uproariously.

"Cussed if it ain't funny!" he gurgled. "'Some smoke cigarettes, some smokes hops, an' some smokes dried loco weed!' Ha-ha-ha! An' I reckon yo're still seein' them woopin' woops."

"You'll see somethin' worse if you moves out into sight," retorted Fleming. "That ghost that *I* just saw was a human that ain't got to th' ghost state yet. If you don't believe me, you ask Ackerman, if you've got th' nerve."

Harrison rose nonchalantly and sauntered over toward the embers. "Come on, Art; I'm cussed near asleep," he yawned.

"You acts like you was plumb asleep, an' walkin' in it," snapped Fleming angrily. "But it's a good idea," he admitted ironically. "You stay right there an' draw his fire, an' I'll pull at his flash. You make a good decoy, naturally; it comes easy to you. A decoy is an imitation. Stand still, now, so he can line up his sights on you. *I*'m all ready."

Harrison grinned and waved his hand airily. "There ain't no human up there," he placidly remarked. "An' I don't care if Benjamin F. *is* there: she goes as she lays. What you saw was a bear or a lobo or a cougar come up to see th' fire, an' hear you orate from th' mountain top. They'll go long ways to see curious things. In th' book, on page eighteen, it says that they has great streaks of humor, an' a fittin' sense of th' ridiculous. Animals are awful curious about little things. An' on page thirty-one it says they has a powerful sense of smell; an' you know you was up purty high. An' I ain't lookin' forward with joy unconfined to gropin' along no moonlit trail with th' boss of th' wolf tribe, or other big varmits sneakin' around. I might step on a tail an' loosen things up considerable. They're hell on wheels when you steps on their tails, poor things."

"La! La!" said Fleming sympathetically. "Just because you have got yore head out of th' window it don't say you ain't goin' to get no cinder in yore eye. A lead cinder. Lemme tell you that animal wore pants an' a big sombrero. I tell you I *saw* him!"

"It was one of them sparks," grunted the other, enjoying himself. "One of 'em that plumb lit on th' back of yore neck. A spark is a little piece of burnin' wood which soars like th' eagle, an' when it comes down makes sores like th' devil. Te-de-dum-dum! Howsomeever, if yo're goin' with me, yo're goin' to start right now—I've done it already," and he walked slowly toward the creek.

Fleming arose and hesitated, scanning the ridge with searching eyes. Then he stepped out and followed his friend, who already was across the creek and climbing the steep bank.

After reaching the top of the steep part of the ridge he

glanced about over the great slope and then paused for breath and reflection, peering curiously toward the tree-shaded hollow where he had seen the much-debated movement. Obeying a sudden impulse he drew his gun and went cautiously forward, bent low and taking full advantage of the cover. A deep groan at his side made him jump and step back. Cautiously peering over a large rock he started in sudden surprise, swearing under his breath. Benjamin Franklin Gates, neatly trussed and gagged, lay against the rock on its far side, and his baleful eyes spoke volumes. There came a soft step behind Fleming and he wheeled like a flash, his upraised gun cutting down swiftly, and came within an ace of pulling the trigger at Harrison, who writhed sideways and snarled at him. Then Harrison also saw the bound figure on the ground and swore with depth, feeling, and vigor.

"Smokes dried loco weed!" he jeered sarcastically, his voice barely audible. "I feels uncomfortable, entirely too present," he whispered, sinking quietly to the ground.

"Which is unanimous," remarked Fleming, with simple emphasis. "Ben, he ain't sayin' nothin'," he added cheerfully.

An angry gurgle came from the bound figure and it rolled over to face them. Harrison grinned at it. "Under other circumstances I could enjoy this unusual situation," he remarked softly.

"Face to face with Ben, an' him not sayin' a word," marveled Fleming, his eyes busy with the rock-strewn slope. "But I can almost hear him think. Twinkle, twinkle, little star—wonder where Mr. Two-gun Nelson is located at this short, brief, an' interestin' second?"

Another gurgle slobbered from the bound man and his heels thumped the ground.

"Hark!" said Harrison, tensely. "I hears me a noise!"

"I hears me it, too," said Fleming. "But not a word; not a soft, harsh, lovin', long, short, or profane word. Not even a syllable. Not even th' front end of a syllable. All is silent; all but that mysterious drummin' noise. An' if it was farther away I'd be quite restless."

A coughing gurgle and a choked snort came from the base of the rock, and then a louder, more persistent drumming.

"An' you said Benjamin had done snuck home," accused Harrison. "I'm surprised at you. He's been here all th' time. How could he snuck when he's hog-tied, which is appropriate? Gurgle, gurgle, little man—I'll untie you if I can." He bent over, cut loose the gag, slashed the belt from the trussed feet and severed the neckerchief from the crossed wrists. "There! There! Not so loud!" he gently chided.

"Blankety dashed blank blank!" said Ben Gates. "Dashed blankety dashed blank blank! What th' hell you want to cut that belt for, you dashed dashed blankety blank of a dash! Three dollars done gone to th' devil! Just because you got a blankety-blank knife do you have to slash every dashed-dashed thing you see!"

"Sh!" whispered Fleming. "We know yo're grateful; but what happened?" he breathed, too busy to look around.

"Shut yore face!" ordered Harrison, trying in vain to stare through a great, black lava bowlder which lay on the other side of a small clearing.

"Dashed blank!" said Benjamin. "It's been shut enough, you damned pie-faced doodle-bug!"

"Yes; yes; we know," soothed Fleming; "but what happened?"

"Leaned over to get my blankety-blank hat and a dashed tree fell on my blank head!" He felt of the afore-mentioned head with a light and tender touch; and the generous bump made him swear again.

"It's that prospectin' rustler," enlightened Fleming, gratis, as he peered into the shadows behind him.

"No!" said Gates. "I reckoned it was General Grant an' th' Army of th' Potomac! Dead shore it wasn't Columbus?" he sneered.

"It was not Columbus, Benjamin," said Fleming. "Columbus discovered America in 1492 or 1942—some time around there. Ain't you heard about it yet? An' somehow I feels like a calf bein' drug to th' brandin' fire. I feels that I'm goin' to get somethin' soon; an' I ain't shore just what it's goin' to be."

"You'll get it, all right," cheered Harrison, anger in his voice withal. "It'll be a snub-nosed .45, if you don't shut up yore trap. You ain't openin' no Fourth of July celebration, or runnin' for Congress."

Ben felt for his gun and cursed peevishly. "My guns are gone: lend me one of yourn!" he said.

"Th' gentleman has quite a collection," chuckled Harrison. "Three Colts an' a Winchester. Good pickin', says he. Good enough, says I. True, says he; but, he says, I have hopes of more. Ta-ta! jeers I."

"Shut *yore* face!" growled Fleming, writhing.

"I want a gun, an' I wants it now!" blazed Gates, pugnaciously.

"Fair sir, how many guns do you think we pack?" demanded Harrison.

"You got a rifle an' a Colt!" snapped Gates. "I wants one of 'em!"

"He only wants one of 'em," said Fleming.

"I was scared you'd be a hog," said Harrison. "Here; take this Winchester, an' *keep* it. Bein' generous is all right; but it has its limits."

Gates gripped the weapon affectionately and sat up. "No use of stayin' here like we done took root," he said, rising to his feet. "We wants to spread out. Mebby he's still hangin' around."

"Yes; an' shoot each other," growled Harrison. "I'm goin' to spread out, all right; an' when I quits spreadin' I'll be in my little bunk. He's a mile away by now; but if he ain't, don't you let him have that gun; he's got enough now."

He stopped suddenly, and their hair arose on their heads as a long-drawn, piercing scream rang out. It sounded like a woman in mortal agony and it came from the ridge above them. From the upper end of the rock-walled pasture below came a howl, deep, long-drawn, evil, threatening. They turned searching eyes toward the nearer sound and saw a crescent bulk silhouetted against the moon. It lay in the top of blasted pine, and as they looked, it raised its chunky head and neck and screamed an answering challenge to the lobo wolf in the canyon.

Ben moved swiftly, and a spurt of flame split the night, crashing echoes returning in waves. The crescent silhouette in the tree-top leaped convulsively and crashed to the ground, breaking off the dead limbs in its fall, and then there ensued a spitting, snarling, thrashing turmoil as the great panther scored the earth in its agony.

Ben's friends forsook him as though he were a leper and melted into the shadows, cursing him from A to Z. They wanted no ringing notice of their presence broadcasted, and the flash and roar of the heavy rifle had done just that.

As they faded into the darker shadows farther back a crashing sounded in the brush and they peered forth to see the great panther plunging and writhing through the bushes, smashing its way through the oak brush in desperate plunges. Reaching the edge of a small clearing it gave one convulsive leap, another harrowing scream and thudded against a bowlder, where it suddenly relaxed and lay quiet.

"There's near a quart of corn juice up in my bunk, an' I'm goin' for it," said Harrison, moving swiftly up the rough trail. "I need it, an' I need it bad!"

"That cat's mate ain't fur away," remarked Fleming thoughtfully. "It's due hereabouts right soon. I'm stickin' closer than a brother, Nat. Lead me to th' fluid which consoleth, arouseth anger and dulleth pain; blaster of homes, causer of—of—headaches, damn it! Ben, he's a great hunter, a wild, untamed, ferocious slayer of varmints; he can stay here an' argue with th' inquirin' mate, if he wants, while we wafts yonder an' hence. It won't be draped up in no tree, neither; somehow I can just see it sniffin' at th' beloved dead an' then soft-footin' through th' brush, over th' ridges an' around th' bowlders, its whiskers bristlin', its wicked little ears pointed back, an' its long, generous tail goin' jerk-jerk, tremble-tremble. Lovely picture. Fascinatin' picture. It is lookin' real hard for th' misguided son-of-a-gun that killed its tuneful mate. Nice kitty; pretty kitty; lovely kitty! I votes, twice, for that whiskey. I votes three times for that whiskey. Lead th' way, Nat; an' for my sake keep yore eyes peeled."

Quick, heavy steps behind them made them jump for cover, turning as they jumped, and to peer anxiously back along the trail.

Ben walked into sight, the rifle held loosely in front of him as he peered into the shadows. "You acts like you has springs in yore laigs," he derisively remarked.

"An' you acts like you had sour dough for brains," courteously retorted Harrison. "An' it's so sour it's moldy. Go away from here!"

"Yo're a great little, two-laigged success," sneered Fleming. "Reg'lar Dan'l Boone. I hopes if any gent ever trails me for my scalp it will be you. You wants to buy yoreself a big tin whistle an' a bass drum when you go out ambushin'!"

"I claims that was good shot," complacently replied Ben. "What with it bein' near dark, an' a strange gun, an' my head most splittin', I holds it was. Must 'a' been to make you long-winded ijuts so damned jealous."

"Trouble is, yore head didn't split enough," grumbled Harrison pleasantly. "It should 'a' been split from topknot to chin. Next time *I* goes manhuntin', *you* stays home with yore pretty picture books."

"Suits me," grunted Ben placidly. "Yore company hurts my ears, offends my nose, an' shocks my eyes. An' as for th' excitement, why I done got enough of that to—*look out!*" he yelled, firing without raising the gun to his shoulder.

An answering flash split the darkness between two bowlders further up the slope and Ben pitched sideways. His companions fired as if by magic; the instant return fire sent Harrison reeling backward. He tripped on a root and fell sprawling, the gun flying from his hand. Fleming leaped toward a huge rock, firing as he jumped, and slid behind the cover, where he sighed, and groped for his gun with trembling hands. Groans and muttered curses came from the trail, and Fleming, raising himself to a sitting position, his back against a rock, saw Harrison dragging himself toward his gun and a clump of brush.

"You stay where you are," said an ominous voice, "an' put up yore hands!"

Lying in a patch of moonlight, Harrison could do nothing but obey; but Fleming nerved himself and picked up his gun, still able to fight and only waiting for his enemy to show himself. Several minutes passed and then a hand darted over the rock and wrenched Fleming's gun out of the weak hand that held it.

"You ain't goin' to get hurt no more if you acts sensible," said the new owner of the gun. "Where you hit?"

"Thigh an' shoulder," muttered Fleming weakly.

The stranger fell to work swiftly and deftly and in a short time he arose and moved toward the two men in the clearing. "You'll be all right after yore friends get you home," he said over his shoulder. Reaching the two figures on the trail he first took their guns and then looked them over.

"This feller with th' lump on his head is my old friend, th' smoker," said Johnny. "He's got a crease in his scalp. Barrin' a little blood an' a big headache, he'll be all right after a while. Where'd I get you?" he demanded of Harrison.

"Arm," grunted Harrison. "Through th' flesh. I done tripped an' fell—must 'a' near busted a rock with my fool head when I lit," he said, as if to explain his subsequent inaction. "We reckoned you'd left th' country till we found th' package you tied up an' left."

"I come back for th' rest of my stuff," replied Johnny. "I was scared to come up th' valley."

"You acts like you'd scare easy," admitted Harrison. "I'm sorry you ain't got more nerve," he grinned despite the pain in his arm.

"Here," said Johnny, squatting beside him, "lemme tie up that arm. I wasn't aimin' to shoot nobody till I was cornered," he grinned. "I heard what you fellers said, back in th' valley, an' that's why. I was plumb peaceful, tryin' to slip away, when that gent up an' let drive at me. Bein' in a pocket made by them fool bowlders I couldn't get out, so I had to cut down on you with both hands. Th' dark shadows helped me a lot; you couldn't see what you was shootin' at. An' anyhow, I *owe* him somethin'. I was under that tree when he up an' dumped that pleasant cougar down on top of me, right in my arms. Never was more surprised in all my life. An' to make matters worse, this is my best pair of pants."

"Show 'em to me!" begged Harrison.

Johnny stepped back for inspection and waved his hands at the trousers; and Harrison had to laugh at what he saw. What was left of them formed a very short kilt, and the underwear was torn into bloody strips.

Harrison wept.

"I'm pullin' my stakes," continued Johnny pleasantly. "This layout is too excitin' for a man of my bashful an' retirin' disposition. You can tell Quigley he don't have to set no more ambushes in that valley, an' also that th' first time I meet him I'm goin' to smoke him up with both hands. I'm honin' for to get a look at him, just a quick glance. Give my regards to yore friend Ackerman; his gun, an' that other feller's, is with Pop Hayes; but mebby they ought to wait till I leave th' country before they go in for 'em."

He turned on his heel and walked slowly away, with a pronounced limp, a present from the cougar. When he reached the edge of the clearing he paused and faced about.

"You two fellers will be all right in a little while, an' if you can't get yore friend home, you can send them that can. I'll take yore six-guns along with me so there won't be no accidents; but I'll leave this rifle over here on this rock, empty. Th' cartridges are on th' ground on th' other side of th' rock. That cougar's mate is some het up about now, I reckons, an' you may need it. Better not come for it for a couple of minutes. There's been enough shootin' already. *Adios*," and he was gone as silently as a shadow.

Harrison sat cross-legged and waited considerable more than two minutes and then walked slowly toward the rifle. As he picked it up there came a haunting scream and a rolling fusillade of shots from the south. Then a distant voice called faintly.

"I got th' mate, an' lost th' rest of my pants. *Adios!*"

"I'll be damned!" grunted Harrison, going toward his friend at the rock. "That feller is one cheerful hombre. If I was Quigley, I'll bet four bits I wouldn't show my face in Hastings till he was a long way off. No, ma'am; not a-tall. Here, Art; you take th' gun till I go back an' see how Dan'l Boone is comin' along. He's a rip-snortin', high-class success, *he* is! I'll bet you he'll *brag* about droppin' that cougar, you just wait an' see. *Hello,* you wild jackass! How you feel!"

"You can go to hell" snorted the man with the creased scalp, sitting up. "An' I don't care a cuss when you starts, or how you goes. I'm fond of excitement, thrive on it an' get fat; but I serves notice, here an' now, that I'm quittin'. Any man that takes th' trail with you two fools is a bigger fool. Great guns! I won't have no head left after a while!"

"You never did have one that amounted to anythin'," said Harrison cheerfully. "I admit that it's a handy place to hang a hat, but when that is said, th' story is ended. Amen. You set right where you are till you are able to walk, an' then we'll get Art home."

"Takin' Art home is what we should 'a' done long ago; we're doin' this thing backwards, th' damn fool!" moaned Ben. "We'd 'a' been home long ago if it wasn't for him."

"Huh?" muttered Harrison. "Well, I'll be damned! Say! If it wasn't for you pluggin' that cat we'd 'a' been home, whole an' happy, sleepin' th' sleep of th' innercent. When you got that bright idea, you shore touched off a-plenty. He was pullin' his stakes, aimin' to get out peaceful, when you dumped that panther right down plumb around his neck! Man! Man! But I wish I'd 'a' seen that! Benjamin, if you only knowed what I'm thinkin' about you! Words ain't capable of revealin' my thoughts; they fall far short; an' if I used enough words I'd strain my vo—vocabulary, till it never would be any good any more. An' I can only swear in English, Spanish, Navajo, an' Ute. An education must be a grand thing."

"Th' breaks was ag'in us," explained Benjamin.

"Lord, please hold me back!" prayed Harrison.

Well to the south of them a limping cow-puncher, with no trousers at all now, and blood-soaked strips of underwear pasted to his torn and bleeding legs, pushed doggedly toward his horse, swearing at almost every painful step and avoiding all kinds of brush as he painstakingly held to the middle of the dried bed of the creek. His shirt tail, cut into ragged strips, flapped in the cold breeze where not held down by the weight of the sagging belts and holsters; and in his hands he carried the captured Colts.

Reaching his horse he fastened the extra weapons to his saddle, carefully drew on his chaps, coiled up the picket rope and climbed gingerly astride.

"Come on, Pepper!" he growled. "Pull out of this. I got a pair of pants wrapped up in that tarpaulin at th' mouth of th' valley; an' I wants 'em bad. You shore missed somethin' this evenin', you lucky old cow!"

When day broke it revealed a shivering, grumbling cow-puncher washing his cuts and gashes in the cold, pure water of Nelson's creek. Retiring to the pebbly bank, he tore up a clean shirt and used it all for bandages, after which he carefully drew on a pair of clean underdrawers and covered them with a pair of well-worn trousers. The chaps came next as a protection against whipping branches and clinging brush. Rolling up the tarpaulin he fastened it behind his saddle and, mounting stiffly, started for Hastings.

Some hours later he lolled at ease and related to the

grinning proprietor the strange and exciting occurrences of the night. Pop was swung from one extreme to the other as the tale unfolded, while Andrew Jackson chuckled, whistled, and laughed until the narrator's scratching fingers lulled him into a deep and soul-stirring ecstasy.

"You shore started some fireworks," chuckled Pop when the tale was finished. "An' yo're cussed lucky, too. When Ackerman showed his hand yesterday I knowed trouble was fixin' to ride you to a frazzled finish. Now what damned fool thing are you goin' to do?" he demanded anxiously.

"I'm goin' to keep out of that valley," reluctantly answered Johnny. "It ain't got no charms for me no more. They've burned my cabin, an' I reckon I got all th' gold there was, anyhow. When my legs get well I'm goin' to try it again somewhere else. Twin Buttes are too unlucky for me."

"Now yo're shoutin'," beamed Pop. "You just set around here an' take things easy for a few days, while me an' Charley fixes that tarp so it'll be a pack cover an' a tent that *is* one. No prospector wants to build a shack unless winter ketches him in th' hills or he finds a rich strike. Me an' you an' Charley will go fishin' a few days from now an' have a reg'lar rest. I'm all tired out, too. Business is shore confinin'." He looked Johnny over and chuckled. "Cussed if I wouldn't 'a' give six pesos, U.S., to 'a' seen that cougar a-fannin' you! He-he-he!"

X

◆

A Change of Base

J ohnny, upon leaving Hastings, struck south from it and spent the night west of the Circle S after a journey of twenty miles on foot. Pepper was again a pack horse, and the diamond hitch which held the bulging tarpaulin in place would have dispelled any doubt as to Johnny's abilities to cut loose from civilization and thrive in the lonely places. And he had cut loose when he placed a note under a rock behind a certain tree near the ford; for when "Hen" Crosby, riding for the mail, saw the agreed-upon sign on the tree, it would not be long before Logan had the note.

Following the line of least resistance, the second day found him bearing westerly, and the next three days found him crowding the pack on Pepper's back and riding due north through a country broken, wild, and without a trail. The way was not as difficult as it might have been because the valleys joined one another, and through them all flowed creeks, which made a trail that left no tracks. To an experienced man who had plenty of time the difficulties were more often avoided than conquered.

At noon of the fifth day he drove Pepper slantingly up the wall of a crumbling butte, and reaching the top, looked around for his bearings. They were easily found, for Twin Buttes looked too much alike, even from the rear, to be easily mistaken; and they loomed too high to be overlooked. Almost on a direct line with the Twins lay Quigley's cabins, a matter of fifteen miles from him; which he decided was too far. That distance covered twice daily would take up too much time. Returning to the valley he built a fire, had dinner, and, hanging the edible supplies on tree limbs for safety, whistled Pepper to him and departed toward the Twins.

Two hours later he left the horse in a deep draw and crawled up the eastern bank. Crossing a bowlder-strewn plateau he not long afterward wriggled to the edge of Quigley's valley and looked down into it.

The size of the enclosed range amazed him, for it was fully thirteen miles long, eight miles across at its widest, the northern end, and three miles wide at the middle, where massive cliffs jutted far out from each side.

The more he saw of it the better he liked it. The grass was better and thicker than even that in the prized and fought-for valley of the old Bar-20. He judged it to contain about eighty square miles and believed that it could feed two hundred cows to the mile. The main stream, which he named Rustler Creek, flowed through a deep ravine and was fed, in the valley alone, by six smaller creeks. There was a sizable swamp and six lakes, one of them nearly a mile long. It was singularly free from bowlders and rocks except at a place near the upper wall, where a great collection of them extended out from a broken cliff.

Except at three places the canyons which cut into the cliffs were blind alleys and he could see that two of them had narrow waterfalls at their upper ends. The three open canyons were the only places where cattle could leave the great "sink," as Johnny called it; and they were strongly fenced. The first was the entrance canyon, near the houses; the second was a deep, steep walled defile at the northwest corner of the range, and it led into another, but smaller valley, also heavily grassed. Through it ran a small stream which joined Rustler Creek at the swamp. The third canyon, at the northeast corner of the valley, was wide enough to let Rustler Creek flow through it and leave room for the passing of cattle; and judging by the gates in the heavy fence which crossed it, Johnny knew this to be the exit through which the drive herds went. Where that drive trail led to he did not know, but he believed it to pass well to the west of Hope.

Taking it all in all, it was the most perfect range he ever had seen. Rich in grass so heavy and thick as to make him wonder at it, naturally irrigated, blessed with natural reservoirs, surrounded by a perpendicular wall of rock which at some places attained a height of three hundred feet, the water courses lined with timber, its arroyos and draws heavily wooded, and with but three places, easily closed and guarded, where cattle could get out, it made the Tin Cup and the Bar-20, large as they were, look like jokes. Its outfit could laugh at rustlers, droughts, and blizzards, grow fat and lazy and have neither boundary disputes nor range wars to bother them. There were no brands of neighboring ranches to complicate the roundups and not a cow would be lost through straying or theft.

Having located the valley, he slipped away, mounted his horse and rode back the way he had come, looking for a good place to pitch his camp. Five miles from the valley he found it—a cave-like recess under the towering wall of a butte, half way up the wooded slope which lay at the foot of the wall. From it he could command all approaches for several hundred yards, while his tarpaulin would be screened by bowlders and trees. It was high enough for purposes of observation, but not so high that the smoke from his fire would have density enough when it reached the top of the butte to be seen for any distance. A spring close by formed pools in the hollows of the rocks below him. The great buttes lying to the east of the fire would screen its light from any wandering member of Quigley's outfit.

"This is it," he grunted. "We'll locate here tomorrow."

The following day, having put his new camp to rights, he rode up the western slope of the great plateau which hemmed in Quigley's ranch, picketed his horse in a clearing, and after a cautious reconnaissance on foot he reached the edge of the cliffs, and the valley lay before him. Cattle grazed near a little lake, but at that distance he could not read the brands. He first had to find out if any of the outfit ever rode along the top of the cliffs, and he struck straight back to cross any such trails. By evening he had covered the western side of the ranch without finding a hoof-print, or a way up the sheer walls where a horseman could reach the top. There were several places where a cool-headed man could climb up, and at one of these Johnny found several burned matches.

The next day was spent on the plateau north of the ranch, and the third and fourth days found him examining the eastern side; and it was here that he found signs of riders. There were three blind canyons on this side, and the middle one had a good trail running up its northern wall, and it appeared to be used frequently. At the top it divided, one branch running north and the other south. It was the only place on that side of the valley where a horseman could get out.

Now that he had become familiar with his surroundings he began his real work. If Quigley had rustled, the operations could be divided into two classes: past operations, now finished; or present operations which were to continue. It was possible that enough cattle had been stolen in the past so that the natural increase would satisfy a man of modest ambitions. In this case his danger would decrease as time passed and eventually he would have a well-stocked range and be above suspicion. If he were avaricious the rustling would continue, if only spasmodically, until he had made all the money he wanted or until his operations became known.

Johnny early had discovered that Quigley's brand was QE and this increased his suspicions, for the E could not be explained. Logan's brand was childishly simple to change: The C could become an O, Q, G, or wagon-wheel; the L would make an E, Triangle, Square, or a 4.

Satisfied that the foundation of Quigley's brand had been the CL, Johnny had to discover if Logan's cattle still were being taken to swell the Quigley herds. Logan's inaction and his easygoing way of running his ranch jarred Johnny, for the foreman had confessed that for the last few years the natural increase, figured in the fall roundups, had not tallied with the number of calves branded each preceding spring. But Logan was not altogether to blame, because the Barrier had given him a false security and there was nothing to fear from other directions. It was the last spring roundup and its tally sheets which had stirred him; and a close study of his drive-herd records and the use of a factor of natural increase suddenly brought to his mind a startling suspicion. Even then he wavered, fearing that he was allowing an old and bitter grudge to sway him unduly; and before he had time to make any real investigations, Johnny had appeared and demanded a job.

Among Quigley's cattle the proportion of calves to cows was so small that Johnny could not fail to notice it. He was satisfied that the QE, so prominently displayed, originally had been CL, but when he caught sight of a crusty old steer near the mouth of the second canyon all doubts were removed. While the mark was an old one, the rebranding had been done carelessly. The segment which closed the original C had not been properly joined to the old brand,

and there was a space between the ends of the two marks
where they overlapped. A look at the ears made him smile
grimly, for Logan's shallow V notch had become a rounded
scallop; and there was no honest reason why Quigley
should notch the ears of his cows when there was no chance
of them getting mixed up with the cattle of any other ranch.
The scallop had been made simply to cut out the telltale V
notch.

XI

◆

Nocturnal Activities

Light gleamed from Quigley's ranch houses and an
occasional squeal came from the corral, suggesting
that "Big Jake" was getting up steam for more deviltry.
Occasionally a shadow passed across the lighted patches
of ground below the windows and the low song of Rustler
Creek could be heard as it swirled into the long, black canyon. Save for the glow of the windows and the rectangles
of light below them everything was wrapped in darkness,
and the canyon, the range, and the rims of the cliffs were
hidden.

"A miner, 'forty-niner, and his daughter, Clementine,"
came from the middle house as Art Fleming dolefully
made known the sorrowful details of Clementine's passing
out. He put his heart into it because he had troubles of his
own, for which he frankly and profanely gave Ben Gates
due discredit.

Ben, tiring of the dirge, heaved a boot with a snap-
shooter's judgment and instantly forsook the heavy in-
hospitality of the house for the peace and freedom of the

great outdoors. He plumped down on a bench and immediately arose there-from.

"Look where yo're settin', you blunderin' jackass!" snarled a hostile voice from the same bench. "Yo're a big a nuisance as a frisky bummer in a night herd!"

"A bull's eye for Mr. Harrison," chanted the man inside.

"You two buzzards are about as cheerful an' pleasant as a rattler in August," snapped Gates belligerently. "Like two old wimmin, you are, *both* of you! Settin' around in everybody's way, tellin' yore troubles over an' over again till everybody wishes Nelson had done a better job. How'd *I* know you was sprawled out, takin' up all th' room? You reminds me of a fool dog that sets around stickin' its tail in everybody's way, an' then howls blue murder when it's stepped on. Think yo're th' only people on this ranch that has any troubles?"

"A miss for Mr. Gates," said the irritated voice within the house. "An' if he will stick his infected head in that door, just for one, two, three, he'll have more troubles," prophesied Mr. Fleming, facing the opening with a boot nicely balanced in his upraised hand. "If it wasn't for him, we—"

"Shut up! *Shut up!*" yelled Gates, enraged in an instant. "If you says that much more I'll bust yore fool neck! For God's sake, is that all you know, Andrew Jackson?"

"If it wasn't for you," said the man on the bench very deliberately as his hand closed over a piece of firewood, "I said, if—it—wasn't—for—you, we'd be ridin' with the boys tonight, instead of stayin' around these houses like three sick babies."

"Another bull's eye for Mr. Harrison," said the man inside.

Gates wheeled with an oath. "An' if it wasn't for *you*

sound asleep in th' valley; an' Fleming sound asleep up on that butte, I wouldn't 'a' been lammed on th' head an' tied up like a sack! It's purty cussed tough when a man with nothin' worse than a scalp wound has to lay up this way!"

"Bull's eye for Mr. Gates," announced the man in the cabin, with great relish.

"If you'd been wide awake yoreself," retorted Harrison, "you wouldn't 'a' been tied up! You didn't even squawk when he hit you, so we'd know he was around. Was you tryin' to keep it a secret?" he demanded with withering sarcasm. "An' as for them bandages, how did *I* know th' dog had been sleepin' on 'em? Cookie gave 'em to me!"

"Bull's eye for Mr. Harrison," said Fleming. "But he was awake," he continued with vast conviction. "He was wide awake. He ain't got no more sense awake than he has asleep. When he's got his boots on, his brains are cramped an' suffocated."

"You got him figgered wrong," said Harrison "His brains are only suffocated when he sets down."

While the little comedy was being enacted at the bunkhouses, the main body of rustlers followed Quigley down the steeply sloping bottom of a concealed crevice miles north of the ranch-house of the CL. The five men emerged quietly and paused on the edge of the curving Deepwater, and then slowly followed their leader into the icy stream. The current, weakened by a widening of the river at this point, still flowed with sufficient strength to make itself felt and the slowly moving horses leaned against it as they filed across the secret ford. Reaching the farther bank the second and third men rode quietly to right and left, rapidly becoming vague and then lost to sight. The three remaining riders sat quietly in their saddles for what, to them, seemed to be a long time. Suddenly a low whistle sounded on the left, followed instantly by another on the right; and like released springs the rustlers leaped into action.

Vague, ghostly figures moved over the open plain, finding cows with uncanny directness and certainty. Two riders held the nucleus of the little herd, which grew steadily as lumbering cows, followed inexorably by skilled riders, pushed out of the darkness. There was no conversation, no whistling now, nor singing, but a silence which, coupled to the ghost-like action and the dexterous swiftness, made the drama seem unreal.

There came an abrupt change. The two men riding herd saw no more looming cattle or riders, which seemed to be a matter of significance to them, for they faced southward, guns in hand, and pushed slowly back along the flanks of the little herd. Peering into the shrouding gray darkness, tense and alert, eyes and ears straining to read the riddle, they waited like sooty statues for whatever might occur, rigid and unmoving.

A sudden thickening in the night. A figure seemed to flow from indefinable density to the outlines of a mounted man. A low voice, profanely irritant, spoke reassuringly and grew silent as the rider oozed back into the effacing night.

"Shore," muttered a herder, relaxing and slipping his gun into its holster. He moved forward swiftly and turned back a venturesome cow. His companion, growling but relieved, shrugged his shoulders and settled back to wait.

Minutes passed and then another lumbering blot emerged out of the dark, became a cow, and found reassurance in numbers as it willingly joined the herd. The escorting rider kept on, pushed back his sombrero and growled: "They're scattered to hell an' gone tonight; but," he grudgingly admitted, "they acts plumb do-cile. S'long."

Another wait, long and fruitless, edged anew the nerves of the herders. Then Quigley, Ackerman, and Purdy moved out of the obscurity of the night and took up positions around the herd, urging it forward. When they had it started on its way, Ackerman dropped back and became lost to sight, engaged in his characteristic patrolling, suspicious and malevolent.

The little herd, skilfully guided over clean patches of rock which led deviously to the water's edge and left no signs on its hard surface, at last reached the river, where a shiver of hesitancy rippled through it and where the rear cows pushed solidly against the front rank, which appeared to be calling upon its inherent obstinacy. The craft and diplomacy of Quigley's long experience won out and the uncertain front rank slowly and grudgingly entered the stream, the others following without noticeable hesitation. As the last cow crossed and scrambled up the western bank, Ackerman rode down to the water's edge, pushed in and crossed silently, only the lengthening ripple on the black surface telling of his progress. As he climbed out he squirmed in his wet clothes and swore from sudden anger, which called forth a low ripple of laughter from the base of the Barrier, where the others took their discomforts lightly.

"Scared you'll shrink, Jim?" softly said an ironic voice.

"Or dissolve, like sugar?" inquired another scoffingly.

"Sugar?" jeered a third. "Huh! He's about as sweet as a hunk of alum!"

Ackerman's retort caused grins to bloom unseen, and the miseries of wet clothes and chilled bodies were somewhat relieved by the thought that Ackerman felt them the most.

Up the crevice in orderly array, docile as sheep, climbed the cattle, and when they reached the top of the plateau they moved along stolidly under guidance and finally gained the outer valley leading to the QE by a trail west of and parallel to the one which showed the way to Hastings.

Back on the QE, Fleming and his friends, having awakened the cook at an unseemly hour by their noise, finally turned in and found some trouble in getting to sleep, thanks to the energetic efforts of the boss of the kitchen, who most firmly believed in the Mosaic Law, and had the courage of his convictions. But things finally quieted down and peace descended upon the ranch.

Outside the bunk-house and behind it, a blot on the ground stirred restlessly and slowly resolved itself into a man arising. He moved cautiously along the wall toward the lighted cook shack and then sank down again, hand on gun, as the door opened.

Cookie threw out a pan of water, scowled up at the starry sky and then peered intently at a chicken-coop, visible in the straggling light from the door, from which a sleepy cackle suddenly broke the silence. Muttering suspiciously he reached behind him and then slipped swiftly toward the shack, a shotgun in his hands. Going around the coop he stood up and shook his fist in the darkness.

"You can dig up my traps, an' smell out my strychnine, but you can't dodge these buckshot if ever I lays th' sights on you. Dawg-gone you, I owes *you* a-plenty!" he growled. Striking a match he looked in the coop and around it. "Had two dozen as nice pullets as anybody ever saw, only three weeks ago; an' now I only got sixteen left. *There,* blast you!" he swore, as the second match revealed the telltale tracks. "There they are! O, Lord! Just let me get my gun on that thievin' ki-yote! Just once!"

He stared around belligerently and went slowly back to the house, swearing and grumbling under his breath. It is the cook's fate to be the sworn enemy of all coyotes, and let it be said without shame to him that he seldom is a victor in that game of watchfulness and wits. And also let it be said that often with tears of rage and mortification, and words beyond repetition, he pays unintentional tribute to the uncanny cunning of the four-legged thieves. With guns, dogs, traps, and poison is he armed, but it availeth him naught. And as bad as the defeat are the knowing grins of the rest of the outfit who, while openly cheering on the doughty cook, are ready to wager a month's wages on the coyote.

The man on the ground moved again, this time toward the canyon, and soon was feeling his way along the great eastern wall. Reaching the other end, he stopped a moment to listen, and then went on again, groping along by the edge of the stream until he stumbled over a dead branch, which he picked up. Then feeling for and finding a certain rock, he stepped on it and with his foot felt for and found another, which was partly submerged in the creek; and by means of this and others he crossed dry-shod to the opposite bank, using the branch as a staff.

Daylight was near when Johnny wriggled to the edge of the cliff opposite the houses and hid behind a fringe of grass on the rim. An hour passed and then his keen ears caught distant sounds. Below him the cook was rearranging his traps and swearing at the cleverness of his four-footed enemy. Suddenly he arose and hastened to the kitchen to serve a hot breakfast to the men who soon drove a bunch of cattle out of the canyon and into the small corral.

While the others hastened in for their breakfast, Quigley and Ackerman loitered at the corral.

"Purty good for five men, with one of 'em playin' sentry," said Quigley. "We'd do better if we didn't have to scout around first."

"Scoutin's necessary," replied Ackerman. "It's too wide

open. This bunch ain't worth gettin' wet for. That river's cussed cold!"

Quigley chuckled. "Huh! I've swum it when th' ice was comin' down."

"You did," retorted Ackerman. "That was th' night Logan burned our houses. You had to swim an' freeze, or stay out an' get shot. You went in *pronto,* that night!"

"You beat me in by forty yards, an' out by sixty!" snapped Quigley.

Ackerman ignored the remark. "Not satisfied with nestin' on a man's range, you had to start a little herd. We didn't bring no cows with us, nor buy any afterward—but what's th' use? Let's eat," and he led the way toward the cook shack.

Johnny waited a few minutes and then, returning to his horse, started for his camp. He was puzzled, for no place near Big or Little Canyons was devoid of shelter, and he knew of no other places where cattle could pass the Barrier. He had noticed that the backs of the cows were dry, which meant that they had forded the river, and he was certain that the crossing had not been made at the ford near Devil's Gap. He had to learn the location of the place they visited and that unknown ford; and he wanted to learn the date of their next raid.

"We'll have to trail 'em, Pepper," he growled. "An' then bust all runnin' records to get Logan and th' boys. Get again'; I'm sleepy."

XII

♦

Yeasty Suspicion

Ackerman walked to the small corral, where two straight irons were in a fire and where three men were cinching up in preparation. Fleming, Harrison, and Gates, lolling on the ground, kept up a running fire of comment, and Ackerman stopped and looked down at them.

"Three cheerful fools," he grinned.

"Here's Little Jimmy," remarked Fleming; "an' by all th' Roman gods, he's actually grinnin'! Look, fellers! Behold an' ponder! Mr. Ackerman wears a smile!"

"Sick?" solicitously inquired Harrison.

"Drunk?" suspiciously questioned Gates.

"Three children," grunted Ackerman. "An' scabby. Two sentries an' a hunter."

Holbrook poked the fire. "Kit Carson, Dan'l Boone, an' Californy Joe. Three scouts. Th' ambushin' trio."

"Faith, Hope, an' Charity," chuckled Purdy.

"You called it," grinned Holbrook.

"If Custer had only had 'em," said Ackerman, "there'd been no massacre."

"Huh!" grunted Gates. "What could *I* do, with them two fools herdin' with me?"

"Not so much herdin' with you, as tryin' to herd you," said Harrison blithely.

Gates sought escape by creating a diversion, and shouted: "Hey, look at him!" and pointing at the cook, who staggered past under a great load of saplings and poles.

"Hey, Cookie!" he shouted stentoriously. "Why don't

you put them birds in th' house nights, an' sleep in th' coop, yoreself?"

"Or give him some of that there strych-nine that we got for you?" yelled Sanford. "There's a lot of it left," he chuckled, remembering the cook's futile rage when he had found the poisoned carcass half covered over with dirt.

The cook, his glistening face crimson, carefully lowered the forward end of the poles to the ground, eased them upright with his shoulder and wiped the perspiration from his face with a grimy sleeve. Turning a red countenance toward his grinning friends he started to speak, muttered something, spat forcibly, shouldered carefully under his load again and staggered away with as much dignity as he could command.

"That's right, Cookie," commended Gates. "Don't you waste no words on 'em a-tall. They're a lazy, worthless, shiftless lot. If they wasn't they'd help you tote them trees. But I wish you'd tell me what yo're aimin' to do, because if yo're goin' to rig up a scaffold for that ki-yote, I want to be around when he's hung." He turned and surveyed the group. "You ought to be ashamed of yoreselves, lettin' him tote that load hisself. He works harder than any man on this ranch, an' I can prove it. I can prove it by him. What with buildin' stockades an' scaffolds, diggin' holes for his traps, poisonin' baits, an' settin' up nights with his shotgun, he's a hard workin' member of this outfit. He ain't got no time to set around an' loaf all day like some I could name if I had a mind to."

"Hard workin'!" snorted Purdy. "That ain't work; that's fun! He's as happy doin' that as others is playin' cards or somethin'. He'd get mopey if that ki-yote died. A man allus works harder at his fun than he does at his work. Allus!"

"Shore!" grunted Holbrook. "I've seen men so lazy that they growled because th' sun kept 'em movin' to stay in th' shade; but show 'em a month's good huntin' an' they'd come to life quick! They'll climb an' hoof it all day to get a shot at somethin'; but if their wife asked 'em to rustle a bucket of water you could hear 'em holler, clear over in th' next county."

"Would you look at him settin' them poles!" chuckled Gates. "He's shore goin' down to bedrock!"

Holbrook pulled an iron out of the fire, glanced at it, shoved it back again and arose. "Let her go," he said.

At the word two men vaulted into their saddles and rode into the corral. A cow blundered out and was deftly turned toward the fire, and at the right instant a rope shot through the air, straightened and grew taut; and the cow, thrown heavily, was hog-tied, branded, its ears cut to conform to the QE notch, and released in a remarkably short time. Arising it waved its lowered head from side to side and stared to charge Holbrook. Gates stepped quickly forward, kicked a spur of dirt in its face and a clever cow-pony sent it lumbering out through the gate in the fence and onto the range.

"Maverick," grunted Holbrook, waiting for the next. "Logan shore is careless in his calf roundups. That's four of 'em we got in th' last two raids. Reckon he thinks brandin' is more or less unnecessary, th' way he's located. An' damned if here don't come another! Nope; it's a sleeper. Somebody took th' trouble to cut th' notch."

Ackerman did his share of the work, silent and preoccupied, and when the last cow had been turned onto the range he wheeled abruptly, looked around, and walked over to Quigley, who was approaching.

"I reckon I better go off on a little scout," he said. "I ain't satisfied about Nelson; an' th' more I mills it over, th' less satisfied I am. You can grin; but *I'm* tellin' you it ain't no grinnin' matter!" he snapped, eyeing the group. "I'm tellin' you what *I'm* goin' to do, an' that's all."

"That's for you to say," smiled Quigley. "Nobody's goin' to try to stop you; but we reckon yo're only makin' trouble for yoreself. He's quit th' Twin Buttes country. I understand he's prospectin' south of town."

"He ain't prospectin' none," retorted Ackerman. "An' he wasn't prospectin' up here, neither; he was runnin' a bluff, an' makin' it stick. *I* looked into that gravel bed!"

Fleming laughed. "He was coverin' his rustlin' operations. His real prospectin' was to be done with a rope an' a runnin' iron."

"Yes," grunted Stanford; "an' now he's doin' th' same thing down south, I'll bet. Th' Circle S has got a lot of sleepers an' mavericks runnin' on their outlyin' range. Holmes has been threatenin' for two years to round 'em all up; but when he's ready, th' Long T ain't; an' t'other way around."

"Our friend is goin' to set right down on a rattler if he starts rustlin' down there," grinned Purdy. "Them two ranches are wide awake. I know, because I've looked 'em over."

"He'll tackle th' job," said Harrison; "because he's somethin' of a pinwheel hisself."

"That's how I figger it," said Holbrook quickly. "A burned child loves th' fire, if it's stubborn. Let him alone; don't stir him up. We don't want him up here, an' that's our limit. What he does down there ain't no game for us to horn into. Let 'em fiddle an' dance an' be damned."

Ackerman regarded them pityingly and shrugged his shoulders. "I pass! Ain't there no way to get it through yore heads that I don't believe he's interested in anythin' but *us?* It's like drillin' in granite. I hammer an' hammer, twist th' drill an' hammer some more; an' after hard work all I got is a little hole, with a cussed sight more granite below it! I feel like rammin' in a charge of powder an' blowin' it to hell an' gone. *Look* at me! *Listen!* Put away yore marbles, an' *think*!"

"Why don't you fellers listen?" grinned Fleming.

"Just because he went south don't say he *stayed* there," hammered Ackerman. "He wasn't scared away; not by a damned sight. *I* know that. Fleming, Gates, an' Harrison know it. We *all* know it. He went south. But he can turn, can't he? If he can't, he's in a hell of a fix! No tellin' where he'll end up—Patagonia, mebby. All right, he can turn. It's only a question of *where*! He's goin' to turn; an' when he does, *I'*m goin' to be there an' see him do it. I'm goin' to make it my business to find him, watch him, an' trail him. If he turns north I'm goin' to *get* him. An' if you'll take any advice from me, you'll *all* begin to take long rides, north, east, south, an' west; mostly southwest an' west. You'll ride in pairs, an' you'll keep yore fool eyes open. Th' time has passed for loafin' around here, shootin' craps an' swappin' lies. Yo're smokin' on an open powder keg; an' *damn you,* you ain't got sense enough to know it!" He raised his clenched fists. "I *mean* it! Damn you—you—ain't—got—sense—enough—to—know—it!"

Quigley laughed, although uneasily; for Ackerman's earnestness carried unrest with it. "Jim, Jim," he said kindly, "we've been up here a long time; an' we've given these hills a name that guards 'em for us. Them that bothered us disappeared; an' th' lesson was learned."

"Was it?" shouted Ackerman. "*He* didn't learn it! *He* come up here, plump in th' face of yore warnin', in spite of what he had heard in Hastings! *Why?* Because it's his *business* to come! Because he's *paid* to come! *He* ain't one of them Hasting's loafers! *He* ain't no sleepy puncher, satisfied to draw down his pay, an' th' hell with th' ranch! I tell you you never *saw* a man like him before. Can't you see it? Logan found out that he was a *real* man, a *gun* man, an' not scared of hell an' high water. Then he quits Logan, an' comes up here. Can't you *see* it? *Can't* you? *Think,* damn it; THINK!"

"I did; have been, an' am," snapped Quigley angrily. "Thinkin' is one thing; goin' loco, another. *I* think yo're a damned fool!"

Ackerman threw up his hands in a helpless gesture. "All right; have it yore own way. I give it up. I pass before th' draw. But I ain't swallerin' no pap an' gazin' at th' moon. I'm goin' to keep my eyes on Nelson."

"You want to; he's a bad hombre," said Fleming uneasily.

Ackerman wheeled and smiled at the speaker. "He is; an' he's a damned *good* man. I takes off my hat to him; an' I wish to heaven we had a few Nelsons up here; this ranch would *hum*. An' you'd 'a' done better if you'd follered yore own advice. I won't make th' same mistake twice. Th' minute he makes a false move I'll plug him. I underrated him before; now I'm goin' to overrate him, to be on th' safe side. But *you* ain't got a thing to say: three to one, an' you let him make fools out of you!"

"I admits it," said Fleming. "An' that's why I'm tellin' you to look out for him. He's as quiet as a flea; an' as harmless as blastin' powder. I wish you luck."

"I ain't so harmless myself," retorted Ackerman. "An' now I know what I'm buckin'. You'll see me when you see me; I'm preparin' to be gone a month or more."

They watched him enter the bunk-house, and when he came out again he had his saddle and a blanket roll; and when he rode into the canyon without a backward glance or a parting word he had his slicker, a generous supply of food, and plenty of ammunition.

Quigley watched him until he rode out of sight beyond

the canyon, and turned toward his outfit, shaking his head. "He's so all-fired set on it that I'm gettin' a little restless myself. Jim ain't no fool; an' he don't often shy at a shadow. It won't do us no harm, anyhow; an' we can take turns at it. I'll start it off by takin' one side tomorrow, an' Holbrook can take th' other. Later on we'll figger it out an' arrange th' shifts. Mebby he's right."

XIII

♦

An Observant Observer

Jim Ackerman strode into Pop Hayes' saloon, where he found the proprietor and Charley James squabbling acrimoniously over the value of a cribbage hand.

"Not satisfied with gettin' a twenty-four hand," snorted Charley, "he tries to make it twenty-seven, shovin' 'em around like he was playin' three-card monte! You old fool! You've counted them runs once more'n you oughter; but I don't care how much you mills 'em; it's twenty-four!"

"I ain't done no more countin' than they'll stand!"

"I dunno what *they'll* stand; but I knows what *I'll* stand. It's twenty-four!"

"Soon as you gets two bits up," sneered Pop, "you lose yore nerve. You can play all day for fun, an' never loose a yelp; but when you've got money up you acts like you was stabbed!"

"That so? You forget how to count when there's money up!"

"When yo're winnin' everything is lovely; but when yo're losin' you go on th' prod!"

"You don't have to go; yo're allus rarin' around on yore hind laigs, a-pawin' th' air an' snortin'. Leave it to Ackerman. I dare you!"

"I'll leave it to anybody but you. You hadn't ought to even play for th' drinks. Jim, look at that twenty-seven hand an' tell that fool what it counts, will you?"

Ackerman moved it around and grinned. "Fifteen eight; two pairs is twelve, an' four runs of three makes that twenty-seven hand count just twenty-four. An' it's a cussed good hand, too; you shore knows how to discard."

Charley nodded emphatically. "There! I told you so!"

Pop raised his hands helplessly to heaven. "How much longer have I got to keep th' peace? Two more like you an' Charley an' this country would go plumb to th' dogs! Yo're two fools."

"Now who's stabbed?" jeered Charley. "You can get more out of one crib hand than most folks can find in two. 'Four, five, six,'" he mimicked. "Why don't you shift 'em around an' work six, five, four; an' five, six, four; an' four, six, five? A genius like you ought to get thirty-six out of a twenty-four hand an' never turn a hair. I'm such a stranger to a hand like that that I'd be satisfied with twenty-four. I ain't no genius at figgers."

"If I told you what you are, you'd get insulted!"

"Anybody that could insult you could make cows live on malpais an' get fat," sneered Charley. "I've done called you a liar, an' a cheat, an' a thief—"

"Hey! Stop that!" interposed Ackerman. "Quit it; an' have a drink with me. You'd let a man die of thirst, *I* believes."

Pop shuffled around behind the bar and sullenly produced the bottle and the glasses. "I know, Jim," he apologized; "but you don't know how my patience gets tried!"

Charley snorted. "If they ever tries yore patience they'll lynch it. Here's how, *Jim*."

"Good luck," said Jim, tossing off the drink.

Charley, walking back toward the card table, caught sight of the well-loaded horse outside; and Pop, taking advantage of the situation, reached swiftly under the bar and slid two Colts toward Ackerman, who frowned and pushed them back. "Some other time," he growled. "Ain't goin' back right away." He pushed his hat back on his head. "Any news?"

"There ain't never any news in this place," answered the proprietor. "But I hear as how th' Circle S has fired Long Pete Carson for stayin' drunk. Long Pete was all het up over it an' lets drive at Holmes. Bein' unsteady he missed Dick an' nicked Harry Kane. Then Dick took th' gun away from him an' give him a beatin'. Dick's hands are shore eddicated. Th' Long T near lost three hosses in that quicksand near Big Bend; an' Smith come near goin' with 'em. An' that Nelson is prospect-in' somewhere near th' Circle S, if he ain't left th' country."

"What makes you think that he's mebby left th' country?" inquired Ackerman casually.

"He had his spirit busted when his cabin burned. Said this country was too full of dogs to live in. But I reckon he'll work around th' Circle S or th' Long T a while before he quits for good."

Charley turned and grunted derisively. "That's all you know about it. He crossed the river near th' Circle S, over Rocky Ford, an' went to Bitter Creek hills."

"How'd you know he did?" demanded Pop.

"I was told by th' man that saw him do it."

"Who was that?" asked Pop, indignant because he had not been told about it before.

"Yo're a reg'lar old woman," jeered Charley. "You can guess it."

"Funny he didn't tell me," sighed Pop.

"Mebby he reckoned it was his own business," retorted Charley. "Mebby he knowed you'd blurt it out to everybody you saw."

"I keep things under my belt!"

"Yes; food an' likker," chuckled Charley, enjoying himself. "If nobody come around for you to tell yore gossip to, cussed if you wouldn't tell it to th' sky, night an' mornin', like a ki-yote."

"So, he's still prospectin'," laughed Ackerman. "He'll starve to death."

"I ain't so shore about that," said Charley. "He weighed his gold on my scales an' it was one pound an' eleven ounces. It was all gold, too; I saw it."

"He-he-he!" chuckled Pop. "If yore scales said one eleven he only had about half a pound. Them scales are worse than a cold deck."

"That's a lie; an' you know it! Them scales are honest!"

"Then they ain't 'pervious to their 'sociations," grinned Pop. He reached behind him, picked up a package and turned to Ackerman. "Did you say you was goin' near th' Circle S?" he inquired.

"He did not," said Charley gleefully. "Didn't I say you was an old woman?"

Ackerman laughed, winked at Charley and went out; and the two cronies listened to the rapidly dying hoof-beats.

Pop wheeled and glared at his friend. "Now you've done it! Ain't you got no sense, tellin' *him* where Nelson is?"

"If I had much I wouldn't hang out with you," grinned Charley. "But I got a little; an' if he crosses th' river he won't find Nelson. A Circle S puncher saw him hoofin' it into th' southwest. *Quién sabe?*"

"Sometimes you do have a spark of common sense," said Pop. "Sort of a glimmer. It's real noticeable in you when it shows at all, just like a match looks prominent in th' dark. Pick up them cards an' don't do no more fancy countin'."

"Countin' wouldn't do me no good while yo're multiplyin'. Get agoin'; I got to get my four bits back before I go home."

Well to the south of the two friends in Hastings, Jim Ackerman loped steadily ahead, debating several things; and as he neared the Circle S range a man suddenly arose from behind a rock. There was nothing threatening about this gentleman except, perhaps, his sudden and unexpected appearance; but Ackerman's gun had him covered as soon as his head showed.

"Turn it off me," said the man behind the rock, a note of pained injury in his voice. "My intentions are honorable; an' plumb peaceful. Yo're most scandalous suspicious."

Ackerman smiled grimly. "Mebby I am; but habit is strong. An' one of my worst habits is suspicion. What's th' idea of this jack-in-th'-box proceedin' of yourn? You've shore got funny ways; an' plumb dangerous ones."

"Reckon mebby it does look that way," said the man behind the rock. "I neglects caution. I should 'a' covered you first an' then popped up. That shows how plumb innercent an' peaceful I am. Yore name's Jim Ackerman, ain't it?"

"You can't allus tell," replied Ackerman.

"That's where yo're figgerin' wrong. I can allus tell. Havin' told me yore name, I'll tell you mine. I'm Pete Carson, known hereabouts an' elsewhere as Long Pete. Some calls me Long-winded Pete; but it's all th' same to me. Pint that a little mite more to th' sky; thank you, sir. I was punchin' for th' Circle S, but th' Circle S punched me; then it fired me. I've got to eat, so I got to work. Th' Long T ain't hirin'; an I'd starve before I'd work for Logan. I ain't no slave, not me.

"I'm settin' there in th' sun whittlin' a stick an' arguin' with myself. I was gettin' th' worst of it when I hears yore noble cayuse. Not bein' curious I riz up instanter an' looked plumb into yore gun—just a little mite higher; ah, much obliged."

"What's all this to me?" demanded Ackerman impatiently.

"That's what I'm aimin' to find out. I saw you comin'—up a little more; thank you. Then I think I got a new chance. I want a job an' I want it bad. Hold it in yore left hand; yore right hand is tired, an' saggin'. Any chance for a close-mouthed man up yore way? One that does as he's told, asks no questions, an' ain't particular what kind of a job it is? Better let me hold that; I can see yo're gettin' tired. Thank you, sir. I'm desperate, an' I'm hungry. What you say? Speak right out—I'm a grand listener."

Ackerman grunted. "Huh! I ain't got nothin' to say about hirin' th' men where I work. As a matter of fact we ain't got work enough for another man. An' I reckon you don't understand nothin' about farmin', even in a small way; but if yo're hungry, why, I can fix that right soon. Got a cayuse?"

Pete nodded emphatically. "I allus manage to keep a cayuse, no matter how bad things busts; a cayuse, my saddle, an' a gun. Why?"

"Climb onto it an' come along with me. I'm aimin' to make camp as soon as I run across water. That's a purty good animal you got."

"Yes; looks good," grunted Long Pete; "but it ain't. It's a deceivin' critter. I'm yore scout. There's a crick half a mile west of here. I'm that famished I'm faint. Just a little more an' I'd 'a' cooked me a square meal off of one of th' yearlin's that wander on th' edge of th' range. That was what I was thinkin' over when I heard you."

"You shouldn't do a thing like that!" exclaimed Ackerman severely. "Besides, you shouldn't talk about it. An' if you *do* it you'll get shot or lynched."

"A man does lots of things he shouldn't. An' as for talkin', I'm th' most safe talker you ever met. I allus know where I'm talkin', what I'm talkin' about, an' who I'm talkin to. Now, as I figger it, I'd rather get shot or lynched than starve in a land of beef. What do I care about killin' another man's cows? I'm plumb sick of workin' on a string that some bull-headed foreman can break; an' I'm most awful sick of workin' for wages. *I* ain't no hired man, damn it! What I wants is an equal share in what I earns. An' you can believe me, Mister Man, I ain't noways particular what th' work is. I never did have no respect for a man that gambled for pennies. No tin-horn never amounted to nothin'. He can't lose much; but yo're cussed right he can't *win* much, neither. If th' stakes are high an' th' breaks anywhere near equal, I'll risk my last dollar or my last breath.

"As to what I am, you lissen to me: When I'm sober I stays strictly sober, for months at a time; an' when I'm drunk I likeways stays drunk for days at a time. I ain't like some I knows of, half drunk most of th' time an' never really sober. Me, I just serves notice that I'm goin' off on a bender, an' I goes. An' when I comes back I'm sober all th' way through. Here's th' crick. An' I never get drunk when there's work to be did. You can put up that Colt now an' watch me get a fire goin' that won't show a light for any distance or throw much smoke. I tell you I know my business."

Ackerman unpacked and turned the horses loose to graze, and by the time he was ready to start cooking, Long Pete had a fire going in a little hollow near the water.

"Now you just set down an' watch me cavort an' prance,"

quoth Long Pete pleasantly. "Reckon mebby you might not move fast enough for my empty belly. Chuck me that flour bag—I'm a reg'lar cook, *I* am. You just set there an' keep right on thinkin' about me; weigh me calm an' judicial."

Ackerman smiled, leaned back against his saddle and obeyed his verbose companion, pondering over what his deft guest had said. He knew of Long Pete by hearsay, and he now marshaled the knowledge in slow and orderly review before his mind.

The cook handed him a pan, a tin cup, and a knife, fork, and spoon. Then he waved at the pan. "Take all you want of this grub, an' take it now. This bein' a one-man outfit I'll eat off th' cookin' utensils—utensils sounds misleadin', don't it?—somethin' like tonsils or a disease. Now I warn you: dig in deep an' take all you kin eat, for there won't be no second helpin' after I gets *my* holt. Want yore coffee now?"

"Later, I reckon," smiled Ackerman. "You shore can cook. Better take th' cup first if you wants yore coffee now. I'll use it later."

"Soon as we open one of them cans I'll have a cup of my own, an' we're goin' to open one tomorrow," grinned Long Pete, opening his pocketknife and attacking the frying pan. When the pan had been cleaned of the last morsel Pete emptied the cup, washed it in the creek, refilled it and handed it to his companion. Rolling a cigarette with one hand, he lit it, inhaled deeply and blew a cloud of smoke toward the sky.

"Cuss me if that don't hit me plumb center," he chuckled. "An' plumb center is th' place for it. I'd ruther eat my own cookin' in th' open, than feed in th' house after some dirty cook got through messin' with th' grub. At first I thought you was another prospector; but when I looked close I saw that you didn't have th' rest of th' outfit. Now don't you say nothin'. I ain't lookin' for no information; I'm givin' it. You see, I shoots off my mouth regardless, for I'm a great talker when I'm sober; an' tight as a fresh-water clam when I'm drunk. A whiskered old ram of a sky-pilot once told me that I was th' most garrulous man he'd ever met up with. After I let him up he explained what garrulous means; an' th' word sort of stuck in my memory. I know it stuck in his; he'll never forget it."

Ackerman coughed up some coffee. "He won't," he gasped. "But what—made you think—I might be prospectin'?"

"Just a little superstition of mine," explained Long Pete. "There's some coffee runnin' down yore neck. You never ought to laugh when yo're drinkin'. Good thing it wasn't whiskey. Things allus comes in bunches. That purty near allus holds good, as mebby you've noticed. I have. I saw one prospector, a cow-puncher gone loco, hoofin' it in th' dirt alongside his loaded cayuse. Of th' two I thinks most of th' cayuse. It was a black, of thoroughbred strain, steppin' high an' disdainful, with more intelligence blazin' out of its big eyes than its master ever had. So when I sees you ridin' along with a big pack I reckoned mebby that you must 'a' eat some of th' same weed an' had got th' same kind of hallucernations. They's different kinds, you know. But this is once th' rule fails. There won't be no bunch of prospectors, an' I know why; but that's a secret. There won't be no third."

Ackerman looked keenly at him through narrowed lids, speculating, wondering, puzzled. Then he leaned back and yawned. "*Is* there a prospector down here?" he asked incredulously. "You don't mean it."

Long Pete coolly looked him over from boots to sombrero. "I'm duly grateful for this sumptious feed, an' I know what is th' custom when you breaks bread with a man; but I *do* mean it; an' I don't lie even when my words are ramblin' free. I reckon, mebby, you ought to remember that. We'll sort of get along better, day after day."

"No offense! I was just surprised. Which way was th' fool headin'?"

"Mebby I am a little too touchy. We all have our faults. He was headin' th' same as us because we're on his trail, right now. I sort of follered it here to keep my hand in. You never can tell when yo're goin' to need th' practice. Our fire is built on th' ashes of hisn. His fire an' smoke was well hid, too. What a two-gun cow-puncher, with a Tin Cup cayuse like that, wants to go hoofin' off on a fool's errand for, is more than I can figger out. But two heads are better than one; an' a man hears an awful lot of talkin' up in Old Pop Hayes' place. Strange old polecat, Pop is."

Ackerman stared thoughtfully into the fire for a few moments. Then he looked squarely and long into Pete's placid, unwavering eyes, and what he saw there must have pleased and piqued him.

"Pete, yore habit of usin' words reminds me of a gravel bed I once panned. It was a big bed an' I panned a terrible lot of gravel; but you'd 'a' been surprised if you knew how much gold there was in it. I was a rich man until I hit town." He waved his hands expressively. "You've said a whole lot, but it pans out strong. Anybody that won't listen to you is a fool. Let's have a powwow, without hurtin' any feelin's. Speak plain; keep cool. What you say?"

Pete waited until he rolled another cigarette and drew in another lungful of smoke. Then he recrossed his long legs, hitched comfortably against his saddle, and nodded.

"Meanin' to swap ideas an' personal opinions, ask questions regardless, an' if things don't come out like we'd mebby like 'em, keep our mouths shut afterwards an' not hold no hard feelin's?"

"Just that," Ackerman acquiesced. "Just what was you aimin' at in yore talk?"

Pete scrutinized the fire. "Well, I hit what I was aimin' at—you allus do with a scatter gun. An' for th' ease of my conscience, an' th' rest of my calloused soul, let me confess that I had a gun on you while I was talkin' to you. One arm was folded across behind my back an' a little old Colt was squeezin' against my side an' th' other arm, lookin' right at you. Carelessness ain't no sin of mine; I got enough without it. But, shakin' some of th' gravel out, let's see what I got.

"I wants a job. It's funny how many times I've wanted a job, an' then threw it sprawlin' after I got it. Bein' desperate, I was aimin' to stick you up an' take your outfit. Then when you got near an' I saw who it was, I knowed I'd have to shoot to kill; an' first, too. That's why I didn't tackle that other feller, too. An' just then my perverted mind says two an' two is four. An' it most generally is. Then I knowed you needed me. So I let th' gun slip an' got real friendly. But, as I was sayin', I want a job. Now you pay attention.

"We knows what's rumored around about Twin Buttes; an' we knows who lives up there; an' we knows there ain't never been no farm products come out of that section. That's th' biggest mistake you fellers ever made; you should 'a' run a garden. Likewise, we knows that tin-horns don't gamble with things that belong to other people, if th' other people packs guns. An' 'specially they don't gamble with no cows an' hosses. 'Tain't popular, an' folks don't like it. A tin-horn ain't man enough to risk a bullet or a rope. Now then, you just let me draw you th' picture of a dream I've often had.

"I can see a bunch of husky cow-punchers, among which I see myself, an' we're punchin' cows that we never bought. We're poolin' our winnin's an' sharin' th' risks. I can even see me rustlin' cows, an' there's men with me that I could name if my memory wasn't so bad. There's a big rock wall, an' a deep, swift river that's so damned cold it fair hurts. An' somewhere back in th' buttes, which is in a section plumb fatal to strangers, all but one, is a little ranch, with a drive trail leadin' north or west. That's th' dream. Ain't it hell what fool ideas go trompin' an' rampagin' through a man's mind when he's asleep, 'specially if he ain't satisfied to work for wages? Did you ever have any?"

Ackerman grinned to hide his surprise. "Yo're a grand dreamer, Pete. I've had dreams somethin' like that, myself; an' so far's I'm concerned yourn can come true; but I only got one vote. An' as I ain't goin' back for some time, I don't know just what to say."

"Not knowin' what to say never bothered me," chuckled Long Pete. "I can talk th' spots off a poker deck; I'll show you how, some day. But as long as you mentioned dreams, it reminds me of another I've had. Not long ago, neither. I saw a two-gun prospector leavin' an unpleasant location. He was a *reg'lar* two-gun man; a wise feller could just see it a-stickin' out all over him. I kept right on bein' hungry. Then, quite a little later I saw another man, a cow-puncher, ridin' along his trail; an' he had so much grub it fair dazzled me. An' bein' friendly, in my dream, I up an' tells th' second man where th' other feller was headin'. An' if th' dream hadn't 'a' stopped there I could 'a' told him which way th' two-gun prospector an' his black, Tin Cup cayuse went on th' mornin' follerin' th' day I saw him. Funny how things like that will stick in a man's memory. An' I've heard tell that lots of people believes in dreams, too. Seems like you only got to know how to figger 'em to learn a lot of useful an' plumb interestin' things. A fortune-teller told me that. Why, once I dreamed that I had shot a feller that had been pesterin' me; an' when I got sober, damned if I hadn't, too!"

Ackerman slammed his sombrero on the ground and leaned quickly forward over the fire. "Pete, I ain't got much money with me—didn't expect to have no call to use it. I ain't got enough for wages for any length of time; but I've got grub, plenty of it. An' if you wants to make that first dream of yourn come true, you stick to me an' with me, come what may, an' I'll see you a member of a little ranch back in some buttes, or we'll damned well know th' reason why. We need brains up there. Are you in?"

"Every damned chip; from my hat to my worn-out boots; from soda to hock," grinned Long Pete. "You got your cayuse, yore shootin' irons, an' th' grub; I got my cayuse, mean as it is, my guns, an' a steady-workin' appetite. Pass them pans over; allus like to wash things up as soon as they've been used. It'll be yore job next meal. I believe in equal work. Better hang up that pack—there's ants runnin' around here."

"Yo're a better cook than me," said Ackerman cheerfully, as he obeyed. "You do th' cookin' an' leave th' cleanin' up to me. I'd rather wrastle dirty pans than eat my own cookin' any day. That fair?"

"As a new, unmarked deck," replied Long Pete contentedly. "An' while we're talkin' about washin' pans, I want to say that that two-gun hombre went due north, ridin' plumb up th' middle of this here crick. An' since yo're trailin' him, I reckon he kept goin' right on north. I allus like to guess when I don't know."

"Yo're a damned good guesser," grinned Ackerman.

"Let's roll up in th' blankets early tonight an' get an early start in th' mornin'."

"Keno. That suits me, for if there is one thing that I can do well, it's rollin' up in a blanket. I should 'a' been a co-coon."

XIV

◆

The End of a Trail

Johnny ducked down behind a bowlder, for a horseman, sharply silhouetted against the crimson glow of the sunset, rode parallel to the edge of the cliff; and, judging from the way he was scrutinizing the ground, he was looking for tracks. While he searched, another horseman rode from the north and joined him. They made a splendid picture, rugged, lean, hard; their sharply-cut profiles, the jaunty set of the big sombreros, their alert and wiry cow-ponies, silhouetted against the crimson and gold sky; but to the hidden watcher there was no poetry, no art, in the picture, for to him it was a thing of danger, a menace. Their voices, carelessly raised, floated to him distinctly.

"Find anythin'?" asked Ben Gates ironically.

"Just what I reckoned I'd find, which was nothin'," answered Harrison. "Ackerman's loco. But I reckon it's better than loafin' around down below. I was gettin' plumb fed up on that."

"It's all cussed nonsense. Nelson's cleared out for good. He ain't no fool; an' there's too many of us."

"Seen th' others?"

"Only when they left. They ought to be ridin' back purty soon I reckon. This finishes this side, don't it?"

"Yes; they'll comb th' west side tomorrow; an' then take th' north end. Ridin' in daylight ain't so bad; but I got a fine chance seein' anythin' at night. An' I hope he *has* cleared out; a man on a bronc looks as big as a house."

"Don't ride at all; lay up somewhere near th' canyon trail an' let *him* do th' movin'. But hell! He's gone out of this country."

"That's just what I was aimin' to do. I could ride within ten feet of a man in th' dark, with all th' cover there is up here, an' not see him. Don't you worry about yore Uncle Nat; he's shore growed up. But it's all fool nonsense, just th' same."

"Oh, well; it'll make things pleasanter down below," grinned Gates. "It'll stop th' arguin'. Quigley's gettin' near as nervous as Ackerman. He's gettin' scared of shadows since Jim laced it into him. Well, I'm goin' on; if I meets Holbrook I'll tell him to take th' south end. So long."

They separated and went their respective ways, and while Johnny watched them he suddenly heard a murmur of voices below him, and he squirmed between two big bowlders as the sounds came nearer.

"Well, we've shore combed this side," said one of the newcomers. "An' that ends part of a fool's errand."

"We shore have," grunted another. "An' it did us good, too. We all have been gettin' too cussed lazy for any account. I reckon a certain amount of work is th' best friend a man has got."

"Mebby; anyhow, I know that my appetite is standin' on its hind laigs yellin' for help," laughed the third. "An' we have th' satisfaction of knowin' everythin' is all right out here. Cussed if I couldn't eat a raw skunk!"

"But that ain't what I'm drivin' at," said the first speaker, his voice growing fainter as they rode on. "I claims if he is workin' for th' CL he only has to get one look in our valley to tell him all he wants to know. If he's up here, or has been up here, that would be enough. He wouldn't stay here day after day like a dead dog in a well."

As the words died out in the distance Johnny started to slip out from between the bowlders, when a sharp *spang!* rang out at a rock near his waist, and a whining scream soared skyward. An opening made by a split in the bowlder had partly revealed his moving body to a pair of very keen eyes on the lookout for just such a sign. A second later the flat report of the shot cracked against his ears, but he was on the other side of the bowlders and leaping down the steep hillside when he heard it. As he cleared a big rock he landed almost upon a slinking coyote, which instantly destroyed distance at an unbelievable speed. It shot up the hill, over the crest, and sped like an arrow of haze across the open table-land. Another shot rang out and a laughing voice shouted greeting.

"Hi-yi! Who-o-p-e-e-e! Scoot, you streak of lightnin'! Cookie's layin' for you with nine buckshot in each barrel. But I'm a drunk Injun if you didn't fool me."

A peeved voice raised loudly in the twilight. "Hey! Damn you! Look out where yo're shootin'! That slug ricochetted plumb between our heads! Ain't you got no sense a-tall?"

"That's right! Start kickin'!" retorted Gates at the top of his voice. "Didn't you ever hear a slug before? Don't you know that th' slug you can hear is past you?"

"That so? How'd *you* like to listen to one *now*?" angrily shouted the objector. "How do *I* know that th' *next* one is goin' past?"

"Ah, go to hell!" jeered Gates. "Little things make big bumps on *you*, you sage hen!"

"*Little* things!" roared a second voice. "*Little* things! Would you *lissen* to him? It sounded like a train of cars to me, damned if it didn't!"

"Thinks he's treed another cougar," laughed a third voice.

The three appeared upon the plateau and rode toward the disgruntled marksman, their hands up over their heads in mock anxiety and surrender. Down from the north rolled a swift, rhythmic drumming, and Harrison, eagerly alert, his rifle balanced in his hands, slid to a dusty stop.

"What is it?" he demanded.

"Reckon it was Cookie's pet ki-yote," grinned Gates. "There ain't nothin' with wings, even, can beat 'em. He just melted."

"Yo're a damned fool!" swore Harrison angrily.

"Huh! I could 'a' told you that long ago," observed Purdy. "You just catchin' on?"

"I saw somethin' move," retorted Gates. "It slid past that crack an' th' sun caught it purty fair, so I let drive. How th' devil do you suppose *I* knowed it was a ki-yote? Think I'm one of them mejums an' has second sight?"

"Never!" chuckled Fleming. "People make mistakes, but th' man don't live, free an' unrestrained, that would think you had second sight. He might even be doubtful about th' first sight. You want to practice second *look*. Look twice, pray, an' then count ten, Dan'l, old trapper."

"He oughta be penned up nights," growled Sanford. "He's a cussed sight more dangerous than a plague."

Another rider joined them from the south. "Dan'l Boone at it again?" he asked, grinning.

"He is!" snapped Purdy.

Harrison quieted his horse. "You fellers take him home with you, an' keep him there. He shoots at anythin' that moves! I'm goin' to make root right here till he gets down below. Mebby he might take me for somethin' suspicious."

"If I'd 'a' got that chicken-thief," placidly remarked Gates, "I'd 'a' slipped it into Cookie's coop tonight, cussed if I wouldn't!"

"You keep away from his coop," warned Fleming, with a solemn shake of his head. "He's another that shoots at anythin' that moves."

Holbrook looked at Harrison. "You takin' th' north end tonight?"

"Yes; but I'm stayin' right here till Davy Crockett gets down on th' range. Don't you move, Frank; he'll likely blow you apart if you do."

"Glad he ain't ridin' in yore place. Good night, fellers."

The group split up and four of the riders rode toward the canyon trail.

"Take th' lead, Art," said Purdy. "You know that ledge better'n we do."

Holbrook and Harrison watched them disappear, consulted a few moments and then separated.

At the bottom of the steep eastern bank of the plateau, Johnny, a vague blur in the fading light, hastened stealthily into the brush. When assured that he was safe from observation he swung north and made the best time possible in the darkness over such ground, eager to reach his horse, which was picketed more than a mile away.

"Huh!" he grunted. "So they're combin' th' country an' patrolin'. Hereafter an' henceforth I've got to play Injun for all I'm worth. An' if they comb th' west side tomorrow I've got to move my camp at daylight."

To the southwest of the rustlers' ranch Ackerman and his new friend had sworn day after day, for they found no tracks to follow. After riding up several creeks to their head-waters they gave up such careful searching and went

blindly ahead in the direction Ackerman thought their enemy would take; and the ashes of dead camp-fires from
time to time told them that they had decided right.

At last they came to a point due west of the little valley
of the burned cabin, and Ackerman did not choose to pass
the stream which flowed from that direction. As the day
was about done they camped on the bank of the little trib-
utary and planned the next day's work. Arising early the
following morning Ackerman divided the supplies and
gave part of them to Long Pete.

"Well," he said, smiling grimly; "here's where we separate. We're north of Twin Buttes, an' that means we are
about even with th' south end of our ranch. He could 'a'
turned off any place from here on because when he got
this far he had just about arrived.

"Now I reckon I better keep on follerin' th' big creek,
for I got a feelin' that I know purty well just about where
he's located. But we can't overlook no bets. You foller this
crick to th' end, or till you see where he left it. An' you meet
me tonight, if you can, at th' south end of that big butte up
there, th' one with th' humpback.

"I've told you he's dangerous, chain-lightnin' with his
guns; an' I'm tellin' you now to make shore you won't
forget it. If you run across him, shoot first, as soon as you
see him. You can't beat him on th' draw; an' while I don't
like to shoot a man that way, I'm swallerin' my pride in
this case because he's a spy, or else he'd never ride up th'
cricks for forty miles. I never heard of anybody bein' so
cautious an' patient *all* th' time. We got to get him; if we
don't there'll be hell to pay."

"Don't you get no gray hair about me," growled Long
Pete. "I know what it means, damn him!" A smile flitted
across his face. "But I shore has to laugh at th' son-of-
a-gun! An' me thinkin' he was a prospector, an' loco! I'd

feel ashamed of myself if I really *did* think he was a prospector. You see, I've seen prospectors before. You mustn't mind me makin' a break like that once in a while; I've had to fool so many folks I can't sort of get my bearin's now. I'd be prouder of gettin' a man like him than anythin' I ever done. Did you gimme plenty of grub? All right; I'm movin' on now. So long."

"So long; an' good luck," replied Ackerman, going north along the creek.

Long Pete rode carefully up his own watery way, thoroughly alert and closely scrutinizing both banks.

"Settin' on a cayuse, out here, don't set well on my stummick," he muttered uneasily. "I'd mebby be more prominent cavortin' around on a mountain top, or ridin' upside down on th' under side of a cloud, but I ain't hankerin' after no prominence. Nope; I'm a shrinkin' wiolet. An' *splash! splash!* says th' bronc. *Splash! splash!* reg'lar as a watch, for th' whole wide world to hear, observe, an' think about. Long Pete, yo're a fool. Long Pete, yo're several, all kinds of fools. What you should oughta do is picket th' bronc an' perceed with more caution, on yore belly like a silent worm, or at least on yore kneecaps an' han's, like a—like a—a—who th' hell cares what? Day after day we been temptin' Providence. 'Hurry up!' says he. 'Hurry be damned!' thought I. But we hurried. Yes sir. But it must be did. Damn th' *must*. All my sinful life there was a *must* or a *mustn't*. It's a *must*-y world. He-he! That ain't a bad one, or I'm a liar!

"All serene. Both banks lovely. Lush grass an' mosquitoes an' *flies. Splash! Splash! Ker*-splash! *Ker*-plash! Slop inter it, bronc. Don't mind my stummick. Keep lungin' on, pluggin' right ahead, stubborn as th' workin's of hell. *Long Pete! Long Pete! Ker-splash! Here's Long Pete!* Tell him, bronc; grease th' chute for yore boss. Even th' frogs got more sense; they shut up when they hears us. It's a gamble, bronc; a toss-up. Our friend, Mr. James Ackerman, says: 'Here, Long Pete. We done reached th' partin' of th' ways. He could 'a' left th' crick any place, now. Over east yonder is where he was burned out. You take that way, an' I'll go on north where I reckon I know mebby where he oughta be.' That's what he *said,* bronc. But what he kept a damp, dark, deep secret was: 'But I know he ain't. He's east, where he knows th' lay of th' land. Where he feels at home. An' anyhow, Long Pete, you know too damned much about our affairs.' He's a friend of ours, bronc; we know that—but he's a better friend of hisself.

"We must watch both banks, bronc; watch 'em close. All right; but this time we'll just bust hell out of Mr. Must. We'll square up, right now, for th' way Mr. Must has horned inter our affairs all our fool life. Come on; get out of this! That's right. Now you stand there an' drip. I'm going to travel humble an' quiet. I don't want no fife an' drum to lead *me* to war; no ma'am; not a-tall."

Long Pete's low, muttered chatter ceased as he wriggled through the cover. Minutes passed as he went ahead, glancing continually at the banks of the small creek for the telltale signs. He wormed around some scattered bowlders and came to the edge of a small, rock-floored clearing, where he paused.

A movement half-way up on a mesa close by caught his eye, and he backed over his trail, wriggled around the little clearing and began to stalk that particular mesa ledge. Yard after yard was put behind him, nearer and nearer he approached the ledge and a nest of bowlders three hundred yards from it. The bowlders were his objective, for, once among them, he would have the view he wished. Leading to them was a brush-covered ridge and toward this he cautiously advanced, rifle at the ready and every sense alert. But he never reached it.

Behind him and two hundred yards to his right a man slowly arose from behind a rock and, resting a rifle on the bulwark, took slow and careful aim at the gray shirt crawling close to the ridge. There was a flash, a puff of smoke, a sharp report. Pete, a look of great surprise on his face, tried to rise and turn to pay his debt, crumpled suddenly and lay inert, sprawled grotesquely on the ground.

The man behind the rock mechanically reloaded and walked slowly toward his victim, waving his sombrero in a short arc. On his face was an expression of triumphant joy. Up on the ledge of the mesa wall another man arose, acknowledged the signal and began to climb down the wall as hurriedly as safety would permit. When he reached the prostrate figure he found the successful marksman standing like a man in a trance, a look of blank wonderment on his face, his lower jaw sagging loosely.

"Good for you!" said the man from above; and then he paused. "What's th' matter?" A ghastly suspicion flashed into his mind and he leaped forward to see who the victim was. He arose relieved, but as surprised as his companion. "Lord! I was scared you'd got one of th' boys, from th' way you looked! Who th' devil is *this* feller? An' what's he doin' up *here*? I've seen him before; who th' devil *is* he?"

The other drew a long breath. "It's Long Pete, of th' Circle S; but what he's doin' up here is past me. Look at his shirt, his hat, an' say he don't look like Nelson from th' back! He only wears one gun, but I couldn't see that; th' grass an' brush hid it. But, just th' same, he was stalkin' you! If you'd 'a' shoved up yore head, he'd 'a' drilled it, *shore*!"

"But why should he stalk *me*?" demanded Harrison. "He didn't have no business up here; he didn't have no reason to sneak along, an' he didn't have no call to stalk me! Say! Mebby he's throwed in with Nelson! If he has, mebby his outfit has throwed in, too! Mebby they're up here strong, an' closin' in from all directions, for a show-down! We better warn th' boys, an' get back to Quigley; an' damned quick!"

"Go ahead," said Gates. "I'll get his cayuse an' foller close. Where's Art an' Frank?"

"They went on north—I'm off after 'em," snapped Harrison. "Let his cayuse be. You hotfoot it to Quigley!"

"Come on!" growled Gates, wheeling. "They may be on both sides of th' ranch!"

Jim Ackerman, riding slowly along the bank of the main creek, saw everything that could be seen by a man with keen eyes; and he felt nervous. There was cover all about him, good cover; and any of it might be sheltering the man he was hunting. There was no sense for him to ride along the bank, an inviting target that a boy hardly could miss; there was no sense in riding at all; so he pick-eted his horse and went ahead on foot.

Gaining Humpback Butte, the meeting place he had mentioned to Long Pete, he worked along its eastern base, noiselessly, cautiously, alertly; and he stopped suddenly as he caught sight of the ashes of a dead fire; stopped and looked and listened and sniffed. It did not smell like a fire that had been dead very long, he thought; and then a play-ful little whirlwind, simulating ferocity, spun across the partly covered ashes and caught up a bit of charcoal which glowed suddenly as if winking about what it knew and could tell.

Ackerman flitted back into the brush and when he again reached the side of the butte he was north of the camp, and had viewed it from all angles. Pausing for a moment he started back again, on a longer radius, and soon found

Pepper's newly made tracks in a moist patch of sand, and hurried along the trail until he saw where it entered the creek. No need for him to wonder which way the submerged and obliterated trail led; for it must lead north. Otherwise he would have met his enemy. Swearing in sudden exultation he whirled and ran at top speed to gain his horse.

Ackerman knew Humpback Butte and its surrounding valley and canyons as he knew the QE ranch, for he had spent days hunting all over that country; and he knew that the great slopes of the valley grew steadily steeper as they reached northward until they became sheer cliffs without a single way up their walls that a horse could master. A mile above Humpback Butte the walls curved inward until only a scant six hundred yards lay between them; and on the southern side of the eastern cliff, which jutted out into the valley, hidden behind an out-thrust point, was a narrow canyon leading into the valley which formed the northwestern outlet of the QE ranch. For nearly five miles north of Humpback Butte extended the valley, now a great, wide canyon; and not one of the several blind canyons in its great walls gave a way out. Anyone passing the hidden canyon would hunt in vain for an exit and have to return again.

Reaching his horse, Ackerman mounted and rode north at top speed, guiding the animal over grass as he threaded his way in and out among the obstructions. Speed was the pressing need now, for if he could gain the hidden canyon before his enemy found it on his return, he had him trapped. There was an up-thrust mass of rock, covered with brush and scrub timber, which lay before the entrance of the canyon; once up on that he could command both the canyon and the valley, the greatest range not over five hundred yards.

Dismounting in a thicket close to the entrance, he slipped to the canyon and looked for tracks. Finding none he clambered up on the mass of rock and searched the valley for sight of Nelson. For a quarter of a mile he could follow the winding creek and he watched for a few minutes, studying the whole width of the valley.

"I've beat him; an' he ain't come back yet," he chuckled grimly. "I got five minutes to look in th' canyon an' be dead shore!"

For a hundred yards the little creek flowed along the north wall of the canyon and he wasted no time on it; any man who would ride for forty miles in creeks would not forsake the water for a mere hundred yards. Running at top-speed he dashed around a bend, eager for what he would find. There was a six-foot drop in the bottom of the canyon, and a small waterfall, where a rider would be forced to forsake the creek to climb the ridge. A quick glance at a wide belt of sand running out from the ledge at a place where it had crumbled into a steep slope told him that no one had passed that way, and he wheeled and ran back to gain the great pile of rock outside.

"Got you!" he panted triumphantly. "Yo're a clever man, Mr. Nelson; but you can't beat a stacked deck. Here's where I pay for a certain day in Hastings!"

As he reached the mouth of the canyon he heard a crashing in the brush near where he had left his horse and he dove into cover like a frightened rabbit. The crashing continued and then he heard the animal tearing off leaves, and the swish of the released branches. As he slipped forward, cursing under his breath, the horse emerged and walked slowly up on a ridge, where it paused to look calmly around.

"Damn you!" raged Ackerman, leaping forward. "I'll learn you to stay where I put you! Hell of a cow-pony *you* are!"

Grabbing the reins he kicked the horse on the ribs and dragged it back into the thicket, where he tied it short to a tree. As soon as the knots were drawn tight he scurried along the ridge, slipped through a clump of scattered brush and climbed frantically up the side of the mass of rock. A swift glance about reassured him, and, settling behind a rock, he patted his rifle and softly laughed.

An hour passed, and then suddenly he heard a plunging in the thicket below him. Pivoting like a flash, he faced about and threw himself flat on the ground, his rifle cuddled against his cheek. To his utter amazement his own horse walked into view again, the broken reins dangling and dragging along the ground. A gust of rage swept over him and he came within a hair of shooting the animal; only the need for silence kept his tightening trigger-finger from pressing that last hundredth of an inch. White with rage, choking with curses, he writhed behind his breastwork, for the horse was on the ridge again, a bold, skyline target for any eye within a mile.

"Th' journey home will be yore last!" he gritted furiously, slipping down the steep incline as rapidly as he dared. "We'll see if you can bust my rope, doubled twice! If you strain at th' rig *I'm* goin' to fix, you'll choke yoreself to death, damn you!"

Driving it back into the thicket he fastened it to a sapling with the lariat, doubled twice; and the noose around the animal's neck was a cleverly tied slip-knot.

"Now, damn you!" he blazed, kicking the horse savagely. "Take *that,* an' *that,* an' *that!*"

Reaching up to readjust the rope he suddenly froze in his tracks as a crisp voice hailed him.

"Keep 'em up!" said Johnny, stepping into view. "Turn around—*keep 'em up!*"

Cool as ice and perfectly composed, Ackerman slowly

obeyed and scowled into the muzzle of a leveled Colt, waiting for his chance.

"A man that treats a cayuse like that ain't hardly worth a bullet," said Johnny. "If you'd 'a' looked at them reins you'd 'a' seen th' knife-pricks."

Ackerman smiled grimly with understanding, but made no answer.

"Sorry that human ramrod ain't with you," continued Johnny. "If I'd knowed he was a friend of yourn I'd 'a' stopped him cold down south of Hastings."

Ackerman scowled. "Talk's cheap. Th' man with th' drop can find a lot to say, if he's a tinhorn."

Johnny slipped the Colt into its holster and slowly raised his hands even with his shoulders. "I want you to have an even break," he muttered. "But I ain't goin' to stay here till that Circle S puncher blunders onto us. I'll wait one minute. It's yore play."

"I've been waitin' for a chance like this," said Ackerman. "Remember how you kicked me? I allus pay my debts. Th' next time—" He sprang aside with pantherish speed and the heavy Colt glinted as it leaped from his holster and flashed in an eye-baffling arc. A spurt of flame flashed from his hip and a rolling cloud of smoke half hid him as he pitched forward on his face.

Johnny staggered and stepped back out of the smoke-cloud which swirled around him and fogged his vision. A trickle of blood oozed down his cheek and gathered in his three-days beard. Peering at the huddled figure, he pushed his gun back into its holster and wiped the blood from his face.

"There ain't many as good as you with a gun, Ackerman," he muttered. "Well, I got to get out of here. Them shots will shore call some of th' others; an' I'd rather let 'em guess than know."

He sprinted to Ackerman's horse, released it and stripped it of saddle and bridle, turning it loose to freedom and good grass; and then, slinging the pack of supplies on his back, hastened to his own horse and rode away.

All day long Pepper moved ahead as fast as the country would permit, first north, then east, and finally south; and when she was stopped in mid-afternoon she was under the frowning wall of the southern Twin, three miles east of Quigley's stone houses and less than half a mile from the trail used by the rustlers when they rode abroad.

The very audacity of his choice of a camp site tended to make it secure; and it was in the section combed by the rustlers only the day before; it was under the most prominent landmark for miles around and practically under the nose of the QE outfit. His camp-fire and its almost invisible streamer of smoke from carefully selected dry wood was screened on the south and east by the great side of the southern Twin, and on the north and west by the bulk of the northern Twin; and by the time the filmy vapor reached the tops of those towering walls it would have become as invisible as the air of which it was a part. And because of the tumbled chaos of rock, ridge, arroyos, bowlders, shrubs, and trees, the little tent easily could be overlooked by anyone passing within twenty feet.

It had been his intention the day before to watch that out-bound trail in hope of following the next raiding party and learning what Logan wanted to know; but now he was forced to change his plans.

"All right," he muttered as he finished putting the new camp to rights. "As long as you know I'm here, an' are huntin' me down, it's time I showed my teeth. I'm goin' gunnin': it's a game two can play."

Having had his supper and lashed a small pack of food

and ammunition on his back, he led Pepper farther down the chasm between the two buttes and let her graze where she pleased, knowing that she would not stray far. Then he plunged into the tangled cover and headed toward the entrance canyon of the QE ranch.

XV

◆

Blindman's Buff

It was nearly dark when he came to the long slope leading to the plateau behind the QE ranch-houses and he went on with infinite caution, at last looking down upon the buildings, which showed no lights.

Had they gone on another raid and had he missed the opportunity of trailing them? He shook his head. There would be no more raids until they were sure that no one was watching them. Suddenly he grinned. The Circle S puncher, when last seen, was going straight toward the ranch-houses. It was simple now. Having been told all that the Circle S man knew, they knew that only one man was watching them and would plan accordingly.

"Layin' low an' settin' traps for me," he grunted. "Bet th' three canyons are guarded—an' that trail down th' blind canyon farther along this wall. That's th' easiest for me, so I'll slip up there an' look around; but first I'll take a look down in th' main canyon."

A short time later he peered over the rim of the chasm and chuckled, for a small fire, cunningly placed so as not to shine in the eyes of anyone in the houses, burned at the base of the great wall and made sufficient light to show a watching marksman every rock and hollow across that part of the canyon.

"They can set in th' house at a loophole an' keep a good watch," he muttered. "There ain't a man livin' could cross that patch of light. An' if they're guardin' one end they're guardin' th' others—an' I'll exchange compliments with one bunch."

Squirming back from the edge he started north, and he stopped only when the plashing of water told him that he was near his objective.

"If *I* was watchin' that trail I'd stay down below," he thought. "It would be near th' narrowest part of the ledge an' where nobody could shoot down on me. I know th' place, too; glad I learned th' lay of th' land around this sink."

He crept forward confidently, his rifle strapped across his back, for he decided to depend on his Colts. Reaching the head of the trail he dropped to all fours and crept onto it; instantly a flash split the darkness ten feet below him, the bullet ripping through his sombrero. He did not reply, but wriggled against the base of the wall, where an outcropping stratum of rock gave him shelter. As he settled down he heard a sound above him and a pebble clicked at his side and bounced out into the chasm.

Here was a pleasant situation, he thought. They were guarding the top of the trail when they should have been guarding the bottom. There was an outlaw below him and another above him, and at the first streak of dawn he would find himself in a bad fix. Glancing up at the sky he saw that the ledge protected him from the man above; but it would take the man above only half an hour to run back along the canyon, round its upper end and appear, ready for business, on the farther side, in which case a certain member of the CL outfit would be neatly picked off at the first blush of daylight.

"I was hell-bent to get down here," he soliloquized in great disgust; "an' now I'm hell-bent to get back again. What business have they got to watch *this* end?"

He looked back up the trail and could see nothing. Then he held out his hand and could not see that. "That fool didn't see me; he *heard* me! I'm glad I didn't shoot back. He'll wait a while, doubt his ears an' think mebby that he's loco."

But Ben Gates, firing on a guess, thought he saw what he fired at when the flash of his gun lit up the trail in front of him. True, the smoke interfered; but Gates was backing both his eyes and his ears.

Johnny waited half an hour, and then grew anxious. His enemies were not doing anything, but appeared to be copying the patience of the noble red men, and waiting for dawn.

"Cuss th' dawn!" mused Johnny fretfully. "If th' feller below still thinks he heard me, th' feller up above may get dubious an' reckon his friend pulled at nothin'; an' he's th' man I got to gamble with an' th' sooner th' better."

He wriggled backward an inch at a time until he had gained a few yards and then he softly turned around. Another pebble fell on the ledge close to the place he had just evacuated. The instant he heard it he moved a little more rapidly because he was now east of the man above. A soft shuffle came to his ears and he swore under his breath when the sounds stopped at the head of the trail. The man above was now east of him, and painfully alert.

Slowly arising, Johnny hugged the wall and felt it over carefully. There were knobs and slight footholds and small cracks in it, and he took the only way open to him, desperate as it was. He judged the rim to be thirty feet above him, and setting his jaws he started to climb it. The shuffling again was heard and it now passed to the west of him.

"Cuss him!" gritted Johnny. "He acts like he don't know what to do with hisself. Why th' devil can't he stay where he belongs?"

Stepping back on the trail again Johnny stooped over and ran silently toward its upper end, thankful that he was wearing moccasins; and he had come within ten feet of it when the shuffling sound again passed him, eastward bound.

"There!" grumbled Johnny. "I *knowed* it. He acts like a bobcat in a cage. All right, damn you! I'll give you some music to shuffle to!"

Finding several pebbles, he threw them, one at a time, over the rim and about over the place where he had found shelter. A muttered expletive came from above and the shuffling went rapidly toward the sounds. Below him on the trail he heard a slight stir, but ignored it as he sprinted up the trail, silent as a ghost, and gained the shelter of a bowlder. Here he waited, grim and relentless, for the sentry's return.

Shuffle Foot was peeved, and cared not a whit who knew it. Just because he was hitched to a fool was no reason why he should endure asinine practical joking; so he peered over the canyon's rim and spoke softly:

"What th' hell do you think yo're doin'?"

The silence below was unbroken; but the astonished Mr. Gates longed passionately for the power of thought transmission. It was all right for Nat Harrison to go wandering around and braying like a jackass; he wasn't lying almost nose to nose with the most capable two-gun man that had ever cursed the Twin Buttes country.

"'Sleep?" queried Harrison. "What did you shoot at; 'nother ki-yote?" Receiving no answer he became exasperated. "If it was anybody but you I'd pay some attention to it. First you shoots a cougar out of a tree when we're all holdin' our breath to keep quiet. Then you let drive at a measly ki-yote, which you opined was a he-man. Next you plugs Long Pete, thinkin' he was Nelson. An' *now* what do you think you see? If I poke my head out far enough, even though I'm *talkin'* to you, I'll bet you'd let loose at it, thinkin' th' Lord only knows what. Why don't you *say* something? Do you think we're playin' some kid's game, where th' feller that keeps still longest gets th' apple? Did you make that noise?"

Gates writhed in impotent rage; but he suffered in silence, which only increased the pressure of his anger.

"Mebby you done shot yoreself," suggested Harrison hopefully. "Didn't see somethin' down by yore feet, an' shoot off yore toes, did you? What's th' matter with yore mouth? You can use it enough, th' Lord knows when nobody wants to hear it. *Say* somethin', you locoed polecat."

The pause was fruitless, and he continued, cheerfully:

"Mebby he's clubbed you again," he said. "Clubbed yore stone head with th' butt of his gun an' gagged you with yore own handkerchief; yore very much-soiled handkerchief. But I hardly reckon he did, because any blow heavy enough to send a shock through that head of yourn would 'a' been heard at th' houses, an' I didn't hear nothin' like that. Goin' to say somethin'?"

Harrison chuckled, and tried again: "Well, if you ain't talkin' I'll bet yo're thinkin'. Bet yo're wishin' I'd find a million dollars, get elected president of th' country an' not have nothin' to worry about all th' rest of my life. Ain't you, Dan'l Boone?

"You must be scared 'most to death," he continued after a pause. "Any time you can't find a chance to talk you shore are in a bad fix. I'm beginnin' to lose my temper. You make me plumb disgusted, you do. What th' devil do you think *I* was doin' out here all night? Think anybody got past me to go down there for *you* to shoot at? If there's anybody down there he come up from below an' crawled over you before you woke up."

Suddenly he cocked his head on one side and listened as a low gurgle sounded in the canyon.

"Cuss my fool hide!" he whispered. "Mebby he *did* see something! Mebby somebody come *up* th' trail, tryin' to get out of th' valley before daylight! Mebby it wasn't Ben at all that did th' shootin'! Hey, Ben; *Ben!* For heaven's sake, *say* something, *any*thing!"

Gates, stung into a blinding rage which swept aside every thought of caution, did say something. Nature seemed to shrink from the stream of throbbing profanity which came shouting up out of the black canyon, whose granite walls flung it back and forth until the chasm reverberated with it.

Harrison listened, entranced, his open mouth, refusing to shut, testifying to the great awe which held him spellbound. Never in all his sinful life had he heard such a masterpiece of invective, epithet, and profane invocation. The words seemed to be alive and writhing with venom; he almost could hear them crackle in the air. He heard himself called everything uncomplimentary which a frontier vocabulary saved for just such situations. He heard his ancestors described back to the time of Adam; sweeping up to the present, himself, his relatives, his ambitions, habits, and personal belongings were dissected by the man below. And then his future and the prophesied future abode of his spirit were probed and riddled and described by a furious, vitriolic tongue. His hair, eyes, ears, nose, gait, and manners were gathered up and torn apart for microscopic examination and the descriptions were shouted at the top of his companion's voice, which bellowed and boomed, rasped and coughed, screeched and shrilled down

in the blackness forty feet below him. Then there fell a
sudden calm, a silence which seemed doubly silent, unreal,
because of the contrast. A convulsive, retching, strangling
fit of coughing broke it, and then a hoarse, rasping voice
asked mildly, anxiously, a mild question:

"Is there anything I forgot?"

Johnny, standing up behind the smaller bowlder that he
might not lose a word or an inflection of the masterpiece,
lost in admiration, forgetful of purpose and the situation,
danced gleefully and gave a joyous shout: "Not a cussed
thing!"

Harrison fired at the sound, and a sharp, lurid flash
replied to his own. He staggered back as he fired again,
and an answering flash doubled him up. Gamely he pulled
the trigger again and two spurts of flame, so close to each
other that they seemed almost to merge, sent him staggering and reeling toward the edge of the canyon. Tripping
over an inequality in the earth he threw out his arms, fought
to regain his balance and with a sob plunged over the wall
into the darkness below.

Down on the trail Gates muttered in sudden horror as
he felt the wind of the hurtling body, and he leaned against
the wall, white, sick, shaken. A muffled, sickening sound
came up from the pit, and Gates dropped to his hands and
knees, not daring to stand erect.

"Nat!" he cried. "*Nat!* Was that you? *Nat! Nat!*"

At the top of the trail a rapier-like flash of fire split the
darkness, and then a series of lurid spurts of flame stabbed
in short jets, rapidly, regular as the ticking of a clock,
marking the place where two heavy guns crashed and
jumped as they poured forth a stream of lead down the
narrow rock shelf that formed the precarious trail. The
canyon roared in one prolonged reverberation and the bullets whined and spatted and screamed in high falsetto as

they cleared the wall or struck it to glance out into the valley below.

Gates, on his hands and knees, shaken, sick with horror, crept slowly downward, oblivious to the crashing, rolling thunder and the flying lead.

"I didn't mean it, Nat!" he muttered over and over again. "I didn't mean it; not a word of it!"

A sharp *spang!* sounded on a rock close to his head and a hot splinter of lead cut through his cheek. He stopped and spat it out, his nerve returning as a cold rage swept over and steadied him. Jerking his gun loose he emptied it up the trail, and, methodically reloading, emptied it again, slowly, deliberately, moving it a little at each shot so as to cover a short arc. Another spurt stabbed the darkness above, and his gun, again refilled, replied to it. Again the canyon sent roaring echoes crashing from wall to wall as flash answered flash. Then suddenly the gun below grew silent, and the guns above spat twice spitefully without a reply, and they, too, ceased.

Gates stirred and slowly raised himself on an elbow, groping blindly for his gun. His trembling hand struck it blunderingly and knocked it over the edge of the trail as his numbed fingers sought to close over it. Dazed, racked with pain, he sobbed senseless curses as he slowly dragged himself down the trail, desperately anxious to reach his picketed horse before his reeling senses left him.

After an unmeasured interval, as vague and unreal as an elusive dream, he stumbled over the picket rope and sprawled full length. Arousing himself he felt along it and managed to loosen it from around the rock which served as a picket pin; and then, slowly, by a great effort he crawled along the rope and staggered to his feet to grasp the pommel of his saddle, where he clung and rested for a moment.

The restless horse, scenting blood, tossed its head and moved forward; but Gates, by a great, supreme effort, crawled heavily into the saddle and bound himself there with his lariat. Then, spurring clumsily, he started the animal toward the ranch-houses, fighting desperately to keep his wandering senses.

An hour later two men stole to the door of the end house and listened, questioning each other. Actuated by a common impulse they slipped out toward the corral, gun in hand, and found Gates, unconscious and weak, but alive, huddled forward on the horse's neck.

XVI

♦

The Science of Sombreros

Johnny rubbed his eyes and sat up, wondering. It was still dark, but a grayness in the east told of approaching daylight. He was puzzled, for it had been mid-forenoon when he had gone to sleep. Unrolling stiffly from the blanket, he sat up to listen and to peer about him. From his thicket he could see the tent, with the soles of his boots and part of his blanket showing. Arising he stretched and flexed his muscles to ease the ache of them, and then approached the ashes of the fire, and found them and the ground underneath to be stone cold. Rubbing his eyes, he laughed suddenly: he had slept for nearly twenty hours!

"Shore made up for th' sleep I been missin'!" he grunted. "An' ain't I hungry!"

Having eaten a hearty breakfast he scouted along his back trail, acting upon the assumption that the Circle S puncher might have gone back again, picked it up and followed it. Reassured as to that he started back to camp, and on the way topped a little rise and caught sight of Pepper grazing in the narrow canyon.

"That won't do, at all," he muttered, thoughtfully. "She's a dead give-away—an' now I can't take no chances."

Returning to his camp he packed up food and spare ammunition, and then, hurrying down the canyon, whistled to the horse, who followed him closely, as he searched in vain for a safe place to put her. He was growing impatient, when he chanced to look closely at the face of the southern Twin, and then nodded quickly. If there was water on its top, that was the place for the horse. Half an hour later, after some careful climbing, he reached the high plateau, dropped the reins down before Pepper's eyes and made a swift examination of the top of the butte. His hopes were rewarded, as he had expected them to be, for in a deep bowl-like depression lying at the foot of a high steep ridge he found a large pool, the level of which was considerably below the high-water mark on the wall. This meant concentration due to evaporation, and he tasted the water to be sure that it was fit to drink. Whistling Pepper to him, he picketed her so that she could reach the edge of the pool and range over enough grass to satisfy her needs, cached the pack and departed.

When he reached the canyon he went around the butte and started for his camp along its southern side, critically examining the sheer wall as he fought the brush and the loose shale under his feet. There was one place where he thought it possible for a cool headed, experienced man to climb to the top, if he put his mind to the task and took plenty of time. Giving it no further thought he plunged on, glad that the horse was out of the sight of any scouting rustler and picketed so she could not get near the edge, where she would have shown up sharply against the sky, visible for miles.

Swinging past his camp and turning to the south he cautiously crossed the rustlers' main trail and climbed the wall behind it, and as he went forward he tried to figure out what his enemies thought of the situation. If they believed that several enemies opposed them they would be likely to stay in the houses, or not stray far from them; but if they thought only one man fought them they would most certainly take the field after him. Such was his summing up; and, bearing in mind that Long Pete, when last seen by him, was headed toward the houses, he took full advantage of the cover afforded.

Approaching the cliff by a roundabout way, he at last wriggled to the edge and peered over. A gun-barrel projected from the crack of the door in the last house; a man lay behind a bowlder on the cliff across the valley, facing eastward; and almost directly below him a sombrero moved haltingly as its wearer slowly climbed up the cliff at one of the few places where it could be scaled.

"They've figgered right," thought Johnny; "an' they're goin' to make things whiz for me. Red Shirt, over there, must be a thousand yards away; but this sink is deceivin'."

He looked down at the climber, who was about half way up the bluff. "Huh! I don't want to shoot him without givin' him a chance; but he just can't come up. Le's see: one, two, three; an' one in th' house, wounded, is four. There's a couple more somewhere, layin' low I reckon, waitin' for me to move across their sights."

He looked across at Red Shirt and grinned. "He's layin' on th' wrong side of that rock an' don't know it. I'll tell him, an' get rid of that climber at th' same time. Hope he busts his neck gettin' down."

Wriggling back from the edge so that the man in the

house could not locate him by the smoke, he took deliberate aim at Red Shirt and gently squeezed the trigger. Red Shirt soared into the air and dove over the bowlder headfirst and with undignified speed.

"Knowed it was deceivin'," growled Johnny. "Shot plumb over him. Can't be more'n eight hundred yards. An' that's a fool color of a shirt to wear on a job like this."

Johnny's shirt had been blue, a long time back; but now its color hardly could be described by a single adjective. Sun, wind, and strong lye soap had taken their toll; and it had not been washed since he had left his little valley.

Wriggling back to the patch of grass, a quick glance below showed the climber frantically descending; and the man in the house was making lots of smoke on a gamble. Across the valley a gray-white cloud puffed out above the big rock and a little spurt of sand forty feet to Johnny's left told him that Red Shirt, too, was guessing.

"Must 'a' been asleep not to see my smoke," muttered Johnny.

More smoke rolled up from the bowlder and soon some pebbles not ten feet away from him scattered suddenly, while a high-pitched whine soared skyward.

"He's pluggin' at every bit of cover he can see," mused Johnny, wriggling back behind a rock. "An' he'll prospect that bunch of grass—*knowed it!* He can shoot," he exclaimed in ungrudging praise; "an' he's got th' range figgered to a foot. An' he's workin' steady from th' north to th' south; an' when he tries for that clump of brush over there he's got to show his head an' shoulder."

A puff of dust and sand fifty feet to his right told him to get ready; and then a bowlder south of the sandpuff said *spat!*

Johnny lowered his rear sight and cuddled the stock of the heavy Sharp's to his cheek. Slowly a red dot moved up in front of his sights and he again squeezed the trigger, and again missed. But he had no way of knowing that Art Fleming was spitting sand and that his eyes had not escaped the little shower.

"I got to guess too much," swore Johnny. "That front sight hides him. I wonder how many times I was goin' to file it sharp?"

As he reloaded, his sombrero suddenly tugged at his scalp and a flat report sounded behind him. He quickly rolled into a shallow depression and another bullet sprayed him with sand.

"Repeater," he growled. "I got as much sense as a sheep-herder!"

There now was plenty of cover between him and Repeater, but there was still too little distance between him and Fleming; and the latter was a disconcertingly good shot. Two quick reports sounded from the house and Johnny smiled; the man at the door was seeing things, and backing his imagination with lead.

Johnny was watching a ridge behind him. "Me an' Repeater are goin' to argue," he remarked, and almost fired when a sombrero slowly arose on the skyline.

"Cussed near bit," he chuckled; "but you got to have yore head in that bonnet before I lets drive."

A matted tuft of grass on the top of the ridge moved so gently that only a very observant eye would have detected it. Johnny's Sharp's roared, and instantly was answered from a point a yard away from the stirring clump of grass, the bullet fanning his face.

"Yo're too cussed tricky," grunted Johnny; "but I got a few of my own."

Leaving his rifle lying so that its barrel barely projected into sight, he slipped into a gulley and crept toward the west, a Colt in his hand.

Repeater again stirred the grass tuft, and then he found a rock about the size of a man's head and pushed it up to the skyline of the ridge. Nothing happened. "If my hair wasn't so red," he murmured, "I'd take a peek. It's an awful cross for a man to bear."

He was a cheerful cattle-thief and did not get easily discouraged. Also, he was something of a genius, as he proved by putting his sombrero on the rock and raising the decoy high enough in the grass for the hat brim to show.

"Shoot, cuss you!" Repeater grunted, leveling his rifle; and then as the uneventful seconds passed he grew faultfinding and used bad language. Suddenly a suspicion flashed across his mind.

"That would fool a man with second sight," he muttered. "Somethin's plumb wrong; an' I think I better move. That bowlder over there looks good." And as he crawled behind it a pair of keen eyes barely caught sight of his disappearing heel.

"That man's got th' right to wear expensive hats," grinned Johnny, squatting behind a great mass of lava; and his grin widened as he glimpsed the sombrero-topped rock. "Yes, sir: he's got a head worth 'em; an' if I don't watch him close I'll grab holt of th' wrong end of somethin'."

Across the valley Fleming, having cleared his eyes of sand, was rapidly recovering his normal vision and was preparing with cheerful optimism to bombard everything which looked capable of sheltering his enemy, when a movement north of and far behind the suspected area acted upon him galvanically. He threw the rifle to his shoulder without elevating the sight, raised it instinctively to the angle of maximum range and squeezed the trigger. He did not expect a hit, and he did not get one; but he caused his friendship to be strongly doubted.

Repeater ducked, and when his face bobbed up again it wore an expression of outraged trust, and he raised a belligerent fist and muttered profanely in hot censure of the distant experimenter. Fleming, chuckling at his friend Sanford's anxiety, raised his sombrero and waved it, seeming to regard this as ample reparation.

"He's gettin' as bad as Gates," growled Sanford, eying a leaden splotch on a bowlder a foot above his head; "but he can shoot like th' hinges of hell with that blasted Sharp's."

He suddenly leaped closer to the bowlder and behind its sheltering bulge, for Fleming, having apologized, fired again. The marksman was frantically waving his sombrero, seemingly indicating a southerly direction.

Sanford scowled at him. "Does he want me to go south, or does he mean that that feller is south of me?"

Fleming, with no regard for the cost of Sharp's Specials, fired again and Sanford heard the slobbering, wheezing hum of a nearly spent bullet turning end over end in the air and trying to ricochet after it struck.

"He's shootin' south of me," said Sanford; "an' I stays here. Somethin' tells me that th' feller that does th' movin' is goin' to die. No red-head ever made a handsome corpse, an' bein' th' red-head which I mentions, I'm goin' to stick to this hunk of granite like a tick to a cow."

Johnny, hands on hips, was glaring defiance at the cheerful spendthrift, sorry that he had left his rifle behind. He regarded Fleming as a meddlesome busybody who took delight in revealing his every movement. Also, the optimist was a good shot; but he derived no satisfaction from the fact that the closest bullet had been ricochet, for a key-holing slug makes an awful mess if it lands.

"I'll bust yore neck!" quoth Johnny, shaking a fist at the persistent nuisance; and then he jumped aside as a sudden sharp *spat!* came from the bowlder. "You can shoot near as good as Red Connors, but if he was here he'd show you what that little difference means." He raised his voice: "Hey, Repeater! Who is that fool?"

Sanford laughed softly and made no answer; but he carelessly showed a shirt sleeve, and when he jerked it back under cover it needed a patch.

"What th' hell you doin'?" demanded Sanford heatedly.

"Who's Red Shirt?"

"Ackerman."

"Then he's better with a Sharp's than a Colt."

"That's a Spencer carbine."

Johnny laughed derisively: "If it is he'll strain it."

"It's a Winchester," chuckled Sanford.

"Yo're a liar!"

"Yo're another! She's a single-shot, .40-90."

"Then he's changed guns. He had a Winchester repeater in Hastings. I saw it."

"You'll see too much some day. You'll see a slug in yore eye."

"I'm waitin'," replied Johnny, and ducked. Fleming was getting good again, and Johnny was glad that he could not see where his bullets were landing, for as it was he was shooting by guess.

"He'll get you yet," encouraged Sanford.

"Think I'm goin' to wait for it?" indignantly demanded Johnny.

"Gimme a look at you," urged Sanford genially.

"Stand up an' take it," retorted Johnny.

"Reckon I'm scared to?"

There was no reply, for Johnny had slipped away and was running at top speed along a gully, where he was out of sight of the hard-working Fleming. A few minutes later he had reached his rifle and was cuddling it against his cheek; and he was causing Sanford a great amount of mental anguish and wriggling progress.

"Some people calls this strategy," muttered Johnny, "but I calls it common sense."

Raising his head cautiously he looked across the valley but saw no sign of Fleming; and he figured that it would be an hour before that interesting person could cross the valley and get close enough to be a menace. What concerned him most were the two rustlers' friends, who must certainly have heard the shooting. Out of deference to the curiosity of those individuals he crawled into a partly filled-in crevice, whose sides were steep rock and whose floor was several feet below the level of the surrounding plateau.

Peering out from between two rocks he saw Sanford's sombrero disappear from the ridge, and then it cautiously arose again; and Johnny's eyes narrowed, for he knew the numerous uses of sombreros.

"Keep stickin' it up," he muttered. "An when I get tired shootin' at it you'll stick yore head in it an' get a good look around. Most generally when a man pokes up an empty hat th' crown don't tip back as it rises; it just comes up level. An honest hat slants back more an' more as it comes up. 'Cause why? Why, 'cause. 'Cause a man uses his neck to raise his head with. Now, if he kept his neck stiff an' raised his whole body, from th' knees up, plumb straight in th' air, then th' hat would come up level. An' I asks you, Ladies an' Gents, if a man layin' down behind a little ridge can raise his whole body stiff an' straight, plumb up an' down? No, ma'am; he can't. He raises his soiled an' leathery neck, an' th' top of th' useful sombrero just naturally leans backward; just like that.

"Look, Mister; there it comes again; an' it don't tip back at all. I shall ignore it, deliberate an' cold. But when it tips back, lifelike an' natural, like a' honest hat should, then I'll pay attention to it, me an' my little Sharp's Special.

"Oh, I've done made a study of appearin' hats. I'm a reg'lar he-milliner. It was Red Connors an' Hoppy that directed my great intelligence to that important science. Tex Ewalt knowed about it, too. Tex was eddicated, he was. He said it is in th' little things that genius showed. He said somethin' about genius payin' attention to details, an' havin' infernal patience. Now, Ladies an' Gents, a hat is a detail; an' right now I've got th' infernal patience. Loo-kee! There she comes again! Level as a table. So, you see; I'm a genius. An' ain't he a persistent cuss? He's got infernal patience, too; but he ain't no genius. He ain't strong on details."

He looked around and grinned. Another hat, to the west of him, was in plain sight.

"Huh! Two hats in sight are two corners of a triangle; an' sometimes th' most dangerous corner is th' third, where there ain't no hat. Somewhere east of me there's a feller sneakin' up; an' he's th' feller I got to ventilate with my long-distance ventilator. An' mebby th' second hat's boss is circlin' around bareheaded; but it is still a triangle. Mebby it's a four or five or six cornered triangle. An' me, I'm all alone; so I'll crawl east an' hunt for company."

He dropped the monologue and took up the science of wriggling swiftly and silently; and when he stopped he was in the middle of a nest of rocks and bowlders at the base of a great pile of them.

The second hat still could be seen, but he gave most of his attention to the opposite direction.

"If I'm wrong, why did Number Two stick up his hat? I'll bet a peso that him, or Red Shirt, or their friends are stalkin' me from th' east. An' I'll bet two pesos that I'll cure him of such pranks. There's only two ways of explainin' that second hat. One is that th' owner is loco. Th' other is that he left his sign hangin' up to show me where he ain't. Th' other is that he left it so I'd think he wasn't there, but he is. An' th' other is that he figgered I'd think he left it to show me where he ain't an' that I'd think he was, so he moved on an' ain't there at all. Jumpin' mavericks! It makes my head ache. Havin' settled it with only four ways left to guess, I'll stay pat, right here, an' let them do th' openin'."

The shadows were growing longer and reaching out from bowlders and brush like dark fingers of destiny, and the sun hung over the western buttes and set them afire with brilliant colors. A lizard flashed around a rock, regarded the prone and motionless figure with frank suspicion until a slight movement sent it scurrying back again.

To the left a bush trembled slightly and he covered a rain-worn crease which cut through the top of a ditch bank. To the right a pebble clicked and behind him came the faint snapping of a twig.

"*Three* of 'em stalkin' me!" he muttered angrily. "I got to shoot on sight an' not waste a shot. An' they knowed where I was, judgin' from th' way they're closin' in on that crevice."

In front of him a red line showed and, rising steadily into view, became the back of a bare head. Then, very slowly, a brown neck pushed up, followed by the shoulders. Johnny picked up a small rock and arose to a squatting position.

Sanford was now on his toes, crouching, the tips of his left hand fingers on the ground, while in his other hand, held shoulder high, poised a Colt, ready for that quick, chopping motion which many men affected.

Johnny took careful aim and threw the stone. Sanford jumped when the missile struck near him, and wheeled like a flash, the Colt swinging down. He saw a squatting figure, a dull glint of metal and a spurt of flame. Johnny wriggled swiftly back among the rocks and awaited developments.

"They don't know who fired," he mused, "an' they dassn't ask."

If it had been a miss the silence would have been unbroken, as before, until a second shot shattered it; and if it had killed the rustler the silence also would remain unbroken; but if Sanford had scored a kill he instantly would have made it known. Being uncertain they were sure to investigate.

"Cuss it, there's at least two left; an' there may be four or five," grumbled Johnny. "I stay right here till dark."

Suddenly he heard a soft, rubbing sound, and he guessed that someone wearing leather chaps was crawling along the rocky ground behind the pile of bowlders which sheltered him. The sound grew softer and died out, and a panic-stricken lizard flitted around a rock, stopped instantly as it caught sight of him, wheeled and darted between two stones. Johnny smiled grimly and waited, the gun poised in his hand. Again the rubbing sounded, this time a little nearer, and he softly pushed himself further back among the bowlders. Something struck his left hand holster and he glanced quickly backward, and paled suddenly as he saw the copperhead wrestling to get its fangs loose. He drew in his breath sharply and his hand darted back and down, gripping behind the vicious, triangular, burnished head; and instantly a three-foot, golden-brown, blotched band writhed around his wrist and arm, seeming to flow beneath its skin. Jerking his hand forward again he broke the reptile's neck, tore it from his arm, shoved it back among the rocks, picked up the Colt again, and waited.

There sounded, clear and sharp, a sudden shirring rattle and the rubbing sound grew instantly louder. Again the fear-inspiring warning sounded and he heard pebbles rolling, where a creeping rustler made frantic efforts to get back where he suddenly felt that he belonged. A rattlesnake ready for war is not a pleasant thing to crawl onto.

"This is a devil of a place!" muttered Johnny, cold chills running along his spine. "It's a reg'lar den! As soon as that cow-thief gets far enough away, that rattler will slip in among these rocks—an' my laigs ain't goin' to be back there when he arrives!"

He wriggled softly out of the narrow opening and found more comfort on a wider patch of ground, where he could sit on his feet. As he settled back he saw the rattler slipping among the stones at his left.

"It all belongs to you an' yore friends," muttered Johnny, getting off his feet. "I'll risk th' bullets, cussed if I won't!" And he forthwith crawled toward the side where he had heard the rubbing sounds.

The shadows were gone, merged into the dusk which was rapidly settling over the plateau, and he had to wait only a little longer to be covered by darkness; but he preferred to do his waiting at a point distant from a snakes' den. Creeping along the edge of the bowlder pile, alert both for snakes and rustlers, he at last reached the southern end and stopped suddenly. A leather-covered leg was disappearing around a dense thicket, and he darted to the shelter of a gully to wait until darkness would hide him on his return to camp.

XVII

♦

Treed

Johnny awakened at the shot and softly rolled out of his blanket. The fire was nearly out, but an occasional burst of flame from the end of the last stick served to show him the outlines of the little tent and the glistening hobnails in the soles of the protruding boots. A bush stirred and a careless step snapped a twig with a report startlingly loud in the night. A voice some distance behind him called out to a figure which appeared like a ghost upon the edge of the little clearing.

"Get him, Purdy?"

Boots scraped on stone at his right and another voice raised out of the dark. "If he didn't, there'd be some cussed rapid shootin' about now!"

"Course I got him!" snorted Purdy.

Johnny cautiously backed out of the thicket while the men behind him crashed through the brush and swore at the density of the growth.

The man at the end of the clearing stopped and stood quietly regarding the vague boots, his rifle at the ready. Somehow he did not feel that everything was as it should be. The boots appeared to be in the same position as when he had espied them a moment before. He must have made a lucky brain or heart shot, or—. He raised his hand swiftly and backed into the oak brush again, where Mexican locust in the high grass stabbed him mercilessly. Again his rifle spoke. The boots did not move.

"You got him th' first time," laughed Fleming, walking rapidly toward the tent; but he was not confident enough in his claim to put up his Colt.

"Shore," endorsed Holbrook. "It was good judgment, an' good luck."

Fleming, Colt ready, leaned swiftly over, grasped a boot and gave a strong pull—and went down on his back, the Colt exploding and flying one way while the boot, showering pebbles and small bits of rock, soared aloft and went the other way.

"Damn him!" swore Purdy, diving back into the brush and giving no thought to the thorns. "Cover, fellers! Quick!" he cried.

His warning was hardly needed, for Holbrook had dived headfirst into a matted thicket and landed on some locust with but little more than passing knowledge of its presence. Fleming bounded to his feet, scooped up his Colt on the run and jumped into another thicket, unmindful at first of the peculiar odor which assailed his nostrils. He had no time, then, to think about skunks, or whether or not they were hydrophobic.

The silence was deep and unbroken, except for an occasional faint swish or scrape, for three men had settled down where they had landed, there to remain until daylight, not far off, came to help them.

Out of the clearing a small, striped animal moved leisurely and defiantly, tainting the air, and entered the tent. It instantly became the cynosure of three pairs of anxious eyes, for while August was a long way off, three worried punchers found small satisfaction in that. They would sooner face an angry silver-tip, or a cougar with young, than to intrude upon the vision of that insignificant but odorous "'phoby cat." Each of them knew of instances, related by others, where men bitten by a skunk had gone raving mad; but none of them, personally, ever had seen any such case; and none of them had any intention of letting the other two see any such a shocking spectacle in the immediate future.

The little animal emerged from the tent and appeared to be undecided as to which way to go; and no roulette ball ever possessed the fascination nor furnished the thrills that took hold of the three staring watchers. It took a few steps one way and a few steps the other, and then started straight for the thicket where Art Fleming shuddered and swore under his breath. Two sighs arose on the air concurrent with the cursing.

"Just my cussed luck!" gritted Fleming. "Get out of here, cuss you!" he whispered fiercely, and raised his Colt. No sane man, with his firm beliefs regarding skunks, would hesitate when forced to choose between probable death from a bullet or certain and horrible death from hydrophobia. The skunk reached the edge of the thicket, five feet from the perspiring puncher, and was blown into a mass of reeking flesh.

Fleming groaned miserably. "They shore dies game!" he swore, half-nauseated. "They're cussed strong finishers! Why couldn't he 'a' headed for one of th' others? I got to move, right now."

He did so, slowly, cautiously, painfully; but the scent moved with him. He stopped, mopped his face, and then held his hand away from him. His sleeve, vest, and sombrero proclaimed their presence with an enthusiastic strength and persistence.

"Cussed if he didn't *hit* me! An' I might just as well go back to th' ranch, so far's huntin' Nelson is concerned. He could smell a day before he caught sight of me!" A sickly grin slipped over his face, for he was blessed with a keen sense of humor. "Won't Gates an' Quigley be indignant when I odors in upon 'em!"

Purdy rolled his head in silent mirth, one hand over his nose; and Holbrook alternately chuckled and swore, wishing that the soft wind would shift and spare him.

THE MAN FROM BAR-20

"Laugh!" blazed Fleming, angry, ashamed, and disgusted, removing his vest and throwing it into the clearing. His sombrero followed it and then there was a ripping sound and a red flannel shirt sleeve joined the other castoffs. The little, persistent flame on the stick blazed higher and revealed the collection of personal effects.

"If he peels off th' rest of his shirt an' shucks his pants, he'll smell near as bad," chuckled Purdy gleefully.

"Dan'l Boone Number Two!" said Holbrook, tears in his eyes. "But I shore wish he had enticed it off aways before he shot it!"

Dawn stole from the east and the magnificent sunrise passed unnoticed. Fleming, sullen, angry, odorous, trudged doggedly to his horse, which regarded him with evil eyes, mounted and rode away at a gallop in his desire to create a breeze; and in this the horse needed no urging. Back in the canyon Purdy and Holbrook scouted diligently, but with caution, covering ground slowly and thoroughly as they advanced.

Under a tangled thicket near the camp there was a sudden movement, and Johnny, hands and face covered with blood from the scratches of thorns, slowly emerged and followed the scouting rustlers at a distance. Satisfied that they would not return he circled swiftly to the south of the camp and caught a glimpse of Fleming as that unfortunate plodded dejectedly over a distant ridge on his way to his horse.

Johnny watched for a moment, and then, turning hastily, slipped back to the camp, where he collected what he could carry, packed it into blankets, put on the well-worn, heavy boots, fastened the pack on his back and dashed into the cover again, desperately anxious to gain his objective.

He knew what would happen. As soon as Fleming

reached the ranch-houses he would reclothe himself and return with those of his friends who were able to accompany him; and it would not be long before the Twin Buttes section would be thoroughly combed. He could not hide his trail, so it was wise to lead them to a place they could not search.

Slipping on the treacherous malpais and loose stones, fighting through the torturing locust and cactus hidden in the grass, he pushed through matted thickets of oak brush and manzanito by main strength, savagely determined to gain his goal well in advance of the creeping, cautious cattle-thieves who crept, foot by foot, down the canyon on the other side of the butte.

A black bear lumbered out of his way and sat down to watch him pass, the little eyes curious and unblinking. Several white-tailed deer shot up a slope ahead of him in unbelievable leaps and at a remarkable speed. He leaped over a fallen pine trunk and his heavy bootheel crushed a snake which rattled and struck at the same instant; but the heavy boots and the trousers tucked within them made the vicious fangs harmless. Flies swarmed about him and yellow-jackets stung him as he squashed over a muddy patch of clay. A grinning coyote slunk aside to give him undisputed right-of-way, while high up on the slope a silvertip grizzly stopped his foraging long enough to watch him pass.

For noise he cared nothing; the up-flung butte reared its rocky walls between him and his enemies; and he plunged on, all his energies centered on speed, regardless of the stings and the sweat which streamed down him, tinged with blood from the mass of smarting scratches. Malpais, cunningly hidden in the grass, pressed painfully against the worn, thin soles of his boots and hurt him cruelly as he slipped and floundered. He staggered and slipped more frequently now, and the pack on his back seemed to have trebled in weight; his breath came in great, sobbing gulps and the blood pulsed through his aching temples like hammer blows, while a hot, tight band seemed to encircle his parched throat; but he now was in sight of his goal.

Beginning at a rock slide, a mass of treacherous broken rock and shale in which he sank to his ankles at every plunging step, a faint zigzag line wandered up the southern face of the butte. He did not know that it could be mastered, but he did not have time to gain the easier trail, up which he had led his horse. Struggling up the shale slope, slipping and floundering in the treacherous footing, he flung himself on the rock ledge which slanted sharply upward.

Resting until his head cleared, he began a climb which ever after existed in his memory as a vague but horrible nightmare. Rattlesnakes basked in the sun, coiling swiftly and sounding their whirring alarm as he neared them; but blindly thrown rocks mashed them and sent them writhing over the edge to whirl to destruction in the valley below. Treacherous, rotten ledges crumbled as he put his weight on them, and he saved himself time and time again only by an intuitive leap nearly as dangerous as the peril he avoided. At many places the ledge disappeared, and it was only by desperate use of fingers and toes that he managed to pass the gaps, spread-eagled against the cliff while he moved an inch at a time, high above the yawning depths, to the beginning of a new ledge.

Scrawny, hardy shrubs, living precariously in cracks and on ledges, and twisted roots found his grip upon them. At one place a flue-like crack in the wall, a "chimney," was the only way to proceed, and he climbed it, back and head against one side, knees and hands against the other, the strain making him faint and dizzy. Below him lay the tree-tops, dwarfed, a blur to his throbbing eyes.

A ledge of rock upon which he momentarily rested his weight detached itself and plunged downward a sheer three hundred feet, crashing through the under-brush and scrub timber before it burst apart. On hands and knees he crossed a muddy spot, where a thin trickle of water, no wider than this thumb, spread out and made the ledge slippery before it was sucked in by the sun-baked rocks. A swarm of yellow-jackets, balancing daintily on the wet rocks, attacked him viciously when he disturbed them. He struck at them blindly, instinctively shielding his eyes, and arose to his feet as he groped onward.

The pack on his back, aside from its weight, was a thing of danger, for several times it thrust against the wall and lost him his balance, threatening him with instant destruction; but each time he managed to save himself by a frantic twist and plunge to his hands and knees, clawing at the precarious footing with fingers and toes.

At one place he lay prostrate for several minutes before his will, shaking off the lethargy which numbed him, sent him on again. And the spur which awakened his dulled senses proved that his frantic haste was justified; for a sharp, venomous whine overhead was followed by the flat impact of lead on rock, and a handful of shale and small bits of stone showered down upon him. The faint, whip-like report in the valley did not penetrate his roaring ears, for now all he could think of was the edge of the butte fifty feet above him.

Never had such a distance seemed so great, so impos-sible to master. It seemed as though ages passed before he clawed at the rim and flung himself over it in one great, despairing effort and fell, faced down and sprawling, upon the carpet of grass and flowers. Down in the valley the persistent reports ceased, but he did not know it; and an hour passed before he sat up and looked around, dazed and faint. Arising, he staggered to the pool where Pepper waited for him at the end of her taut picket rope.

The water was bitter from concentration, but it tasted sweeter to him than anything he ever had drunk. He dashed it over his face, unmindful of the increased smarting of the stings and scratches. Resting a few minutes, he went to the top of the easier trail, up which he had led the horse, and saw a man creeping along it near the bottom; but the rustler fled for shelter when Johnny's Sharp's suggested that the trail led to sudden death.

Having served the notice he lay quietly resting and watching. The heat of the canyon was gone and he reveled in the crisp coolness of the breeze which fanned him. As he rested he considered the situation, and found it good. He was certain that no man would be fool enough to attempt the way he had come while an enemy occupied the top of the butte; the trail up the north side could easily be defended; the other Twin, easy rifle range away, was lower than the one he occupied and would not be much of a menace if he were careful; he had water in plenty, food and ammunition for two weeks, and there was plenty of water and grass for the horse.

Safe as the butte was, he cheerfully damned the necessity which had driven him out of the canyon: the question of sleep. Dodging and outwitting four men during his waking hours would not have been an impossible task; but it only would have been a matter of time before they would have caught him asleep and helpless.

Returning to the pool, he saw how closely Pepper had cropped the grass within the radius of the picket rope, changed the stake and then built a fire, worrying about scarcity of fuel. Since he could not afford to waste the wood he cooked a three-days supply of food.

Eating a hearty meal, he made mud-plasters and applied them to the swollen stings, binding them in place by strips torn from an undershirt, and then he sought the shade of the ledge by the pool for a short sleep, which he would have to snatch at odd times during the day so as to be awake all night, which would be the time of greatest danger.

XVIII

♦

At Bay

It was late in the afternoon when he awakened from a sleep which had been sound despite the stings. Removing the plasters he made a tour of the plateau, satisfying himself that there was really only one way up and that the rustlers were not trying to get to him. Returning to the camp, he filled a hollow in the rock floor with water, bathed, put on his other change of clothes, and then made a supper of cold beans and bacon. Filling another hollow, he pushed his soiled clothes in it to soak over night.

When he passed a break in the rampart-like wall near the top of the trail, which at that point shot up several feet above the top of the butte, a bullet screamed past his head, so close that he felt the wind of it. Peering cautiously across the canyon he saw a thin cloud of smoke lazily rising over the top of a huge, black lava bowlder on the crest of the other butte. A head was just disappearing and he jerked his rifle to his shoulder and fired.

"Five hundred an' little more," he muttered. "I got it now, you wall-eyed thief!"

Another puff of smoke burst out from the lower edge of the lava bowlder, the bullet striking the rampart below him. His reply was instantaneous, and was directed at a light spot which ducked instantly out of sight, just a little too quickly to be hit by the bullet, which tossed a fine spray of dust into the air and put a leaden streak where the face had been. He fired again, this time at the other side of the bowlder, where he thought he saw another moving white spot, and he thought right.

After a quick glance down the trail, Johnny took a position a hundred yards to the left, trying to find a place where he could catch a glimpse of the hostile marksman. But Fleming had a torn and bloody ear and a great respect for the man on the southern Twin, and henceforth became wedded to caution. Curiosity was all very well, but his was thoroughly satisfied, and discretion meant a longer life of sinful activities.

"I had my look, three of 'em," growled Fleming. "An' three looks are enough for any man," he added quizzically, binding up his bloody ear with a soiled and faded neckerchief, which should have given him blood-poisoning, but did not.

"Now that we got him treed, there ain't no use goin' on th' rampage an' gettin' all shot up tryin' to get him. All we got to do is wait, an' get him when he has to come down. It'll be plumb easy when he makes his break. A man like him is too cussed handy with his gun for anybody to go an' get reckless with. If we keep one man near th' bottom of that trail, he's our meat. I don't know how he ever got up that scratch on th' wall; but I'll bet there ain't a man livin' that can go *down* it."

Johnny grew tired of watching for Fleming, and

wriggling back to where he could safely get on his feet he arose and made the rounds again. When he reached the place where he had floundered over the edge to safety he critically examined the faint trail from cover, and the more he saw of it the more he regarded his ascent as a miracle.

"Only a fool would 'a' tried it," he grinned. "It's somethin' a man can do once in a hundred times; only he's got to make it th' very first time, or th' other ninety-nine will shore be lost. I'll never forget it, not never."

Watching a while, he wondered if it were guarded, and grinned at the foolishness of the idea; but he slowly pushed his sombrero out around a rock to find out. An angry *spang!* and a wailing in the sky told him the answer. The flat report in the valley became a mutter along the distant hills.

"Good shootin'," he grunted. "Glad you was out of breath, or excited, or somethin' this mornin'."

Back at the top of the other trail he found two large rocks lying close together near the edge, and he crawled behind them and peered out through the narrow opening for a closer look at the canyon.

It was a chaos, dotted with bowlders of granite, sandstone, and lava, some of them as large as small houses, their tops on a level with the tops of the nearest trees. It was cut by rock ridges, great backbones of stone that defied Time; and dotted with heavily wooded draws which extended up to the foot of the great pile of detritus embracing the foot of the buttes. Down its lowest levels ran a zigzag streak of bright, clean rock, the water-swept path of the torrents sent roaring down by melting snows and an occasional cloudburst. Several pools, fed by a dark trickle of water from the springs back in the upper reaches, could be seen. Of timber there was plenty, heavy growths of pine extending from the edge of the creek bed to the edge of the detritus, with here and there an opening made by the avalanches which had cut into the greenery for short distances. At other places even the stubborn pines could not find a grip, and a thinning out of the growth let him see the rocky skeleton below; but these were so few that he easily memorized their positions. Trouble would come a-winging to any careless rustler who blundered out onto any of them.

The opposite butte took his attention and he marveled at it. Under its lava cap and the great layer of the limestones was a greater layer of clay and shale and other softer sandstones. These had been harassed and battered by the winds and rains and frosts of ages and the resulting erosion had chiseled out wonderful bits of natural sculpturing. At one place he could see, and with no very great strain upon his imagination, part of a massive building with its great buttresses, where a harder, more enduring streak of rock had offered greater resistance to the everlasting assaults.

Farther to the right was a wonderful collection of columns and pinnacles, and some of the openings between them ran back until shrouded in darkness; great caverns in which houses could be built.

As the sun sank lower the shadow effect was beautiful, and even Johnny's practical mind was impressed by it. The color effect he had seen before—the streaks of black, gray, red, green, maroon, and white. Bits of crystal and quartz were set afire by the sun's slanting rays and some of them almost dazzled him.

To the west the sky was a blaze of color and the lengthening shadows made an ever-changing picture. Below him the dusk was beginning to shroud the bottom of the canyon, creeping higher and higher as the minutes passed. To see better, he wriggled closer to the edge, and a venomous whine passed over his head to die out swiftly in the air.

"Huh!" he grunted. "Fine target I must 'a' been for that thief down there, with such a sky behind me. I've got to remember things up here, or I'll lose my rememberer. I'm on a skyline that *is* a skyline. An' I ain't goin' to answer every fool that cuts loose at me, neither. I got plenty of cartridges, but I won't have if I start gettin' foolish with 'em. An' before dark I'm goin' to rustle me a blanket; it's gettin' cooler by jumps."

He made another visit to the south side of the butte for a glance down the trail of misery, and then dismissed it from his mind. In view of his experiences with it in daylight, he knew that no human being could climb it in the dark.

"It's as safe, day *an'* night, as if Red or Hoppy was layin' right here—an' that's plenty good enough for me," he smiled. "William, Junior's, bobcat kitten won't never grow big enough to climb that place—an' it's th' only thing on earth that he can't climb, blast him!"

Returning to his camp he had a drink and a smoke, and then, taking up a blanket and a pan of cold beans, he went to the head of the trail, there to keep a long and wearisome vigil.

Darkness had descended when he reached his chosen spot, and wrapping the blanket around him he sat down cross-legged, laid his rifle near him, and leaned back against a rock to watch the trail and wait for daylight. Faint, long-drawn, quavering, came the howl of a wolf, and from a point below him in the blackness of the canyon a cougar screamed defiance. He was surprised by the clearness with which occasional sounds came up to him, for he distinctly heard the crack of dead wood where some careless foot trod, and he heard a voice ask who had the second shift on the south side of the butte.

"Turn in," came the answer. "We ain't watchin' that side no more. You relieve me at midnight, an' don't forget it!"

For some time he had been hearing strange, dragging sounds which seemed to come from the foot of the trail; and had been fooled into believing that an attack was under way. Then several low crashes gave him the distance, and he again leaned back against the rock, slipping the Colt into its holster.

A tiny point of light sprang up in the darkness, whisked behind a bowlder as he reached for his rifle, and grew rapidly brighter. Then it soared into the air and curved toward the foot of the trail, and almost instantly became a great, leaping flame which soon lit up the trail, the towering walls of the buttes, and the glistening bowlders in the canyon.

He stared at it and then laughed. "They ain't satisfied with watchin' th' trail an' listenin' with both ears, but they has to light it up! There ain't no danger whatever of me tryin' to get down now; an' I'd like to see anybody try to get up it while that fire's burnin'! They're shore kind to me."

"You be careful an' keep it out of th' brush," warned a faint voice. "If she catches, this canyon will be a little piece of hell. Everythin's so dry it rustles."

"Ain't you turned in yet?" demanded the guard. "You never mind about th' fire. You get to sleep; an' you get awake again a twelve."

"Huh!" came the laughing retort. "We can *all* go to sleep while *that's* blazin'. Go gnaw yore bone an' quit growlin'."

Johnny laughed loudly, derisively. "I may set it on fire myself!" he jeered. "An' if I don't, th' rainy season is purty near due—an' when it comes you'll need a boat. Fine lot of man-hunters you are. All you can shoot is boots an' skunks!"

A flash split the darkness, and the canyon tossed the

report from side to side as though loath to let it die. When the reverberations softened to a rolling mutter he jeered the marksman and called him impolite names. The angry retort was quite as discourteous and pleased him greatly.

An hour passed, and then Johnny arose and crept softly down the trail, hugging the rock wall closely. When he reached a small pile of broken branches, caught in a fissure, he gathered an armful and carried them up on the butte. Firewood was too scarce for him to neglect any opportunities. A second trip enabled him to find a few scattered pieces and they were added to his store. Then he went to his horse, removed the picket rope, and going to the edge of the cliff at a spot over the trail he tied one end of the rope around a rock and lowered the rest of it over the rim. Another trip down the trail was necessary to make the free end fast to a dead fir that lay along the wall, and having tied it securely he slipped back to the plateau, hurried to the rope and pulled on it in vain. Try as he might he could raise only one end of the log.

"Cuss it!" he grunted; then he grinned and whistled a clear note. A few minutes passed and soft hoofbeats came slowly nearer. Then a black bulk loomed up beside him and nuzzled his neck. "I forgot th' saddle," he said. "You wait here, Dearly Beloved," and he slipped away, the horse following him.

They returned together and Johnny made the line fast to the pommel of the saddle, took hold of it himself to show his good will, and spoke to the horse.

"Oh, you don't know nothin' about haulin', huh?" he grunted, dropping the rope and taking the reins. "Come on, now—easy does it. Easy! Easy! Keep it there—th' cussed thing's got stuck on th' edge." In a moment he returned. "All right! *Over* she comes."

The man at the foot of the trail hurled more wood on

the fire and then tried a few shots when the noise above caught his ear. Then as the flames shot up he grunted a profane question and stared at the animated tree trunk which climbed sheer cliffs in the dark.

"Well, I'm cussed!" he grumbled. "Firewood! An' me lettin' him get down there to tie that rope!"

Johnny peered over the rim and noticed that the flashes came from one place, and getting his rifle he kicked a few rocks over and fired instantly at the answering flash. Two guns in the canyon awakened the echoes and he stepped back to let the whining lead pass over his head.

"There I go!" he snorted. "Wastin' cartridges already! But I wish—gosh! *I* got it!"

Grinning with elation he felt his way along the butte until he was directly over the fire, where he stopped and began to search for rocks and stones, and he did not cease until he had quite a pile of them. Approaching the rim he peered over cautiously and searched the canyon within the radius of the firelight, but without avail. He noticed, however, that there seemed to be a nest of rocks and bowlders on the outer edge of the circle of illumination and he surmised that it was there the guards were lying. He heaved a big stone and watched it whiz through the lighted arc. It fell short and he tried again. The second rock struck solidly and made quite a noise, and choice bits of profane inquiry floated up to him. Several more rocks evoked a sudden scrambling and more profanity, and a lurid bayonet of fire flashed from a dark spot.

"Now he's took to heavin' rocks!" growled a peeved, angry voice. "Damned if he ain't th' meanest cuss I ever saw!"

Johnny threw a few more missiles and a deep curse replied from the pit. Close to the edge of the wall was a large rock, nicely balanced. It was the size of a small trunk, and a grin crept across his face as he walked over to it. Putting his shoulder, all his wiry strength, and plenty of grunts into the task, he started it rocking more and more, and, catching it at the right instant, he pushed it over and rolled it to the edge, where it threatened to settle back and remain; but another great effort rolled it slowly over the edge and it disappeared as if by magic. Striking a sharp bulge in the great wall when about half way down, it bounced out in an arc; and when it struck the bowlder pile it was a real success, judging from the noise it made. The canyon roared and seemed to shudder as the crash boomed out; and the huge missile, shattering into hundreds of fragments, lavishly distributed itself through the brush and among the bowlders like a volley of grape.

Deep curses roared from the canyon and several flashes of flame darted out.

"Lay on yore stummicks, fightin' mosquitoes, an' heavin' wood on that fire at long range, huh?" jeered Johnny, throwing another rock. "These are better at night than cartridges, an' they won't run out. I'll give you some real troubles. I only wish I had a bag of yellow-jackets to drop!"

Another jet of flame stabbed upward, but from a new place; farther back; and a voice full of wrath and pain described the man on the butte, and with a fertile imagination.

"What's th' matter with *you*? An' what's all th' hellaballoo?" indignantly demanded another and more distant voice. "How can a man sleep in such a blasted uproar?"

"Shut up!" roared Purdy with heat. "Who cares whether you sleep or not? He cut my head an' near busted my arm with his damned rocks! Mebby you think they ain't makin' good time when they get down here! Only hope he stumbles an' follers 'em!"

"He's a lucky fool," commented Fleming, serene in the security of his new position. "Luckiest dog I ever saw."

"Lucky!" snorted Purdy. *"Lucky!* Anybody else would 'a' been picked clean by th' ki-yotes before now. For a cussed fool playin' a lone hand he's doin' real well. But we got th' buzzard where we want him!"

"Lone hand nothing'," grunted Fleming. "Didn't he have that drunken Long Pete helpin' him?"

Purdy growled in his throat and gently rubbed his numbed arm. "There's another. It just missed th' fire. Say! *That's* what he's aimin' at!"

"Mebby he is," snorted Fleming; "but if he is he's got a cussed bad aim. Judgin' from where they landed, I bets he was aimin' 'em all at me. I got four bits that says he wasn't aimin' at no fire when he thrun them little ones. One of 'em come so close to my head that I could hear th' white-winged angels a-singin'."

"White-winged angels a-singin'!" snorted Purdy. "Hell of a chance *you'*ll ever have of hearin' white angels sing. Yore spiritual ears'll hear steam a-sizzlin', an' th' moans of th' damned; an' yore spiritual red nose will smell sulphur till th' stars drop out."

"I'm backin' Purdy," said the distant voice. "They don't let no skunk perfume get past th' Pearly Gates."

"They won't let any of you in hell," jeered a clear voice from above. "You'll swing between th' two worlds like pendulums in eternity. Cow-thieves are barred."

A profane duet was his answer, and he listened closely as Holbrook's voice was heard. "Say!" he growled, killing mosquitoes with both hands and sitting up behind his bowlder. "Can't you hold your powwow somewhere else? Want him to heave rocks all night? How can I sleep with all that racket goin' on? Yo're near as bad as these singin' bloodsuckers; an' who was it that kicked me in th' ribs just now?"

"If you wouldn't sprawl out in a natural path an' take up th' earth you wouldn't get kicked in th' ribs!" snapped Fleming.

"Yo're a fine pair of doodle-bugs," sneered Holbrook, sighing wearily as he arose. He lowered his voice. "Here he is over this end of th' trail an' givin' you a fine chance to sneak up an' bushwhack him; an' all you do is dodge rocks, cuss yore fool luck, an' kick folks in th' ribs. Don't you know an opportunity when you see one?"

"Is *this* an opportunity?" mumbled Purdy sarcastically, rubbing his arm and fighting mosquitoes.

"With that fire showing up everything for rods?" softly asked Fleming with heavy irony. "Who's been puttin' loco weed in *yore* grub?"

"'Tain't loco weed," growled Purdy. "It's redeye. He drinks it like it was water."

"No such luck," retorted Holbrook; "not while yo're around. It ain't no opportunity if yo're aimin' to have a pe-rade past th' fire," he continued in a harsh whisper; "but it shore was a good one if you had cut down through th' canyon a couple of rods below th' end of th' trail, an' then climbed up to it an' stuck close to th' wall. You could 'a' been up there now, a-layin' for him when he went back on guard. It's cussed near as simple as you are."

"You must 'a' read that in that joke book what come with th' last bottle of liniment," derided Purdy. "Fine, healthy target a man would make if he didn't get over th' top in time! Lovely job! You must think he's a fool."

"Don't be too sarcastic with him, Purdy," chuckled Fleming. "He does real well for a man that thinks with his feet."

"You fellers make me tired!" muttered Holbrook in sudden decision as another rock flew into pieces on a bowlder and rattled through the brush. "I'd just as soon get shot on a good gamble as die from these whinin' leeches. I'm all bumps, an' every bump itches like blazes. I never thought there was so many of 'em on earth. You watch me go up there—an' cover me if you can. Jeer at him an' keep him up there heavin' rocks as long as you can."

"Watch you?" grunted Purdy. "That's just what I'm aimin' to do. I'm aimin' to watch *you* do it. We don't have to take chances like that. His grub will run out an' make him come down. Time is no object to us. We can afford to wait."

"You can't do it, Frank," said Fleming, dogmatically, ducking low as another rock smashed itself to pieces against a bowlder.

"Huh!" snorted Holbrook, picking up his rifle and departing.

His friends chose their positions judiciously and shouted insults at the man on the butte; and after a few minutes they saw Holbrook, bent double, dart swiftly across a little open space, disappear into the brush and emerge into sight again, vague and shadowy, near the base of the wall a dozen yards below the end of the trail. He crept slowly over a patch of detritus which sloped up to the wall, and began his climb, which was not as easy a task as he had believed.

The wall, eroded where rotting stone had crumbled away in layers, was a series of curving bulges, each capped by and ending in an out-thrust ledge. He forsook his rifle on the second ledge and went slowly, doggedly upward, but despite all his care to make no noise, he dislodged pebbles and chunks of rotten stone and shale which lay thick upon the rocky shelves. When half way up he paused to search out hand and foot holds and became suddenly enraged at the amount of time he was consuming; and he realized, uneasily, that he had heard no more crashing rocks. The knowledge sent caution to the winds and drove him at top speed, and it also robbed him of some of the jaunty assurance which had urged him to his task. Fear of the ridicule and the jeers of his sarcastic friends now became a more compelling motive than the hope of success; and he writhed and stretched, twisted, clawed, and scrambled upward with an angry, savage determination which he would have characterized as "bull-headed" in anyone else. Then another smashing rock revived his hopes and made him strain with renewed strength.

At last his fingers gripped the crumbling sandstone of the trail's edge and by a fine display of strength and agility he swung himself over it and rolled swiftly across the slanting ledge to the base of the wall, where he arose to his feet and leaped up the precarious path. The ascent was twelve hundred feet long and it swept upward at a grade which defied anyone to dash along it for any distance. Walking rapidly would have taxed to the utmost a man in the pink of condition; and his pedal exercise for years had been mostly confined to walking to his horse.

The footing was far from satisfactory and demanded close scrutiny in daylight, while in the dark it was a desperate gamble except when attempted at a snail's pace. Ridges, crevices, stones, pebbles, drifts of shale and rotten stone, treacherous in their obedience to the law of gravity when the pressure of a foot started them sliding toward the edge of the abyss; places where the soft sandstone had split in great masses and dropped into the canyon, taking parts of the trail with them and leaving only broken, narrow ledges of the same rotten stone, all these conspired to make him use up precious minutes.

Below him to his right lay a sheer drop of two hundred feet; above him towered the massive wall; behind him and unable to help him, were his friends, and the fire, which was not bright enough to let him see the footing, but too bright for his safety in another way; before him stretched the heart-breaking trail, steep, seemingly interminable, leading to the top of the butte, where the silence was ominous, for somewhere up there was an expert shot defending his life. He had heard no more crashing rocks, and the insults of his friends had not been answered; and to hear such an answer or the crash of a rock he would have given his season's profits.

He paused for breath more frequently with each passing minute and his feet were like weights of lead, the muscles in his legs aching and nearly unresponsive. He was paying for the speed he had made in the beginning.

The great wall curved slightly outward now and he hugged it closely as he groped onward, and soon emerged from its shadow to become silhouetted against the fire below. And then a spurt of flame split the darkness above him and a shriek passed over his head and died out below as the roar of the heavy rifle awoke crashing echoes in the canyon.

Below him lurid jets of fire split the darkness and singing lead winged through the air with venomous whines, which arose to a high pitch as they passed him and died out in the sky. He knew that his friends were firing well away from the wall, but he cursed them for the mistakes they might make. Another flash blazed above him, and the sound of the lead and the roar of the gun told him that his enemy was now using a Colt. Ordinarily this would have given him a certain amount of satisfaction, for everyone knows that while a rifle is effective at such range, a hit with a revolver is largely a matter of luck; but as he leaped back into a handy recess a second bullet from the Colt struck the generous slack of his trousers and burned a welt on that portion of his anatomy where sitting in a saddle would irritate the most. It was a lucky shot, but Holbrook was too much of a pessimist at the moment to derive any satisfaction from the knowledge.

"I'm in a hell of a pickle!" he growled as the shadows of the recess folded about him. "I can't go up, an' I can't go down—I can't even *sit* down. I got to wait till that fire dies out—an' suppose they don't let it die? Five minutes more an' I would have won out."

"Hey, Frank! Are you all right?" asked a voice.

"That's Fleming, th' fool," growled Holbrook. "I suppose he wants me to step out on th' edge of the platform an' speak a piece for him."

A laugh rang out at the head of the trail. "Answer th' gentleman," said Johnny in a low voice, fully appreciating Holbrook's feelings. "Don't it beat all how some folks allus pick th' wrong time in their yearnin' for conversation? I've been there; more'n once. You promise to go down an' give him a lickin' an' I won't pull a trigger on you while yo're on th' trail!"

"Hey, Frank! *Oh, Frank!*" persisted Fleming.

"Tell him to shut up," chuckled Johnny. "Here, I'll do it for you: Hello!" he shouted. "Hello, you loquacious fool! Frank says for you to shut up!"

Fleming's retort was unkind.

"Frank says he ain't smelled no skunk since he left th' canyon!" jeered Johnny. "Don't you get upwind of me!"

Fleming's retort was even more unkind.

"Hey!" yelled Purdy, cheerfully. "You ought to 'a' heard what Quigley said when Art odored into th' house! Dan'l Boone was scared it would get in his wounds an' poison him to death."

"Yo're a sociable ki-yote!" jeered Fleming.

Johnny laughed. "I'm that sociable I carries callin' cards, like you read about in th' mail-order catalogues. They're snub-nosed an' covered with grease, which I mostly rubs off because of th' sand stickin' to it. I'm 'most as sociable as th' dogs that drove me out of my valley, burned my cabin, stole my cows, an' put me out of th' game. I'm 'most as sociable as th' three skunks that laid for me that night. I told Quigley in Pop Hayes' saloon what I'd do if I was pestered; an' I've been doin' it. An' I ain't through yet, neither. Here's one of my cards now," he jeered, sending a .45 down the trail to let Holbrook know that he was not forgotten.

"You stopped my play, an' stole my cows," he said. "So I'm goin' take all them that you got in yore sink. When I gets through *I'll* be th' owner of th' QE ranch, all by myself; an' there won't be none of you left to bother me. Hoggin' a free country is a game two can play at, an' you shore got a good pupil when you taught me th' game. I'm aimin' to set up a record for th' cow-country. I never heard tell of a man shootin' off a whole outfit an' takin' their ranch; but that's just what *I'm* goin' to do unless you fellers get out of th' country while you can."

Jeering laughter and ridicule answered him; and then Purdy had an inspiration and voiced it with unnecessary vigor and quite a little pride.

"Hey, Frank!" he yelled. "If yo're all right, heave a rock over th' edge!"

There was a moment's silence and then a faint crash sounded in the canyon.

"There," called Johnny pleasantly. "Does that satisfy you, or shall I heave another?"

Fluent swearing came from below, in which Holbrook fervently joined, *sotto voce,* and he heaved another rock.

Johnny laughed loudly. "There's another in case you didn't hear th' first. I'm tellin' you about it because I don't want to deceive you. Mebby one of you fellers would like to sneak up here an' drag yore friend down?"

Holbrook reviewed the situation and could not see that he gained anything by keeping silent.

"*I* heaved them rocks!" he shouted savagely. "I'm all right. Now you put out that fire an' gimme a chance. I don't want to stay up here forever!"

"All right, Frank," called a new voice, which Johnny recognized as belonging to Quigley.

"Shore," jeered Johnny. "Run out an' kick it apart an' smother it with sand," he invited, reaching for his rifle. "But you want to do a good job. An' if he's still there at daylight you won't have to bother about him no more. I mean business now. I gave three of you thieves yore lives th' night you burned my cabin; but I'm shootin' on sight now."

"You got too cussed much to say!" snapped Holbrook angrily.

"An' I'll have more to say if yo're there at sunup," retorted Johnny. "An' lemme tell you, fire or no fire, you ain't down in th' canyon yet!"

Holbrook laughed. "You'll be as savin' of yore cartridges as you are of yore grub. How long do you reckon you can hold out?" he sneered.

"It only takes four bullets to clear a way for me," retorted Johnny.

New sounds came from the canyon. Rock after rock curved into the arc of illumination and landed in the fire, knocking it apart and sending blazing sticks flying toward the wall of the butte. Quigley warned his men to be careful and not set the brush on fire. There was a sudden puff of steam and the light dimmed quickly. Several other hatfuls of water turned the blazing embers into a black, smoking mass, where only an occasional red speck showed in the darkness.

The trail was blotted out and Johnny sent a .45 whining

along it. A flash from below replied to him and he listened for a sound which would tell him that Holbrook had started on the return trip. But that individual, boots in hand, made no noise as he slipped along the wall. Coming to another recess, he sought its shelter, tied the boots together with his neckerchief, slung them over his shoulder and started down again.

Quigley ordered his companions not to shoot. "You might get Frank; an' he's in danger enough as it is. Yore flash will give that coyote a fair idea of where th' trail is."

"Did you hear what that ki-yote said about takin' our ranch?" asked Purdy.

Quigley laughed. "Yes; an' I admire his gall. He's got three of us, if he got Ackerman; but we wasn't awake to his game then." Another flash came from the top of the butte, and he growled when he heard the spat of the bullet. "He ain't lost th' trail yet, but he's puttin' 'em high."

"He'd be a handy man to have around," said Fleming. 'I wonder if he'd 'a' throwed in with us, 'stead of rustlin' by hisself?"

"I'd 'a' found that out if Ackerman hadn't 'a' been so dead set ag'in him," grunted Quigley, not refusing to take credit for an idea that was not his own. "I wonder," he mused.

"Offer him a share," suggested Purdy. "If we change our minds later, that's *our* business. We're losin' a lot of time with him; too much."

There was a sudden rattle of shale and pebbles, low-voiced profanity and a crash of breaking branches. "Cuss them rotten ledges!" said a voice not far distant. "An' damn these cactus an' locusts! I owe him more than he can ever square up, blast his hide!"

"Thank th' Lord," muttered Quigley in sudden relief.

"But mebby he *is* workin' for Logan," objected Fleming. "Hey, Frank! Over here."

"If he is it's about time for th' CL to hunt him up," Purdy growled anxiously. "We'd shore be in a fix if they caught us down here!"

"CL or no CL, we stays!" snapped Holbrook, rounding a bowlder and swearing at every step. "We got him now; an' we ain't goin' to let him go!"

"Shore!" endorsed Quigley. "They drove me off th' range; but I'll stay in these hills if I dies for it. Once we get this feller out of th' way an' get back to th' ranch we can put up an awful fight from th' houses, if we're forced to. They're stocked good enough to last us six fellers over four months. It's a show-down for me, come what might; but any man can take his share of th' money an' get away, if he wants."

Growls answered him, and he laughed. "That's th' way! Well, Frank; now what do you think of th' grand opportunity?"

"It was there; I started too late!" snapped Holbrook angrily. "If Art an' Purdy had any sense, one of 'em would 'a' jumped for that trail when th' first rock came down, instead of duckin' around these bowlders like a pair of sage hens. I didn't wake up till th' show was 'most over; an' I got within a hundred yards at that. Five minutes more an' I'd 'a' been layin' behind a rock waitin' for him to come back. It would 'a' been all over by now."

"Well, don't try it again," said Quigley. "He's got all th' best of it up there. We'll give him a week for his grub to peter out before we force things. An' there ain't no use of all of us stayin' out here. This is th' only way he can come down. Two of us out here is plenty, takin' turns watchin' th' trail. An' if you keep a fire burnin' you both could almost sleep nights. He'd never tackle it. Purdy, you an' Art clear out for th' ranch at daylight. Me an' Holbrook will stay here tomorrow an' tomorrow night, when you fellers can relieve us. I'd feel better, anyhow, if there was somebody besides Ben an' th' cook in them houses. You can't tell what might happen. It'll be light in an hour, so I'll go over an' start some breakfast."

"Say, Tom," said Fleming. "Make yore camp up on th' other Twin, an' get out of this cussed hole with its heat an' its pests. Th' man off guard could get a real sleep up there. But, of course, you'll have to do th' cookin' down here, where there's water handy."

"See about that later," answered Quigley. "Anyhow, we can sleep up there without shiftin' th' camp," and he disappeared in the darkness.

Fleming rolled a cigarette by sense of touch and thoughtlessly struck a match. *Spang!* said a bowlder at his side. *Ping-ing-ing-g-g!* sang the ricochet down the canyon.

"Put it out!" yelled Holbrook, diving for cover.

"You damned fool!" sputtered Purdy from behind a pile of rocks.

"Beats all how careless a feller will get," laughed Fleming as he slid behind a rock. "I plumb forgot!"

XIX

◆

An Unwelcome Visitor

Dawn Broke, and as the light increased Holbrook saw a column of smoke arising from the southern Twin like a faint streamer of gauze. A slender pole raised and stood erect, and his suspicious mind sought a reason for it.

"Wonder if he's tryin' to signal somebody? Long Pete! I reckon he don't know Pete's dead. He'll not see *him* this side of hell," he muttered, settling in a more comfortable position to go to sleep.

The pole swayed as a rope shot over it and grew taut, and then a faded shirt, heavy with water, came into view and sagged the rope.

Holbrook grinned and picked up his rifle. "Gettin' th' wash out early. An' he must have plenty of water, to waste it like that."

He raised the sight a little and tried again. "Can't tell where they're goin'," he grumbled, and tried the third time. The edge of the shirt flopped inward as the garment momentarily assumed the general shape of a funnel.

"He ain't th' only ki-yote that can shoot," chuckled the marksman. "Fleming couldn't 'a' done any better'n that. Bet he's mad. Serves him right for havin' two. He ain't no better than me, an' I only got one, since Ackerman took my other one. Cuss it!" he swore, blinking rapidly and spitting as a sharp *spat!* sent sand into his face.

He shifted, wiped his lips, and peered out at a spot on the other butte where a cloud of smoke spread out along the ground. Then he poked his sombrero over the breastwork and wriggled it on a stick, but waited in vain for the expected shot.

"He ain't bitin' today; an' he's savin' his cartridges. Well, *I* got plenty; so here goes for that shirt again."

Again the inoffensive garment flopped; and then a singing bullet passed squarely through Holbrook's expensive sombrero.

"You stay down from up there!" grunted Holbrook at the hat. "Plumb center! I got a lot of respect for that hombre. He got th' best of th' swap, too. I spoiled a worn-out shirt, an' he ventilated a twenty-dollar Stetson. He owes me a couple more shots!"

The next shot missed, but the second turned the shirt into another funnel.

"Hey!" shouted an angry voice. "What you think yo're doin'?"

Holbrook's grin turned into a burst of laughter as the pole swiftly descended, and he again poked up his hat, hoping for a miss and another wasted cartridge; but, failing to draw a shot, he gave it up and crawled back to a safer and more comfortable place where he lay down to get some sleep.

Johnny, full of wrath, worked along the edge of the butte in a vain endeavor to catch sight of his enemy, and he took plenty of time in his efforts to be cautious. Any man who could hit a shirt plumb center and nearly every time, at that distance, shooting across a deceptive canyon and against the sky, was no one to get careless with. After waiting a while without hearing any more from his humorous enemy, he looked down each trail and then went to the other end of the butte.

Not far from him a slender column of smoke arose from a box-like depression which lay beyond a high ridge and was well protected from his rifle. Peering cautiously over the rim of the butte, his head hidden in a tuft of grass, he critically examined the canyon, bowlder by bowlder, ridge by ridge. A puff of smoke spurted from a pile of rocks and a malignant whine passed over his head. Wriggling back, he hurried to another point fifty yards to his right, where he again crept to the edge and looked down. Another puff of smoke and a bloody furrow across his cheek told him that the marksman had good eyes and knew how to shoot. Johnny drove a Sharp's Special into the middle of the smoke and heard an angry curse follow it.

"Hey, Nelson!" called a peeved voice from the rocks. "Nelson!"

"What you belly-achin' about?" demanded Johnny insolently.

"How'd you like to join us instead of fightin' us?"

"Yo're loco!" retorted Johnny. "Can't you think of anything better'n that? I cut my eye-teeth long ago."

"I mean it," said Quigley, earnestly. "Mean it all th' way through. We talked it over last night. It's poor business fightin' each other when we might be workin' together. Laugh if you want to; but lemme tell you it ain't as foolish as you think. It's a lazy, independent life; an' there's good money in it. You'd do better with us than you'd 'a' done alone."

"I've shore fooled 'em!" chuckled Johnny softly. Aloud he said: "I can't trust you, not after what's happened."

"I reckon you *are* suspicious; an' nobody can blame you," replied Quigley. "But I mean it."

"Why didn't you make this play when I was in my valley, pannin' gold an' gettin' a little herd together?" demanded Johnny. "*You* knowed I wasn't after no gold; an' you knowed what I *was* after. But no; you was hoggin' th' earth an' too cussed mean to give a man a chance, an' make another split in yore profits. You burned—oh, what's th' use? If you want my answer, stick yore head out an' I'll give it to you quick!"

"I know we acted hasty," persisted Quigley; "but some of us was ag'in it. Three of 'em are dead now; Ackerman's missin'. We'll give you th' share of one of 'em in th' herd that we got now; an' an equal share of what we get from now on. That's fair; an' it more than makes up for yore cabin an' them six cows. As far as *they* are concerned, we'll give you all of what they bring. How about it?"

"Reckon it's too late," replied Johnny. "I ain't takin'

nobody's share. I'm aimin' to take th' whole layout, lock, stock, an' barrel. Why should I give you fellers any share in it? What'll you give me if I let you all clear out now?"

"What you mean?" demanded Quigley.

"Just what I said," retorted Johnny. "There's six of you now. It ought to be worth something to you fellers to be allowed to stay alive. I'll throw off half for th' wounded men—let 'em off at half price. What are you fellers willin' to pay me if I let you leave th' country with a cayuse apiece an' all yore personal belongin's?"

"This ain't no time for jokin'!" snapped Quigley angrily.

"I ain't jokin' a bit! I'll have yore skins pegged out to dry before I get through with you. Yo're a bunch of sapheaded jackasses, with no more sense than a sheepherder. I'm 'most ashamed to get you; but I'm stranglin' my shame. You pore muttonheads!"

Quigley's language almost seared the vegetation and he was threatened with spontaneous combustion. When he paused for breath he swung his rifle up and pulled the trigger, almost blind with rage. Johnny's answering shot ripped through his forearm and he felt the awful sickness which comes when a bone is scraped. Half fainting, Quigley dropped his rifle and leaned back against a rock, regarding the numbed and bleeding arm with eyes which saw the landscape turning over and over. Gathering his senses by a great effort of will, he steadied himself and managed to make and apply a rough bandage with the clumsy aid of one hand and his teeth.

"I'll give you till tomorrow mornin' to make me an offer," shouted Johnny; "but don't get reckless before then, because th' temptation shore will be more than I can stand. Think it over."

"Damn his measly hide!" moaned Quigley, his anger

welling up anew. "Give him our ranch, an' cows, an' *pay* him to *let* us leave th' country! Six of us! Six gun-fightin', law-breakin', cattle-liftin' cow-punchers; sane, healthy, an' as tough as rawhide rope, payin' *him,* a lone man up a tree, to let us leave th' country! All right, you conceited pup; you'll pay, an' pay well, for that insult!"

He still was indulging in the luxury of an occasional burst of profanity when Holbrook approached the bowlders on his hands and knees.

"I'm still hungry; an' I can't sleep unless I'm full of grub," apologized the rustler. "An' I heard shootin'. What's th' matter, Tom? Yore language ain't fit for innercent ears!"

"Matter?" roared Quigley, going off in another flight of oratory. "Matter?" he shouted. "Look at this arm! An' listen to what that —— carrioneatin' squaw's dog of a —— had th' —— gall to say!"

As the recital unfolded Holbrook leaned back against a rock and laughed until the tears washed clean furrows through the dust and dirt on his face; and the more he laughed the more his companion's anger arose. Finally Quigley could stand it no longer, and he loosed a sudden torrent of verbal fire upon his howling friend.

Holbrook feebly wiped his eyes with the backs of his dusty hands, which smeared the dirt over the wet places and gave him a grotesque appearance.

"Why shouldn't I laugh?" he choked, and then became indignant. "Why shouldn't I?" he demanded. "I've laughed at yore jokes, Fleming's stories, Cookie's cookin', an' Dan'l Boon's windy lies; an' now when something funny comes along you want me to be like th' chief mourner at a funeral! I'm forty years old an' I've met some stuck-up people in my life; but that fool up there has got more gall an' conceit than anybody I ever even heard tell of! I'm glad *I* didn't hear him say it, or I shore would 'a' laughed myself plumb to death. Did you ever hear anything like it; drunk or sober, *did* you?"

"No, I didn't!" snapped Quigley. "An' if you've got all over yore nonsense, suppose you take a look at my arm, an' fix this bandage right!"

"Sorry, Tom," answered Holbrook quickly; "but I was near keeled over. Here, gimme that arm; an' when I get it fixed right, you make a bee-line for th' ranch. There ain't no use of you stayin' out here with an arm like that. Good Lord! He shore made a mess of it! Them slugs of his are awful; an' that gun is th' worst *I* ever went up ag'in. *I* want that rifle; an' I speaks for it here an' now. When we get him, I get th' gun."

"It's yourn," groaned Quigley. "Gimme a drink of whiskey before I start out. But I don't like to leave you to handle this alone. I can stick it out."

"It's a one-man job until somebody comes out," responded Holbrook. "All I got to do is lay low an' not let him come down that trail. A ten-year-old kid can do that durin' daylight. But you ain't goin' to go till you feel a little better," he ordered, producing a flask. "You wait a while—th' sun won't be hot for a couple of hours yet. An' would you look at th' mosquitoes! They must 'a' smelled th' blood. Here, wrap yore coat around it or they'll pump it full of pizen."

Two hours later, Quigley having departed for the ranch, Holbrook lay on the top of the northern Twin, glad to have escaped from the attacks of the winged pests which had driven him out of the canyon; and hoping that his enemy would try to take advantage of the situation, if he knew of it, and try to escape. He had decided that he could guard the trail as well from the top of the butte as he could from the canyon, for the whole length of the steeply sloping path lay before him. Cool breezes played about him, there were neither flies, mosquitoes, nor yellow-jackets to plague him, and the opposite butte and the whole canyon lay under his eyes. And he also had better protection than the canyon afforded, for there was always present a vague uneasiness, no matter how well hidden he might be, while his good-shooting enemy was five hundred feet about him. Food and water were close to his hand and he enjoyed a smoke as he lazily sprawled behind his protecting breastwork of rocks and set himself the task of keeping awake and alert.

He had seen no sign of his enemy, although he had closely scrutinized every foot of the opposite butte. Quigley, he thought, must have reached the ranch by that time and no doubt Fleming or Purdy was on the way to relieve him. As he glanced along the canyon in the direction that his friend would appear he saw a movement of the brush near the bottom of the much watched trail and he slid his rifle through an opening between the rocks covering the center of the disturbance.

It was too early for Fleming or Purdy, he reflected; and his eyes narrowed as he wondered if it could be some friend of the man he was watching.

The bushes moved again and a grizzled head thrust out into view, slowly followed by pair of massive shoulders as a great silver-tip grizzly pushed out into the little clearing where the guarding fire had been, and slowly turned its head from side to side, sniffing suspiciously. Satisfied that there was nothing to fear, it crossed the clearing and ripped the bark off of a dead and fallen tree trunk, licking up the grubs and the scurrying insects. Shredding the bark and thoroughly cleaning up the last of the grubs, it sat down and lazily regarded the towering butte.

Holbrook watched it with interest, for there was something almost human in the great bear's actions, a comical gravity and a deftness of paws which brought a grin to his face.

The bear arose clumsily, scratched itself, and proceeded toward the trail in that awkward, lumbering way which conveys such a vivid impression of tremendous strength and power. Holbrook knew that the lazy, clumsy shuffling, the indolent thrust of the rounded shoulders and the slow, deliberate reaching of the great legs, the forefeet flipping quickly forward, hid an amazing, deceptive quickness and agility, and a devastating strength. Sleepy, peaceful, and good natured as the beast appeared, its temper was always on edge and its heart knew nothing of fear when that temper was aroused; and he also knew that the vitality in that grub, insect, and berry-fed body was almost beyond belief, that a clean, heart shot would not stop it instantly.

The animal waddled onto the trail and paused to turn over a rock, licked up a few scurrying bugs and waddled on again, the great shoulders rising and falling with each deliberate step. A pause, and the red tongue wiped out a procession of hard-working ants, and again it lumbered upward.

"Nelson is due to have company; an' plenty of it!" chuckled Holbrook; "an' if he slides any lead into th' wrong place under that flea-bitten hide he'll find that butte is a cussed lot smaller than he ever thought it was. Ah-ha! Cussed if th' yellow-jackets ain't declarin' war on him! Just wait till his snout gets well stung, an' he'll be ready an' eager to fight anything that lives!"

The bear was moving swiftly now, but pausing frequently to scrape his smarting snout with one paw or the other, and it was beginning to show signs of irritation as the swarming yellow-jackets warmed to the attack.

"Gettin' riled more every minute!" grinned Holbrook. "I'd hate to run foul of him now! Mr. Nelson shore is goin' to have a grand an' busy little seance up there, unless that Sharp's of his gets home plumb center th' first crack. He'll mebby wish it was a repeater. That old varmint must be nine feet long, an' just plumb full of rage. I can imagine them wicked little eyes of hisn gettin' redder an' redder every minute. An' one swipe of them paws would cave in th' side of th' biggest steer on th' range. It's a cussed good thing grizzlies ain't got th' speed an' habits of mountain lions—they'd be th' most dangerous things on earth if they had."

The bear sat down suddenly and dragged himself a few feet, and then ran on at top speed.

Holbrook roared with laughter. "Ho! Ho! Ho! This is goin' to be as much fun as a circus! Damned if I'd miss it for a week's pay! Go on, Old Timer; steam up!"

Free at last from the stinging attacks of the yellow-jackets, the great bear suddenly stopped, squatted back on his haunches and rubbed his head and snout with both paws; and then, looking across the canyon at the place the laughter was coming from, slouched back on four legs and waddled rapidly upward, his huge body twisting ponderously at each step. Reaching the top he paused while he surveyed his immediate vicinity, looked back down the trail, glanced across the canyon again, and then slowly disappeared among the rocks and bowlders.

Holbrook shifted his rifle to a more comfortable position across his knees and leaned forward expectantly, grinning in keen anticipation, his cigarette cold and forgotten between his lips. It was just possible that there might be more in the coming show for him than amusement, for Mr. Nelson, intent, very, very intent, upon his part of a game of tag among the bowlders, might forget for a moment and carelessly show himself long enough to become a promising target.

"Wonder how much he'll take, purty soon, to *let* Ol' Silver-tip leave th' country along with us?" he chuckled. "I wish Tom was here!"

Johnny opened his eyes at Pepper's snort and glanced at the horse, which trembled in every limb and whose big eyes were ablaze with terror. She had jerked the picket rope loose from under the rock which had held it, but was rigid with fear. Sitting bolt upright as he jerked out a Colt, Johnny glanced in the direction of Pepper's stare and then left the blanket to take care of itself. Twenty paces distant was the Sharp's, loaded and lying on a rock, and he hotly cursed the stupidity and carelessness which had caused him to go to sleep so far away from the weapon. It was the first time such a thing had happened in weeks, and he instantly resolved that it never would happen again. Between him and the rifle was the biggest, meanest looking grizzly it ever had been his misfortune to face.

The unwelcome visitor had finished a pan of beans and a pan of rice and had its nose jammed in the last can of sugar that Johnny owned. Observing his unwilling host's acrobatic leap and the flying blanket, the huge animal pushed the sugar can from its swollen nose with a cunningly curved paw, and heaved itself onto its four legs, regarding the puncher with a frankly curious and belligerent stare. The little eyes were wicked and bloodshot and one of them was nearly closed from the stings of the yellowjackets. Altogether it was as unpleasant a sight as anyone would care to look upon at such close range.

Behind Johnny was the rock wall, rising fifteen feet above the bottom of the little rock basin, and it curved slightly outward at the top. On one side were scattered several great bowlders, and he kept these in mind as he glanced quickly behind him at the wall, which was smooth and devoid of hand-holds.

He had killed a grizzly with a six-shooter, but no such animal as the one facing him; and a Colt was not a weapon to be eagerly used, especially at such close quarters, where a sudden rush might be fatal to the user. He knew the thickness of the bone over the little brain, and keenly realized the smallness of the eyes as a target in the slowly moving head; if he could maneuver the animal to give him a heart shot he would have a fair chance.

"G'wan away from here!" he ordered peremptorily, with an assurance in his voice which he did not feel. "Pull your stakes, you big tramp, or I'll bust yore neck!"

Bruin refused to heed him; instead, the animal shuffled forward, its head wagging, and Johnny also stepped forward, on his toes, yelled loudly and waved his arms. Bruin paused and looked him over. Johnny side-stepped toward the rifle, but the bear pivoted quickly, swung around and declared its intentions with a low but entirely sufficient growl.

Johnny figured quickly. He might beat his visitor to the gun, but he strongly doubted if he would lead by a margin large enough to have time to swing the weapon to his shoulder and obtain the nicety of aim necessary to stop his pursuer as suddenly as the occasion demanded. The bowlders remained as his other alternative, and as the bear took its second step, which was the beginning of the rush, Johnny made a very creditable leap in the direction of the bowlders, gained the first by ten feet to spare, vaulted the second, dashed around the third and streaked up the slope leading to the top of the rocky wall behind the pool.

As he gained the top a bullet hummed past his head,

but it received no recognition from him, for the bear also was hustling up the slope, thoroughly aroused and abrim with energy and ambition. Jerking out his Colts, he emptied one of them into the rushing animal as he leaped aside to get behind another bowlder. The bear slowed for an instant as the six heavy slugs ripped into it, and then, loosing a roar that awoke the echoes, it gathered speed and slid around the rock, clawing desperately to make a short turn. Johnny emptied his second gun into the enraged animal as he dodged around another rock, and then, dropping both Colts into their holsters, he sprinted for the top of the wall as Holbrook's second bullet loosened a heel and almost threw him.

Reaching the edge he launched himself from it, recovered his balance like an acrobat and dashed for his rifle as the grizzly, reaching the edge, checked himself barely in time and hunted hurriedly for a way to get down the wall. Giving it up in an instant, the animal drew up its forelegs with a pivoting swing, and started at full speed along the edge, to go down the way it had come up. This exposed its left side, and the Sharp's, already at Johnny's shoulder, steadied upon the vital spot as he timed the swing of the great foreleg. There was a sharp roar, and an ounce and a quarter of lead smashed through skin and flesh, squarely into the animal's heart. The great beast collapsed, slid around and raised its head; but again the heavy rifle spoke and the massive head dropped limply, for the stopping power of a Sharp's Special is tremendous.

Johnny jerked out the smoking shell, slid another great cartridge into place, and then sat down on the rock, wiping his face with his sleeve.

"Hey!" called a distant voice. "Want any help with th' varmints?"

Johnny grabbed his rifle and slipped to the edge of the butte. Holbrook called again, carelessly exposing his shoulder; and then cursed the bullet which grooved it.

"Can I do anything more for *you*?" jeered Johnny.

XX

♦

A Past Master Draws Cards

Back on the CL the foreman was worried about his new, two-gun man, and had almost made up his mind to order the outfit into the saddle and to lead it up into the Twin Buttes country to aid Johnny. While he was turning the matter over in his mind he entered the bunkhouse and saw Luke Tedrue, the oldest man on the ranch, dressed in a clean shirt, new trousers, and a pair of new boots. Luke looked surprisingly clean and he was busily engaged in cleaning and oiling the parts of an old .44 caliber Remington six-shooter, one of those early models which had been transformed from its original cap-and-ball class into a weapon shooting center-fire cartridges. It had been the butt of many joking remarks and the old man cherished it, and had defended it in many a hot, verbal skirmish. Considering its age and use it was in a remarkably fine state of preservation.

Luke had played many parts in his day, for he had been a hunter, frontiersman, scout, pony-express rider, miner, and cavalryman, and as an Indian fighter he had admitted but few masters. Tough, wiry, shrewd, enduring, of flawless courage and bulldog tenacity of purpose, he had behind him long years of experience; and his appearance of age was as deceptive as the pose of a basking rattler.

The lessons of such a long, precarious, and daring life as he had led were not easily ignored, and now as a cowpuncher, riding out his declining days on the range, there were certain habits which clung to him with the strength of instinct. One of these was his faith in a weapon almost universally condemned on the range. It mattered nothing to him that times and conditions had changed; he had proved its worth in years of fighting, and now he refused to lay it aside. There had been a day when Bowie's terrible weapon had entered largely into the life of the long frontier.

Logan, worried and preoccupied as he was, could not keep from smiling at the old man's patient labor.

"Luke, you waste more time an' elbow grease on that worn-out old relic than most people do with *real* guns. Th' whole outfit, put together, don't pamper their six-guns th' way you do that contraption. Why don't you throw it away an' get a *good* gun?"

Luke snorted, and screwed the walnut butt-plates into place. Then he slipped the cylinder into position, slid the pin through it, swung up the old ramrod lever and snapped it into its catch under the barrel. Spinning the cylinder, he weighed the heavy weapon affectionately, and looked up.

Luke grunted. "Huh! Mebby that's why old Betsy is a better gun today than any in this outfit. Why should I get a new one? This old Rem. had been a cussed good friend of mine. She's never balked nor laid down, an' she puts 'em where she's pointed. An old friend like her ain't goin' to rust if I can help it."

"Rust?" inquired Logan, chuckling. "Why, there ain't been enough moisture in th' air lately to rust anything, let alone any gun that's as full of grease an' oil as that contraption. Wait till th' rainy season hits us before you worry about rust. An' what are you all dressed up for? When I saw you this mornin' you was th' dirtiest man on th' ranch; an' now you fair shines! Ain't aimin' to go an' hitch up with no female, are you?"

Luke shoved home the last greasy cartridge, snapped shut the hinged flange, laid the gun aside, and pointed to a pile of wet clothing on the floor near his bunk.

"There ain't no female livin' can put a rope on me no more," he grinned. "See them clothes? I done fell in th' crick. Some slab-sided nuisance shifted th' planks an' was too lazy to put 'em back right. They tip sideways. I got half way acrost an' up she turns. Lost my balance an' lit belly-whopper. But I put 'em back just like I found 'em."

"An' you'll get an innercent man."

"There ain't none in this outfit," grunted Luke. He searched the foreman's face with shrewd eyes. "John, worryin' never did help a man. Get shet of it, or it'll get shet of you."

"Easy said, Ol' Timer; but it ain't so easy done," replied Logan.

Luke kicked his wet holster toward the clothes and took down one belonging to someone else, and calmly appropriated it, belt and all.

"Two most generally splits a load about in half," he observed, shoving the gun into the sheath. "An' it allus helps a lot to talk things over with somebody."

"Well, I ain't heard a word from Nelson since he left that note tellin' me where he was goin' an' for me not to bother about our five-day arrangement; an' he shore started off to wrastle with trouble."

"Huh!" snorted Luke grimly. "Dunno as I'd do much worryin' about him. Real active, capable hombre, he is. Chain lightnin', an' an eye like a hawk. A few years more an' he'll steady down an' get sensible. Lord, what a fool *I* was at his age! Beats all how young men ever live long enough to become old ones."

"But he's been gone a month," replied Logan. "It's been two weeks since I heard from him, an' longer. He's playin' a lone hand ag'in them fellers, an' it ain't no one-man job, not by a damned sight! He was to find out certain things an' then come back here an' report. Why ain't he got back?"

"Busy, mebby," grunted Luke. "I have an idea th' job would keep one man purty tolerable busy, with one thing an' another turning up. He don't want to get seen an' tip off his hand; an' keepin' under cover takes time."

"I should 'a' taken th' outfit up there an' combed th' hills, regardless what anybody said about squarin' up old scores."

"What you should 'a' done, an' what you *did* do don't track," replied Luke. "An' I ain't shore that you oughta 'a' busted loose like that a-tall. It's a good thing most generally to know where yo're goin' to light before you jump. What you should 'a' done was to 'a' sent me up there, either alone or with him. 'Tain't too late to deal me a hand. Where'd he say he was goin'?"

"West of Twin Buttes. But if you go it'll be a one-man job again, an' I don't like it."

"Uh-huh!" chuckled Luke. "That's just what it is; an' I *do* like it. I drove stage, carried dispatches through Injun country, an' was th' boss scout for th' two best army officers that ever fit Injuns. Reckon mebby if th' Injuns couldn't lift my scalp, no gang of thievin' cow-punchers can skin it off. An' I'm cussed tired of punchin' cows. I ain't no puncher by nature, hopes, or inclinations. I'm a scout, *I* am; an' I'm goin' up there somewhere west of th' Twins an' find Nelson, if he's still alive, get them facts an' bring 'em back."

"I don't like th' idea," muttered Logan.

"Huh! I ain't got them fool notions that Nelson has. I ain't no Christian when I'm on a war trail. He worries about givin' th' other feller an even break; but I worries if I lets him have it. Mexicans, thieves, an' Injuns—they're all alike; an' they don't get no even break from me if I can help it. I puts th' worryin' right up to them. I'll bet he's alive, an' workin' all th' time; but he ain't got no chance to get quick results; an' it's his own handicappin', too. When a man's scoutin' around a whole passel of rustlers, a gun has got its limits. Gimme a pair of moccasins an' ol' Colonel Bowie."

"I likes you purty much; but damned if I thinks much of any man that uses a knife!"

Luke laughed grimly and got the knife from his bunk. "There he is. He don't make a man no deader than a bullet; an' he don't make no noise. There ain't nothin' handier in a mix-up—an' a good man can drive it straight as any bullet, too. I'm gettin' het up considerable about all this palaver about this knife an' me; an' I'm goin' to lick th' next man that rides me about it. It's a' honest weapon. It was ground out of a two-inch hoof file, an' when it cuts through th' air it takes considerable to stop it. When I was younger I could send it so far into a two-inch plank that you could feel th' pint of it on th' other side. Just feel th' heft an' balance of that blade!"

"Feel it yoreself!" snapped Logan. "That ain't fair fightin'; an' if you don't like that, you can start in here an' now an' lick me."

"I never said I was a fair fighter," grinned Luke, slipping the weapon into a scabbard sewed to the inside of his boot; "but old as I am, I can put yore shoulders in th' dust. We'll argue instead. Them fellers ain't fair fighters; they dassn't be even if they wanted to be; an' when I'm tanglin' up with 'em I ain't polite a-tall. I just fights, knife, gun, teeth, hands, feet, an' head, any way as comes handy. That's why I'm still alive, too. Now I'm goin' up somewhere west of th' Buttes an' look around from there; an' Colonel Bowie goes with me, right where he is. Tell th' cook to give me what grub I wants. An' I reckon I better take Nelson some ca'tridges an' tobacco."

"Tell him yoreself; an' if he won't do it, I'll tell you who moved th' planks," grinned Logan. "But I hate to see you go alone."

"An' I'd hate to have anybody along," grunted Luke. "I'll be busy enough takin' care of myself without botherin' with a fool puncher."

The old scout sauntered into the kitchen. "Mat, you sage hen; th' next time you shifts them planks, put a stone under th' edges that don't touch th' ground. You near drownded me in three inches of water an' a foot of mud. Now you gimme a chunk of bacon, couple pounds of flour, three pounds of beans, couple of pounds of that rice, 'though I ain't real fascinated by it, couple handfuls of coffee, handful of salt, an' a pound of tobacco. I may be gone a couple of months an' get real hungry. Nope; no canned grub. I want this fryin' pan, that tin cup, an' a fork."

He sniffed eagerly and strode to a covered pan. "Beans, ready cooked! Mat, you was hidin' them! Dump some of 'em into a cloth—now I won't have to cook my first couple of meals. Stick all th' stuff in a sack, them on top," and he hurried out.

Fifteen minutes later Logan entered Mat's domain. "Where's Luke? What, already? Must 'a' been scared I'd change my mind. Why, he left his pipe an' smokin' behind," pointing at the table.

Mat grinned. "He says a smoker can't smell, an' gets smelled. An' he says for somebody to go up to Little

Canyon for his bronc. He's leavin' it there tonight, hobbled. An' take that pipe out of here; I don't want them beans ruined."

Luke was crossing the CL range at a gallop, anxious to cross the river and get past the Hope-Hastings trail before dark. Reaching the Deepwater he forced his indignant horse into it and emerged, chilled, on the farther bank. Hobbling the animal, he put his boots on the saddle, slipped on a pair of moccasins, fastened the pack on his back and swung into the canyon, his mind busily forming a mental map of the country.

Placing Hope at one end and Hastings at the other, he connected them by the trail, putting in the Deepwater, the Barrier, and Twin Buttes.

"They comes to Hastings 'stead of Hope, which says Hastings is nearest. He said west of Twin Buttes. Then I'll start at th' Buttes an' go west till I find his trail; an' if I don't find it, I'll circle 'round till I finds *something*! I'd know that black cayuse's tracks in a hundred.

"Logan sent Nelson up here because nobody knowed him an' that he was workin' for us. Huh! What good will it do 'em to know a man if they never see him? An' they won't see me, 'less I wants 'em to. That water feels colder than it ought to—reckon I'm gettin' old. I shore ain't as young as I uster be. Got to move lively to get thawed out an' dry these clothes."

Crossing the main trail after due observation, he saw an old and well-worn trail leading westward into a deep valley.

"Huh! Hit it first shot. You just can't beat luck!"

Choosing the cover along one side of the smaller trail, he melted into it and plunged westward, swinging along with easy, lazy strides that covered ground amazingly and with a minimum of effort. His long legs swung free from his hips, the hips rolling into the movement; his knees were rather stiff and as his feet neared the ground at the end of each stride he pushed them ahead a little more before they touched. This was where the swaying hips gave him an added thrust of inches. And like all natural, sensible walkers, his toes turned in.

Night was coming on when he neared Twin Buttes and a rifle shot in their direction drew a chuckle from him. Throwing off the pack he ate his fill of Mat's cooked beans, shoved the wrapped-up remainder into his shirt, hid the pack and slipped into the deeper shadows, his rifle on his back, the old Remington in one hand and Colonel Bowie lying along the other, its handle up his sleeve and the keen point extending beyond his fingers.

A coyote might have heard him moving, but the task was beyond human ears; and after a few minutes he stopped suddenly and sniffed. The faint odor of a fire told him that he was getting close to a camp, and a moment later a distant flare lit up the treetops in the canyon proper. Looking down he noticed the buckle of his belt, thought that it was too bright, and wrapped a bandanna handkerchief around it. Slipping the six-shooter into its holster he moved forward again, bent over, going swiftly and silently, his feet avoiding twigs, branches, and pebbles as though he had eyes in his toes. Rounding the southern Twin he melted into the darkness at the side of a bowlder and peered cautiously over the rock.

A great, crackling fire sent its flames towering high in the air from a little clearing at the lower end of a path which went up the side of the butte and became lost in the darkness. Examining the scene with shrewd, keen, and appraising eyes, he waited patiently. A burst of fire darted from the top of the northern Twin and a strange voice jeered softly in the distance. From the top of the southern butte came an answering jeer in a voice which he instantly recognized.

"Treed, by God!" he chuckled gleefully. "Reckon he'll be tickled to see me. Wonder how long he's been up there?"

A piece of wood curved into the circle of illumination and landed on the blazing fire, sending a stream of sparks soaring up the mesa wall.

"There's Number Two," soliloquized Luke cheerfully, "feedin' th' fire an' watchin' th' trail. Cuss him for a fool! Some of them sparks will get loose, an' hell will be a nice, quiet place compared to this canyon. Well, now I got to rustle around an' locate 'em all; an' this ain't no place or time for no shootin', neither."

Half an hour later Fleming tossed more wood on the fire and settled back to fight mosquitoes. A glittering streak shot through the air and he crumpled without a sound. A shadow moved and a silent form wriggled through the brush and among the bowlders and retrieved the knife, took the dead man's weapons and wriggled back again. It slipped noiselessly across the canyon, searched along the base of the northern Twin, found the wide, up-slanting trail and flitted along it, pausing frequently to look, sniff, and listen. Reaching the top of the butte, it wriggled from bowlder to bowlder, ridge to ridge, systematically covering every foot of the plateau, and steadily working nearer the southern rim.

Holbrook yawned, stretched, and yawned again. He picked up his rifle and scowled into the canyon, where the fire engaged his critical attention.

"That lazy cuss is lettin' it burn too low," he growled. "Wonder if he's asleep!" He laughed and shook his head. "Nope; don't believe even Art could sleep down there, with them mosquitoes pesterin' him. *This* suits me, right here!"

He looked around uneasily. "I do so much layin' around

out here in daytime that I can't sleep nights," he grumbled, not willing to admit that he felt uneasy. "Funny how a man's nerves will get hummin' when he's on a job like this. It shore is monotonous." Looking around again, he shifted so that he could see part of the mesa top behind him, and tried to shake off the premonition of evil which persisted in haunting him.

"How many cows you thieves sold so far?" called a voice from the other butte.

"Nowhere near as many as we're goin' to get," retorted Holbrook, laughing. "Changin' yore mind?" he jeered.

"Not me; I wouldn't work with no teethin' infants. I'd rather work alone. I associates with *men, I* do."

"You'll 'sociate with dead men purty soon," sneered Holbrook. "We got you just where we—" the words choked into a gurgle and a lean, vague figure moved slowly forward from behind a ridge.

"What's th' matter?" ironically demanded the man on the southern Twin. "Swaller yore cigarette? That's a good thing. You want to practice swallerin' hot things because tomorrow yo're goin' to swaller a snub-nosed Special." Pausing, Johnny waited expectantly for an answer, but receiving none, he grunted cheerfully. "All right; go to blazes!"

The fire burned lower and lower and Johnny became suspicious. If the rustler on the other butte hoped to keep him engaged in snappy conversation when the fire grew low, there was no telling what the man in the canyon might do; so he crept to the top of the trail and peered down it, scanning the wall intently, half expecting to glimpse some swift, shadowy movement; but his alertness was not rewarded.

"Wonder how long Hoppy or Red would loaf on a game like this," he grinned, "if they was down there! But there ain't many of their breed runnin' around."

An hour passed and the fire was a mass of glowing embers, now and then relieved by a spasmodic burst of flame, which flickered up and died. Across the little clearing a shadowy form moved slowly backward, chuckling softly. If there were any more rustlers around, one of them certainly would have investigated why the fire was allowed to die; and Luke felt quite confident that he had accounted for all of them who were in the vicinity. Still, he argued, nothing was a certainty which depended upon circumstantial evidence, and he did not relax his caution as he moved away.

Johnny, straining his eyes in trying to discover signs of enemies on the trail, suddenly stiffened, listening eagerly with every nerve taut. Again came the voice, barely audible. Moving to the other edge of the butte he peered over cautiously, well knowing that he could see nothing.

"'Tell Red his pants wear well,'" floated up to him out of the canyon.

Johnny moved a little and leaned farther over after a glance at the black sky assured him that he would not be silhouetted for a marksman below.

"'Does William, Junior, chew tobacco?'" persisted the whisper.

Johnny wriggled back and sat bolt upright, incredulous, doubting his senses. "What th' devil!" he muttered. "Am I loco?"

"'We was scared he'd die,'" continued the canyon.

Taking another good look down the threatening trail, Johnny wriggled to the edge and again looked down.

"'Pete paid Red th' eight dollars,'" said the chasm, a little louder and with a note of irritation.

"Who th' devil are you?" demanded Johnny loudly.

"Not so loud. Luke Tedrue," whispered the darkness. "How many of them skunks are around here?"

"Yo're a liar!" retorted Johnny angrily. "An' a fool!"

"Go to th' devil!" snapped the canyon.

"Come around in daylight an' I'll send you to him!" growled Johnny. "Think I'm a fool?"

There was no answer, and, fearful of a trick, Johnny wriggled back to his snug cover at the head of the trail, finding that the fire had become only a dull, red mass of embers which gave out almost no light.

"You shore got me guessin'," he grumbled; "but I reckon mebby I'm guessin' purty good, at that. You just try it, cuss you!"

Luke explored the canyon again to make assurance doubly sure, and again approached the great wall.

" 'Does William, Junior, chew tobacco?' " he demanded.

Johnny squirmed, but remained where he was. "You can't fool me!" he shouted peevishly.

"Reckon not; yo're as wise as a jackass, a dead one," said Luke. "You stubborn fool, listen to this: 'Don't look for no word from me. I'm goin' west, to try it from back of Twin Buttes. They've drove me out.' " The voice was plainer now. "How many of 'em are out here?"

Johnny grinned suddenly, for in the increase in the power of the voice he recognized a friend.

"Hello, Luke, you old skunk!" he called, laughing. "Glad to see you. There's four been hangin' around but there's only two now, or three at th' most. Look out for 'em. Goin' to try to come up?"

"No, not a-tall," replied Luke. "There's enough of our outfit up there now. I only found two of th' thieves, but th' third may be hid som'ers well back, 'though I've shore hunted a-plenty."

"Found two?"

"Yep; one down here, an' t'other up there. Colonel Bowie pushed 'em over th' Divide. Comin' down?"

"When that fire's out."

"How'd they come to drive you up there?"

"I come up myself. Couldn't watch while I slept; an' I had to sleep. Now that there's two of us it's all right."

"You called th' turn. Get yore traps together an' I'll fix th' fire. Where's yore cayuse?"

"Up here. Don't bother with th' fire. Be right down."

Half an hour later Johnny reached the bottom of the trail and paused.

" 'Red's pants,' " said a humorous voice.

"Come on, Luke. We'll hold up somewhere an' get th' relief shift when it comes out from th' ranch."

"Shore. Where's th' ranch?"

" 'Bout three miles west; an' it's a cussed fine one, too."

"All right; get movin'. I want to dry out these pants. They must be all cotton from th' way they feel. We'll go back a ways an' start a fire."

"No, we won't; too dangerous," growled Johnny decidedly. "We got this game won right now if we don't let 'em know there's two of us."

Luke grinned in the dark. "Suits me. You wait here a minute," he said, disappearing. When he returned he grunted with keen satisfaction, for Fleming's trousers felt snug and warm. "How many are left?" he asked, leading the way toward his hidden pack.

"Quigley, Purdy, Gates, an' th' cook."

"Them names don't surprise me," grunted Luke. "How'd you get so wet?"

"Swimmin'," growled Luke.

"Yore shirt feels dry."

"It is, around th' shoulders; but th' tail feels like th' devil. But it's wool, all through."

"Was you trailin' Ackerman an' Long Pete?"

"Nope; didn't trail nobody a-tall. How many cows they got?"

"Plenty, damn 'em!" growled Johnny.

"What you been doin' up here all this time; an' how many have you got?"

"Three; I've been busy."

"Why, you had time to get 'em all."

"Didn't dare do any shootin' till I had to," replied Johnny. "Didn't want 'em to know I was up here. A gun makes a lot of noise."

Luke chuckled grimly. "Shore! That's what I *allus* said; an' that's why I use Colonel Bowie. He don't even whisper."

Johnny snorted with disgust. "Huh! I ain't knifin' or shootin' from ambush. There's *some* things I won't do!"

"Uppish, huh?" chuckled Luke. "Well, young man; mebby ambushin' ain't yore style, but I feels free to remark that it's mine in any game like this. Them pants feel good. That river's gettin' colder every year."

"River!" said Johnny, pausing in his surprise. "What river?"

"Deepwater, of course. How many rivers do you reckon we got out here?"

"Th' devil!" muttered Johnny. "Say! When did you leave th' ranch?"

"'Bout three o'clock. I'd 'a' been here sooner, only I hoofed it from th' river. Cayuses can't go where a man can; they make a lot of noise, an' a man sticks up too cussed prominent in a saddle. They ain't worth a cuss in this kind of country when trouble's afoot."

"Well, I'll be hanged!" grunted Johnny.

"Pull up; here we are," said Luke, stopping and bending over some rocks, which he rolled aside. "Rocks are reg'lar telltales. They has a dark side an' a light side; an' th' deeper they're set in th' ground, th' bigger th' dark side is. When you want to cache with 'em, you picks them that sets *on* th' ground; an' you don't turn 'em wrong side up, neither. Then a little sand used right will fix things so that only me or an Injun can tell that anything's been moved. Here's yore ca'tridges an' tobacco. Tote 'em yoreself."

"Much obliged. But how did you find me so cussed quick?" demanded Johnny, breaking open the boxes and distributing their contents about his person.

"Smelled you," chuckled Luke, fixing the pack on his back.

"Yo're an old liar!" retorted Johnny. "Tell me about it."

"Can't; there ain't nothin' to tell," replied Luke, winking at the sky. "It's just experience, instinct, brains, knowin' how, an' a couple more things. Us old-timers done better'n that, forty years ago. I'm glad to get my hand in ag'in; punchin' cows shore does spoil a man. Now, you know this layout; where we goin' now? An' what you goin' to do with that four-laigged nuisance?"

"Put her in a draw east of here. She'll stay where I leave her."

"Then she ain't no fe-male. It just can't be did. I know 'em!"

"You an' our Pete oughts get acquainted with each other," chuckled Johnny. "You fellers has th' same ideas 'bout some things."

"Foreman, or owner?"

"Just a plain puncher."

"He oughta be th' foreman; he's got sense. I buried one, an' left two more. You can't fool me about th' sex."

"Yo're a reprobate. Come on, Pepper," said Johnny, whistling to the horse, who heeled like a dog. "It'll be light purty soon, an' we want to hide this cayuse."

"It's yore say-so; I'll string along, ready to chip."

XXI

◆

Scouting as a Fine Art

Quigley, favoring his injured arm, led the way toward Twin Buttes to relieve the men on guard, Purdy close behind him; and he did not stick to the trail, but cut straight for his objective along a way well known to both. He was not in good shape for hard work or hard fighting, but he felt that his place was on the scene of action, as befitted a chief; and he had stubbornly battered down all the reasons advanced by his companions at the ranch by which they sought to dissuade him. It had to be either him or the cook, for he was not as seriously wounded as Gates.

The chief was the best man for leader that the outfit contained, and if he had erred in being slack and over-confident it was only because they never had been molested seriously since they had taken to the Twin Buttes country, and, with the exception of Ackerman, he secretly felt less security than any of the others. Thanks to his earlier activities and clever distortion of facts as to why he had crossed the Deepwater to live in the Buttes, the outfit had not been bothered; and the Twin Buttes section had become taboo, in recent years, to everyone, no man caring to risk his life in penetrating that locality until Johnny Nelson appeared. And although Ackerman had preached disaster, he had preached it so long and so much that he was regarded as a calamity howler.

There were two comparatively safe ways to reach the Buttes, when once the last high, intervening ridge was attained. One led to the far side of the northern Twin and was hidden by it from the sight of anyone on the other butte; the second course swept to the south, running through arroyos and draws, and sheltered by the dense growths of pine; and it not only was a shorter and easier course, but allowed an occasional glimpse of the way Johnny had scaled the great southern wall.

Reaching the ridge, Quigley paused to rest, and weighed the merits of the two approaches. He could be as clever and cautious as the next man when he felt that the occasion demanded it; and the events of the last few days told him that such an occasion had arrived. Easing the bandages, he chose the southern course and led the way again.

"There's his smoke," grunted Purdy, trudging along in the rear. "Wonder how much grub that ki-yote's got?"

"Don't know; an' don't care much," replied Quigley. "It don't make no difference. Th' time will come when he's *got* to come down, an' bein' there when he does is our job. If I was plumb shore he was workin' on his own hook my worries would simmer down a whole lot; an' until I *am* shore, I ain't overlookin' nothin'."

"You ain't got no business comin' out here with an arm like that," growled Purdy. "Three of us are enough."

"I ain't got no business bein' nowhere else," retorted Quigley. "An' as long as yo're ridin' that subject again, lemme tell you that from now on till we get him, I'm goin' to stay right there. My eyes are all right, an' my Colt arm is th' same as ever. Bend low here an' foller my steps close—on th' jump, *now*!"

Reaching the end of the wide valley they came to a great widening of the lower levels, where the canyon emerged from between the Buttes and became lost in the great sink which surrounded the Twins. Quigley knew the sink from former explorations, and he chose ridges and draws without hesitation and kept well hidden at all times from anyone up on the butte. In order to continue in this security it was necessary to go almost to the eastern wall of the sink in a wide detour, and the chief unhesitatingly chose that route.

Because of an instinct born from years of woodcraft, Quigley's eyes missed nothing. Had he been riding down Hastings' single street he unconsciously would have observed every tin can, every old boot, and his memory, automatically photographing them with remarkable fidelity, would have filed the pictures away for future reference. Crossing a sage hen's track he unconsciously observed it minutely, and he could have told quite an interesting and intimate tale of what the bird had been doing.

Plunging into a deep gully, he swung up the opposite slope on a diagonal, and stopped suddenly, his busy mind instantly sidetracking its cogitations to take care of a matter immediately under his eyes. Three small stones lay, dark and damp, against the sun-dried, whitish rock stratum which formed the surface of the ridge. Above the level of his shoulders several green twigs were well chewed, two of them bitten clean off, and a dried lather still clung to them. Shoving his elbows out from his sides to check his companion, he looked closely at both signs, and then, bending over, hurried along the slope searching the ground and swiftly disappeared around a bowlder. Purdy followed and bent over beside him. In a small patch of sand and clay which filled a hollow in the rock floor was the print of a hoof, and extending in front of it lay the imprint of the forward half of a moccasin.

Quigley glanced up quickly at his companion. "Fresh made!" he grunted. "Leads away from th' butte. Might be two men, one of 'em ridin'. Wait here, an' lay low!"

Going on a few steps he shook his head slowly and disappeared around a thicket. Ahead of him was a wide streak of sand and gravel and he hurried to it.

"*Two* men on foot, leadin' a hoss!" he growled. "Wish I had time to foller these tracks; but there's no tellin' how far they go." He paused a moment in indecision, tempted to go on, but shaking his head he wheeled and ran back to Purdy, cursing the increased throbbing of his arm.

"Purdy!" he whispered incisively; "somethin's rotten! One cayuse; two men. Wait a minute!" and he sent his thoughts racing over every possibility. "They can be strangers that blundered through here; or friends of Nelson's. If they was strangers, an' passed th' Buttes, as that back trail indicates, they wouldn't try to keep hidden, an' either Art or Frank would 'a' seen them, an' follered them. If they was friends of his—damn it! Wish I had taken th' trouble to hunt up th' tracks of that black cayuse some place where they showed up plain an' deep!"

Purdy thoughtfully rubbed his head. "Mebby that cayuse wandered down, an' th' boys led it off to hide it."

"*Both* of 'em?" snapped Quigley. "One had to stay on guard. An' they can't turn boots into moccasins. Cuss it! Why would innercent strangers wear moccasins in this kind of country? They wouldn't, unless they was up to some deviltry. Purdy, we got a job on our hands. First, we'll see Art an' Frank—no *we* won't: *I* will. You foller these tracks an' find out what you can. Don't foller 'em longer than an hour. We'll meet right here. If you hear three shots so close together that they sound like a ripple, you cut hell-bent for th' ranch, by a roundabout way," and he was gone before Purdy could answer him.

Purdy ran forward, his gaze on the ground, and every time the trail became lost on clean, hard rock, he swore impatiently and ran in ever-widening circles until he found it again. Suddenly he crouched low and froze in his tracks.

In an opening at the bottom of a deep, heavily wooded draw lying just ahead of him he caught sight of a black horse, saddled, cropping grass. The animal threw up its head, looked at him, flattened its ears and backed away, ready to bolt. And under his eyes lay four pairs of moccasin prints, two of them pointing back toward the Buttes.

"It's *his* bronc!" growled Purdy under his breath. "How th' devil—!" Wild conjectures filed into his mind in swift confusion, and, wrestling with them, he wheeled sharply and dashed back the way he had come, his Colt ready for action.

Quigley, calling into play every trick of woodcraft that he knew, kept on toward the Twin Buttes canyon, silent, alert, never once leaving cover. The smoke of the fire up on the butte was barely discernible now and the smoke from the rustlers' fire at the foot of the trail could not be seen at all. Eagerly he scrutinized the tops of the two buttes, but in vain.

Working steadily forward with the caution of an Indian, he followed and kept close to the eastern wall of the sink until directly back of the place where the trail guard should be, and in line with that and the lower end of the trail. His progress now became slow, and he exercised an infinite caution and patience. Cover followed cover, and every few yards he stopped and waited, his senses at the top pitch of their efficiency. Drawing near the position used by him and his men in guarding the mesa trail he passed within fifty feet of Luke Tedrue, and neither knew of it. Had he gone ten feet farther forward he would have died in his tracks.

He stopped. It was now Art's or Frank's turn to show some sign of life. Neither of them had any need to remain quiet, and he knew that under such circumstances a man is almost certain to make some kind of a noise within a reasonable length of time.

The minutes passed in absolute silence, and finally he could wait no longer, for each passing minute was precious to him, and he silently backed away, to approach from another direction. As he crept past a bowlder, avoiding every growing thing and every twig or loose pebble, he glanced along a narrow opening between some rocks and a thinning of the brush, and saw two sock-covered feet, toes up. It took him a long time to maneuver so that he could see enough of the body to be sure of its identity, and when he was sure he choked back a curse.

"Fleming!" he breathed. "Knifed through th' throat! An' they took his pants an' left a pair of blue ones. Nelson wore black! An' Frank, up there on th' other butte—I can't get up *there* without bein' seen. Frank, my boy; if yo're alive, you'll have to look out for yoreself!"

As he crawled and wriggled and dashed back over his trail his racing thoughts threw picture after picture on his mental screen, until every possible solution was eliminated and only the probable ones remained; and from these two there loomed up one which almost bore the stamp of certainty. The CL outfit, either wholly or in part, had arrived on the scene, and even now might be attacking the ranch-houses. Dashing around a pinnacle of granite, he sped down the slope of the draw where Purdy, behind a thicket, awaited him.

"Here, Tom!" softly called the waiting man, arising.

"Quick!" panted Quigley. "Hell's broke loose with all th' gates open! What you find?"

"Nelson's bronc. Th' two men that led it cached it in a draw an' went back again towards th' Buttes. What's up?"

"Everything, I reckon. Fleming's dead—knifed," panted Quigley, leading the way westward. "Frank—I don't know—about him. Never—had a chance—Art didn't. Good thing—I reckon we come—th' way we did.

There—ain't no tellin'—what we might a' run—up ag'in. Damn 'em! I'll never leave—th' hills! Dead or—alive, I stays!"

"I've located here—permanent myself," growled Purdy. "Fleming knifed, huh? Mebby—mebby they're Injuns! Knife-play an' moccasins! I—betcha!"

"Damn fool!" gritted Quigley savagely; and then, remembering his companion's declaration of permanent location, he relented. "He wasn't—scalped!"

"Apaches—don't scalp!" grunted Purdy doggedly.

"But they make—tracks, don't they?" blazed Quigley. "I tell you—I know Injun tracks—like I know my name. They're—white men!"

XXII

◆

"Two Ijuts"

Luke Tedrue brushed flies. Since a little after dawn he had brushed them continually, insistently, doggedly, with an enforced calmness and apathy which only an iron, stubborn will made possible; and had they suddenly desisted in their eager explorations he would have kept on brushing from sheer force of habit. But while his hands and arms were moving mechanically, his mind was having an argument with itself concerning his ears, and a vague uneasiness made him restless.

He suspected that he had heard a sound, one which only a moving body would have made; but it had been so slight that he had not recognized it at the time, and it was only through the persistent, indefatigable urging of some subconscious sense that he was now trying to force his memory to repeat it for him, to give him a hold upon it that he might describe and classify it. Exasperated, fretful, uneasy, he called himself a fool with too zealous an imagination; but he kept straining at his reluctant memory, trying to force it to leap back and grasp the elusive impression. Vexed and anxious, he at last wriggled back among the bowlders which sheltered him, determined to prove or disprove the haunting subconscious sense. It had become maddening, a ghost he simply had to lay.

Realizing that the moving object is the more readily seen, Luke moved slowly and with no regard for dignity; and he proceeded, an inch at a time, upon his lean, old stomach. Nothing was too small or insignificant to escape his notice, for his eyes, close to the ground, first took in the entire field of vision with one quick, sweeping glance, and then, beginning with the more distant objects, examined everything in sight as though he had lost something of great value and of size infinitesimal. Another few inches of slow, laborious progress, and another searching scrutiny, his ears as busy as his eyes. In half an hour he had covered ten feet, and at the end of an hour he had made it to twenty. And then, as he glanced around to obtain a general and preliminary view of a new vista, his eyes passed over a little patch of sand, and instantly flashed back to it, regarding it with an unwinking intentness.

He hitched forward again, more rapidly, and gained three feet before he stopped to peer about him. At last he came to the sand patch, which lay between a bowlder and a clump of dry, dead, and rustly brush, which accounted for its having a story to tell. It was the only way a cautious man could have proceeded, and the print of the heel of a hand and the five little dots where the tips of thumb and fingers had rested was well to one side of it. Furthermore, there was a smooth streak across it which contained two other streaks along the outer edges of the first one. The story was plain: a stomach, followed by two legs, had been dragged across the little patch of sand.

Luke raised his educated eyes and looked around him, but now his field of vision was considerably constricted, for he paid attention only to those few spaces in the brush and among the rocks which a clever man would be likely to use; and being a clever man himself, he unerringly picked certain openings and almost instantly riveted his gaze on a sign: a toe print at his left. Close to it was another, and the way in which the sand had been pushed up told him that the first had been made by a man crawling west; and the other announced to him that it had been made by a man moving east. Luke deduced that the same man, returning over his own trail, had made the second as well as the first.

Luke was relieved, and, having a safe trail to follow, he pushed on rapidly but silently, soon reaching the place where it ended; and in plain sight of him, through the thin growth of brush, was Fleming's body. One glance at it and Luke turned, following the trail back as he had come; and an hour later, having learned a great deal, he ran and crept, leaped and wriggled up to the place where his friend lay and petulantly cursed the flies.

"Ijut Number Two," said Luke pleasantly, "where are you?"

"Talkin' to hisself again," grumbled a low voice from the mysterious passages under a great, tumbled mass of bowlders. "If a body meet a body, reachin' for th' rye," continued the vexed voice, "whose treat is it?"

"Depends on who can't keep still," answered Luke brightly. "We are two ijuts," he said positively and flatly.

"Well, I allus like a man that speaks his mind, even if

he *is* a liar," commented the mysterious voice. "Damn these flies! I crawled in here to get rid of 'em; but they come right along. An' a little while back I smelled a striped kitty-cat. I knowed what it was because th' wind wasn't blowin' from yore direction."

"Cuss his impudence!" said Luke. "He takes me for a wild flower! A rose, mebby. An' me comin' out here to save his worthless life!"

"You didn't do nothin' of th' kind," contradicted the sepulchral voice. "You come out here to practice with Colonel Bowie! I can prove it before any fool jury. Damn th' flies!"

"What flies?" innocently demanded Luke, his voice suggesting a hot curiosity and a thirsty yearning for knowledge.

"Time," said the other. "Time flies; an' I've had these flies all th' time. It's time they flies away, to fly back another day. You leave yours behind you, Cow Face, if you visit me."

"Ain't got none; an' ain't seen none," replied Luke cheerfully.

"Twice a liar," observed Johnny pleasantly. "Why don't you learn to speak th' truth sometimes? I'm worried about yore soul."

"I'm worried about my belly an' my knees. They're scraped clean, wrigglin' over rock."

"'Tain't possible; not at yore age," commented Johnny. "Th' accumulations of years can't be got rid of so easy, Old Timer."

"No wonder they chased him off th' Tin Cup," grinned Luke. "We are two ijuts."

"Listen to th' jackass," said Johnny. "Th' flies that flew an' flied; th' flies that crawled an' died; th' flies that buzzed an'—an'—holy hell! Did you *ever* see so many of 'em?"

"I done listened to th' jackass," grunted Luke. "An' now I observes, gentle but firm: We are two ijuts."

"We are *one* ijut," corrected Johnny. "You are th' one. A soft answer turneth away wrath."

"I am an injut; an' you are an injut," replied Luke with exaggerated patience. "That makes two; an' so we are *two* ijuts."

"Can't you say nothin' else, One Ijut?" demanded Johnny peevishly. "Yo're tiresome; yo're a repeater, rim fire, Chestnut, model of 1873. I'm lazy by nature; but doin' nothin' *all* th' time is hard work. It don't set right. They have taken her to Georgia, there to wear her life away. An' my neck aches from lookin' up, an' holdin' my head out on th' end of it. My stummick an' my elbows, my knees an' my toes all, all ache. They are rock-galled. As she toils 'mid th' cotton an' th' corn."

"Cane," corrected Luke. "Yore appalin' ignerence is discouragin'. We are two ijuts."

"All right; I quit," said Johnny wearily. "Have it yore own way; mebby we are. But it could 'a' been corn just as well as cane, anyhow. Why are we two ijuts?"

"Because we are holdin' th' bag," said Luke sadly.

Johnny turned around and stuck his head out. "Yes?" he inquired, with a rising inflection. "I'm plumb insulted. I ain't never held no bag; not never!"

"'Tain't never too late to learn," said Luke sorrowfully. "Th' snipe has come, an' went; an' we're *still* holdin' th' bag."

"Let's fill it full of flies," suggested Johnny. "Say! If you ain't seen no flies, how did all of them get squashed on yore face?"

"Come flyin' out of yore cave just now an' bumped into me full speed," replied Luke, grinning. "We have been out-guessed, we have. They smelled us out. We're two tenderfeet in a wild, bad camp. Somebody's likely to hurt us, first thing you know. What did you see when you wasn't killin' flies?"

"Th' sky, th' canyon, an' th' butte."

"Uh-huh; so did I. I saw th' butte, th' canyon, an' th' sky. Then I moved an' saw hand prints, belly prints, toe prints, knee prints, an' other kinds of prints. Yore friends stacked th' deck on us an' dealt 'em from th' middle. Now what?"

"First, we eat," said Johnny, arising with alacrity. "Then, mebby, we eat again. We drink an' we wash. I'm near half as dirty as you. What have you found out?"

"Did you ever see two calves, wobble-kneed, friskin' around lookin' saucy an' full of hell an' wisdom; but actin' plumb foolish?"

"I shore did. I never saw no other kind, unless it was sick. Stiff back, humped in defiance; tail tryin' to stand up; stiff-laigged, when they didn't buckle unexpected; jumpin' sideways, tryin' to butt, an' allus hungry. I did, Old Timer; lots an' lots of times."

"Well, them's us," sighed Luke. "You hold yore trap an' listen while I speaks my piece. I saw them signs, like I said. Th' cuss that made 'em sneaked right up to my back door, went around th' side of my house, stopped just in time for his health, backed off, saw his friend's body, an' my pants, an' backed off some more. Then he climbed up on two good feet an' made toe prints plumb deep. He didn't run; no, ma'am; he just telegraphed hisself; never stopped for nothin'. He sped, he shot, he *moved*!"

"An' us two ijuts layin' out here in th' sun till we was cussed near jerked meat!" growled Johnny. "I call that blamed unpolite."

"Didn't I tell you we was two ijuts? When an older man speaks you want to keep yore mouth shut an' yore ear tabs open. Th' young bucks go out an' steal th' horses an' lift th' scalps; but th' old fellers make good talk around th' council fires. Stick *that* in yore peace pipe an' smoke it. Might be good for your health some-time."

"Yo're a purty spry scalper yoreself," admitted Johnny. "Regular old he-whizzer; but you got no morals, an' a very bad, disgustin' habit. I'm surprised you didn't take scalps, too!"

"You let the Colonel alone," warned Luke. "Now, that rustler is some he-whizzer hisself, an' he won't need no-body to tell him what he saw. He's done told his tribe about that; an' bein' a stranger here I'm only guessin'. Say what's on yore mind."

"Th' young buck will now talk at th' council fire," grinned Johnny. "Yo're right, for once. It wasn't th' cook. I never saw a cook yet that could move around so nobody could hear him. It wasn't Gates, because he's wounded sev-eral; an' I don't think it was that other feller, because some-how I ain't feverishly admirin' his brains. That leaves Quigley; an' he ain't no fool *all* th' time. I can see him beatin' hell an' high-water to his three stone shacks, where his friends are, an' where his guns, grub, clothes, an' other things are. I can see four men lookin' out of four loop-holes. They are if they ain't jumped th' country; an' if they has, we'll let 'em go.

"Takin' a new, fresh holt, I'd say that they don't know that we'd let 'em go; an' they don't know how many we are, or where all of us are located. They don't aim to lead us a chase; that is, mebby they don't. Them shacks are shore strong; an' they don't know how far they might get if they run for it. 'Tain't like open country—they got just four places to ride out of that sink an' they all can be easy guarded."

"They won't come out th' way they went in," said Luke.

"That would be risky an' foolish; so they's only three places left."

"A wise man never does what he ought to do," said Johnny. "Now, I'll bet they are either in them stone houses, or some place else," he grinned. "Th' only way, after all, to see a good man's hand, is to call it. Me an' you, bein' amazin' curious, will do just that. If they're in them houses they'll be expectin' us; they'll turn th' 'Welcome' sign to th' wall an' smoke up them loopholes. Don't interrupt me yet! I'm long-winded an' hard to stop. Th' question is: Are you primed to wrastle this thing out, just me an' you, or shall I watch 'em while you go back to th' CL for help? That—"

"I *will* interrupt!" snorted Luke heatedly. "If it wasn't that yo're only a fool infant, damned if I wouldn't fan yore saddle end! I ain't never yelled for help when it wasn't needed; an' lots of times when it was needed I forgot to yell. Too busy, mebby. You've been running things with a high hand out here, an' yore head reminds me of th' head of a cow bit by a snake. It's swelled scandalous. I'm goin' to show you how to get four men out of them loopholes. Bein' young an' green, you'd likely want to crawl in an' pull 'em out. But me, bein' wise, will use brains, an' more brains. I can make a cat skin itself."

"You want to be plumb shore that it ain't one of them striped kitties—they look a lot alike in a poor light; an' that entrance canyon is shore poor light. I reckon we won't eat, yet. We better rustle for their ranch."

"But Logan wants to know them facts that he sent us after," growled Luke regretfully.

"We ain't got 'em; an' we can't get 'em. Them fellers won't do no rustlin' now, so how can we trail 'em? They're too cussed busy lookin' out for their skins about now. An' only two of 'em ain't wounded; Purdy an' th' cook."

"How many cows they got?"

"Near two hundred."

"Holy Jumpin' Jerusalem!" snorted Luke. "We're lucky that we still got th' ranch-house an' th' river!"

"We're wastin' time," growled Johnny, impatiently. "There's no telling what they're doin'. Come on. Bein' desperate, mebby they're round-in' up to make a drive. Come on!"

It was past mid-afternoon when the two punchers looked down into the QE valley and found relief at the sight of the cows lazily feeding. They were scattered all over the range and both men knew that no attempt had been made to round them up.

Going down the blind-canyon trail, they crossed the range, climbed the opposite cliff and finally stopped in front of the stone houses. A gun barrel projected from a loophole in the south wall of the house nearest the canyon, and four saddled horses were in the smaller corral.

"There they are," said Johnny. A bullet stirred his hair and he drew back from the rim. "We got to get 'em. Start skinnin' that cat, Old Timer."

"It'll shore take a lot of skinnin'," growled Luke.

"Not if we uses 'brains an' more brains,'" jeered Johnny. "Th' young buck will now be heard shootin' off his mouth at th' council fire; an' you listen close, One Ijut!"

"Have yore say," said Luke, covering a loophole which showed signs of activity.

"We've got to move fast, before they learn that there's only two of us," said Johnny. "When them houses was built they was laid out with th' idea of men bein' in *all* of 'em; an' they'd be cussed hard to lick, then. But I reckon they're all in that one house. There ain't men enough to hold 'em all; an' so they favored th' one near th' canyon. We got to keep that door shut so they can't get out an' away. I'll do that after dark; an' I'll stampede them cayuses. That leaves 'em no chance to make a dash an' ride for it. Now you see that little trickle of water flowin' under th' houses? That's their water supply; I know something about that crick; but that's another job for th' dark. Take a look over there, where it turns. See that dirt bank, on th' bend? That's where they turned it out of its course an' sent it flowin' in th' ditch leadin' to th' houses. Do you reckon you could cut that bank with Colonel Bowie an' throw a little dam across th' ditch? 'Tain't wide; only a couple of feet. I—"

Luke fired, and grunted regretfully. "Missed him, damn it!" he swore, reloading. "Gettin' so you can find work for my knife, huh?" he chuckled. "Not bein' blind, I see th' bank an' th' bend. An' if I can't turn that water back th' way it used to go, I'll fold up an' die. This is like old times. You must 'a' had a real elegant, bang-up time out here, crawlin' around an' raisin' hell with 'em. What a grand place for th' Colonel! I shore missed a lot; but I'm here now, an' with both feet! Sing yore song; I'm listenin'."

"It's sung," grinned Johnny; "an' now we got to dance."

"I ain't as spry as I used to be," grunted Luke; "so I'll have to make them fellers do th' dancin'."

XXIII

◆

"All but th' Cows"

Gates, the wounded, tossed restlessly in his bunk, and finally rolled over and faced the dark room.

"Never was so wide awake in my life," he grumbled. "Been settin' around too much lately. If I wanted to stay awake I'd be as sleepy as th' devil."

"Better try it again," counseled Quigley, shifting from his loophole. "You don't want to be sleepy tomorrow when yo're on guard."

"Tom," said Gates, ignoring the advice. "I've been doin' some thinkin'. A feller does a lot of thinkin' when he can't sleep. We made a couple of mistakes, holin' up like this. In th' first place, if we had to hole up, we should 'a' occupied *both* end houses, 'stead of only one. This way, they can walk right up to within twenty feet of us, use th' cook shack, th' grub in th' store-house, an' them store-house loopholes, which is worse. If we had both end houses, two men in each, they couldn't get anywhere close to us except along th' crick an' up on th' cliff."

"Yes; I reckon so," said Quigley. "'Tain't too late yet, mebby. I didn't like th' idea of splittin' up our forces. As far as grub is concerned, we're near as well off that way as we are in our water supply. We got grub in here for two months, an' plenty of cartridges if we don't get reckless with 'em. Of course, I wish that other case was in here, too; it'd give us another thousand rounds for th' rifles; but I ain't worryin' none about that. An' I'm purty near shore, now, that there's only two of 'em fightin' us: Nelson an' that Tedrue, judgin' from th' knife-work."

"That's th' way I figger it," agreed Gates. "An' that's why we shouldn't 'a' holed up like this. Me an' th' cook could 'a' held this house, while you an' Purdy was on th' outside stalkin' 'em. Any man that can stalk like you can is plumb wastin' his time cooped up in here; an' you could 'a' made things sizzlin' hot for them two fellers, good as they are. This way, they've got us located, an' they only have to look for trouble in front of 'em. They know where to expect it all th' time. It was a big mistake."

"Mebby," grunted Quigley. "We'll try it in here tonight an' tomorrow, an' then if we don't have no luck, I'll fade away tomorrow night an' give 'em a taste of Injun fightin'.

There ain't no moon this week, so we can pick our time to suit ourselves."

Purdy leaned his rifle against the wall and groped for the water bucket. "I'll make a try for that extra case of cartridges right now, if you say th' word," he offered. "Huh! We shore drink a lot of water," he grunted. "I filled this pail before sundown, an' it's near empty now. Too much bacon, I reckon."

Quigley laughed softly. "Water is one thing we don't have to worry about at all. That ditch was a great idea."

Could he have followed the ditch in the dark he would have been surprised to have seen the dam across it, and the cut through the artificial bank, where Luke Tedrue and a commandeered shovel had released the little stream and let it flow to Rustler Creek along its old, original bed down a shallow gully. That was Johnny's idea; but after the old scout had carried it out, he had an idea of his own which pleased him greatly, and he acted upon it without loss of time.

The cook stirred and sat up, feeling for his pipe, which was always his first act upon awakening. He grunted sleepily and sat on the edge of his bunk. "This is a whole lot like bein' in jail," he yawned. "An' what do you think? I dreamed that somebody had just tapped a keg of beer, an' when I sidled over to see that none of it was wasted, why I woke up! That's allus my luck. How soon'll it be daylight? That dream made me thirsty. Where's that cussed water bucket?"

"Right where it was th' last time you found it," grinned Purdy. "It ain't moved none at all."

"Yo're right, it ain't," grumbled the cook, scraping a tin cup across the bottom of the pail. "It never does unless *I* do it. I'll bet four bits that I've filled it every time it got empty; an' I'll bet four bits more that I ain't goin' to fill it *this* time," he chuckled. "There's just enough here for me. Th' next gent that wants a drink will be observed bendin' over th' trapdoor an' fillin' it for hisself. Here's how! An' damn th' beer what only comes in dreams."

Gates crawled out of his bunk and limped to the bucket. "Get out of my way," he growled. "Speakin' of beer started my throat to raspin'. No you don't; not a-tall," he grumbled, pushing the cook aside. "I'll wait on myself, slugs or *no* slugs. I ain't no teethin' infant, even if I *am* full of holes." He crossed to the trapdoor and fumbled around in the dark. "Huh! I knowed it couldn't get far away. I've been kneelin' on it all th' time!"

"Better lemme do that," offered the cook, advancing.

"Better yore grandmother," said Gates. "No, ma'am; you put on too many airs, you do." He raised the door. "You might strain yore delicate back, Cookie, old hoss. An' anyhow, I'm aimin' to spite you for that unnecessary remark about openin' a keg of beer. This ain't no time to talk about things like that." He leaned down and swung the bucket, but there was no splash, only a rattling, tinny thump. "Why," said his muffled voice, "there ain't no water here! Mebby I missed it. Why, damn it, there ain't no water here a-tall! What th'—" His voice ceased abruptly and a solid, muffled thump came up through the opening.

The cook, leaning forward in the position he had frozen in when he had grasped the significance of the sound of the striking bucket, moved toward the trap, feeling before him. He touched the edge of the opening and swiftly felt around it. Gates was not there.

"Damn it, he's fell in!" he muttered. "It wasn't no job for a wounded man like him, bendin' over that way. Here, Purdy!" he called. "Gimme a hand with Ben. He plumb keeled over an' fell in." He reached down impatiently and felt around. "Hell!" he yelled as an up-thrust hand gripped him, jerked him off his balance and pulled him down through the opening. "Look out, fellers!" he shouted.

A second thump, softer than the first, ended the cry and Purdy, leaping forward, slammed shut the trap and bolted it. "More knife-work!" he gritted, pale with rage. Arising, he leaped toward the cabin door, yanked it open and dashed along the house, staggering as a finger of flame spurted from a loophole in the wall of the store-house, but recovered his balance and turned the corner. As he did so he caught sight of a thickening in the darkness, which moved swiftly and silently along the ditch, and he fired at it. Something whizzed past his neck and rang out, sharp and clear as a bell, on the end wall of the house. He answered it with another shot and saw the blot stagger and fall.

From the ditch came a spurt of fire and Purdy plunged forward, firing as he fell. Another shot answered him and again he fired, but with a weak and shaking hand. Then from a loophole behind him Quigley's rifle poked out and sent shot after shot along the ditch, firing on a gamble.

As the rifle spoke, a shadow flitted past the corner of the store-house, passed swiftly and silently across the space between the two houses and plunged through the open door of the rustlers' stronghold. It tripped over a box and sprawled headlong just as Quigley wheeled and sent a bullet through the space Johnny had occupied an instant before.

Leaping to his feet, Johnny hurled himself upon the rustler, wrenched the rifle loose and gripped the owner's throat. Plunging, heaving, straining, they thrashed around the room, smashing into bunks, breaking dishes; hammering, gouging, biting, choking, they bumped into the door, plunged through the opening and carried the struggle out under the sky.

Quigley, his face purple and his eyes popping out, almost senseless on his feet, and fighting from instinct, managed to break the grip on his throat and showered blows on his enemy's face. Sinking his teeth in Johnny's upper arm, he got both of his hands around Johnny's throat and closed his grip with all his weakened strength.

Across the yard they reeled, bumped into the corral and along it, following the slope of the ground without thought. Johnny, suffocating, thrust the heel of his right hand against his enemy's nose and pushed upward and back, while his left hand, leaving the gripping fingers around his throat, smashed heavily into Quigley's stomach. The hands relaxed, loosened their grip and fell away, and before they could regain their hold, Johnny's chin settled firmly against his chest and protected his windpipe. Just in time he caught Quigley's gun hand and tore the Colt out of it, whereupon Quigley hammered his face with both hands. Shoving, wrestling, reeling, they came to the edge of the ravine through which flowed Rustler Creek, and, plunging over the steep bank, rolled to the bottom and stopped in the mud and water of the creek itself, where they fought lying down, each trying desperately to remain on top.

Quigley's hand brushed one of Johnny's guns, gripped it, drew it out and shoved the muzzle against his enemy's side. As he pulled the trigger Johnny writhed swiftly and turned the muzzle away. Squirming on top, he again turned the muzzle away as Quigley fired the second time. At the roar of the shot the rustler grunted and grew suddenly limp.

Logan pushed back from the dinner table and glanced out of the window. Shouting an exclamation he leaped for the door, the rest of the outfit piling pell-mell at his heels.

A black horse, carrying double, stopped near the door and eager hands caught Luke Tedrue as he fell from Pepper's back. Johnny, covered with mud, dust, blood, and powder grime, his clothes torn into shreds and his face a battered mass of red and black and blue flesh, swayed slightly, grasped the saddle horn with both hands and sat stiffly erect again.

"Good Lord!" shouted Logan, jumping to him. "What th' hell's up?"

"Rustlin'," muttered Johnny. "Luke's brains got foundered in th' head an' he pulled three of 'em out of a hole; but I made Quigley skin th' cat."

"Are they *all* gone under?" yelled Logan incredulously.

"All but th' cows," sighed Johnny, and strong arms caught him as he fell.

Johnny
Nelson

◆

I

◆

A Rolling Stone

The horse stopped suddenly and her rider came to his senses with a jerk, his hand streaking to a six-gun, while he muttered a profane inquiry as he swiftly scrutinized his surroundings. Had it been any horse but Pepper he would have directed his suspicions at it, but he knew the animal too well to do it that injustice. The valley before and below him was heavily grassed, and throughout its entire length wandered a small stream. Grazing cattle were scattered along it, and riding up the farther slope were three men, who appeared to be peaceful and innocent of wrong intent. These his eyes swept past, and they passed a small cluster of bowlders down on the slope below him, but instantly returned to them, a puzzled look appearing upon his face. In that nest of rocks a woman lay prone, peering at the distant horsemen, and she slowly brought a rifle to her shoulder, cuddling its stock against her cheek. What he did not see, and could not, at that angle, was the menacing head of a rattlesnake not twenty feet from her, the instinctive fear of which put a chill in her heart and urged her to shoot it, even at the risk of being heard by the men she was watching. Johnny Nelson unconsciously estimated the range and shook his head.

He could do it with his Sharp's single-shot, a rifle of great power; but he had yet to see any repeater that could. Knowing the futility of a shot, he coughed loudly, and had the satisfaction of seeing a flurry below him, and a rifle muzzle at the same instant. Slowly he raised his hands level with his shoulders, spoke to the horse and, mustering all the dignity possible under the circumstances, rode slowly down the slope.

"That's far enough," said a crisp voice, pleasant in timbre even though business-like and angry. "Haven't I told you punchers to keep off this ranch?"

"Never to my knowledge, Ma'am," he answered.

"Have you the brazen effrontery to sit there and calmly tell me that?"

"I don't know, Ma'am; but I never heard about no such orders."

"Who are you? Where do you come from? What are you doing here?"

Johnny smiled apologetically. "Fifteen hundred shore would strain that gun, Ma'am. An' mostly a shot wasted is worse than none at all. I'm here to offer you one that bites hard at that distance, 'though I can't say I generally recommend it for ladies—it kicks powerful hard, heavy as it is."

"Answer my questions. Who are you?"

"A stranger, Ma'am; a pilgrim, seekin' what I can devour. But now it's nearer sixteen hundred," he suggested, lowering a hand to get the Sharp's from its sheath under his leg.

"That will do!" she warned. "The range which interests me is ten yards. You may rest them on your hat," she conceded.

He locked his fingers over his head and grinned. "Why, I'm a rollin' stone from Montanny, Ma'am. So far I've rolled into trouble all th' way, an' it looks like I'm still a-rollin'. I want to apologize for bustin' up your party—they've done faded."

"'Done faded' never was born in Montana," she retorted, suspicion glinting in her eyes. She lowered the gun until it rested on her knees, but its muzzle still covered Johnny.

"Neither was I, Ma'am," he replied, smiling. "I was born in Texas, an' grew up there. My greatest mistake was goin' north—but now I'm tryin' to wipe that out. It's a long trail, Ma'am; an' I've wasted a powerful lot of time."

"You shall waste some more; after that the speed of your departure will doubtless largely compensate you. How do I know you are telling the truth?"

"As to that, not meanin' no offense, I ain't none interested. An', Ma'am, neither are you. I might say, as a general proposition, that no stranger has any business askin' me personal questions; an', also, that in such cases I reserve th' right to lie as much as I please, 'though I ain't admittin' that I'm doin' it here. Pepper warned me that somethin' was wrong, which it was by several hundred yards—an', Ma'am, shootin' across a valley is shore deceivin'. Also I saw that one young lady was goin' to mix up serious with three growed-up men—pretty craggy individuals, from what I know of punchers. That was not th' right thing for a lady to do—but I'm allus with th' under dog, I'm sorry to say, so I horned in an' offered you a gun that would fill them fellers with righteous indignation, homicidal yearnin's, an' a belief in miracles. I knowed they wouldn't get hurt at that distance—you see, there's little things like windage, trigger pull, an' others. But, Ma'am, th' sound of that lead an' th' noise of that gun shore would pester 'em. They'd get most amazin' curious, for men, an' look into it. An' when they found me with a gun

on 'em they'd get more indignant than ever. Now, Ma'am,
I've busted up yore party, which I had no right to do. If
you wants them fellers right up close so you can look 'em
over good an' ask 'em questions, say so, an' I'll go get' for
you. I owe you that much. But I don't aim to be no party to
a murder," he finished, smiling, and slowly and deliberately lowered his hands and rested them on his belt.

She was staring at him with blazing eyes, a look on her
white face such as he never had seen on a woman before;
and he realized that never before had he seen an angry
woman. His smile changed subtly. It softened, the cyni-
cism faded from it and kindly lines crept in; and there
was something in his eyes that never had been there before. He looked out across the valley, at the few cows,
where there should have been so many in a valley like
that. Then he gazed steadily at the point where the three
horsemen had become lost to sight—and the smile gave
way to a look hard and cold. Pepper moved, and Johnny
drew a deep breath, squaring his shoulders in sudden reso-
lution. Swinging from the saddle he walked slowly forward toward the threatening rifle muzzle, took the weapon
from its owner's knees, lowered the hammer, and placed
the gun against the rock at her side. Straightening up, he
whistled softly. Pepper, advancing with mincing steps,
shoved her velvety muzzle against his cheek and stopped.
He swung into the saddle, wheeled the horse and rode
around a nearby thicket, soon returning with a saddled
SV pony, which he led to its owner. Mounting again, he
backed Pepper away and, removing his sombrero, wheeled
and sent the horse up the slope without a backward glance,
sitting erect in the saddle as a figure of bronze until hidden
by the crest and well down on the other side. Then he
pulled suddenly at the reins with unthinking roughness
and dashed at top speed to the left until the crest was

again close at hand. With his head barely on a level with the top of the hill, he sat staring across the little valley at the point where the horsemen had disappeared; and there was a look on his face which, had they seen it, would have turned their conversation to subjects less trivial.

II

◆

Bit by Bit

The sun was near the meridian when Johnny rode into Gunsight, a town which he took as a matter of course. They were all alike, he reflected. If it were not for the names they scarcely could be told apart—and it would have been just as well to have numbered them. A collection of shacks, with the overplayed brave names. The shack he was riding for was the "Palace," which only rubbed it in. Out of a hundred towns, seventy-five would have their Palace saloon and fifty would have a Delmonico hotel. Dismounting before the door, he went in and saw the proprietor slowly arising from a chair, and he was the fattest man Johnny ever had seen. The visitor's unintentional stare started the conversation for him.

"Well, don't you like my looks?" bridled the proprietor.

Johnny's expression was one of injured innocence. "Why, I wasn't seein' you," he explained. "I was thinkin'— but now that you mention it, I don't see nothin' th' matter with your looks. Should there be?"

The other grunted something, becoming coherent only when the words concerned business. "What's yourn?"

"A drink with you, an' some information."

"Th' drink goes; but th' information don't."

"I take it all back," soliloquized Johnny. "This town don't need a number; it don't even need a name. It's different. It's th' only one this side of Montanny where the barkeeper was hostile at th' start. I'm peaceful. My han's are up, palm out. If you won't give me information, will you tell me where I can eat an' sleep? Which of th' numerous hotels ain't as bad as th' rest of 'em?"

Davis Lee Beauregard Green slid a bottle across the bar, sent a glass spinning after it, leaned against the back bar and grinned. "Gunsight ain't impressin' you a hull lot?" he suggested.

"Why not? It's got all a man needs, which is why towns are made, ain't it?" Johnny tasted the liquor and downed it. "I allus size up a town by th' liquor it sells. I say Gunsight is a d—d sight better than I thought from a superficial examination."

Dave Green, wise in the psychology of the drinking type, decided that the stranger was not and never had been what he regarded as a drinking man; and even went so far in a quick, spontaneous flash of thought, as to tell himself that the stranger never had been drunk. Now, in his opinion, a hard-drinking, two-gun man was "bad;" but a coldly sober, real two-gun man was worse, although possibly less quarrelsome. He was certain that they lived longer. Dave was a good man with a short gun, despite his handicap; but a stirring warning instinct had told him that this stranger was the best who ever had entered his place. This impression came, was recognized, tabbed, and shoved back in his memory, all in a mechanical way. It was too plain to be overlooked by a man who, perhaps without realizing it, studied humanity, although he could not lay a finger on a single thing and call it by name.

Dave put the bottle back and washed the glass. "Well," he remarked, "every man sizes things up accordin' to his own way of thinkin', which is why there are so many different opinions about th' same thing." Letting this ponderous nugget sink in, he continued: "I reckon th' bottom of it all is a man's wants. You want good liquor, so a town's good, or bad. Which is as good a way as any other, for it suits you. But, speakin' about eatin'-houses, there's a hotel just around th' corner. It's th' only one in town. It butts up agin' th' corner of my rear wall. Further than sayin' I've et there, I got no remarks to make. I cook my own, owin' to th' pressure of business, an' choice."

"It ain't run by no woman, is it?" asked Johnny.

"No; why?"

Johnny grinned. "I'm ridin' clear of wimmin. It was wimmin that sent me roamin' over th' face of th' earth, a wanderer. My friends all got married, an'—oh, well, I drifted. Th' first section I come to where there ain't none, I'll tie fast; an' this country looks like a snubbin' post, to me."

"You lose," chuckled Dave. "There's one down here, an' some folks think she's considerable. What's more, she's lookin' for a good man to run her dad's ranch, an' get an outfit together, as will stay put. But if you don't like 'em, that loses th' job for you. An' I reckon yo're right lucky at that."

"Shore; I know th' kind of a 'good' man they want," said Johnny, reminiscently. " 'Good,' meanin' habits only. A man that don't smoke, chew, drink, cuss, get mad, or keep his hat on in th' house. Losin' th' job ain't bendin' my shoulders. I ain't lookin' for work; I'm dodgin' it. Goin' to loaf till my money peters out, which won't be soon. You'd be surprised if you knowed how many people between here an' Montanny think they can play poker. Just now I'm a eddicator. I'm peddlin' knowledge to th' ignorant, an' I ain't no gambler, at that!"

Dave chuckled. "There's some around here, too. Now,

me; I'm different. I can't play, an' I know it; but, of course, I'll set in, just for th' excitement of it, once in a while, if there ain't nothin' else to do. Come to think of it, I got a deck of cards around here some'rs, right now."

The rear door opened and closed. Johnny looked up and saw the worst-looking tramp of his experience. The newcomer picked up a sand-box cuspidor and started with it for the street.

"Hi, stranger!" called Johnny. "Ain't that dusty work?"

The tramp stiffened. He hardly could believe his ears. The tones which had assailed them were so spontaneously friendly that for a moment he was stunned. It had been a long time since he had been hailed like that—far too long a time. He turned his head slowly and looked and believed, for the grin which met his eyes was as sincere as the voice. It made him honest in his reply.

"No," he said, "this here's sand."

"But ain't yore throat dusty?"

Two-Spot put the box down. "Seems like it allus is. If these boxes *get* dusty, I'll know how it come about, me bendin' over 'em like I do, an' breathin' on 'em."

Johnny laughed. "I take it we're all dusty." He turned to Dave. "Got three left?"

Two-Spot walked up to the bar. Usually he sidled. He picked up his glass and held it up to the light, and drank it in three swallows. Usually it was one gulp. Wiping his lips on a sleeve, he pushed back the glass, dug down into a pocket and brought up a silver dollar, which he tossed onto the bar. "Fill 'em again, Dave," he said, quietly.

At this Dave's slowly accumulating wonder leaped. He looked at the coin and from it to Two-Spot. Sensing the situation, Johnny pushed it farther along toward the proprietor. "Our friend is right, Dave," he said, "two *is* company. Make mine th' same."

Two-Spot put down his empty glass and grinned. "I'll now go on from where I was interrupted, Gents," and, picking up the box, went toward the door. As he was about to pass through he saw Pepper, and he stopped. "Good, Lord!" he muttered. "What a hoss! I've seen passels of hosses, but never one like that. Midnight her name oughter be, or Thunderbolt." He turned. "Stranger, what name do you call that hoss?"

Johnny looked around. "That's Pepper."

Two-Spot grinned. "Did you see that?" he demanded, tilting the box until the sand ran out. "Did you *see* it? She knows her name like a child. Well, it's a good name—a fair name," he hedged. "But, shucks! There ain't *no* name fit for that hoss! How fur has she come today?"

"Near forty miles," answered Johnny.

"I say it ag'in—there ain't *no* name fit for that hoss. She looks like she come five," and he passed out.

"Don't mind him," said Dave. "But where did he git that dollar? Steal it? Find it? Reckon he found it. I near dropped dead. Pore devil—he come here last winter an' walks in, cleans my boxes an' sweeps. Then he goes 'round to th' hotel an' mops an' cleans th' pans better than they ever was before. He was so handy an' useful that we let him stay. An' I've never seen him more than half drunk—it's amazin' th' liquor he can hold."

"Sleep here?"

"No; an' nobody knows where he does sleep. He's cunnin' as a fox, an' fooled 'em every time. But wherever it is, it's dry."

Johnny produced a Sharp's single-shot cartridge. "Where can I get some of these Specials?" he asked.

Dave looked at it. "'.45-120-550'—you won't get none of 'em down in this country."

"Post office in town?"

"Not yet. Th' nearest is Rawlins, thirty mile east, with th' worst trail a man ever rode. Th' next is Highbank, forty mile south. We use that, for th' trail's good. We get mail about twice a month. Th' Bar H an' th' Triangle take turns at it."

"Then I'll write for some of these after I feed. I'll tell 'em to send 'em to you, at Highbank. What name will I give?"

"Dave Green, Highbank-Gunsight mail. But you better write before you eat. This is goin' away day, an' th' Bar H will be in any minute now."

Johnny arose. "Not before I eat. I ain't had nothin' since daybreak, an' it's afternoon now. I hate letter writin'; an' if I don't eat soon I'll get thin."

"Then don't eat—'though I wasn't thinkin' of you when I spoke," growled Dave. "Wish I was in danger of gettin' thin."

"What you care?" demanded Johnny. "Yo're healthy, an' yore job don't call for a man bein' light."

"That's th' way you fellers talk," said Dave. "I'm short-winded, I'm in my own way, an' the joke of th' country. I can't ride a hoss—why, cuss it, I can't even get a gun out quick enough to get a hop-toad before he's moved twenty feet!"

"Pullin' a gun has its advantages, I admits," replied Johnny, who had his own ideas about Dave's ability in that line. Dave, he thought, could get a gun out quick enough for the average need—being a bartender, and still alive, was proof enough of that. He walked toward the door. "If you was to get a big hoss—a single-footer, you could ride, all right."

He went around and entered the hotel, mentally numbering it. Arranging for a week's board and bed for himself and Pepper, he hurried out to the wash bench just outside the dining-room door, where he found two tin basins, a bucket of water, a cake of yellow soap, a towel, and two men using them all. Taking his turn he in turn followed them into the dining-room and chose the fourth and last table, which was next to a window. The meal was better than he had expected but, hungry as he was, he did not eat as hurriedly as was his habit. Fragments of the conversation of the two punchers in the corner reached and interested him. It had to do with the SV ranch, as near as he could judge, and helped him to build the skeleton upon which he hoped to hang a body by dint of investigation and questioning. The episode of that morning had occurred on the SV ranch if the brands on the cattle he had seen meant anything. The woman's name was Arnold, and she had a father and a brother, the latter a boy. There was a fragment about "th' Doc," but just what it was he did not hear, except that it was coupled to the Bar H. Also, something was afoot, but it was so cautiously mentioned that he gained no information about it. Finishing before him, the two men went out, and soon rode past the window, mounted on Triangle horses.

He rattled his cup and ordered it refilled, and when the waiter slouched back with it, Johnny slid a perfectly good cigar across the table and waved his hand. "Sit down, an' smoke. You ought to rest while you got th' chance."

The waiter lost some of his slouch and obeyed, nodding his thanks. "Are you punchin'?" he asked.

"When I'm broke," answered Johnny. "Just now I'm ridin' around lookin' at th' scenery. Never knowed we had any out here till I heard some Easterners goin' mad about it. I've been tryin' to find it ever since. But, anyhow, punchin' is shore monotonous."

"If you can show me anythin' monotoner than *this* job, I'll eat it," growled the waiter. "It's hell on wheels for me."

"Oh, this whole range is monotonous," grunted Johnny. "Reckon nothin' interestin' has happened down here since Moses got lost. But there's one thing I like about it—there ain't no woman in thirty miles."

"You foller Clear River into Green Valley, which is SV, an' you'll change yore mind," chuckled the waiter. "She'll chase you off, too."

"I'll be cussed. An' she's suspicious of strangers?"

"Don't put no limit on it like that; she's suspicious of everythin' that wears pants."

"How's that?"

"Well, her cows has been wanderin' off, lookin' for better grass, I reckon, an' she thinks they're bein' drove."

Johnny pictured the valley, but hid his smile. "Oh, well; you can't blame the cows. They'll find th' best. Any ranches 'round here run by men?"

"Shore; three of 'em. There's th' Bar H, an' th' Triangle, an' over west is th' Double X, but its ranch-house is so fur from here that it's a sort of outsider. It's th' biggest, th' Bar H is next, an' then comes th' Triangle. Th' Triangle don't hardly count, neither, 'though it's close by."

"What about th' SV you mentioned? An' what's yore name?"

"My name's George. Th' SV has gone to th' dogs since it was sold. It ain't a ranch no more. Of course, it's got range, an' water, an' some cows, an' a couple of buildin's— but it ain't got no outfit. Old Arnold, his gal, an' his kid— all tenderfeet—are tryin' to run it."

"But they've got to have punchers," objected Johnny.

"They can't keep 'em, though I ain't sayin' why," replied George mysteriously.

"Does th' Doc own th' Bar H?" asked Johnny.

"Lord, no! It owns him—but, say; you'll have to excuse me. I got work to do. See you at supper. So long."

Johnny left and rode back the way he had come that morning, lost in meditation. Reaching the rim of the valley he looked down over the rolling expanse of vivid green, here and there broken by shallow draws, with their brush and trees. He noticed an irregular circle of posts just south of him and close to the river. Experience told him what they meant, and he frowned. Here was a discordant note—that enclosure, small as it was, was a thing sinister, malevolent, to him almost possessing a personality. Turning from the quicksands he sat and gazed at the nest of rocks below him until Pepper, well trained though she was, became restless and thought it time to move. Stirring, he smiled and pressed a knee against her and as he rode away he shook his head. "Yes, girl, I'm still a-rollin'—an' I don't know where to."

After supper he talked with George until they heard the creaking of wheels and harness. Looking up they saw four heavy horses slowly passing the window, followed by a huge, covered wagon with great, heavy wheels having four-inch tires. A grizzled, whiskered, weather-beaten patriarch handled the lines and talked to his horses as though they were children.

"Now I got to make a new fire an' cook more grub," growled George, arising. "Why can't he get here in time for supper? He's allus late, goin' an' comin'."

"Who is he, an' where's he from?"

"Ol' Buffaler Wheatley from Highbank. He's goin' up to Juniper an' Sherman."

"He come from Highbank today?" demanded Johnny, surprised.

"Shore—an' he must 'a' come slow."

"Slow? Forty miles with *that* in a day, an' he come *slow*?" retorted Johnny. "He was lucky to get here before midnight. If you'd 'a' done what that old feller has today, you'd not think much of anybody as wanted you on hand at supper time."

"Mebby yo're right," conceded George, dubiously, as he went into the kitchen.

Johnny arose and went out to the shed where the driver was flexing his muscles. "Howd'y," he said. "Got th' waggin where you want it?"

"Howd'y, friend," replied Buffalo, looking out from under bushy brows. "I reckon so. 'Most any place'll do. Ain't nothin' 'round'll scratch th' polish off it," he grinned.

Johnny laughed and began unhitching the tired, patient horses, and his deft fingers had it done before Buffalo had any more than started. "Fine hosses," he complimented, slapping the big gray at his side. "You must treat 'em well."

"I do," said Buffalo. "I may abuse myself, sometimes, but not these here fellers. They'll pull all day, an' are as gentle as kittens."

"How do you find freightin'?" asked Johnny, leading his pair into the shed.

"Pickin' up, an' pickin' fast," answered Buffalo, following with the second team. "It's gettin' too much for one old man an' this waggin. An' top of that I got th' mail contract I been askin' for for years. So I got to put on another waggin an' make th' trip every week 'stead of only when th' freight piles up enough to make it worth while. Reckon I'll break my boy in on th' new waggin."

"I'll leave th' feedin' to you," said Johnny, leaning against the wall. "You know what they need."

"All right, friend; much obliged to you. I just let 'em eat all th' hay they can hold an' give 'em their measures of oats. I have to carry them with me—can't get none away from Highbank, everythin' up here bein' grass fed."

"I feed oats when I can get 'em," replied Johnny. "I allus reckon a corn-fed hoss has more bottom."

"Shore has—if they're that kind," agreed Buffalo.

"Travel th' same way all th' time?"

"Yes. I won't gain nothin' goin' t'other way 'round," answered Buffalo, busy with his pets. "You see I allus come north loaded. Th' first stop, after here, is Juniper, where I loses part of th' load. That's thirty miles from here, an' th' road's good. Then I cross over to Sherman, lose th' rest of th' load, an' come back from there light—it's fifty mile of hard travelin'. Goin' like I do I has th' good, short haul with th' heavy load; comin' back I have a light waggin on th' long, mean haul. If I went to Sherman first, things would just be turned 'round."

"What do you do when you have passengers for Sherman?"

"Don't want none!" snorted Buffalo. "Wouldn't carry 'em to Sherman, anyhow. Anybody with sense that can sit a hoss wouldn't crawl along with me in th' heat an' dust on that jouncin' seat. But sometimes I has a tenderfoot to nurse, consarn 'em. They ask so many fool questions I near go *loco*. But they pays me well for it, you bet!"

"Anythin' else I can give you a hand with?" asked Johnny, following the old man out of the shed.

"No, thankee; I'm all done. Th' only man that can give me a hand now is that scamp, George. I'm goin' in to eat, friend. Got to be up an' be on my way before th' sun comes up. I get th' cool of th' mornin' for my team, an' give 'em a longer rest when she gets hot. If you see Jim Fanning, tell him I'm buyin' hides as a side line now. I pays spot cash for 'em, same price as Ol' Saunders would pay, less th' freight. He has quit th' business an' went to live with his married da'ter, ol' fool!"

"Fanning sell hides?"

"No; I just want him to know so he can tell th' Bar H an' th' Triangle an' mebby th' Double X. I want to have a good load goin' back from here. There ain't no profit in goin' all th' way back with an empty waggin. Well, good night, friend! I'm much obliged to you."

"That's all right," smiled Johnny. "I'll tell him. Good night; an' good luck!" he added as an afterthought, and then drifted around to the saloon, where he found several men at the bar.

Dave performed the introductions, and added: "Nelson, here, says he ain't goin' back punchin' cows as long as his money lasts. He's a travelin' eddicator in th' innercent game of draw—or was it studhoss, Nelson?"

"Draw is closer to my heart," laughed Johnny. "My friend, Tex, told me I might learn draw if I lived long enough; but I'd have to have a pack of cards buried with me an' practice in th' other world if I aimed to learn studhoss."

"It grieves me to see a young man wastin' his time in idleness," said Ben Dailey, the storekeeper. "Th' devil is allus lookin' for holts. Young men should keep workin'. Might I inquire if you feel like indulgin' in a little game of draw? You'll find us rusty, though."

"We don't play oftener than every night, an' some afternoons," said Fanning.

"I'm a little scared when a man says he's rusty," replied Johnny. "But I reckon I might as well lose tonight as later. I hope Dave is too busy to cut in—he said he don't know *nothin'* about it."

"Dave's still cuttin' his teeth," chuckled Jim Fanning; "but he uses my silver to cut 'em on. When he learns th' game I'm goin' to drift out of town while I still got a cayuse."

Two punchers came stamping in and Dave nodded to

them. "Here's yore victims; here's them infants from th' Double X. Boys, say 'Howd'y' to Mr. Nelson. Nelson, that tall, red-headed feller is Slim Hawkes; an' that bow-legged towhead is Tom Wilkes. They ain't been in here in three months, an' they've rid twenty miles to rob us."

"An' we might walk home," retorted Wilkes. "Let's lay th' dust before we starts anythin'. Nelson, yo're in bad company. This gang would rob a church. You want to get a kneehold an' hang onto th' pommel after *this* game starts. Here's how!"

As the game progressed the few newcomers who straggled in felt their interest grow. As each finished his drink, Dave would lean forward and whisper: "There's what I call a poker game. Four highwaymen playin' 'em close. To listen to 'em you'd think they never saw a card before."

Johnny was complaining. "Gents, I know I'm ignorant— but would you advise me to draw to a pair of treys? Shall I hold up an ace, or take three cards? I'll chance it; I never hold a sider. Gimme three."

"Ain't that just my luck," sighed Ben. "An' me with three of a kind."

A little later Johnny picked up another hand and frowned at it. "Well, seein' as I allus hold up a sider, I'll have two, this time."

Hoofbeats drummed up and stopped, and a voice was heard outside. Dave looked at the calendar. "Big Tom's a day ahead—he ain't due for his spree till pay-day. Hello, Huff! What you doin' so fur from home?"

"Hello, Dave! Hello, boys!" said the newcomer. "I feel purty good tonight. Just got word that McCullough wants two thousand head from us fellers up here. He'll be along with his reg'lar trail outfit in a few weeks. Sixteen men, a four-mule chuck waggin, an' nine saddle hosses to th' man. I'm sendin' word that I can give him a thousand head, an' th' Triangle is goin' to give him five hundred; so he'll want five hundred from th' Double X, which Slim an' Tom can tell Sherwood."

"Shore," growled Slim, and his ranch mate nodded.

"Goin' up to Dodge again?" queried Dailey.

"He didn't say," answered Big Tom. "Who's doin' the scalpin'?" he asked, going over to the table, where he gradually grew more restless as he watched.

"Some of these days, when I grows up," grinned Wilkes, "I'm goin' up th' trail with a herd, like a reg'lar cowpuncher. Dodge may be top-heavy with marshals, but I'd like to see it again, with money in my pockets."

Slim grunted. "Huh!" He looked over his hand, and drawled: "Th' last time you went up you put on too many airs. Just because Cimarron let you play *segundo* once in a while when he went on ahead to size up th' water or some river we would have to cross, you got too puffed up. I'm aimin' to be th' second boss th' next trip, an' I'll hand you a few jobs that'll keep you out of mischief."

Big Tom watched the winner rake in the chips and could stand it no longer. "Say," he growled, "anybody gettin' tired, an' want to drop out?"

Dailey looked up. "I only won two dollars in two hours, an' I got some work to do. Everybody bein' willin', I'll go out an' bury my winnin's."

Big Tom took his place. "I'm shore of one thing: I can't lose th' ranch, for I don't own it."

A round or two had been played when Big Tom drew his first openers. Johnny raised it and cards were drawn. After it had gone around twice, the others dropped out. Big Tom raised and Johnny helped it along. The betting became stiffer and Big Tom laughed. "I hope you keep on boostin' her."

"You can't get me out of this pot with dynamite," replied Johnny, pushing out a raise.

Big Tom's gun was out before he left his seat. His chair crashed backward and he leaned over the table. "Meanin'?" he snarled.

Johnny, surprised, kept his hand on the chips. "What I said," he answered, evenly.

"Tom!" yelled Dave. "He don't mean nothin'! He's a stranger down here."

Big Tom's scowl faded at the words. "I reckon I was hasty, Nelson," he said.

Johnny spoke slowly, his voice metallic. "You was so hasty you come near never gettin' over it. Put down th' gun."

"I'm a mite touchy at—"

"If you has anythin' to say, put—down—that—gun."

"No offense?"

"For th' third time: Put—down—that—gun."

Big Tom shook his head and appeared to be genuinely sorry. He slid the gun back and picked up his chair. "You raised?"

"I did. I advise you to call—and end it."

"She's called. Five little hearts," said Big Tom, lying down his cards.

"They're hasty, too. Queen full, count 'em. Let's liquor."

The foreman paused in indecision. "Nelson—"

"We all get touchy," interrupted Johnny, scraping in the winnings. "Will you drink with me?"

"I'll take the same," said Big Tom, and he bought the next round, nodded his good night and went out.

Johnny turned to Dave. "Will you oblige me by tellin' me what Mr. Huff got huffy about?"

Dave hesitated, but Slim Hawkes laughed and answered

for him, his slow drawl enhancing the humor of his tale, and wrinkles playing about his eyes and lips told of the enjoyment the picture gave to him. "Clear River crossed our range, flowed through Little Canyon, made a big bend on th' Bar H, passed out of East Canyon, an' flowed down the middle of th' SV. Three years ago a piece of Little Canyon busted loose an' slid down, blockin' th' river, which backed up, gettin' higher an' higher, an' began to cut through its bank about three miles above. Big Tom got busy, *pronto*. He sends for a box of dynamite, sticks it around in th' *débris* an' let's her go—*all* of it. When th' earthquake stopped there was a second one in th' dust an' smoke—we all thought it was a delayed charge. It wasn't. It was a section of th' canyon wall, near a hundred feet long an' almost two hundred feet high. There was a shale fault runnin' down from th' top, back about forty feet. Everythin' in front of that was jarred loose an' slid. Th' canyon was choked so hard an' fast that it won't never get open again. Clear River kept right on a-cuttin', an' it now flows on th' other side of Pine Mountain, which means th' Bar H ain't got no water of its own, except a few muddy holes south an' west of th' ranch buildings. That's why he's touchy. But that's a long speech, an' a dry one. Let's all liquor again."

III

♦

An Objection

Johnny looked forward eagerly to the coming of the outfits for their monthly celebration, and he was not certain that he would not make enemies before the night was over, which impelled him to visit the Bar H and the Triangle while he would be welcome. He had familiarized himself with the SV valley and the country close to the town. Therefore he mounted Pepper after an early breakfast and rode south, passing the shack occupied by the Doc, about two miles south of Gunsight, The Doc was squatting on SV land, had a small corral, a hitching post, and a well. Johnny stopped at the latter and had a drink while he mentally photographed everything in the immediate vicinity. When he started on again he had the choice of two trails. One wound up over Pine Mountain, a high, wooded hill, and was the more direct route to the Bar H; the other followed the river bed around the base of the mountain, and was the trail used by the Triangle. Deciding on the shorter, if more difficult route, he gave Pepper her head and started up the slope. The trail was fair, following, as it did, the line of least resistance and threading through rocky defiles, rocky clefts, and skirting steep walls.

Riding down on the south side he found himself in a deep ravine and when he left it he came to the old bed of the river, and a grin came to his face as he pictured the episode of the dynamiting. Following the dried-up bed he entered East Canyon and found its north wall to be perpendicular and remarkably smooth; the other side sloped more, showed great errosion and was scored by clefts and wooded defiles running far back. Emerging from the canyon he rode over a hilly, rolling range and some time later recrossed the old river bed and arrived at the Bar H ranchhouses. Two men were in sight, one mending riding gear and the other had just fixed the fence around the wall. They nodded, and he asked for Big Tom.

"He's around some'rs," said "Squint" Farrell, whose name had been well bestowed.

"Git off an' set down," invited the other. "He won't be long. Ridin' fur?"

"Gunsight," answered Johnny.

Bill Fraser's eyes were on Pepper. "Ever think of swappin' cayuses?" he asked.

"Not this one," smiled Johnny. "She's too dumb—won't learn nothin'. But I had her since she could stand up, an' she's rapid for short distances."

"Meanin' several short distances hooked together," suggested Squint. "I can see she's dumb—it's writ all over her."

"I don't care," said Fraser. "I'm a great hand with th' dumb ones. I'm doin' wonders with Squint."

"Shore," grunted Squint. "He owes me so much money I got to do what he says. Here comes Tom, now. He's some touchy this mornin'. Must 'a had a session with them poker deacons last night."

"He holds 'em too long," chuckled Fraser. "He figgers that if three little deuces are worth a dollar, why two aces an' two kings is worth a hull lot more."

"Does sound reasonable," said Squint, "three deuces makin' only six, an' th' others makin'—a king is thirteen—twenty-six, an' two more is twenty-eight. That the way you been figgerin' all these years, Tom?"

Big Tom smiled. "Howd'y, Nelson. What brings you down here so early?"

"Curiosity, mostly," answered Johnny. "That an' not havin' nothin' to do. An' I'm grievin' about them two dollars Dailey took away from me last night."

"Nobody that wiggles away from Dailey an' only leaves two dollars behind can associate with me steady," objected Fraser. "I got my rights."

"Mebby we'll see him get two more tonight," said Squint. "We're ridin' in with money in our pockets."

"An' you'll travel light returnin'," said Big Tom.

"An' most amazin' noisy," laughed Squint.

After a little more idle conversation Johnny pulled his hat more firmly down on his head. "Well, I just thought I'd drop in an' say hello. Any place else to go?"

"Don't be in no hurry," said Big Tom. "But if yo're set, you might get acquainted with th' Triangle—it's only an hour's ride. They'll be in town, too, tonight."

Johnny nodded all around and rode off the way they pointed. He looked carefully at the brands of the cattle he passed, stopped at the Triangle for a drink and a few minutes' conversation with a puncher who was saddling a fresh horse and returned by the trail around the eastern end of Pine Mountain, to Gunsight, where he spent the afternoon playing seven-up with Dave, with indifferent success.

Night had scarcely fallen when a whooping down the trail heralded the approach of an outfit. It was from the Triangle and they stamped in eagerly. Dailey, Fanning, and several more of the townsfolk followed them, and it was not long before liquor and cards vied with each other for the honors of the evening.

Johnny, declining cards, and going easy with the liquor, watched the games and became better acquainted all around.

"I'm losin' my holt," mourned Dailey. "Reckon I'm sick."

"When you get so sick you can't move," grunted Hank Lewis, foreman of the Triangle, "I'm comin' in an' take yore clothes. You'll be left like you was born."

"You ain't got a chance, Hank," asserted Fanning. "I live next door to him, an' I'll get him first. Here's a little more to freeze him out."

"No man with three jacks ought to sit in this here game at all," muttered Gardner, sorrowfully, "But I'm trailin'."

"Now that I know what Sam's got, I'll trail, too," grinned George Lang. "Here comes Huff an' his angels."

The Bar H arrived tempestuously. Big Tom's voice could be heard above the noise and he was the first to enter, followed closely by his outfit. He nodded to the crowd and ordered drinks all around. Exchanging a few words with Dave, he approached Johnny.

"Reckon you can hold onto that last pot, Nelson?" he asked.

"I'll do my best," replied Johnny. "I'll have a better chance with Dailey out of our game."

"Let's make up another table," said Big Tom, looking around.

Fraser joined them, followed by Lefty Carson. "I'm after more'n two dollars," he laughed. "Dailey allus did play a kid's game."

"Somebody else is pickin' on me," came Dailey's voice. "If that Fraser'll come in some evenin' I'll try to suit him. Hey, Dave! What's th' matter? Somebody tie you to th' bar?"

Dave's retort was not what fiction attributes to a fat man. He was not genial; he was stirred up. "You go hang! I'm so cussed busy I can't see. *I* ain't no jack rabbit!"

"He says so hisself!" shouted Squint, roaring with laughter. "If I ever sees a jack rabbit lookin' like Dave, I'll give him all th' trail!"

"Hey, Two-Spot!" yelled Dave, with a voice which shook the bottles. "He's allus around when there's nobody here—but when there's a crowd to be waited on, he flits. Hey! Two-Spot!"

Dahlgren held his hand over the bar. "Gimme a glass of liquor, Dave, an' I'll trap him," he laughed, looking at his foreman, who had forgotten all about cards and was drinking steadily.

Dave looked at him, grinned, and complied. Dahlgren turned, glass held up. " 'Order, Gents! Order! Less noise! I'm goin' to trap a bum-bum an' have him on show right before you for two bits a head."

The crowd took it as a wager and would not let him explain. "All right, you coyotes; let it go that way, then: Two bits apiece that I do," he cried, and, the cynosure of all eyes, pranced to the door where he placed the glass on the sill and then lay down along the wall, his hand raised to grasp his quarry. Laughing, he faced the crowd. "They are 'lusive animals, Gents; but they can't—oh! ho!— resist th' enticin' smell of—"

Another roar went up as a hand stole around the glass and whisked it from sight. All oblivious to this, Dahlgren took the shout as a tribute to his humor, and when he could be heard, continued: "They can't resist th' smell of liquor, Gents. When th' wary bum-bum scents this here glass of fire water," pointing—he stopped as another roar went up. "Well, I'm d—d!" he grunted. Scrambling to his feet, he plunged out into the night as Two-Spot entered the rear door, carrying the liquor at arm's length. Two-Spot stopped, gulped down the fiery liquid and, placing the glass on the bar, started to serve the card players, his face grave and serious.

The place was in an uproar when Dahlgren returned and he was met by a howling mob of creditors. Shaking his fist at Two-Spot he exhausted his change as he bobbed around in the crowd, got more from Dave and at last managed to pay off. Emitting a yell, he jumped for Two-Spot, grabbed him and began to manhandle him playfully. Others joined in and the sport grew fast and furious, rougher and rougher. Johnny, seeing how things stood, and thinking that Two-Spot was in danger of being hurt, plunged head-first into the mass of merrymakers, grabbed Two-Spot and, at the first opportunity, threw him reeling toward the door. Leaping after him, he grasped the confused tramp, whispered: *"Vamoose!"* and then yelled out: "I *can't,* huh? We'll *see!*" There was a flurry and Two-Spot shot out of the door as though he had left a bow. Johnny turned and faced the crowd. "Did you *hear* him?" he demanded. "I showed him if I could, or not. Blast his nerve, to talk like that to *me!*"

"Wish he'd said it to me," growled Big Tom, whose liquor was making him surly and uncertain. "I'd 'a' busted his cussed neck. This here country is gettin' too d—d independent. That's it—too independent. Th' Bar H runs this country, an' *I* run th' Bar H," he boasted, resting against the bar. "That's it, an' it's got to learn it. It's got to learn that th' Bar H runs this country, an' *I* run th' Bar H. Anybody say I don't?" he demanded, looking around.

Just at this auspicious occasion, Squint was unfortunate enough to step on the foot of a man who had little use for him and who, several times in the last few years, had been restrained only by force from carrying out his thinly veiled threats. Wolf Forbes, the deadliest man on the Bar H, more than disliked Squint, and only their common interests had averted bloodshed. Now he snarled and reached for his gun, but found it held in the holster by Little Tom Carney, who hung to Forbes' arm like a leech until others came to his aid and succeeded in taking the killing edge from Wolf's anger.

Wolf struggled, gradually getting free. "I don't want him *now,*" he panted. "Let go of me! I'll get him when he's sober." He wrestled free and went over to his foreman. "You heard what I said?" he demanded. "There won't be no interference this time!"

Big Tom rocked back on his heels and scowled down at his gunman. "I heard you," he replied. "An' I says yo're makin' a fool of yoreself. *I*'m runnin' this ranch, an' I'm tellin' you that I'll see that he is *good* an' sober an' gets an even break, if it ever comes to gunplay between you two. Take my advice, an' forget about it." He pushed Forbes to one side and waved his arm. "Everybody have a drink with Big Tom Huff, th' boss of th' Bar H. Set 'em out, Dave."

They responded, but the soberer heads began to feel uneasy. Dave looked at Dailey, who exchanged glances with him; and at Johnny who, lounging against the farther wall near the card players, was missing nothing. Johnny allowed a faint smile to show, and winked at the proprietor, a knowing, significant wink. If it was meant to bring ease to Dave's troubled mind, it failed utterly. Worse than that, it acted the other way.

"D—n it!" thought Dave. "He's sober as a hoss an' cold as h—l" which anomaly did not strike Dave's too-busy mind. "Is he aimin' to get Huff? Is he nursin' last night's play? Here I was hopin' none of th' Double X would ride in, an' Trouble was campin' under my fat nose all th' time! H—l will shore pop at the first shot—they'll shoot him to pieces, an' no tellin' who else!"

The card game died gradually and the players nearest the crowd shoved their chairs back. Dave noticed it and shook his head imploringly, trying by sheer willpower to force them back to the game. He failed, and his fears looked to be justified. Big Tom, turning ponderously, looked at them and then stared as their strange inactivity slowly impressed itself on his befuddled mind.

"Go on an' play!" he roared. "I run th' Bar H—an' Bar H runs th' country."

Dave leaped into the breach. "They can't. Dailey's got all th' money."

"Dailey's got—Ha! Ha! Ha!" roared Big Tom. "He's th' ol' fox. Goin' to shake han's with th' ol' fox!" He weaved across the floor and shook Dailey's hypocritical hand. "An' he's got Nelson's two pesos! Me an' Nelson's goin' to play a two-hand game for th' limit—an' th' winner'll tangle up with Dailey."

That plan did not suit Dave at all. He refilled a glass and slid it across the bar. "Hey, Tom!" he called. "Hey, *Tom*!" As the foreman turned clumsily and stared at him, Dave held up the glass. "I never thought you was so stuck up as to ask th' boys to drink with you, an' then throw 'em like that!"

"Who's stuck up?"

"Then why didn't you drink with 'em?" demanded Dave, severely.

Huff looked at him and lurched forward. "Beg boys' pardon. I'm with th' boys. I allus drink with th' boys, an' I ain't stuck up!" He gulped the liquor and, spreading his feet, leaned against the bar. "Th' Bar H runs this country, an' *I* run th' Bar H. I'll learn 'em, too!" He threw off two of his men who tried to quiet him, fearing he would say too much. "I'm all right," he assured them. "I'll learn 'em," he continued. "There's that minx on th' SV. I'll learn her, too. I've been layin' low; but I'll learn her. I'm not stuck up; but *she* is. First night I called she tried to sneak out an' leave me holdin' th' sack. But I showed her who was runnin' this country. She's a wiry minx, but I kissed—"

"That'll do!" snapped Johnny, the words sounding like the crack of a whip. He leaned forward, away from the wall, his hands hanging limply at his sides. The crowd jumped, and Dave's heart was severely taxed. "I don't know th' woman, but I objects. The Bar H may run this country, an' you may run th' Bar H; but if I hears any more about wimmin I'll take th' job of runnin' you, an' th' Bar H, an th' country besides, if I has to! I've got some rights an' I ain't goin' to have my evenin' spoiled by wimmin! An' that goes as she lays!"

Big Tom had pushed away from the bar and swung around unsteadily. He blinked, and focused his eyes on the man who had interrupted him, and who spoke about running him. Steadily the meaning of the words hammered at the liquor-paralyzed brain cells, and at last was recognized and understood. His blood-red face wrinkled like the muzzle of an angry dog and the red eyes blazed with murder. Memory tried to inflame him further, and succeeded. He snarled an oath and reached for his gun.

There was a flash, a roar, and a cloud of smoke at Johnny's hip and before the crowd could move they were facing two guns, from one of which trailed a thin wisp of smoke. Big Tom, holding his benumbed hand against his body, looked from it to his gun, which slowly ceased sliding and came to a stop on the floor at the other end of the bar. He appeared to be stupefied.

"I didn't touch him!" snapped Johnny. "I hit his gun. You all saw him draw first. I'm aimin' to make this personal between him an' me—an' so far's *I*'m concerned, it's over now. But if anybody has any objections, I'll hear 'em." Receiving no reply, he continued, looking out of the corner of his eye at the Bar H foreman:

"Tom, I don't aim to do you no injury, an' you can palaver all you wants, an' have all th' fun you wants, regardless. That is yore right. But I've got rights, too. An' so has all th' boys. An' we ain't goin' to hear nobody talk about wimmin. Wimmin is barred, all th' way to th' ace. I ain't goin' to listen about 'em, at all. They lost me th' best job I ever had, on the best ranch I ever saw. They drove me clean out of Montanny, to h—l an' gone. All my troubles have been caused by wimmin—an' you hear me shout that there ain't goin' to be no palaverin' about 'em where I got to hear it. That's flat; an' I got two six-guns that says it is. I ain't holdin' no grudge ag'in' you—no more'n yo're holdin' ag'in' me for my mistake last night. We all of us make 'em, not meanin' to.

"This is a man's town, a man's saloon, an' we're all of us men. We ain't goin' to be follered around by no wimmin in talk or otherwise. All in favor of barrin' wimmin, have a drink with me."

The invitation was accepted, and Dave followed it by a treat on the house. Then he mopped his head and wearily let his hands hang down at his side. He looked at Johnny and heaved a sigh. "D—d if you ain't a he-wizard!" he muttered. "A reg'lar sheep-herder!"

Johnny walked over, picked up the gun and handed it to its owner, slapping him on the back at the same time. "Here, Ol' Timer," he grinned, "take yore gun. She's a beauty an' ain't hurt a bit. Don't it beat all how me an you get all mixed up without meanin' to? I says it's funny—cussed if it ain't!"

Big Tom fumbled at the holster, slid the gun into it, and a grin crawled across his face. "Seems like we *are* allus buttin' our fool heads together," he replied. "I'm with you, Nelson. I'm with th' boys. Th' h—l with wimmin. They're barred, an' I won't listen about 'em. We're all men—ain't we, boys?"

"I reckon so," said Dave. He motioned to Squint and Fraser, nodding at Big Tom, and then at the door.

"Hey, Tom," called Fraser, "let's go home!"

"Won't—won't go home!" objected Big Tom, lurching forward. Reaching a chair in a corner he fell into it and in a few minutes was snoring sonorously.

Dave slid his elbow on the bar and rested his head in his hand. His pose bespoke great weariness. He looked at Johnny and shook his head in bewilderment. Johnny dragged a chair up to the unused second table, made a face at the fat proprietor, and piled up a sizable stack of coins in front of him.

"Any Bar H or Triangle *hombre* think they can get any of this?" he demanded, grinning. Four men thought so at the same time; and soon a third game was going on beside them.

Two-Spot poked his face up to the window again and looked in. Then he came in with an air of nonchalant confidence. Having seen all that had happened he believed the stormy weather to be over and if it wasn't, why Nelson seemed to be a friend of his, which sufficed. Dave slid him a partly filled bottle.

"Take it away and don't bother me," said the proprietor. 'I'm restin' up for th' next storm."

Two-Spot looked around. "You can go to sleep, Dave," he said. "I'll tend bar for you. There won't be no more. My friend over there is like his black cayuse—everythin' in this country is hid back in his dust." Turning away, he glanced quickly around, stuck out his tongue at the snoring Mr. Huff, put his bottle on a chair, sat down on another one, rested his feet on the recumbent form of Squint, who snored tenor to his boss' bass, and appeared to be well pleased with himself.

IV

◆

With His Shadow Before Him

The following morning was a quiet one in Gunsight and a stranger entering the town would have thought an epidemic of sleeping sickness had raided it, for yawns would have met him wherever he turned, and quite some headaches, the owners of which were short of temper and ugly in words. Dave dozed in his chair and his countenance was not a smiling one. He opened his eyes from time to time and fell asleep again with a scowl. Ben Dailey petulantly cursed everything his clumsy fingers bungled, and it can be said that clumsiness was not the normal condition of those digits. Art Fanning, whose hired man could run the routine affairs of the hotel as well without him, turned and tossed on his bed, finally getting up and poking his head out into the hall. Thinking he heard a noise in Nelson's room, he went to the door and hammered on it.

"House afire?" demanded Johnny, sleepily.

"No; but my head is," growled Fanning. "What you say about a bucket of roarin' strong coffee for us sinners?"

"I say yo're shoutin'. Comin' in?"

"Naw; I got to put on some clothes—an' find some socks; these here are roundin' my heels an' climbin' up my laigs. I'm shore hard on socks," he growled. Leaning over the stairs he let out a bellow, "Hey, *George!*"

"I'll swear he heard you," said Johnny. "Mebby th' Bar H did, too. I never saw nobody go under so quick from liquor as Big Tom an' Squint."

"Hey, *George!*" yelled Fanning. "Oh, they was well ribbed before they hit town. Where th'—"

"What you want?" asked a voice from below.

"What you think I want!" retorted Fanning. "Yore gran'mother's aunt? You brew us a quart of coffee apiece, and brew it *my* way. I been bit by a snake."

"*I* don't want none of that paint," objected George, surprised.

"Who said you did?" snapped Fanning. "Who cares what *you* want? Nelson an' I'll handle that. Jump lively or I'll shoot down th' stairs."

"Shoot, if you wants. They don't belong to me. You can

shoot down th' house, if you wants!" George slammed the door with vim. " 'Bit by a snake!' Bet it was a hydrophoby skunk. I'll brew him some coffee that'll stunt his growth, blast him!"

After breakfast, during which his companion found fault three times with everything in sight, Johnny wandered around and dropped in to see Jerry Poole, the harness-maker. Jerry's mouth tasted of burnt leather and alum from his night's indiscretions and he was so unendurably ugly that his visitor, twiddling his fingers at him, dodged a chunk of wax and departed, going into Dailey's.

"Hello, yoreself!" growled Dailey. He fumbled a ball of cord, dropped it, and kicked it through a window. "Now look what you done!" he yelled.

Johnny wheeled, slammed the door, and wandered to the Palace. Peering in, he assayed a test of Dave's hospitality.

"How do you feel?" he asked, loudly. "You was goin' too fast with th' juniper."

Dave straightened up, glared at him for a moment and found a more comfortable position. "You can go to Juniper, or h—l, for all *I* care!" he grunted, and went off to sleep again.

Johnny leaned against the wall in momentary indecision. Hearing shuffling steps, he looked up to see Two-Spot rounding the corner. His face brightened. Here was someone with whom he could talk.

"Howd'y, Ol' Timer," he said, cheerily.

"Howd'y," grunted Two-Spot, and passed into the Palace. There was a noise within, a crashing of chair legs, and a thunder of words. Two-Spot came out again in undignified haste, crossed the street in three leaps and, turning, shook his unwashed fist at Dave, Johnny, Gunsight, and Creation, and told his opinion of them all.

Johnny shook his head and went around the corner.

"Pepper's th' only company fit to 'sociate with; an' a ride won't do me no harm. Reckon I'll go down an' wander around that hill between th' SV an' th' Triangle. I ain't been south of that valley yet." He looked up at the sun. "Cussed if it ain't noon already!"

While Gunsight slept or swore, the day's work was going on as usual on the SV. Arnold had finished a hurried breakfast and ridden out to the north boundary of his ranch, at that point not more than a mile from the house, to continue setting posts for a fence. His boundary ran along the foot of hills heavily covered with brush and timber and he had grown tired of turning his cattle from them. Having found several rolls of wire left by the former owner of the SV, he determined to use them and make them go as far as they would. If they reached no farther than across the Devil's Gulch section and the creek, he would be repaid for his labor.

Reaching the gulch, he started to work and found the task disheartening. The ravine was rocky and bowlder-strewn and he had difficulty in finding places for the posts. More than half of the morning had passed when he reached the bottom of the gulch and began to look for a place where his shovel would do more than scratch rock. After a fruitless search he abandoned the idea of digging and determined to build a cairn around the post. Taking a crowbar, he attacked the side of the gulch and sent several rocks rolling down. He was prying at a small bowlder with indifferent success when the rock under it, giving way unexpectedly in a small slide of gravel and shale, freed the bowlder suddenly and sent it crashing downward before he could get out of its way. It passed over his left leg and he dropped in agony, the leg broken below the knee. There was only one thing for him to do and he tried it, despite the excruciating pain. He had to drag himself to his horse and get into the saddle somehow. There was no way to call for help with any chance of being heard, for he did not pack a gun, believing himself safer without one. Not being able to use a six-gun well, he knew he would have no chance against men who used them as though they were an integral part of themselves; and to carry a weapon under those circumstances would be suicidal, for he then would become an armed man and have to assume the responsibilities of one.

After what seemed to be an age, he finally reached the top of the gulch, and saw his horse. Resting for a few minutes, he again dragged himself forward. The horse wheeled, pricked up its ears and stared at him in panicky fear. Snorting, the animal dashed away at top speed, the injured man calling after it in despair.

Back in the ranchhouse Margaret set the table for the noon meal. The dinner was nearly cooked when she glanced out of the window and saw her father's saddled horse standing at the corral. Going to the door, she called out that dinner was ready, well knowing her father's habit of not coming until the food was nearly spoiled. Her brother appeared from the tool shed and splashed with the wash basin, which he firmly believed was all that was necessary; but his sister, wise in the ways of boyhood, thought otherwise.

"Don't you dare to touch that towel," she warned. "If you want any dinner, wash your hands and face with soap—get them wet, anyway. Charley, for a ten-year-old boy you are hopeless!"

"An' for a twenty-year-old woman you are a nuisance," retorted Charley. "You women don't do nothing but find fault. Where's dad?"

"I don't know. When you have washed go tell him that dinner will be spoiled if he doesn't hurry."

Charley growled something, made a creditable effort at revealing his face, and departed to find his father. After a short but fruitless search, he returned and reported his failure. "Wonder where he went?" he demanded.

Margaret felt a chill of apprehension. Fears of this kind were not strangers to her, for she had felt many of them in the last two years. "Perhaps Lazy wandered home without him," she suggested. "It wouldn't be the first time. You would better saddle Pinto, and go see. Take Lazy with you."

"Go yourself."

"If you want any dinner you'd better be starting. The sooner you return, the sooner you will eat," she declared, with vexation. "You know that I cannot leave now."

"All right!" growled Charley. He slouched to the corral, saddled Pinto, caught Lazy, and loped toward the gulch.

Margaret's impatience gave way to a nameless fear as the minutes passed without sign of the "men." Going to the door again, she looked out, caught her breath, and then ran toward the corral. Her father, supported in the saddle by her brother, was riding slowly toward the house.

"Dad's broke his leg, Peggy; a big rock come down on it," said Charley, gloomily. "Help me get him into the house."

Between them they soon had him on his bed and Margaret told her brother to ride to Gunsight for the doctor.

"He won't come," groaned the injured man. "If he wouldn't come when you needed him, he won't come for me. Don't waste any time with Reed—I wouldn't have the blackguard if he would come! Charley, you'll have to make that ride to Highbank again. I hate to ask it of you, but there is nothing else to be done. Forty-five miles is too long a ride for Peggy, and besides, I need her here. Eat your dinner, sonny, and then start as soon as you can. I only hope Doctor Treadwell is sober enough to sit a horse when you get there."

"Gee, Dad! I can do it!" Charley asserted. "I did it before in five hours—I'll do it in less this time. Pinto can run all day, for she's a good little horse. Take good care of him, Sis; I'm off."

Grabbing a chunk of meat, and stuffing his pockets with bread, Charley dashed out of the house, climbed into the saddle, and rode off. "Come on, Pinto!" he pleaded. "It's goin' to be a long, hard wait for dad!"

Fording the river, he took the slope of the hill beyond at a walk and, reaching the crest, shot down the other side. Soon he came to a better trail, where the Triangle punchers rode when they went out to their north line. He had not gone far along it before he saw a horseman ahead of him, and when the rider turned and looked back, Charley felt a thrill of fear. It was Squint Farrell.

Squint was still going home from Gunsight and he was not yet sober. Worse than that, he was in a savage mood. When his outfit had started for the ranch, in the early, dark hours of the morning, he had fallen behind them, stupid with drink. At the end of one of his spells of mental oblivion he suddenly realized that he was alone, and urged his horse forward in hope of overtaking his friends. If left to itself the animal would have followed the trail to the ranch; but in his sodden frame of mind the rider knew better. "G'wan!" he ordered, pulling savagely on the reins, and barely managing to ride out the ensuing bucking. "Where you—goin'? *I*'m boss of this—here outfit an' I'm goin' home. I'll—point this here herd. G'wan!" The result was that when day broke and Squint aroused himself and looked around he had no idea of where he was. "It's further'n I reckoned," he muttered. "Don't care: I'm goin' to sleep." He dismounted, made the horse fast to a sapling, and soon was asleep. When he awakened he looked around in bewilderment and began to take note of his surroundings. Mounting his horse, he rode around and finally got his bearings. He was miles east of the ranch-house and, with a savage burst of profanity, he turned the horse and started for home. As he crossed the SV-Triangle trail he heard the rapid drumming of a horse's hoofs and, drawing rein, waited to see who it was.

"Wonder if he got lost, too?" he muttered, and then the hard-riding horseman turned the corner and shot into the narrow defile. "Cussed if it ain't that brat from th' SV," he exclaimed, and became instantly though hazily suspicious. "Here, you!" he shouted. "What you doin' on this range? Where you goin' so fast?" He turned his horse across the narrow trail, effectually blocking it. "You speak up, an' don't give me none o' yore lip! Where you goin'?" He reached for the pinto's bridle, but missed it as Charley pulled the pony back on its haunches and backed away.

"I'm going to Highbank for the doctor; dad's broken his leg," answered the boy, trying to get past.

"Oh, are you?" snarled Squint. "Wish he'd busted his neck! Go 'round an' git on th' trail where you oughter; you can't cross this ranch."

"You don't belong to it," argued the boy. "This is the Triangle; and I haven't got time to go back now. Please, Mr. Farrell, let me past. I can't waste any time!"

"Can't you?" sneered Squint. "I say yo're goin' 'round th' way you should. G'wan, now! Turn 'round, an' d—d quick, before I does it for you! D—d brat!"

"Please, Mr. Farrell," pleaded the boy. "Let me past. Dad's suffering, and I've got to hurry."

"'Please, Mr. Farrell,'" mimicked Squint, savagely. "You goin' to do what I say?" he demanded, drawing his Colt and waving it menacingly. "I got a notion not to let you go at all, no way. You turn that cayuse, an' move fast. Hear me?"

In his desperation Charley forgot his fear. There was only one way to save the precious miles, and he took it. The sides of the defile were steep, and studded with bowlders, but he dug his heels into the pony's sides and sent him scrambling like a goat up the left-hand bank. He was ten feet above Squint before that surprised individual realized what had occurred; but with the realization came a burst of drunken rage. The heavy gun chopped down and flamed. Pinto rose straight up on his quivering hind legs, stood poised for an instant, and then crashed backward and rolled down to the trail, his rider barely having time to throw himself from the saddle.

"Now you can hoof it!" shouted Squint, brandishing the gun. "Next time you'll listen, an' do what yo're told. G'wan home, now!"

"D—n you!" blazed Charley, groping his way down the bank, and kneeling at the side of the little horse. Realizing what was at stake, he flung himself down on the dead pony and sobbed as though his heart would break.

Squint kneed his horse forward. "Don't you cuss me!" he warned. "Don't you do it, you brat! Serves you right: now you can hoof it!" He urged his horse into a lope and rode down the trail, arguing with himself, and finally burst into uproarious laughter at the trick he had played.

Johnny, riding as quietly as possible along the side of the big hill, just below and south of the SV-Triangle boundary, looking for rebranded cattle and other signs of range deviltry, pulled up short at the sound of a distant shot. It fitted in very nicely with his suspicious frame of mind and, thinking that he might catch some one red-handed in some of the things he had been searching for, he sent Pepper tearing down the slope and arrived at the trail shortly after Squint had departed. Rounding a turn, he

saw the defile and the pitiful scene it held, and he pulled
Pepper to her haunches and leaped from the saddle.

"Well, sonny," he said, cheerfully, "yo're in tough luck,
but cryin'—" then he saw the wound in the horse and his
eyes narrowed. "Who shot that cayuse?" he demanded.

Charley told him between sobs.

"Tell me all about it," demanded Johnny, but when the
tale was half over he sprang into the saddle and started
down the trail at top speed. "Stay there, sonny," he shouted
over his shoulder. At the speed he was making he did not
have to ride long before he caught sight of his quarry and
he loosened his rope, shook it free, and leaned forward in
the saddle.

Squint, still arguing, had a Colt in his upraised, waving
hand, and was making so much noise with his mouth, and
was so interested in and spellbound by his own eloquence
that he failed to hear the rolling hoofs behind him until
too late. As he turned, the sailing loop dropped over his
upraised arm, tightened and pulled him from his horse
which, slowing down, soon stopped and fell to grazing.
Squint landed on his back, the gun exploding and flying
from his hand, his sombrero going to the other side.
Johnny came up along the taut rope, swung down, and
scooped up the gun, and then released the lariat, recoiling
it for future use. Squint opened his eyes, considerably
more sober than he had been for twelve hours, and sat up,
dazed and angry.

"What th'—" he began.

"Shut yore face!" snapped Johnny. "Pick up yore hat an'
hoof it to yore cayuse. You was headed wrong, so I stopped
you. Move rapid, or I'll provide some dance music!"

Squint tried his legs and arms, found them still to be
working, and sullenly plodded to his horse. Mounting, he
surrendered his rifle in compliance to orders, and then

loped back the way he had come, Johnny riding one length in his rear.

"Squint," said his captor in a hard, level voice, "if you give me th' least excuse I'll blow you apart. I've seen some mangy humans, but I never run across a two-laigged polecat like you. I hate to tell you anythin' that'll save yore life, an' I'm hopin' you'll forget it. I'll tell you just once: You behave yoreself like you never did before, an' move lively when I speak. *Keep lookin' ahead!* You don't have to look around to hear, do you?"

Squint preserved an unbroken silence and soon they reached the scene of his outrage and stopped. Johnny ordered him to ride on for a hundred feet.

"That's him, Mister!" excitedly cried Charley. "That's th' big bum!"

"I agree with you, buddy," answered Johnny. "Now you tell me all of it, over again." He listened in grave silence until the pitiful tale was told and then pointed to Pepper's back, behind him. "Climb up, sonny. Squint an' me are passin' close to yore house an' we'll take you as far as we can. You don't mind walkin' a few miles, do you?"

"But I can't go!" protested Charley. "I got to go to Highbank for th' doctor. I only hope he ain't drunk when I get there."

"How you goin'?" quizzically demanded Johnny.

"Don't know; but that don't make no difference—I just *got* to go, *somehow*! Mebby I could take Squint's horse," he suggested, emboldened by desperation.

Johnny shook his head. "You don't never want to ride a Bar H cayuse; 'tain't healthy. But, say, bud, we don't have to go to Highback at all—we can get th' Doc at Gunsight. You been eatin' loco weed?"

"He won't come," said the boy, whispering, and looking at Squint.

"Did you ask him?" asked Johnny in a low voice, taking the cue.

"No; but he wouldn't come when Peggy was sick—an' dad says to get Dr. Treadwell from Highbank."

"He wouldn't come when—when *Peggy* was sick?" demanded Johnny.

"No, sir; he said he'd treat cows an' horses, but he wouldn't sling a leg across a saddle if the whole SV was dying."

Johnny sat up very straight. "Climb up here, sonny. I'll get th' doctor for you—I can get to Highbank on this cayuse so quick you'd be surprised. First, I'll take you nearer home. *Pronto,* buddy. Yo're holdin' up th' drive. That's th' way; up you come!" He picked up the reins. "Squint," he called, "lead th' way, an' don't stay too close. We travel along th' foot of th' hill, on th' other side, goin' east after we get there."

"That ain't th' way to Highbank," said the boy.

"I know," replied Johnny. "When you grow up an' ride around th' country as long as I have, you'll find there's lots of ways gettin' to places. I'll have th' doctor at yore house by ten o'clock tonight, which is some hours before you could get him there. Now, don't you tell anybody who it was that helped you out. Plumb forget what me an' Pepper looked like. An' one thing more—if you say anything about what happened to that drunken coyote ahead, be sure an' tell 'em that he wasn't goin' to be killed, an' that they'll do th' stranger a great favor if they says nothin' about th' whole thing to nobody, nobody at all. Will you do that?"

"Shore, Mister," assured Charley. "Ain't he gettin' pretty far ahead?"

"Not as far as I'm hopin' he'll try to get. But he's got a most unpleasant memory, he don't forget nothin'—not nothin' you tell him."

Reaching the edge of the valley, they turned east and soon afterward Johnny checked his horse. "Here's where you get down, buddy. I hate to make you hoof it, but it won't be near as hard as ridin' down to Highbank an' back. Tell your sister to look for th' doctor at ten o'clock: I can't get him there any sooner. So-long, buddy."

"Thanks, Mister, but my name's Charley. I'm Charley Arnold."

"Glad to meet you, Charley," gravely replied Johnny. "I'll see you again some day, I hope. So-long, an' don't forget nothin'."

"No, sir. Thank you."

Johnny pushed forward until he was close behind his prisoner. "Hit it up, you!" he ordered. "Nice, easy lope; I ain't got all day, if I'm goin' to Highbank. That's something else I owe you for, you coyote. An' I'll have to wear out my cayuse, an' come back on a strange one. Oh, if you'll only make a break, or give me half an excuse to throw lead!"

The trail grew slowly but steadily worse, and when they finally reached the bottom of a long, rough slope Johnny ordered a halt.

"I figger we're twenty miles from Gunsight, near as I can judge," he said, "which leaves only ten to Rawlins. Get off that cayuse. You heard me. *Yes; get off!* Now, any man as shoots a fine little pinto pony an' tells a kid to walk, ought to do some of that walkin' hisself. Rawlins is ten miles; it's twenty to th' Triangle, an' with a lot of hills, an' a bad trail. Also, there's my six-guns. If I ever hear of you comin' back, or see you this side of Rawlins I'll *get* you. I want to make that plain. If it's th' last thing I do on earth, *I'll—get—you!* I ain't got no love for th' SV, but h—l ain't good enough for th' man that'll shoot a fine hoss to keep a kid from gettin' a doctor. Thinkin' as mebby you forgot last night, I'll give you another sample of my gunplay." He jerked out a gun and a hole appeared in the crown of Squint's hat. "When I say I'll get you, you know what it means. Turn around, an' keep yore shadow before you. *Vamoose!*"

Watching the hurrying Squint until satisfied that he intended to keep on in the right direction, Johnny turned back, leading the Bar H horse. He had watched the animal closely while driving Squint, and believed it to be in good enough condition to answer the demand he wished to make upon it. He could tell better when he got back to the SV range, in a certain woody draw near the main trail. This point was reached at dusk and he examined the horse, nodded his head, and picketed the animal to a tree with Squint's lariat. The two hours would do wonders for it. Leaving the Bar H horse, he led his own farther back in the draw and tied it to a tree with his lariat. Returning to Squint's mount, he took the slicker from behind the saddle and unrolled it, picking up the worn gloves which rolled out of it. Finishing his preparations, he went on a reconnaissance on foot, smiled as he saw the dim light in the Doc's house, and quickly returned to the horse.

V

◆

A Lesson in Medical Ethics

Doc reed, finding his tobacco pouch nearly empty, led his horse around to the door and went in to replenish the pouch. He plunged his hand into the big tobacco jar—and let it remain there, the tobacco slipping from his fingers, for a guttural, muffled voice suddenly said:

"Hands up! Shut up! Come here, backwards!"

An argument in one's own mind can be exhaustive and reach a conclusion in a very short space of time. It took the Doc about a second to weight matters and abandon the idea of hurling the jar, and with the decision his hand came slowly out and went up, with the other, above his head. While he was doing this his eyes had not been idle and they saw everything there was to be seen, for he was trained in observation. They saw: A man of his own height, dressed in an old, well-worn, yellow slicker; a sombrero so covered with gray dust as to resemble a hat only in shape and function, its brim pulled well down in front; a pair of common black trousers reaching from the slicker down to common boots, so thickly covered with gray dust as to resemble the hat in everything but the above-mentioned characteristics; a common cotton kerchief, of a pattern found on half of the kerchiefs on the range, was tied across the caller's face, hiding it from chin to eyes; a narrow strip of the intruder's face, so indistinct in the shadow of the hat brim as even to hide the color of the eyes; a pair of gloved hands, the right of which was held in front of the intruder and on a level with his eyes; and last, but emphatically not least, a heavy, common-calibered Colt, with ivory grips yellowed by use and age, which weapon was firmly gripped by the upraised hand. The hammer was up, and a crooked, gloved finger lay in the trigger guard. As the Doc moved to obey, as he turned around, he caught a glimpse of a heavy, black line running from the lower edge of the ivory grip uncovered by the curling fingers. It looked as though it was a crack filled with dirt, which was a little thing, but not too small a thing to be forgotten.

"Whoa!" growled the man in the door.

The Doc obeyed. "What do you want?" he asked coolly.

"Nothin' you can lose," came the answer. "Back up a little more!"

The Doc backed, stopped when the gun pressed into his back and stood motionless while a heavy hand felt him over. It took a Colt out of his shoulder holster, and then the victim felt the gun at his back move a little. He smiled slightly, for the fact that his captor had shifted it to the left hand so he could use the right to empty the captured gun and then toss it across the room onto the bed was no clue, for the reason that all of the men he knew were right-handed. The pressure changed again as the right hand went back on the offensive, and then the intruder gave him his second surprise.

"Pack yore tools—broken laig—take everythin' you need. Hurry!"

The Doc stepped forward and picked up a satchel, glancing out of the corner of his eye as he did so. Only a hand, a foot, and part of the hat and face were in sight, the rest of the visitor's body being behind the outside wall. Filling the bag with what he would require, he took a bundle of splints from a shelf, for he was a methodical person, usually had plenty of time on his hands, and believed in having things to suit him.

"It was not necessary to go to all of this trouble," he smiled, as he reached out to turn down the lamp.

"Stop! Let it burn!" warned the visitor.

"Very well, although I only intended to turn it down. As I said, it was needless for you to go to all this trouble and risk. I am in the habit of going on professional calls at any hour, in any weather, merely upon a simple request, or a statement of fact. If this is a practical joke I may or may not enjoy it—usually the victim doesn't—but I really don't mind, if you are careful with this bag and its contents. You might be the man to need it first—*quién sabe?*"

"I shoot at th' first false move," warned the other. "You are goin' to th' SV—now—with me—an' fast. I'll lead yore hoss—mine's out yonder. Go ahead of me, an' don't look back."

The Doc obeyed and his captor, feeling around the saddle for weapons, grasped the bridle and led the animal to where his own was picketed. Mounting, he ordered the Doc to do likewise, and soon they were pounding along at a good pace, too good to suit the Doc, considering how dark it was.

Their coming had been prophesied by the stranger that afternoon, and now it was heralded by the rolling hoof-beats; and as they neared the house two figures, one considerably shorter than the other, appeared in the lighted doorway, while behind them a clock slowly struck ten.

The captor growled a command and, surprised, the Doc pulled up quickly. "There won't be no charge for this call," he said, "an' remember that I'm stayin' outside, near th' window. You make a false move an' I'll shoot you through it. If th' job ain't well done, I'll shoot you when I find it out. You don't know me, so you won't know who to watch for; but I know you well—all h—l can't save you. Don't talk more than you have to, an' then only about yore trade. Get off, an' go in—hurry, before they come out here!"

The Doc dismounted, turning for a look at his captor's horse and saddle, and walked forward, adjusting his hat and pulling at his coat sleeves. Handing the bag to the boy who ran to meet him, and who seemed to be very much surprised, he led the way to the house, bowed to Margaret and went inside. The boy, looking back reluctantly, slowly followed him, and as the man in the saddle tied the Doc's horse to a sapling and swung around to leave, he saw the slender figure of Margaret reappear, softly outlined against the mellow, yellow light of the room and framed by the darkness, for all the world like a jet cameo against an old ivory background. She looked without moving while the horseman in the dark, the glint of whose brass saddle ornaments barely reached her, bent low in the saddle and removed his hat. She could not see this, nor his slow departure, 'though she faintly heard the soft tread of his horse on the sod, steadily growing fainter. A voice from within called her, and turning, she shook her shoulders as if to throw off a restraining force, and hastened to answer the summons.

Reaching the main valley, Johnny rode at a lope, and when he believed himself to be well past the quicksands, he entered the river, following it close to the bank. Leaving the water at the main trail, he dismounted, removed the saddle and bridle and, slapping the horse on its rump, sent it homeward. Picking up the saddle and seeing that the stirrups did not drag, he stepped only on rock as he went up the mountain, where he stopped at the base of a great pine. When he came down again to go to his own horse he had left behind him everything belonging to Squint, the saddle in the brush, and the weapons and gloves well-wrapped in the slicker and buried in a sand drift.

Some time later, in Gunsight, Two-Spot heard a rider and, waiting a few minutes, slipped into the horse shed, where he spoke softly to Pepper before running his hand over her.

"Huh! What made Dave say he went to Juniper?" he muttered. "She's warm, but not much; her back is near dry. Juniper?" he scoffed. "Thirty miles there, an' thirty mile back, since noon? He was *some* place; but I'll bet my jewels he ain't been to Juniper. There's deviltry afoot— but I ain't talkin', little hoss."

VI

♦

Information Wanted

Two-spot rested on the broom. "Wonder what happened to Nelson?" he queried. "Ain't seen him since you went on th' prod yesterday."

Dave held up the glass he was polishing and looked at it. "What you mean, on th' prod?"

"When you chased me, at noon."

Dave picked up another glass, breathed on it and rubbed it vigorously. "He stuck his head in th' door an' said he was goin' to Juniper. Ain't he got back yet?"

"Don't know," grunted Two-Spot, going to work again. "Ain't his hoss back?"

"Don't know." He listened. "Mebby this is him, now, comin' up th' trail." He looked out and shook his head. "Nope, it's only that d—d pill-roller from the flats. What's *he* comin' here for? He's got more liquor in his shack than we've got. I don't like no man that swizzles it secret. As I was sayin', it ain't every—why, hello, Doc! What brings you up here so early in th' mornin'?"

"My horse," grunted the Doc, passing him without a glance. "Hello, Dave! How are things?"

"Smoother'n h—l, as th' old lady said when she slipped on th' ice. What'll yours be?"

"Cigar apiece," said the Doc; "for you an' me," he amended.

Two-Spot turned back and resumed his sweeping.

"Dave, I was kidnapped last night," said the Doc, bluntly. Waiting for Dave to get his expression part way back to normal, he told the story. Dave's expression was under control again and bespoke surprise and sympathy, gradually assuming a stern, uncompromising aspect at the thought of such a grave breach of law and order. Two-Spot, after the first shock, did not dare to look around, for his grin was unholy and altogether too sincere for his health, should the victim of the unheard of atrocity see it. *Swish! Swish!* went the broom; *he! he!* went his throat, low and in time with the sweeping. Doc finished and hammered the bar with his fist. "It's a d—d outrage!" he declared, with heat.

Dave nodded emphatically; "It shore is! Do you know who did it?"

"No; if I did I'd be on his trail."

"See anythin' that might identify th' coyote?"

"Perhaps; I'll know more about it before the day is over," answered the Doc. "Big Tom has some of his men out now looking for tracks on the Double X. Those fellows don't like me very much."

"Blast their eyes!" commented Two-Spot, sweeping with renewed vigor.

Doc glanced at him, frowned, and went on. "Some things lead me to think one way; other things, other ways. It's complicated by Squint's disappearance."

Two-Spot assimulated the second shock with avidity. He was beginning to be glad that he was alive, and his brain was putting two and two together at top speed. His ears fairly ached for more, and he waited for the third. When there were two, there should always be a third, he hopefully assured himself.

Dave's face showed real surprise again and then marched to orders and revealed his sympathy and disapprobation. "Why, there won't be nobody safe!" he exclaimed. "Do you mean he's missin'?"

"He is. Have you seen him since the night they were all here?"

"No; I ain't."

"Sorrers an' calamities never come singly," said Two-Spot, energetically digging a match stick out of a crack.

"Mebby it was Squint," suggested Dave, "as captured you."

"Well, the evidence points that way, but it isn't reasonable," replied the Doc, going to a chair and sitting down. "Squint wasn't the sort of a man who would go out of his way to do anyone a favor, especially if it was for someone he did not like; and most especially if it involved a large element of risk. But this man had on Squint's slicker, rode Squint's horse and saddle, and even had Squint's gloves and gun."

"He must 'a' et Squint," suggested Two-Spot, spitting violently at the thought.

"Shut up, you!" said Dave, sternly. "But, Doc, he was shore petrified when he left here; an' what he had in his person would stay with him for a long time. He allus was economical in his drunks: he made 'em last quite a spell. Now, when a man's full of liquor he'll likely do anythin'—no tellin' what."

"This man was not drunk," asserted the Doc in his best professional manner, "and he had not been drunk for over a week. His hand was as steady as mine, and he did not make a single false move. I'm sure it was not Squint; Big Tom cannot make up his mind; Wolf Forbes swears it was, but Wolf was no friend of his, as we all know. Some of the boys suggested the Double X, knowing the strong dislike some of that litter has for me. Three of the boys are over there now lookin' for tracks."

"What good will that do 'em?" demanded Dave. "A man has a right to make tracks on his own ranch, an' they're allus ridin' around over it. But, then, if they found tracks leadin' from th' Double X to yore place, or from th'

Juniper trail to th' Double X, why, then you'd have some-thin'."

"There are none of the first category," replied the Doc, "and there will be none of the second: I told you that this man rode Squint's horse, and any tracks on the Juniper trail could have been made while we rode over it together. We can't find where he got onto the horse, or where he got off of it; but it must have been in the river somewhere. He was a fiend for riding on rock—he knew this country like a book. We've tried trailing, but it got us nowhere. So, Dave, I rode up here to ask you a plain question: Who were in here last night between quarter of nine and, say, a quarter after ten? You may save some innocent person from a lot of trouble."

"Well," said Dave, pursing his lips. "Th' poker gang was here. Two-Spot an' I was here. Jerry Poole came in to set his watch—that was just at nine-twenty. Nelson poked his head in th' door about ten minutes after Jerry, wrig-gled his fingers at me, cuss his impudence, an' disap-peared. Where he went I don't know. I guess that's all."

Two-Spot gripped the broom convulsively and then slowly relaxed. The third shock had arrived. The prob-lems of his sorely taxed brain were jammed by the sud-den arrival of more. Never before had he heard Dave deliberately lie; and here the proprietor was lying coolly and perfectly, with trimmings to make it stick. In turn sur-prise, wonder, and satisfaction swept across his boiled countenance like driven clouds across the coppery sun. He gradually worked closer to the Doc and soon his stroke became longer and harder. When he began trying to sweep a tobacco stain out of the flooring the Doc suddenly leaped from his chair.

"What—the h—l do—you think—you're doing?" he coughed.

"Huh?" said Two-Spot, looking up.

"What do you mean, sweeping like that, over here?"

"I was only sweepin' where th' dirt was," answered Two-Spot.

The Doc regarded him keenly. "Oh, is that it? Well, hunt for it somewhere else, or I'll kick you through the window!"

Two-Spot flared up. "You got my permission—"

"Shut up!" snapped Dave. "Now, Doc, as I was sayin'— what'n h—l *was* I sayin'? Well, anyhow, I said it," he asserted, belligerently. "What you aimin' to do now?"

"Dance on th' quicksands, I hope," grunted Two-Spot, savagely. Then he listened, and said: "Here comes Nelson on that fine little hoss." Under his breath he muttered, "I bet he'll be surprised to find out he was in here at nine-thirty, last night." He straightened up. "Huh! Mebby he won't. Mebby he fixed it with Dave. Well, if he's wise, he'll tip me off next time—I might tell th' truth, an' make a lot of trouble, if I didn't know."

Johnny walked in. "Hello, Ol' Timer!" he said, jabbing Two-Spot in the ribs.

Two-Spot grasped the broom handle firmly. "Hello, yoreself! An' you lookout who yo're punchin'," he grinned. "Squint's dead," he said, mournfully.

"What?"

"Oh, well; he's missin', anyhow," amended Two-Spot.

"Missin' what?" asked Johnny.

"Missin' hisself!"

"Then he's drunker than I thought," replied Johnny. "I never heard of nobody bein' so far gone in liquor that they missed themselves."

"Oh, you go to th' devil!" snorted Two-Spot, turning around so he could snicker in safety.

Johnny glanced casually at the Doc, walked up to the

bar and bought a cigar, which he lit with scrupulous care.

"Meet th' Doc, Nelson," said Dave.

Johnny turned. "Glad to meet you, Doctor. I've heard of you, an' passed yore place."

"Saw you," replied the Doc, "and I coveted that black mare."

"Nice little cayuse," admitted Johnny.

"The Doc was kidnapped," said Dave, watching closely.

"That so?" replied Johnny, politely. "An' how old was you, Doctor?"

"What do you mean?"

"Why, when you was kidnapped," Johnny explained.

"I was kidnapped last night," replied the Doc.

"You—last night?" demanded Johnny, incredulously. "Well, I'm d—d! What did they get?"

"They got me."

"I mean, what did they get that was valuable?" persisted Johnny.

Two-Spot turned away again and missed the floor twice.

"They stole th' Doc," explained Dave. "They was takin' him away just about th' time you looked in at me. They took him over to th' SV, to set Ol' Arnold's busted laig."

"What you talkin' about?" snorted Johnny, seating himself across from the Doc. "I never heard of a doctor bein' kidnapped to set a busted laig. What am I supposed to say? I'll bite, if it does cost me th' drinks."

"No, Nelson, that's the truth," earnestly asserted the Doc, and he told the story over again.

"You say he was on Squint's cayuse, wearin' Squint's slicker, an' usin' Squint's gun?" asked Johnny. "Then where was Squint? A man don't just drop things like that without knowin' it. What was that Two-Spot was tryin' to tell me?"

The Doc explained the matter and finished by saying that he felt sure that it had not been the missing puncher who had visited him.

"I don't think so, neither," asserted Johnny. "He'd be a fool to go like that. No, sir, I'll bet it wasn't Squint—but, wait a minute! If he counted on leavin' th' country right after, why, he might a' done it, at that. If it wasn't Squint, then where was he?"

"Sleepin' off his liquor," said Dave. "Why, that's it! While he slept somebody took his outfit an' kidnapped th' Doc. H—l, it may all be a joke!"

"You wouldn't think so if you observed that man as I did," replied the Doc. "He was in deadly earnest. I could *feel* it."

"Well, there's two ways to start at it," said Johnny, ordering drinks all around, including Two-Spot. "He had a grudge ag'in' you, an' he was extra friendly to th' SV. Run back in yore mem'ry for somebody that hates you enough to want to get square. If that don't work, then hunt for th' feller that likes th' SV. Anybody 'round here that's sweet on that Arnold gal, that you knows of?"

"No; not that we know of," answered the Doc. "Big Tom was the last one who called there; but he quit, quite some time ago."

"Got throwed so hard he still aches," gloated Two-Spot.

"Well, I can't help you," said Johnny. "I don't know anythin' about th' people around here. An', bein' a stranger, an' likely to be suspected of any orphaned devilment, I'm shore glad I looked in here, last night. But I ain't worryin' about Squint," he deprecated. "He's an old hand at takin' care of hisself, if I'm any judge. He'll turn up with a headache, an' yell fit to bust for his saddle, an' gun."

"I hope so," said Dave. He turned to the Doc. "Did you fix up th' laig?"

"Certainly; it was a simple fracture," answered the Doc. He paused. "Cussed if I know what to think," he growled, arising. He had observed Johnny closely, saw that he was left-handed, found the voice not quite what he had hoped for, and Dave's statement cinched the matter. He nodded good-by and went out, but he looked at Johnny's saddle, where he found silver ornaments instead of brass, and plain stirrup guards instead of the fringed ones he had noticed the night before. Shaking his head he mounted and rode homeward.

Two-Spot placed the broom across a table and sat down. "Dave," he said, almost reverently, "what made you say that?"

"Say what?" demanded the proprietor, belligerently. "You hearin' things?"

"Mebby; but I ain't *seein'* 'em."

"What did I say that's ridin' you so hard?" demanded Dave.

"What you did about Nelson lookin' in last night."

"What was that?" asked Johnny, with pardonable curiosity.

"Why, Dave up an' tells th' Doc that you poked yore head in at that there door at nine-thirty *last night*," explained Two-Spot.

"Well, suppose I did?" asked Johnny. "What about it?"

"Well, now," mourned Two-Spot, "if I ain't got th' cussedest mem'ry! It's got Texas fever; a tick must a' crawled up my ear. Of course you did; and didn't you say 'Two-Spot, when I sees you tomorrow I'll buy you a drink?'"

"I reckon I might 'a' said somethin' like that," laughed Johnny. "She's yourn, Ol' Timer—with a cigar to punish me for forgettin'.'"

Two-Spot enjoyed his drink and pulled contentedly on the cigar. Then he turned toward the rear door. "Time for me to give George a hand. Shall I take Pepper around out of th' sun?"

"Why, yes; an' much obliged," answered Johnny.

Dave pointed his finger and his whole arm at the broom lying across the table. "That yourn?" he demanded.

Two-Spot looked. "I told you that my mem'ry was bad," he chuckled. Putting the broom away where it belonged he went out and led Pepper around to the shed.

Johnny looked hard at Dave. "That was a good turn, Dave," he said. "What made you do it?"

Dave rumpled his hair. "Squint's missin', which means one customer less. Bein' a stranger down here I reckoned they'd pass th' buck to you. That meant they'd likely do it here—th' Doc come up to locate you, I figgered. Besides losin' a lot more customers I'd have to clean up a slaughterhouse. I just made up my mind I wouldn't do it. Anyhow, I'd like to shake hands with th' coyote that lugged th' Doc off to fix that laig. I would so."

"Don't blame you," said Johnny, holding out his hand. "We can shake on that, all right. I say a doctor is a doctor an' ought to go where he's needed."

Dave looked him full in the eyes, a quizzical smile playing around his mouth, and shook hands gravely, solemnly. It was almost a ceremony. "My sentiments, exactly," he responded. "Wonder if Squint was hurt?"

"I'd bet he wasn't," answered Johnny. "I'd even bet he went to a different part of th' country. Mebby he got caught in some devilment. Punchers are great for roamin'—just look where *I* am." He shook his head sadly and went out through the rear door for the hotel, leaving Dave with a grin on his face which threatened to disrupt it. He had not gone more than a few steps when he turned and went back. Poking his head in at the door, he said: "Dave, when I'm drinkin' in here, an' it can be done easy, just see that mine is some watery. I like th' delicate flavor it has that way; th' delicater, th' better."

Dave chuckled and nodded. "Yo're drinkin' it. If yo're satisfied, I am. I can't do it at th' bar, where th' bottle passes; but it'll be easy if yo're playin' cards."

VII

♦

Hunting with the Hounds

Johnny entered the kitchen, looked at the stove and went into the dining-room, where George was playing solitaire. "That's a bad habit, George," he said, shaking his head. "It don't get you nothin'."

George made a play and looked up. "Aimin' to get me into a two-handed game of somethin'?" he queried.

"No; I ain't," answered Johnny. "I was just wonderin' how long you was goin' to play it."

"I'm goin' to play it till I have to start cookin'," said George, determinedly.

"Then you ain't goin' to stand over that hot stove for more'n an hour, are you?"

"No, sir; I ain't."

"You talk like it was somethin' to dodge!" snorted Johnny.

"I'd like to see *you* do it!" retorted George.

"Huh!" sniffed Johnny. "I got a good notion to do it."

George made another play. "Notions!" he sneered. "Notions ain't doin' it!"

"Then I *will* do it," said Johnny, going into the kitchen and throwing wood into the stove. He took down a lid made up of rings, substituted it for one of the stove lids, lifted out the middle section and put in its place an iron ladle.

A chair scraped out in the dining-room and George poked his head in. "What you think yo're doin'?" he demanded.

"Callin' yore bluff. Go on back to yore solitaire. I'm goin' to run some bullets."

"Why, cuss yore nerve!" said George. "Who told you to mess up my kitchen?"

"You said you'd like to see me stand over this stove," answered Johnny. "Run around an' get me two pounds of lead from Dailey."

"Get it yoreself!" snapped George. "You clean up when you get through," he warned.

"Shore," replied Johnny, and he went out to get the lead.

Dailey looked up. "Hello, Nelson!"

"Howd'y, Ben! Got two pounds of lead, an' some Kentucky powder?"

"Shore, answered Dailey. He slid a bar of lead onto the counter and took a can from a shelf. "This ain't Kaintuck—but it's as good. How much?"

Johnny put a few grains in the palm of his hand and rubbed them with a forefinger. "I don't want this at all," he said, showing the black smudge. "I want th' kind *you* use."

Dailey grumbled, but felt under the counter and produced another can. "Here's th' best made," he said.

Johnny tested it, and nodded. "Half a pound will do."

Returning to the kitchen he used George's axe to cut the lead into smaller pieces, and dumped them into the ladle, after which he paid a hurried visit to his room for tools.

Two-Spot shoved his head in at the door. "What you doin'? Runnin' slugs?"

"Shoein' a hoss," said Johnny.

Two-Spot grinned. "Where'd you get th' lead?"

"Dailey's," answered Johnny, punching out old primers.

"Buy primers, an' powder, too?" demanded Two-Spot.

"Powder," grunted Johnny.

"Off'n th' shelf behind him?"

"Under th' counter."

"Yo're lucky; he must like you. Well, then some of 'em will go off," said Two-Spot. "But if you'd bought his primers, none of 'em would." He looked around and started to resize some of the shells. "These here ain't shells. They're— they're kegs." He picked up the mold and opened it. "My G—d!" he snorted. "You're a bloody-minded cuss. Yore gun got wheels an' a limber?"

"It'll make th' other feller limber gettin' out of th' way."

Two-Spot hurt his finger and quit. "Reckon Dave wants me," he observed.

"I'm shore *I* don't," grunted Johnny, beginning to re-prime the shells.

"*Do* it yoreself, then!" snapped Two-Spot, going out. He looked carefully around and, going into the narrow space between the kitchen and the rear of the saloon, disappeared from sight.

Around in front of the Palace four punchers were dismounting. They were disgruntled, but in one way they felt relief. After a morning's search for tracks on the Double X, along its eastern line, they had given up the job and had started to Gunsight to carry out a task which they felt would require a great amount of tact to keep it from becoming a shambles. But on the way they had stopped at the Doc's and found that it would not be necessary to cross-question Johnny. There remained one further duty to perform and they decided to slake their thirsts before attempting it. Big Tom wanted information from those who he felt would be able to give it, since they were directly benefited by the kidnapping of the Doc. He felt sure that the committee he had appointed were qualified to get it for him, especially if they had a proper amount of liquor before they started after it. Hence he had supplied them with the funds and told them that it was his treat. Carson and Dahlgren had fat blanket rolls behind their saddles; "Smitty" and Fraser, nothing but their usual paraphernalia.

They stamped in to the bar and lined up. To Dave's inquiry, they replied that their morning's work had been in vain, but boasted that the afternoon would not be wasted.

"We're goin' where th' information is," said Carson, "an' we're goin' to get it. If it comes easy, all right—*but* we're *goin' to get it,* savvy?"

"An' when we *do* get it, it will be forty feet of rope an' a sycamore tree for th' coyote that got rid of Squint an' kidnapped th' Doc," boasted Dahlgren.

"Nobody gives a whoop about th' kidnappin', 'cept th' Doc," said Fraser; "but this was a poke at th' Bar H, an' that's where we set in. If we finds out who got rid of Squint, we know who kidnapped th' Doc; an' if we learns who kidnapped th' Doc, we likewise finds th' coyote what got rid of Squint. An' I'm tellin' *you* that we're goin' to find out who he is. Doc said he done a good job on that busted laig, an' it would be a mean trick on him to undo it; but we're goin' to find out! Give us another round."

"I got to laugh about th' Doc," said Smitty, "a growed man, lettin' hisself be stole that way. An' what's he doin' now? Is he out a-huntin'? He ain't. He's settin' in that shack of his'n waitin' for *us* to get his kidnapper. Fill 'em again, Dave."

"Forty feet of rope an' a sycamore tree," repeated Carson. "If he puts up a fight we'll give him *this*!" He yanked out his gun and fired at the floor.

Could they have seen the result of the shot they would have been greatly surprised. Two-Spot, under their feet, lying on his pile of stolen blankets and discarded clothing, and drinking in every word they said, had just shifted to a more comfortable position when the gun roared and the bullet, ripping through the flooring, cut a welt on his cheek. Panic stricken, he started to roll and crawl toward the hotel, and was too excited to notice the pair of legs at the wash bench, where Johnny was cooling bullets in the basin, but rolled out and against the bench, upsetting it and Johnny, too, as well as the basin, bullets, and the water bucket. There was a mad scramble for a few seconds and Two-Spot lost a tooth before Johnny saw who it was. Then both leaped to their feet, Two-Spot angrily spitting blood and dirt.

"What you think yo're doin'?" blazed Johnny, reaching for Two-Spot's collar. "Playin' earthquake?"

"Who you hittin'?" snarled Two-Spot. "Leggo my shirt; I got somethin' to tell you!"

George came running and stuck his head out of the door. "Go it, Ol' Timer!" he encouraged. "Serves him right for th' mess he's made!"

Two-Spot thanked him by kicking backward, guided by sound and instinct. George, receiving one whole foot just below his short ribs, doubled up forthwith and disappeared. There was a crash and the sound of falling stove wood, and George had interest in nothing outside of himself.

"They're goin' to th' SV, an' make 'em tell who's raisin' th' devil on th' range," said Two-Spot in Johnny's ear. "If they ain't told easy, then they'll take th' splints off'n th' ol' man's laig. G—d only knows where they'll stop, for they're gettin' full of liquor."

"Who are they?"

"Carson, Dal, Smitty, an' Fraser," answered Two-Spot. " 'Forty feet of rope an' a sycamore tree,' they says," he mimicked, "an' shot through th' floor. I got it in th' cheek, d—n 'em." A frightened look came to his face. "Don't tell 'em where I was," he begged, for the hiding-place was his only refuge and without it his life would be miserable.

"I'll swap secrets," said Johnny. "Keep mum about tellin' me this. Take Pepper around front an' mix her in with their cayuses. Then pick up th' slugs an' keep 'em for me."

A piece of firewood whizzed past his ear, and then a stream of them. George, still throwing, emerged from the kitchen, blood in his eye. Johnny grabbed him.

"We was playin' a joke on you, George," he said, hurriedly. "Two-Spot kicked you accidental. Here's somethin' to square it," and George opened his hand to see a coin nestling therein.

"Joke!" he muttered, feeling around his belt. "Accidental! *You* may think so, but I'm cussed if *I* do! My G—d, his relations must be mules!"

Dave and the committee looked up as the door flew back and slammed against the wall, to see Johnny enter, a little too erect, stepping a little too precisely and wide, his mind obviously concentrated on his legs. His face was owlishly serious and he nodded to each in turn with great gravity. Describing a wide curve he stepped carefully to the bar, where he stopped, sighed, and braced himself.

"Dave," he said, waving an arm, "th' best in th' house for us. Didn't know what to do with m'self; but now we can have some 'citement. Here's how. Here's to pore Ol' Squint."

"Here's to pore Ol' Squint," repeated Dave. "I allus liked Squint."

"Everybody liked Squint," responded Johnny. "Everybody, 'cept—'cept what's his name? Pore Squint, kidnapped; an' the Doc, kidnapped; nobody's safe no more. *You* might get kidnapped—*you*—an' *you*—an' *you*—an' Dave! No, not Dave!" he burst into laughter. "Not *Dave*! He! He! Less'n it was Ol' Buffalo an' his waggin!"

Smitty rocked to and fro: "He! He! He!" he roared. "Ol' Buffalo an' his four-hoss team! Freight for Juniper!"

Carson slapped Johnny on the shoulder. "Nobody's safe but Dave!" he shouted. "Ol' Buffalo would have to *roll* him in, like a bar'l."

"Don't you care, Dave," said Fraser. "I'm yore friend, an' nobody's goin' to kidnap you, waggin or no waggin. Not while Bill Fraser's aroun'. No, sir. Give us another. Big Tom's blowin' his boys."

"Couldn't get along without Dave, not nohow," said Johnny. "Here's to Dave—everybody's fr'en'. Just th' same I ain't forgettin' pore Squint. I'd like to know who kidnapped him—just so I could get my rope on him. That's all. Jus' that. Got notion to go find him. Come on, le's *all* go!"

"Forty feet of rope an' a sycamore tree," burbled Smitty. "Forty feet of—"

"We're goin' to find him," boasted Dahlgren. "Goin' to righ' now. Le's have one more drink, Dave. Just one more, an' then we go git him."

"That's th' way!" cried Johnny. "Come on—one more, Dave, ol' kidnapper. Then forty feet of sycamore rope. Want to come, Dave? Come on! Come on with us!"

"I better stay here," said Dave, earnestly. "I better be right here when you bring him in. *Somebody* ought to be."

"That's Ol' Dave, all righ'," cried Smitty. "Good Ol' Dave."

"Give us a bottle, Dave," said Johnny. "Give us *two* bottles. Nothin's too good for my fren's."

"If pore Squint was only here," burbled Smitty, eyeing the bottles. "Pore Squint. We'll bring that coyote in for you, Dave. We'll drag him to town."

"Him an' Ol' Arnold," supplemented Carson. "*Both* of 'em!"

"That's it!" cried Johnny. "That's where we'll go— come on, fellers! Goo'-by, Dave; goo'by!"

They surged toward the door, milled before the opening, and then shuffled to the street. Fraser threw an arm around Johnny's neck and slobbered about poor Squint. Johnny slipped the six-gun from Fraser's holster, dropped it on his own foot to deaden the fall, and then pushed it under the saloon. He staggered, with Fraser, out toward the horses and bumped into Dahlgren, who grabbed them both to save himself. Fraser's other arm went around his friend's neck and he protested his love for them both. Dahlgren's gun also struck Johnny's boot and was quickly scraped over with sand.

Under the saloon Two-Spot changed from all ears to mostly ears and some eyes, for his view was limited to below the hips of the maudlin gang. When Fraser's gun slid under the floor he became, for an instant, all eyes, and wriggled in greedy anticipation. Then he saw the second gun strike Johnny's boot and become covered over with sand, and he rocked from side to side with silent mirth, his boiled countenance acquiring spots of mottled purple, especially his nose. As soon as the crowd mounted, he crawled forward, wriggling desperately when the space became too small for hands and knees. He had to get those guns before the proprietor got them, for Dave would not allow him to own a weapon. When he had gone as far as he dared, he stopped and waited until the bunched group whirled away up the trail, and then wriggled more desperately than ever. Suddenly he stopped and writhed sideways behind a pile of dirt, for the heavy steps above his head ceased as a pair of enormous legs waddled into his field of view. Dave kicked around in the sand, found the weapon, and laboriously picked it up. The huge legs remained motionless for a moment as their owner watched the cloud of dust which rolled eastward on the trail.

"He's takin' chances," muttered Dave. "An' I can almost smell him from here. Six glasses of whiskey down his sleeve—great guns, but he must feel comfortable! Well, boys, I don't know where yo're goin', but nothin' would surprise me." He paused a moment in indecision, thoughtfully regarding the Colt. "I reckon I ought to lose this gun down th' well—but I'll wait till he comes back."

The fat legs waddled out of sight and the floor creaked again. Two-Spot wriggled forward, snatched the Colt and backed to his nest, where he looked at his prize and gloated.

"Dave never saw you fall," he chuckled. "Oh, yo're a beauty; an' only two are gone. Cuss it! This is th' gun that shot *me*!" He considered a moment. "Now I got to get some .45's from th' store when Ol' Eagle-Eye ain't lookin'."

Meanwhile the exuberant committee tore over the trail until Fraser, wishing to let off some extra steam, felt for his gun. He reined in so quickly as almost to cause a catastrophe. Dahlgren now discovered his own loss and there was a wrangle about going back to look for the missing weapons. Their insistence won out and the committee wheeled, spread out, and cantered back almost to Gunsight, wrangling all the way. Yielding at last to the acrimonious suggestions of the other three, they gave up the search and set out again, beginning on the second bottle. When they finally arrived at the SV ranchhouse the afternoon was over half gone and they were so under the influence of liquor that it was all they could do to get to the door of the house. Staggering in, they went to Arnold's room and all began talking at once. There were no preliminaries—Margaret and Charley, caught in the room, were forced into a corner and had to hear the brutal threats. Johnny was the loudest of them all, but there was no profanity in his words; and he took the first chance that offered to wink at the helpless man on the bed. Arnold, ignorant of what he was supposed to know, pleaded in vain. Carson rolled up his sleeves and announced his intentions, staggering toward the bed. He collided with Johnny and they both fell. As Johnny scrambled to his feet he caught Margaret's eye and winked slowly. Then he let out a roar and blamed Carson for the fall. His eye caught sight of a calendar on the wall and he objected to the red numerals representing Sundays. Jerking out his guns he shot the numbers out, the bullets passing so close to Smitty that that valiant committeeman nearly broke his neck falling over a chair he backed against. A glass of water was shattered and then the guns became wobbly, covering everything in sight. Boasting that he could shoot out a fly's eye without touching the rest of the insect, he shot a spur off of Carson's boot and put a hole through Dahlgren's hat when he presumably aimed at the lamp on a shelf. Roaring and jumping, he accused Arnold of doing the kidnapping himself, and fired at a knot in the floor, missing it, and clipping a button from Fraser's vest. The committee was very drunk, but it was not so far gone that all instincts of self-preservation had fled, and it made haste to get out of the room. Smitty, finding the door blocked, and being in a hurry, went through the open window with remarkable directness for one in his condition.

"He ain't here!" shouted Johnny. "He's got away! Come on, fellers; we got to get him—*pronto!*"

"Where'd he go?" shouted Carson, stumbling over a

chair. He kicked it across the room and sat down suddenly. Being assisted to his feet, he staggered out toward the horses, the rest stringing after him. "Where'd he go?" he demanded at the top of his voice.

"Don't know," answered Johnny, hanging onto Dahlgren. "But he'll come back. Let's ambush him!"

"A'right; I'm tired of ridin'," declared Smitty. "Got forty feet of rope an' sycamore tree. Where'll we go?"

"Up on th' Juniper trail," said Johnny. "We know he don't hide in th' south; we'd a' seen him long ago. I know a good place, come on!"

It was a wonder how they ever mounted, but they managed it, all but Smitty, who had to be assisted to the saddle. Once seated, they were fairly well at home and followed Johnny along the ranch trail. An hour later Johnny and three of them were lying in the bushes at the edge of the Juniper trail, Smitty having been lost on the way. The sun was still warm, and the liquor potent, which was in no way checked by their inactivity, and snores soon arose. Johnny, smiling cynically at the prostrate figures, made a soft bed out of Carson's and Dahlgren's blankets and lay down to see it through. The night passed quietly and the early morning light showed four soundly sleeping figures. Higher and higher climbed the sun and one by one the men awakened, consumed by raging thirsts. Johnny raised himself on one elbow and looked around.

"I want a drink," he announced. "Gimme a drink, Fraser!"

"Ain't got none; I'm dyin' of thirst!"

Staggering to their feet they looked around, got their bearings and made a rush for their horses; and soon a miserable, sick committee pounded along the trail at its best speed, bent only on one thing—to get to Dave's.

Dave heard them coming and knew what would be wanted. He met them at the door and passed out a bottle;

consuming it eagerly, they straggled off toward their ranch, ugly and profane.

Johnny watched them go. "I was in desperate company, Dave," he said. "They was all primed to raise h—l out there, but I saw that nobody belongin' to that ranch knew anything about Squint, or th' Doc, that we didn't know, so I sort of coaxed 'em away. An' would you believe it, Dave, we was so petrified we got lost an' finally climbed down an' went to sleep right where th' idea struck us?"

"I allus was a great believer, Nelson," answered Dave. "That's mebby why I'm a pore man at my time of life. An' I admits that you has persuadin' ways. Now, I figgers it this way: Th' Doc up an' kills Squint; Squint gets even by kidnappin' th' Doc; after which th' Doc buries th' corpse an' throws away th' grave. But, I says, an' it's th' 'buts' that raise th' devil, how does Big Tom figger it? He ain't got my trustin' nature. An' how will Wolf figger it? An' all th' rest, after they get together an' wrestle things out? I'm glad you got a fast hoss, an' a clear trail. Where's Smitty?" he demanded.

"He was a weak brother," Johnny sorrowfully declared. "Th' last I saw of him he was fallin' off his cayuse about five miles northwest of th' ranch. First he fell back over a chair, backwards; then he fell out of a window, frontwards; an' when he fell off his cayuse he was goin' sideways. When it comes to fallin' I'll back him against anybody. What do I owe you for them two bottles of whiskey? They was amazin' medicine."

"Whiskey?" queried Dave. "Did you taste it?"

"I didn't," confessed Johnny. "I handed th' first bottle to Dahlgren, an' by th' time it got back to me there wasn't nothin' in it. Th' second bottle I gives to Smitty, an' I got left again. If I'd had a couple more I might a' got a drink. What makes you ask?"

"The first was brandy, an' th' second was gin," said Dave. "I reckoned mebby they'd like a change. Sorry you didn't get none of 'em."

Johnny looked at him reproachfully. "*I* ain't," he said. "Good Lord! Come, Pepper, there ain't no tellin' what this man'll do next. Mebby we won't see Smitty till next week—come, little hoss!"

VIII

♦

A Man's a Man

Having eaten enough to arouse the unqualified admiration of George, Johnny went to the kitchen and became busy with patch paper, tallow, and loading cup, and had just finished the twenty-fifth, and last, cartridge, when Two-Spot wandered in. George was out attacking the wood pile.

"Got 'em done, huh? Ain't it better to buy 'em?" asked Two-Spot, looking into the dining-room.

"It is, Ol' Timer, when you can. Just now I can't get 'em, so I got to make 'em."

His companion looked at the belt full of .45's. "Gimme a couple of them? I want to try somethin'."

Johnny complied. "Want to see if they fits?" he asked.

"What you mean?"

"Carson dropped his gun under Dave's floor. Who got th' one in th' road?"

"Don't say nothin'," begged Two-Spot. "Dave's an old woman, an' I don't want nobody to know I got it. He got th' other."

"What you goin' to do with yourn?"

"Keep it in my bunk. I might need it, sometime. I ought to have a rifle, though."

"I'll get you one," promised Johnny.

"What you goin' to do this afternoon?" asked Two-Spot, his face beaming at the thought of owning a rifle.

"Don't know yet."

"It's time you knowed about things out here. You ride up th' Juniper trail to th' second draw, in about an hour, an' I'll fix yore case rack so you'll know what cards are out. Yo're guessin' good, but Faro ain't th' only game where keepin' cases is better."

"Why go up there?"

"Well, purty soon it ain't goin' to be healthy for anybody to be too friendly with you," said Two-Spot, reflectively. "Anyhow, I'll be worth more if I ain't suspected of bein' too talkative."

"Th' best way to get suspected is to hide out when you don't have to," said Johnny. "You wander over to that grass spot across th' road from Dave's an' Dailey's in about an hour, an' lay down to rest yore lazy bones, with yore head toward th' saloon, so nobody can see that yo're talkin' steady. I'll try to get there first. It'll be innocent as sheep. Pepper hankers for live grass—an' she deserves what she hankers for."

"She does," responded Two-Spot. "Big Tom was in yesterday talkin' to Dailey. I heard him say somethin' about no supplies. They had an argument, an' finally Dailey says: 'All right; if you say so.'"

Johnny nodded. "I'll see you around front in about an hour."

About the time agreed upon Two-Spot stopped sweeping and looked out of the door. "Things look plumb peaceful, Dave," he said. "There's Nelson lyin' on his back over there in th' sun. He's too comfortable. Got a notion to stir him up."

"You stir up that broom an' get through," replied Dave. "You're sweepin' later an' later every mornin'."

The sweeper sighed and went to work again, with a vigor so carefully figured that Dave was on the verge of speaking about dust several times, but thought better of it each time. Finishing his chores, Two-Spot shuffled out and threw a can at the recumbent figure over on the grass. It stirred and raised its head.

"I'll turn you inside out," it threatened.

"You couldn't turn a glove inside out," retorted Two-Spot.

Johnny grunted. He was silent for a moment, and then inquired, "What you doin', Feather Head?"

"Workin'."

"Then you can't do it," regretted Johnny.

"What?"

"Bring over a couple of cigars."

"Show me yore money."

Johnny rolled over on his side and produced a coin, which he held up.

"Chuck it over," said Two-Spot.

"Yo're too busy," jeered Johnny.

"Chuck it, an' see."

Johnny sat up and sent the coin glittering through the air, Two-Spot making an unexpected catch. He went into the saloon, soon reappeared, and shuffled across the road. Sitting down at Johnny's side with his back to the buildings, he lit his cigar and lazily reclined. "I shore appreciates this rest," he sighed.

Johnny laughed outright. "Yo're worked to death," he jibed.

"Ol' Simon Verrier," began Two-Spot, "was th' first

owner of th' SV. He run it for twenty years, an' there wasn't nobody in all that time done any devilment an' wanted to repeat it. He was testy, big, an' powerful, an' he reckoned th' gun he packed was made to be used. He had Buck Sneed for his best man, an' an outfit what believed th' same as he did about guns. At that time there wasn't no boundaries, not fixed. Th' ranches sort of mingled along th' edges. Then th' Bar H got notions. It sort of honed for that valley, an' made a play or two for it. There wasn't no third. Ol' Simon an' Buck rid down to th' Bar H house an' spoke plain. Failin' to have any lines didn't bother them two. They picked th' ridges of th' dividin' hills an' says: 'Them's th' lines; stay on yore own side.' "

Johnny laughed for the benefit of any of the curious on the other side of the road.

"Ol' Frank Harper owned th' Bar H in them days. Poker an' drink was his failin's. His poker took Dailey out of th' saddle an' put him into th' store, an' it did th' same for Dave. It also put a mortgage on th' Bar H. More'n that, it kept him drinkin' harder an' harder—an' he was found dead one day in East Canyon; he had fell off his cayuse an' busted his neck. Th' mortgage was foreclosed an' th' present owners of th' ranch bought it in an' hired Big Tom to run it.

"Th' first thing Big Tom did was to forget all about them boundary lines. Ol' Simon an' him had words, an' when th' smoke cleared Big Tom had four slugs out of five into him; but he's got th' strength of a grizzly an' pulled through. About th' time he was ridin' around ag'in, on his own side of th' lines, Simon got his feet wet an' died in four days. I says that is downright funny. He had weathered stampedes, gunplay, northers, an' th' Lord only knows what for sixty years, an' then he goes an' dies from wet feet!"

Johnny nodded and pushed Pepper's muzzle from his

face. "Keep a-feedin', girl," he ordered; "I won't sneak away."

"Well," continued Two-Spot, "Buck buried th' ol' man, an' went right on runnin' things for th' heirs. He kept th' outfit together, an' th' ranch was payin' fine. Then th' heirs, eastern mutton-heads, didn't like his spellin', an' his habit of writin' letters when he was mad. They fired him, an' th' outfit, feelin' insulted personally, quit th' ranch an' went with him."

"I've knowed outfits just like that," murmured Johnny, reflectively.

"Th' new foreman came, an' went. Likewise th' second. They had a mark to live up to—it lays along th' top of them hills—an' they wasn't big enough to do it. Meanwhile th' SV was goin' to th' dogs. Then Ol' Arnold bought it an' came out to run it. He was a tenderfoot, an' came out for his health. Things was happenin' all th' time. His herds was shrinkin'. Rustlin', shootin', maverick huntin', an' them quicksands kept a-cuttin' his herds. Just about that time Big Tom dynamites th' rock slide in Little Canyon, an' forthwith loses his water. Then things happen faster than ever. He makes a play toward th' Double X; but th' Double X talks plain an' he reckons he better get th' SV."

Johnny sat up and stretched. "Let's play mumble-peg," he suggested, producing a clasp knife. "This steady talkin' is lastin' a long time, though I don't believe they hear you. I better cut in an' ask fool questions for th' looks of it."

"That'll come easy to you," retorted Two-Spot. "Well, things was goin' from bad to worse on th' SV. They couldn't keep an outfit. Them that wasn't scared away was bribed to quit. Dahlgren, Lang, an' Gurley all was SV men. Ol' Arnold borrowed three thousand dollars on his note in Highbank two years ago. Big Tom bought it an' holds it now. I think it's due next spring. Arnold has had to sell cows in small bunches to buy grub. There ain't no nat'ral increase, an' th' Bar H has a lot more calves an' yearlin's than Nature gave it. For th' last year th' SV ain't been bothered very much. It's so close to dyin' that I reckon Big Tom would rather wait a little longer an' have somethin' left to take when he does get it."

"Pleasant sort of a buzzard, Big Tom," said Johnny. "You missed then—gimme th' knife."

"Once in a while Lang or Gurley drive a cow into th' quicksands, just to keep their hands in. They work for th' Triangle, but really for Big Tom. They're handy for him, seein' that they has th' Triangle range next to th' SV."

"Them names are easy to remember," observed Johnny, surrendering the knife.

"Big Tom wants th' SV for its water," said Two-Spot. "That's what most folks think. *I* think him an' some friends he's got somewhere aim to get it cheap an' run it themselves."

"What's th' Doc doin', squattin' where he is?" queried Johnny.

"There was some talk about th' SV's title to that end of it lyin' west of th' main trail, an' I reckon he's there to file a homestead claim if it's needed; but I really don't know."

"An' these other ranches are settin' back an' watchin' a sick man, a woman, an' a kid get robbed?" asked Johnny.

"Th' Triangle is scared of th' Bar H," answered Two-Spot. "It had its lesson ten years ago, an' ain't forgot it. Hank Lewis ain't got no nerve—it's only gall. Sam Gardner is sore about th' game, but he's all alone. Lefferts an' Reilly don't care much, an' Lang an' Gurley are in Big Tom's pay."

"What about th' Double X?" demanded Johnny.

"They are so far off they don't take no interest. They keeps over there purty much an' don't meddle, an', besides, they has troubles of their own, with th' rustlin' goin' on along their west edge."

"How do you know all this?" said Johnny.

"I worked for Ol' Simon fifteen years ago. I drifted back last winter, an' I've been here ever since. Nobody knows me."

"Why are you tellin' me?"

"I hears a lot under th' floor, before you come, an' after," said Two-Spot. "My ears are good, an' I got some brains left—not much, but enough to put two an' two together. Likewise I'm feelin' sorry for them Arnolds. I don't like to see a gang of thieves robbin' helpless critters like them. An' there's more. When I was comin' down here I got ketched in a storm an' like to froze to death. I would have, too, if that Arnold gal hadn't rid across me, pulled me out of a snowbank, an' toted me to th' ranch. They took care of me till I was strong ag'in, an' fed me up. I was near starved when th' storm got me."

"But why are you tellin' all this to me?" demanded Johnny.

Two-Spot stretched and handed over the knife. "I'm an ol' man, now," he said, "but there was a time when I wasn't. You are a young man, an' square, fur's I know. You been hangin' 'round here playin' a lone hand against a bunch that'd cut your throat if they knowed what you've been doin'. There's a purty gal over on th' SV. She's square, too, an' helpless, an' lonely. She don't know what to do, nor where to turn. She layed in a nest of rocks one day an' was watchin' three Bar H punchers. A rattler showed up close to her, in a dead line with th' men. Scared to death of snakes, she was drawin' a bead on it, when a stranger offers her his cannon, an' his help. Then he gives her h—l about murder, an' goes away. But he don't go fur, only to Gunsight. He drives Squint out of th' country, kidnaps th'

Doc, an' keeps a bunch of hoss thieves from killin' her ol' man. I never saw you before; I don't know how many cattle you've rustled nor how many trains you've stuck up. What's more, I don't care. I know a white man when I sees one, an' I'm not gamblin' when I shoots off my mouth to you. I'm only a two-spot; but even two-spots has their good points. You can allus remember that there's a two-spot holdin' a six-gun under that there floor any time you need him."

Johnny sat up: "I'm sayin' you ain't no two-spot, neither."

"Before I forget it, I want to tell you th' rest of it," went on Two-Spot, anger heightening his color. "As I was sayin', th' gal's white, an' square. She's plumb different from some I've seen in th' cow-towns. Big Tom wants th' SV, but he wants her, too; an' 'though he ain't pesterin' her now, I know him too well to think he's give up th' idea. He never lets loose. Th' only reason he's let up is because he figgers he's got a better way; an' he's patient. Can you imagine a whiskey-smellin', big brute like him courtin' *her*? Can you imagine how he'd do it? An' lemme tell you, Nelson: I *am* a two-spot, for if I'd been any good at all I'd 'a' put a knife into him an' then took my medicine, like a man. I was near sick with disappointment when you shot th' gun out of his hand."

"How do you know anythin' about that nest of rocks, an' th' three men?"

"I know lots of things I ain't supposed to, an' one of 'em is that Big Tom ain't give up th' notion of gettin' th' SV, nor her, neither. There ain't no parson in thirty miles—an' Big Tom is terrible lazy. Sometimes I near sees red!" He glanced up the trail. "Here comes little Charley, leadin' a pack hoss. He's after supplies at Dailey's—" he stopped short and looked at Johnny, who was looking at him through narrowed lids. The same thought had come to them both at the same time. "I'm bettin' he don't get 'em," Two-Spot prophesied.

Johnny arose and stretched. "I'm bettin' he does," he drawled. "Reckon I'll go over an' swap gossip with Dailey," he explained, striding away.

Two-Spot watched him and also arose, going across the road and around the saloon. "I called it wrong," he muttered. "I'll copper that bet: *I* bets he does." A grin stole across his face as he shuffled toward Dailey's back door. "This'll be worth hearin', an' mebby I can get me a box of .45's; Ol' Eagle-Eye may be too cussed busy to pay any attention to *me*!"

Johnny sauntered into the store and seated himself on a box. "Howd'y, Ben."

Dailey smiled a welcome. "Been sunnin' yoreself?"

Johnny yawned. "Yeah; I'm shore lazy." He glanced out of the door at the boy who had ridden up and dismounted. "Reckon this is that Arnold kid," he observed.

Dailey hid a frown, and nodded. "I'm awful short of supplies today," he said. "Ol' Buffalo didn't bring me any—now I got to wait till he comes again."

Charley entered and handed a paper to the storekeeper, who took it, studied it, and then shook his head. "Bud, if you'd hunted through th' store you couldn't 'a' picked 'em any worse. I ain't got nothin' this calls for."

Charley's face fell. "Gee!" he said, "Peggy's out of almost everything. She said she just had to get these today." He looked around inquiringly. "Ain't that flour?" he asked, pointing to several filled sacks behind the counter.

"Them's flour sacks," answered Dailey, "but there ain't no flour in 'em now." He handed the list back to the boy. "No use, bud, you'll have to wait till Buffalo comes up again. He's too old to be of any account, anyhow, th' ol' fossil: he's allus forgettin' somethin', allus!"

Johnny held out his hand, his right hand. "Let's see it, Charley," he said, and looked it over. "I'll be cussed if that ain't funny!" he exclaimed. "This here is th' very same as I was goin' to get filled for myself, only mine wasn't all writ down like this. How'd you come to pick these things out, Charley?"

"Quit yore fooling," grinned Charley. "I didn't pick them. Peggy wrote that."

Johnny reached out and put the list in Dailey's hand. "Better begin at th' top, Ben, an' run right down," he suggested. "We won't get 'em mixed that way, or leave nothin' out. Let's start with one of them flour sacks, no matter what's in 'em."

Dailey flushed. "But I just said I was all out—"

"Yo're th' most forgetful man I ever knowed, except, mebby, Buffalo," said Johnny. "You ain't got no mem'ry at all. Don't you remember you found a lot of things you'd poked away an' forgot you had? An' don't you remember that nobody ain't told you, yet, not to sell me nothin'? That there paper is mine, now. I'm borrowin' it because I ain't got my own list writ out. That's writ so pretty an' plain, that it's pretty plain to read. If anybody gets curious, which they won't unless you tell 'em, you say that I gave you that an' wanted it filled. Now, we'll start with th' flour, like I was sayin'."

Dailey looked down the list and then up at Johnny. He was asking Fate why Nelson had to pick that particular time to visit the store. Johnny was smiling, but there was a look in his eyes which made the storekeeper do some quick thinking. He had no orders not to sell to anyone but the SV; and if Big Tom became curious he could put his questions to the two-gun man and get what satisfaction he could. In his heart he was in sympathy with the SV, and he had argued against refusing to sell to it.

"Nelson," said Dailey, slowly going behind the counter, "It's a good thing you remembered about that stuff. Are you takin' it to th' hotel?"

"Reckon not," answered Johnny. "Reckon I'll borrow Charley's pack hoss an' him to take it off to a place I knows of, where there ain't no mice. You'd be surprised, Ben, if you knowed how many mice there are in that hotel."

Charley looked from one to the other and, not knowing what to think or say, grinned somewhat anxiously.

"How's yore dad, an' yore sister?" Johnny asked him.

"All right," answered Charley. "But they was scared half to death yesterday when you an' them fellers came tearin' in, 'specially when you started shooting. You was awful drunk, wasn't you?"

"I don't remember much about it," confessed Johnny, "so I reckon mebby I was. We all got lost an' had to sleep out in th' brush all night. We was after th' coyote what kidnapped th' Doc, but we couldn't find him."

Dailey forgot to continue filling the list. He was holding a sack of sugar in his hand and drinking in every word. Johnny turned to him.

"Say, Ben," he said, "did I ever tell you th' story about Damsight?"

"You never did," answered the storekeeper, "not if my mem'ry ain't playin' me false again."

"It was scandalous," began Johnny, drumming with his fingers on the butt of a gun. "There was a bunch of hoss thieves fightin' a lone woman an' her crippled dad. An' what do you reckon th' men in Damsight did about it? Nothin'. Nothin' at all. They was so miserable, so coyote-livered, so scared to death that they didn't raise a finger.

No, sir; there wasn't a *man* in th' town. They were just yellow dogs, runnin' around in men's clothes an' pertendin' they was humans—a lot of yellow dogs, an' not a cussed thing more."

Dailey bungled a knot, and swore under his breath.

"Things went on like that for quite a spell," continued Johnny, "then a big storm come up, an' one by one them fellers who didn't see th' error of their ways was struck by lightnin'. They never knowed what hit 'em. It was just like th' miracles I've heard sky pilots tell about. Some of 'em did see th' error of their ways in time. They had a hard time in th' storm, but they pulled out alive. There seems to be a moral to that story; there ain't no use tellin' a story like that if th' moral is left out. An' I reckon th' moral of this one is: A man might be able to dodge lots of trouble, 'specially when it ain't near him all th' time; but when he's livin' right next door to th' lightnin', he can't dodge that. What do you think about it, Charley?"

"Gee! That's like the things Peggy reads to me out of the Bible," he replied. "Only it wasn't lightning, but floods, and pestilences, and things like that. Why, once a whole ocean opened up right in the middle and let a lot of people walk across it, but when their enemies got halfway over it, closed up, *smack!* and they were all drowned."

Johnny nodded gravely. "There's strange things happenin', even today, Charley, an' nobody knows when or where they *will* happen. Now, leavin' miracles out of it, let's put those packages on that hoss out here, an' see if Ben has forgot how to throw a diamond hitch. I'm bettin' a dollar he has."

"I'll take that dollar, parson," grinned Dailey. "Gimme a hand with th' stuff."

They filed out to the horse, loaded with packages, as Two-Spot slipped in the back door, and Dailey won the dollar. Watching the boy ride away, he turned and started for the store.

"Well," he said, over his shoulder, "I've put up my lightnin' rods, an' now I'm goin' to spit on my hands an' hold fast, for if this storm busts she'll be a whizzer. I'm aimin' to tell people right to their faces that Dailey's store sells to anybody that's got th' cash. You better look to yore tent pegs, young man."

IX

♦

Rolling Faster

The next morning Johnny mounted Pepper and rode toward the SV. He had some thinking to do and chose the conditions which he had found were most conducive to clarity and continuity of thought—the saddle. As he left the town behind he took Pepper into his confidence.

"Little hoss," he muttered, "we've gone just about as far as we can go without stirrin' up active an' personal troubles. We can't play our hand much longer without folks knowin' what we are doin'. What you an' me has got to do is plan things, choose th' leads, an' then stick to 'em in spite of h—l an' high water. An' we ought to figger on doin' somethin' solid for th' SV. Any fool can tear around an' smash things, an' we've got to do that; but you an' me ain't satisfied with no worthless pile of rubbish; we got to smash so we can pan that rubbish, sort of, an' get somethin' out of it. An' when a feller pans free an' wide on a cattle range, he most likely will get cows. What else can

he get? A man rocks gravel an' gets gold, if there's any
gold in it. A puncher, rockin' ranches, ought to get cows.
There ain't nothin' else *to* get. So we got to get cows, an'
now we got to find out how many cows we want. We can't
find out exact, but we can do better than guess at it. There's
a limit to this pannin' of ours—an' it ought to be what was
lost an' stolen. There's only one place where we can find
that out, an' we're ridin' that way now. Havin' decided
what we're aimin' for, we'll let it rest an' turn to somethin'
mighty close to us, ourselves; somethin' plumb personal,
an' terrible riled.

"You remember Tex Ewalt, don't you? You ought to, because he said some mighty nice things about you; I was
scared he'd turn yore head. Now, Tex was a wise boy; he
was amazin' wise. Do you remember what he told young
Slim-Shanks, that there Baxter kid, who was all tangled
up with tender feelin's? Mebby you don't; but *I* do. Slim-
Shanks, he was fair wallerin' in misery, an' actin' like a
sick calf. He hung around that gal's house like a dogie
'round a water hole. She must 'a' got sick of th' sight of
him. Every place she looked, there was Slim-Shanks, an'
his hope-I-die look. She couldn't get away from th' big
calf. Tex never missed anythin', 'specially if it was under
his eyes, an' one day young Slim-Shanks got bleatin' to
him, moanin' an' groanin' about his busted heart. What
did Tex tell him? I'll tell you. He says, slow an' deliberate:
'Slim-Shanks, some you got to rush; others you got to
pique—an' th' best way to do that, in most cases, is to let
'em think you can look at 'em, an' not see 'em. It takes
nerve—an' not one man in a hundred has got th' nerve.
Make 'em keep a-thinkin' of you without chasin' after
'em. Yore medicine ain't no good—you might try th'
other.' Now, just because Slim-Shanks didn't have th'
nerve ain't sayin' Tex was wrong. I've got to decide which

way is best, an' it's tough ridin'. Now you keep right still while I wrestle this thing out," and he became so wrapped up in the problem that he paid no attention to where Pepper was going; and she took him to the vantage point on the valley's rim from whence he had looked down at the posts and their enclosed quicksands; and arriving there, she stopped. Johnny was aroused from his abstractions by a voice which brought him back in touch with his surroundings, and with a jerk.

"Good morning," said Margaret.

He looked up, hauled off his sombrero and muttered something, his face in one instant giving up his secret. Then by an act of will almost brutal in its punishment, he mastered his feelings and nodded calmly.

"Good mornin', Ma'am," he replied. "You found me off my guard; I was miles away."

"Why aren't you?" she retorted, smiling.

"Meanin'?"

"If I were a man I'd stay near my friends as long as I could."

"I did, Ma'am; but there was too many wimmin', so I drifted."

"Ah! A woman-hater; or are you trying to forget?"

"They was all married," he grinned, "that is, all that had any chance to be. They married my friends, which took down th' bars on me. I was fair game when there was any blame which should 'a' been saddled on their partners. So I drifted. You can't use a gun on a woman, you know."

"So you came down here to be a mystery?"

"Mystery?" he laughed. "Me! Why, Ma'am, I'm so open I'm easy pickin' in every poker game I sets in. Folks know what I'm goin' to think before I start thinkin' at all."

"Then I must be even denser than I feared. I am very much interested in what you have been thinking, and haven't the slightest clue to it. Perhaps if I confess my helplessness you will take pity on me, and tell me what you are doing down here; and why?"

"Th' 'why' shows you ain't guessin' much, Ma'am," he replied, quizzically.

"Why did you join that crowd of drunken rowdies, and act worse than any of them?"

"Because when I acts bad, I'm harmless, an' they was not."

"Perhaps; but why did you join them?"

"I was afraid they might hurt themselves, or get lost."

"Father says that we owe you a debt of gratitude; I'm sorry that I shall have to disillusion him."

"I wouldn't give him no shocks, Ma'am, till his laig gets well. He ain't as young as he was."

"Why did you go to the trouble of seeing that we had supplies?"

"Invalids has got to eat, Ma'am."

"Why did you stop that—that brute—when he was entertaining his companions with his idea of humor?"

"A man would just naturally do that, Ma'am; it's an instinct."

"Why did you do what you did the day, and night, that my brother was stopped from going to Highbank for the doctor?"

"A man would do that, too; an' any doctor that forgets his duty deserves to be stole an' *made* do it."

"You realize, of course, that you are getting yourself into great danger?"

"I wouldn't hardly call it that, Ma'am," he replied, smiling. "There are different breeds. A man might get scared at a pack of wolves, an' not worry about coyotes, at all."

"Nevertheless, the danger exists; no man is proof against ambush. Why are you courting it?" she persisted.

"Folks don't ambush till they're purty shore about things; an' tryin' to keep 'em from gettin' shore is th' hardest part of it."

"Why are you courting it?"

"Ma'am, some things are so raw that they rile an honest man; I admits I'm riled considerable, which, of course, don't prove me to be honest. Even Two-Spot says he don't know how many cows I've rustled, nor how many trains I've stuck up. Th' number might surprise him."

"Somehow I feel that I should thank you for the favors you have done us," she replied; "but my opinion of western men, as *I* have found them, urges me to seek the motive first."

He flushed, and looked at her steadily. "Mebby that's th' motive yo're askin' about," he said gravely, and slowly continued: "You've asked me a lot of questions; can I deal a few?"

"It depends on what they are."

"They're personal—plumb personal. I'm wantin' to know if Big Tom holds yore dad's note for three thousand dollars." He waited a moment and, receiving no reply, asked two in one. "How many cows was on th' SV when you bought it, an' how many are on it now? Th' tally sheets ought to give that purty close—close enough, anyhow."

"Mr. Nelson, the first seems to be public knowledge. Mr. Huff holds my father's note for that amount. The number of cows, then or now, I do not know."

"Is th' note endorsed, an 'what security was given?"

"I endorsed it. The ranch is in my name."

"Uh-huh," commented Johnny. "Do you know where th' tally sheets are?"

"If you mean the books, they are on a shelf in the house."

"Ma'am," he said, earnestly, "I wonder if you would

mind copyin' off what there is about th' number of cows on th' ranch after th' last trail herd left, th' year before you took possession? An' how many cows there was this spring, or th' number of calves branded then?"

"Why do you want this?" she demanded. "Why should I go to that trouble, or tell you such things?"

"I don't know," he answered, "less'n you want to. You see, I'm curious about things, *too*. It's a failin' most humans have, a bad failin'. An', before I forget it, I'm goin' to ask you another: Judgin' from them posts down there along th' river, that's quicksand. Why ain't there more wire strung to keep th' cows out of it?"

"Because it is torn off as fast as it is put up. We have given up the effort; it is useless. *If you only knew—*" she checked herself, but the tears of helpless anger in her eyes could not be kept from forming.

"That's just it, Ma'am—if I only knowed," he replied, nodding. "I know a lot about that, but not about th' number of cows you have lost. I'm what you might call morbid, an' like to grieve about calamities. Would you mind gettin' them figgers for me? I'll be here about ten o'clock tomorrow for 'em, if you will."

"Yes; but *why* do you want them?" she demanded.

"I'm aimin' to put th' fear of God where it ain't been knowed for a long time, Ma'am," he answered, "an' be rewarded by th' company."

"What company?"

"I'll tell you that later, Ma'am. It will be th' last thing to be told, an' you'll never guess it alone. You'll have to be helped. An' when I tell you, you'll be surprised, an' wonder how it was that you couldn't guess such a simple thing as that. I'll be leavin' you now, to keep on a-rollin'."

She looked after him longer than he was in sight, lost in the solving of the riddle, which grew more formidable the more it was attacked, unless the instinct of her sex was given a fairer hearing. It hammered and hammered for admittance and gained entry enough to cause a flush to steal across her face, and was instantly thrown out bodily. But if it was refused its day in court, it could at least stand outside the walls and make its plea, and so it did. Somehow, when she was in the presence of this man she felt a sense of security that was almost like a lullaby. His easy, graceful poise, the quiet reverence which lay smiling behind his eyes and crept into his voice, the un-obtrusive but unwavering confidence he had in himself, and the feeling of tremendous reserve power which ema-nated from his every word, look, and movement seemed almost to bathe her with peace and security. And for one instant his eyes had looked at her and made her go sud-denly limp: she had felt suffocated, and the feeling had not been rebuked. Turning her pony's head, she rode slowly homeward, knowing that she would do whatever he re-quested, in spite of herself—and, strangely, she felt no fear.

Johnny, the vortex of an emotional whirlpool, rode into Gunsight and dismounted before the Palace, the action purely a matter of habit. Suddenly he shook his head with savage energy. "You fool!" he growled. "Keep yore mind on yore job, or somebody'll find you easy pickin'!" He looked around and saw Two-Spot grinning at him, and felt a quick irritation. "Well," he demanded sharply, "what's on *yore* mind?"

Two-Spot rubbed the disgraceful stubble on his face and grinned wider than before. "I was just a-thinkin' you need a guardian," he retorted. "Through with Pepper?"

Johnny regarded him unfavorably. "A man usually gets what he needs, if he tries hard enough. Tote that away an' gnaw on it! I'm through with Pepper."

Two-Spot watched him enter the saloon, and reflectively

scratched his chin. "Mebby there is some meat on that bone, but he didn't have to call me no dog, did he? Cuss him an' his trick of leavin' me knots to untie. He's crazy—crazy as a fox!"

X

◆

Freight for Highbank

While Johnny had been talking to Margaret there was being enacted a far different scene down on the Bar H. The foreman's anger at the condition of his three men when they had ridden in the day before was newly aroused by Smitty the following morning, when he arrived and shamefacedly slunk into the bunkhouse. Big Tom stormed about the room, demanding to know why he had to have such sheep in his outfit. He wanted to know what they had done, and they could not tell him; he asked where they had gone, and they replied to the SV. What had they done there? They could not recall. Dahlgren spoke vaguely of "going after th' feller," but had no idea who he was, or anything about it; but they all remembered that Nelson had been with them, in the same condition as themselves, and that he had terrorized the SV household. Smitty corroborated the last and rejoiced at the agility which had twice saved him. There were some things to which his memory clung.

Little Tom Carney and Wolf Forbes enjoyed their friends' discomfiture, at the same time sharing in some of Big Tom's disgust.

Wolf looked at them pityingly. "You make me sick!" he

sneered. "Fine bunch of sage hens—all you think about is liquor. How many times have I told you to let th' stuff alone, as long as you couldn't drink like humans?"

"Parson Forbes has th' floor," growled Carson. "Bein' human, he—"

"That'll do!" snapped Wolf. "You know how much parson there is to me. Who shot you out of a lynchin' bee back in Texas?" he demanded.

"Who got me into it?" demanded Carson. "They was watchin' that bank, an' I told you so!"

"You said so because you got scared at th' last minute!" retorted Wolf. "If I didn't have to waste half an hour arguin' with you—oh, what of it! That ain't excusin' you from bein' a fool day before yesterday, is it?"

"Mebby you could 'a' done better?" ironically queried Dahlgren.

"If he couldn't, I'd fire him!" snapped Big Tom.

"You wouldn't have to fire me; I'd quit!" replied Wolf.

"Then why don't you *do* somethin', 'stead of loafin' along that northwest line, pertendin' you has got to watch for rustlers an' them Double X fellers?" sneered Fraser.

"I will!" shouted Wolf. "I'm goin' to watch one man—not everybody on th' range. There's only one man in this country that ain't got a good reason for bein' here—that's Nelson—an' I'm goin' to watch him till I get what I want. Then mebby you fools will be able to bury him for me. Think so?"

"I'm wishin' you luck," said Smitty. "You'll need it. You be careful who it is that gets buried."

Wolf looked at him pityingly. "You pore sheep!" he said, "I'm sorry you was so lively in th' SV house, cussed if I ain't!" He turned to Big Tom. "Do I go?"

"You do," said the foreman. "Somethin' is wrong, an' we got to fix it. Stay as long as you has to. I'm not worryin' about *you*—but I *am* scared th' cows will eat these four chumps. They shore is green an' tender. When you startin'?"

"Right soon," answered Forbes, going out.

Big Tom stood in the doorway and watched his two-gun man enter the corral. His confidence in the wiry killer was not built upon hearsay. Cold, venomous, and quick, he was more like a rattler than his namesake. Up to now every man who had faced Wolf Forbes had faced death, a death swift and certain.

In due time Wolf rode northward and arrived in Gunsight, where he loafed around exchanging gossip with everyone he knew. George was coaxed to talk, but his stupidity did what a mediocre cleverness might have failed to do. He yielded nothing that Wolf could use, and a few things which did not suit Wolf's needs. With Jerry, the harness-maker, the conversation was a husk without a kernel, and the second-hand saddles were of no value to Wolf, who was searching down things which were against his own convictions. Two-Spot smoked his cigar and rambled aimlessly in his garrulous monologue. He was hopeless from Wolf's viewpoint. Dave's admissions were barren of information of a constructive sort. Fanning did not know anything, and Dailey was as bad. Wolf finally gave up the effort and went back to the Palace, there to await the coming of Nelson.

Johnny entered the saloon some time later, nodded to its occupants, but kept on going toward the rear door. "Be back after I eat," he said.

George looked out to see who was washing. "This ain't no time to come in for dinner," he growled.

"There's never no time like th' present. Can't help it," retorted Johnny. "While I'm washin' you rustle th' chuck."

"Wolf was here askin' about you," said George.

"That so? Well, that ain't no crime."

"Can he shoot better'n you?" queried the cook. "He says he'll shoot against anybody in this country with six-guns, any fashion, for a dollar a shot. Does it sound like money?"

"If I could shoot that good I'd be too rich to be restin' up between cow-punchin' jobs," gurgled Johnny through a double handful of water. "Reckon he knows what he's talking about, or he wouldn't risk bein' took up."

"Well," said the cook, "I've heard somethin' from them that seen it. If you aim to go ag'in' him, let me know ahead of time, will you?"

"I ain't aimin' to," replied Johnny.

"Hey! Wait!" exclaimed the cook, disappearing. He returned with a clean towel. "Use this. That ain't fit for a dog no more."

Johnny looked at the old one and smiled. It was quite some distance from the condition which called for a change of towels at the Delmonico. "Thanks. Th' dirt won't come off this one. What about dinner?"

"Gosh! I forgot," said George, dodging into the kitchen.

Johnny had company while he ate, for the cook entertained him with an account of Wolf's visit, to all of which Johnny paid polite interest, but he hastened his meal. Then he slowed again, for George was beginning to get at the kernels.

"Has he lost his saddle?" asked the cook.

"Don't know."

"Must a' busted it. He asked me if I knowed where there was a good second-hand one, gold or brass trimmed. An' say, keep yore eyes on yourn; he asked me if you tote it up to yore room nights. I didn't tell him you keep it in th' kitchen, but I did say there wasn't no room in yore room for no saddle. He wants one, I reckon, because he went to Jerry's when he left here."

"He wouldn't take my saddle," said Johnny. "He was havin' fun with you."

"Mebby," admitted George. "He was in a jokin' humor, 'cause he laughed an' says he reckoned you'd get th' courtin' bug, like all th' rest, an' go callin' on that Arnold gal. An' he says he'll bet you get throwed as hard as th' rest of 'em. I gave it to him right back an' says that you an' me are both alike—we hates wimmin."

"They've got to hustle if they rope you or me," laughed Johnny. "What else did he say?"

"That's all, that an' what I told you before. Where you goin' now?"

"Round to Dave's for a game of cards, mebby. Wolf an' Fanning are there," answered Johnny, taking his hat from the floor and arising.

"You ain't repeatin' what I said, are you?" asked George, somewhat anxiously. "He didn't mean nothin' by it."

"No; why should I? We all like to joke. I ain't got nothin' against Wolf. See you at supper," and Johnny went out the back door. As he neared the corner of the kitchen Two-Spot turned it and bumped into him. "Wolf's askin' about you all over town," he muttered, and then, louder: "Why'n blazes don't you look out?"

"Some day I'll chuck you over th' roof," retorted Johnny. "If you'd keep yore head up you'd see where you was goin'!"

"Keep yore own head up! You don't own this town!"

Johnny turned as he reached Dave's door. "If I did I'd run *you* out of it," and entering, he slammed the door behind him.

There was a laugh from the bar, where Wolf and Fanning were still chatting with Dave. Wolf swung the conversation around to the SV and kept it there as long as he could after Johnny joined them. He worked around to Squint, and to the kidnapping of the Doc, and endeavored to get a careless admission from Johnny; but the latter evaded the traps. He showed no disinclination to talk about Wolf's pet subjects and even helped the other to keep the conversation on them. He disposed of the committee's visit to the SV by saying that either the Arnolds knew nothing at all about recent events, or else they had been terrorized by the visitors' actions and had been unable to think clearly or even to talk. He admitted that the committee was in no condition to handle the situation, and that he was as bad as any member of it. As to what had really occurred out there the details were lost to him because he had been too drunk to know much about anything; and in this he was backed up by what Wolf, himself, knew about the other members of the committee. He remembered that he had got rough and that someone, he thought it had been Smitty, had yelled something about getting somebody, and they had followed him to do it.

"Give us another round, Dave," said Wolf. "I ain't losin' no sleep about th' Doc—" he began again.

Johnny interrupted him and led the way to a table. "Ain't no use standin' up all afternoon. We'll drink 'em over here, Dave."

Fanning and Wolf followed and the afternoon passed in cards, drinking, and talking. Johnny drank his liquor every round without losing his head, for which he was indebted to the proprietor. When supper time came around Fanning pushed back the table.

"I just can't make nothin' these days," he growled. "I never saw a game break so even; bet nobody's lost ten dollars."

"I won somewhere 'round four," laughed Wolf, arising.

"I'm out five," grinned Johnny. "Jim has played all afternoon to get that dollar. Goin' home, Wolf, or you aimin' to make a night of it?"

"Got to go," answered Wolf, "but I got sense enough to get my supper in town," he smiled. "Lead th' way, Jim."

"Hey!" called Dave,' "somebody gimme a hand with this keg?"

Johnny, who was last in the line, turned. "Be right after you fellers," he said, over his shoulder. "Where do you want it, Dave?"

"Up on th' buck, under th' bar. Easy, now! *Up!* Good."

"That was fine baby stuff I was drinkin' all afternoon," chuckled Johnny. "How'd you keep th' color?"

"Young man," smiled Dave, "yore business is punchin' cows; mine's sellin' liquor. Go on, now, an' eat. Keep yore wits sharp."

While they were at supper there was a commotion outside and four punchers from the Double X stamped in. "Hello, fellers!" said Slim Hawkes, throwing his sombrero on a table.

"It smells good," grunted Wilkes, and turned to the other two. "Boys, this is Nelson: Nelson, shake han's with Gus Thompson an' Bill Sage." He nodded coldly to Wolf, who returned it with reserve.

"What brought you hoodlums to town?" asked Fanning. "You fellers act scared of Gunsight. Ol' Dailey got you buffaloed?"

"I reckon it's th' twenty miles," said Slim, dragging a table up to the one then in use. "Hey, George! Can't you move faster'n that?"

"Go roll in a ditch," came the polite reply.

"Well," said Wilkes, "we was riding near th' east line when we discovers we was goin' to be late for supper, an' th' ranchhouse bein' near twenty miles, an' th' town only a couple, we votes for a *ho*-tel feed an' a session in Dave's." He turned toward the kitchen. "Hey, George! We saw dust above th' Sherman trail an' figgers it's Buffalo. Is he due tonight? Thought I'd tell you so you could get ready for th' old codger."

George stuck his head in the doorway. "Any more hard luck comin' this evenin'?" he demanded. "Can't somebody trail in after him so I can keep on a-workin'?"

"You get back in there an' go to work!" warned Thompson. "We're hungry!"

Wolf arose, paid his bill, and took up his hat. "Well, I'm off. So-long, fellers," and he strolled out.

"Which ain't causin' me no tears," muttered Slim. "He likes us 'bout as well as we like him. Here comes th' cook. Good for you, George!"

When the Double X squad had nearly finished, the rumble of a wagon was heard, rapidly getting nearer. Soon it passed the side of the hotel, and ceased.

"There's Ol' Allus-Late!" grumbled George.

"I'll give him a hand," said Johnny, arising and going out. "It'll save you time."

"Don't strain yoreself on *my* account," replied George.

"Hello, Buffalo!" said Johnny, starting to unhitch. "I'll put these boys in th' shed an' you go eat. George is ready for you. You can feed 'em later. If you'll trust me, I'll do it for you; I watched you last time."

"Much obliged, sonny," smiled the old man. "Yo're right obligin', but I allus eat last. They've done good today, considerin' th' load, an' nothin's too good for 'em."

"Thought you came back light?"

"Got near a load of hides—can't you smell 'em?"

"I shore can; but I'm so slow witted they didn't mean anythin' to me. Green, too?" he suggested.

"Yep," replied the freighter. "Picked 'em up all along; but I won't get no more this trip. Th' Triangle won't have none—an' I ain't goin' to go out of my way to call at th' Bar H. Got enough, an' I'm goin' right through. I'm allus glad to git home."

"I bet you are," replied Johnny. "Ain't anythin' more I can do, is there?"

"No, sonny; thankee. I appreciate yore help. I ain't as young as I used ter be, nor as quick. Thankee; good night."

Johnny went to the saloon, where a sudden outburst of voices told him he would find Fanning and the Double X men. As he opened the door a roar of laughter greeted him.

"Cussed if that ain't rich!" shouted Slim, jumping up and down. "Th' Doc stole from his peaceful fireside. Oh! Ho! Ho! An' to 'tend to his *friends,* th' SV! By th' Lord! Mebby we'll do it over again, ourselves, sometime, when we feel extra good!"

"I'd give ten dollars to shake han's with th' man that done it," laughed Sage. "I bet Big Tom rolled on th' floor when he heard it—an' bit th' furniture!"

"But how'd he get Squint's outfit?" demanded Wilkes.

Dave told of Squint's disappearance and of the deep sorrow darkening the sun, whereupon an eager discussion took place. This lasted until Dailey came in and impatiently pounded on a table with the butt of his gun.

"Order, Gents; order!" he shouted. "My time's valuable— who are goin' to be th' victims?"

"Shore we'll order!" yelled Slim. "All up, boys! Dailey's treatin'," and despite his protests, he found that he was. Soon after this a six-handed game got into full swing.

Dave's vexation grew steadily and passed the anger point without stopping. He was tired, and now his labors were only beginning. Two-Spot was living up to Dave's opinion of him, for he had not been much in evidence around the saloon since noon, and had not appeared at all since the Double X punchers had come in. Dave went to the front door and called, and then he went to the rear door and yelled, but received no response. Thinking that he saw a shadowy figure skulking in the darkness, he yelled again, and with no honeyed promises as the burden of his message. Glancing around in the darkness as if to penetrate it by an act of will, he shouted a threat and stamped back to the bar, slamming the door so hard that the windows shook.

"Come on, Dave!" cried Dailey, cheerful in view of his ownership of the last pot. "What you so slow about?"

"If he'd quit pickin' on Two-Spot," said Thompson, "an' tend to business, folks would like it better."

"Anybody that don't like it can get out!" retorted Dave. "He's *never* around when there's work to be did!"

The evening passed swiftly and midnight was not far off when Dave found it necessary to draw on the contents of the new keg, and he disappeared below the bar for a few minutes. Hardly had his head passed from sight when Two-Spot, closely watching the bar, slipped quietly through the back door and went silently to Johnny, where he poked his face close to the puncher's ear and muttered for a moment. Johnny nodded and looked over his hand again, while Two-Spot scurried for the door and safety, being silently threatened by Fanning, who thoroughly enjoyed the situation. Two-Spot looked fearfully around and closed the door behind him. He barely had time to get under the saloon when Wolf Forbes, returning from his short tour around the buildings, turned the corner of the kitchen and peered in at the window.

Johnny folded his hand, pushed out the required number of chips and grunted. "I'm trailin'—but I shore wish that man would stop. He must have about thirteen aces."

"I'm limpin', but I'm there," remarked Thompson. "Th' dust back here is awful."

"There ain't no call for you to put on airs," growled Slim, pushing in what he was shy. "I got four kings, but you don't see *me* quittin', do you?"

"You must a' picked up what I throwed away," said Dailey. "Havin' felt yore pulses I'm buildin' a house right out there in th' middle, where you all can see it, an' get covetous."

"Th' coyote that wins this pot," said Slim, "will shore have to get Ol' Buffalo an' his freight waggin' to haul—"

A roar of laughter burst from Johnny and he pushed back from the table, lying back in his chair so his lungs could have plenty of room. Dailey put his hand over the pile of chips he had just shoved in, Slim jumped and stared at the roaring puncher, the others manifesting their astonishment each according to his own manner. There was a resounding *whack!* from the bar and Dave, holding the top of his head with both hands, moaned as he looked wildly about, and then, glaring at the convulsed puncher, he made several pointed, pertinent, profane, and personal remarks and slowly went down again to finish his task.

Slim scratched his head. "Well," he drawled, "I allus knowed I was bright an' witty, but I never knowed that I was *that* good. I likes a man that pays me a compliment like that."

"Th' loud an' screechin' roarin' of th' wild jackass is heard nightly over th' land," observed Sage. "It has scared me plumb cold—I'm layin' down as fine a pair of four-spots as I've ever held. I ain't got th' nerve to give 'em the backin' they deserves. Will somebody lend me their gun?"

"I cussed near shot," said Wilkes.

"What's that?" demanded Dailey. "Don't you do nothin' like that! He's a part of my profits. Now, if some-body will stuff a hat in that cave, I'll proceed from where I left off. I've raised her till she sags in th' middle—who's got any props?"

"I allus play poker by th' weather," said Thompson. "When it's dry an' hot, I calls, an' when it's hot an' dry, I raises. Bein' dry an' hot, I hereby calls. Dave, bring me a box to put it in."

"Don't you bother Dave," chuckled Dailey. "He's puttin'

hoss liniment on his bald spot—from ear to ear, an' eyes to spine. I can tote this home in a couple of trips."

Johnny, weak and tearful, drew up to the table. "I was just a-thinkin'," he said. "Where are we now?"

"Was you?" queried Fanning. "Then don't you never do no thinkin' nights after I've gone to bed."

Dave emerged again, grinning. "Beats all," he muttered, "how our sins foller us around. Pore Squint; I reckon his mem'ry's with us. I won't rest till I knows what was done with him."

In the middle of the next game Johnny broke out again and Dave reached for the mallet.

"I ain't what you'd call superstitious," said Dailey, "but I lost that last pot to a man who didn't even know where he was. Every time I hears a jackass warble I has bad luck. I'm obeyin' th' warnin' an' gettin' out of this game while I have th' holes left in my belt. What's more, I'm goin' home; I know when it's time to let go."

"Pore Dailey," moaned Fanning, "we all got a little of it tonight—an' I'm sleepin' with a gun under my piller, you bet!"

"It's time we quit," said Slim, arising. "We got twenty miles to go—an' while mebby it ain't so dark as I've seen it, it'll be dark enough to keep us from racin'. But before I go I'd like to find out somethin': Will somebody please tell me what I said, that second time, that was so funny?"

"It wasn't nothin' you said, Slim," answered Wilkes; "it was yore face—but I holds that it's cussed unpolite for anybody to laugh right out loud about a man's misfortunes."

"Nelson, I begs yore pardon," said Slim. "You has a proper an' fittin' sense of humor. Let's have one more round before we ride home an' wake up th' boys to tell 'em what happened to Dailey. How'd you come out, Nelson?"

"I got plenty—a great plenty, thank you," answered Johnny, throttling the laughter which threatened to burst out again. "I'm heavy with it. Dailey will foller me around tomorrow tryin' to get me into a seven-up or Californy-jack game in his store, where he's got lookin' glasses an' cold decks. Well—here's how." Putting down the half-emptied glass he turned, nodded, and went out. When he closed the door behind him he became alert as a cat in a strange cellar and slipped around the kitchen, hand on gun. Once inside the hotel he began laughing again, silently this time, and went hurriedly up to his room, where he lit the lamp and began to undress. Removing his boots he stood up, and in such a position that the shadow on the wall would tell any watcher that he was removing his shirt. Blowing out the light, he hurriedly put the garment on again and, carrying the boots in his hand, slipped silently down the stairs and into the kitchen, where he took the lariat from his saddle and went swiftly to the front door, where he listened as he slowly opened it. Satisfied that no one was watching, he slid out sideways, closed the door gently behind him and, going along the side of Dailey's store, he slung the lariat around his neck, put the boot straps between his teeth and, dropping on all fours, crossed the road and disappeared into the darkness on the farther side.

The noise around at Dave's took on sudden volume as the Double X punchers went out to their horses. Laughing and joking, they swung down the trail at a lope. Fanning and Dailey said good night to Dave and departed.

Gunsight instantly grew quiet and soon a figure emerged from Dave's horse shed and was swallowed up in the darkness to the east of the main trail, and soon thereafter the hoofbeats of a horse were heard by one pair of listening ears in town. Two-Spot crept out from under the saloon and stood up, shaking his fist at the sound, which moved southward. Then the hoofbeats grew more rapid as Wolf increased the pace of his horse.

Down the trail, where it narrowed to pass between two clumps of bush, a coatless, hatless figure crouched in the left-hand thicket, the coil of rope in his left hand held low down. At irregular intervals he seemed to be suffering from an attack of ague, for he quivered and shook; and there came from him strange, subterranean rumblings and rusty wheezes which he tried to muffle with an arm. As the hoofbeats coming from town grew rapidly louder and nearer he tensed himself. The pounding rang out loudly now, the soft jingling of chain and ornaments distinguishable in the greater sound, and soon the vague figure of a mounted man burst out of the darkness and swept past the clumps of brush. The waiting man on foot straightened his body and arm at the same moment, and at the instant the rope grew taut he pulled it sharply and leaned back with all his strength. There was an exclamation and a crash, and the man who had waited ran swiftly forward, hauling the rope in hand over hand. Kneeling at the side of the prostrate figure he slipped the guns from their holsters and threw them into the brush, and then fell back to work with the rope and the victim's kerchiefs. With the gagged, bound, and blindfolded man on his back he went up the trail toward town.

Gunsight had been quiet for over an hour when a strangely shaped figure staggered across the road west of the hotel and steadily neared the shed. It came slowly around the corner and stopped at the side of the big freight wagon, where part of it went to the ground, while the remainder, appearing in the form of a man, worked at the ropes closing the tarpaulin at the rear of the wagon, and soon had it open. He stepped back for a moment as a reminder of what lay behind it struck his nostrils, and again he was seized with a recurrence of the peculiar malady which had seized him frequently in the last hour. At the muffled sounds which came from him, the figure on the ground writhed as if in sympathy and endeavored to repeat them. The attack passing, he drew a long breath and plunged his head and shoulders into the opening he had made and worked hard for a few minutes; and when he stepped back he had several pieces of rope in his hands, which he had taken from a bundle of skins. Drawing a few deep breaths he moved around the wagon and bent over the figure on the ground, exchanging the pieces of rope for his own lariat, but not without a struggle which made it necessary for him to sit on the figure and exert his strength. Tying good knots in the dark on arms and legs which writhed and twisted was slow work, but it was necessary that it be well done, and when he arose to his feet he was assured as to that. Bending over, he picked up the figure and carried it to the rear of the wagon, where he pushed it headfirst into the opening made for it, despite its contortions and gurgled profanity. Again his head and shoulders disappeared under the tarpaulin, and when he straightened up he knew that his victim was so securely lashed to the wagon box that it would be impossible for him to move around, no matter how much he bridged and wriggled, no matter how much the wagon jolted. It was a job which demanded care, and had received it. Satisfied as to the conditions inside the wagon, he now turned his attention to the outside, which must be proof against telling anything to the observing eyes of the old buffalo hunter. He carefully replaced the tarpaulin as he had found it, even to its folds, and he duplicated the knots he had untied. Pausing a moment to think, he dusted canvas and ropes, cogitated as to his own footprints, which Old Buffalo would not fail to notice, if the light permitted. He got his rope, coiled it, and with this for his tool he effaced the prints and then went to the horse shed. When he reappeared he was leading a horse whose color melted into the darkness like a lump of charcoal in ink. They passed in the dark like the passing of a cloud and it was not until some minutes later that the drumming of hoofs rang out on the trail, bound southward in search of a saddled, but riderless, horse, which should be found in that direction. It would not do for it to be seen by anyone but themselves while it bore the riding gear of Wolf Forbes.

A blot on the ground near the horse shed arose. Two-Spot was in pain and the tears were flowing down his unwashed cheeks, while spasm after spasm racked him. Holding a six-gun limply in his hand, he stumbled and staggered away from the buildings, to some place where he could give free vent to the agonizing mirth which threatened to choke him. Coming to a weed-filled gully he sank into it and lay with his face buried in his arms. Minutes passed before he got control of himself and then he rolled over weakly and stared up at the star-filled sky, inert and sore, for he knew not how long.

"If it was anybody but Wolf," he moaned, "it would be bad enough, but it's ten times worse as it is. Wolf Forbes, th' killer; Wolf, th' two-gun badman, th' terror of th' range; th' cool, deliberate, stuck-up Wolf, who walks with stiff-laigged dignity, an' holds his nose up in th' air! Wolf Forbes—oh, my G—d! Gimmie air! Snoopin' wise-like all over town, fillin' his ears; smart an' chipper, cold an' wise! Oh, me! Oh, my! Sneakin' 'round from winder to winder, listenin' at th' cracks—as if I didn't see his bow laigs passin' back and forth. Tryin' to learn if it was Nelson who stole th' pill-roller, an' did for

Squint. Hearin' what them Double X fellers had to say about it, an' *him*; standin' there bilin' with rage! Oh, when this night's work gets spread over th' range there'll go up a laugh that'll shake th' sky! If he's got th' nerve to come back an' face that music he'll have to *use* them guns of his'n. An' he can't fight 'em all, good as he is. *Wolf*, huh? He started out as a wolf, but he'll change his spots afore he gets to Highbank, an' his scent, too! He! He! He! He'll turn into a polecat—a hydrophoby skunk! Oh! Me! Oh! My! Polecat Forbes, th' strong man! Oh! Ho! Ho!"

While he rested, his merriment slowly died and gave way to venom, and he sat up to shake his fist in the direction of the wagon.

"You earned it, cuss you!" he snarled. "Bound up like a bundle of rags, an' headed for Highbank, you are! Forty mile, it is; forty mile of sun, an' jolts, an' stink, an' flies, an' achin' bones, an' cuttin' ropes. Forty mile of heat an' dust an' thirst; forty mile of rage, of thinkin' it all over; forty mile of h—l on wheels—that's what it is—forty mile of h—l on wheels! Fourteen hours, says I, but I hopes it's twenty. Time enough for thinkin', you blackguard. 'Member th' time you kicked me off'n Dave's hitchin' rail? 'Member how funny it was, huh? 'Member how I said I'd get square with you, an' how you kicked me ag'in, an' made me dance to yore blasted guns? I was a harmless ol' man; but it was funny, just th' same. Oh, I'm wishin' I dast go over there an' tell you all I'm thinkin'—yore ears would bother you more'n yore nose if I could. If I only knowed you wouldn't come back; if I only knowed that! It was *me* that did it. I told Nelson about you, an' I was hopin' you'd get blowed apart; but this is better, cuss you! When yo're dead yore troubles are over—an' you'll wish you was dead when *this* story gets out. An' if you keeps yore nerve, an' finds out who done it, you *will* be! Wolf? Wolf? Huh? I got a better name for *you*!"

He arose and went back toward the saloon, and had not quite reached it when he heard the soft steps of a horse on the sand and he dropped to the ground, his gun lightly held and ready. In a moment he made out a man leading a horse and he arose, which turned the approaching figure into a blur of action. He could feel the menace of the other's gun.

"It's me—Two Spot," he whispered hoarsely.

The other relaxed and came nearer. "You tryin' to get shot?" came a low, tense voice. "What you doin'?"

"I had to be *dead shore* who it was that's tied up like a bundle of trash in th' waggin," answered Two-Spot. "You ridin' south bothered me. I'll never forget this, *never*!"

"That's th' first thing you got to do—till you hear about it from somebody else," replied Johnny, feeling at his saddle. "Here," he said, untying a Winchester and holding it out. "I promised you a rifle—an' this is somethin' else you want to forget. I got one of his six-guns tied under my slicker roll—you see that you don't forget that it belongs to me. I'll give you th' cartridges tomorrow—they're in th' belt over my shoulder. You rustle under that floor, it's near daylight."

A grin of delight swept over Two-Spot's face as he grasped the weapon, and he scurried to his nest. But there was one thing more to make his happiness complete—he had to see the start of the wagon. And he did not have to wait long. With the first blush of day Old Buffalo appeared, hitched up his horses and urged them to begin their long pull to Highbank. The wagon squeaked and rumbled and passed from the watcher's sight; and when the last sound died out in the south,

Two-Spot went to his blankets to lie on his back and gloat over the miseries of Wolf as his vivid imagination pictured them.

Down on the Highbank trail, bound and helpless, and exhausted by his frantic efforts to free himself, Wolf Forbes seethed with rage, which later would burn itself out and bring an inert apathy to ease him; and two things seared his memory: The mirth of the man who had trapped him, and the sound of a horse's hoofs pounding at top speed down the trail. They had gone southward, toward the Bar H, the Triangle, and the faint trail leading to the Double X. With these meager clues he built several edifices of speculation, not one of which could be singled out in preference to the others. His friends were notorious practical jokers, and he had done his share at it. The Double X outfit hated him, and Nelson had cause to wish him out of the way if his suspicions concerning Nelson were well founded. Would his unthinking friends carry a joke so far; would the Double X think of and carry out the play; and if Nelson felt that he was in danger, would he be fool enough to do a thing like that? In his place Wolf would have killed. But he would hunt out the perpetrator, whoever he was, when he came back—*and he was going back!*

XI

◆

"The Tinkling of the Camel's Bell"

Johnny had a late breakfast, according to George.

"You look like you made a night of it," said the cook.

"I reckon I did," replied Johnny, yawning; "I didn't get much sleep."

"Did Wolf make any remarks about shootin'?"

"When?"

"Last night."

"Didn't you see him start for home?"

"Thought mebby he come back to play."

"He didn't come back to play," replied Johnny. "I'm goin' for a ride an' see if I can wake up," he said, and he did.

As he loped along the Juniper trail he made a confidante of Pepper.

"Dearly Beloved," he muttered, "we are goin' to be th' center of a whole lot of eyes before long. People will pay attention when they sees us. We are going to be right popular—an' *un*popular. If you knowed all th' trouble I'm brewin' for us, you'd reckon I wasn't no friend at all. But I know yo're with me to a finish, an' not worryin' about whose finish it's goin' to be. I've got to do some thinkin'. You listen.

"Wolf was sent up to find out who's been ticklin' th' Bar H with a prong, an' he didn't have no luck. Knowin' he was losin' patience, I knowed what a man like him would do when he came to th' end of it. He'd pick a fight an' start shootin'. Now you know I ain't scared of Wolf, but you don't know that I wasn't ready to start no open war just yet. I'll admit I hope I don't have to start none, but I wouldn't bet two bits on *that*. So what did I do? I sent him away, Pepper, but he'll come back. Uh-huh, he'll come back if he's got th' nerve—an' it'll take some. An' if he does you an' me'll have to step around right lively. If he figgers right he'll come back a-shootin', for he'll be all riled up. I couldn't have him trailin' me wherever I went, could I? Th' man wasn't reasonable—he didn't allow I had any rights.

"Now, then: Wolf won't be back before tomorrow mornin'. I'm bettin' he won't be able to sit a saddle before mornin', an' that brings him here tomorrow afternoon. Th' Bar H won't hunt for him, thanks to what you helped me do last night. If they find his cayuse without his saddle they'll think he come down an' got a fresh hoss. An' all we want is to see that little Peggy girl, an' go over to th' Double X. Then we'll turn th' Bar H upside down, an' let Wolf square up for his buggy ride if he wants. An' I'll give odds that he'll want to."

When he reached the rendezvous he was early and he grinned as he realized his unusual impatience. "Pepper, things are shore happenin' to me. I'm what you might call sober-drunk. Just settin' here quiet, lookin' at that little valley is plumb thrillin', little hoss—an' *would* you cock an eye at that gent down there! An' cussed if there ain't a cow in them sands! I reckon, mebby, it's goin' to be *real* thrillin' before long."

He jammed his sombrero tight on his head and waited, tense and eager for the overt act he felt sure would come, and send him down the hill like the swoop of a hawk.

Down in the valley Lang looked searchingly around and then, tying his rope to the remaining strand of wire, urged his horse ahead. He was standing up in the stirrups, his weight on one leg, leaning to one side to keep the rope from pressing against his other leg, his back to the hill, and he did not see the black thunderbolt dropping down the green slope; and so intent was he upon the work in hand that his ears did not give him warning of the charging enemy in time to attempt deliberate and well-sighted long-range rifle shooting. The wire had been torn loose from the first post and was straining at the staples in the next one before he had any intimation of the swiftly approaching danger. Surprised and galvanized into action by the sound of rolling hoofs pounding over a stretch of bare, hard ground, he turned in his saddle, flung a glance at the racing thoroughbred and jerked his rifle from its sheath. His horse, feeling the rope rub against one of its hind legs, kicked viciously and pranced. Twisting from one side to the other, rifle at his shoulder, Lang found himself in too awkward a position for well-aimed shooting against the racing enemy, who lay along the back of his horse and presented a discouragingly small target. Sliding the rifle back into the sheath, Lang worked desperately at the rope, trying to free it from the saddle. Cursing his clumsy fingers, he suddenly realized the trouble. "D—n my soul, if somebody ain't *knotted* it! Oh, th' cussed fool!"

Giving up the attempt, he reached again for the rifle, swiftly changed his mind and pulled angrily on the reins to back his horse so he could get the other end of the rope and free it from the wire. "Staked out like a calf!" he gritted. Hauling in the rope, he at last grabbed the knot, and swore again. It had pulled so tight that precious seconds were wasted before he could free it, and his temper was not sweetened any by the two bullets which Johnny, firing at long range, sent on a gamble. They missed him by feet, but had their effect. Dropping the freed wire, he spurred around to face the swiftly nearing danger and jerked out his Colt, firing hastily. Johnny now was standing up in his stirrups to offset the bouncing of the horse and his shots were coming nearer all the time. Lang swerved his horse suddenly and fired again, but the animal was prancing. Johnny's reply struck the horse and the pain-racked animal, leaping convulsively, bolted for the gap between the posts, straight for the quicksands. Lang, frantic at this new danger, fought the animal with one hand, trying desperately to turn it, and used the gun with his other hand, doing neither well. Johnny, drawing his second Colt, replied to Lang's last shot and the Triangle puncher, dropping his weapon, sagged forward in the saddle and fell sideways into a grassy hollow, where he sprawled grotesquely as his horse, freed of his weight, leaped forward at greater speed and dashed out onto the treacherous sands, stopping only when it became mired beyond the possibility of further progress. It floundered and strained with frantic energy until exhaustion made it pause, and then stood trembling, doomed by the inexorable sands which slowly crept up its quivering legs and caused its eyes to become wide with terror.

Johnny flashed past the prostrate puncher and then suddenly became aware of his danger. Pepper, holding her speed, kept straight on for the sandy trap. Johnny tried to swing her and she responded, but not enough in the restricted space and when he had pulled her back on her haunches she had crossed the quicksands' edge and slid, wallowing and struggling, to a stop far from safety. Her instinct warned her of her peril and she struggled frantically to retrace her steps, but succeeded only in turning part way and had to give up the fight momentarily, with her side to the firm ground she had just quitted. Panting and shaking with terror, she looked around appealingly at her rider, who shook his head.

"No use, Pepper Girl," he said. "You'll only get in deeper. Rest yourself an' wait—I'm th' only one who can help you now—an' I never thought I'd do a thing like that to you; an' I ain't goin' to do it till I has to. Good little cayuse—th' best I ever laid eyes on, an' I've seen th' best there was. We've had our last ride together, little hoss, an' mebby we'll go down together, too. Easy, girl; easy," he coaxed, and not wholly in vain. "You just rest an' mebby we'll make another try after I see what there is to be seen. We got th' coyote that caused it, anyhow!"

His words were contradicted almost as soon as spoken, for a derisive voice from the grassy hollow rang out in exultant laughter. Johnny, fearing a shot, although the fear was from instinct rather than from reason, fired instantly at the sound, and then lowered the gun. Lang was unarmed and could not get to his Colt without exposing himself.

"He won't get it while I'm alive," muttered Johnny, reloading his other gun.

"Shoot!" exulted Lang; "but you better save th' last for yoreself. That's right, *shoot!*" he jeered, as Johnny, stung by the words, wasted another cartridge. "Yo're comin' as close as anybody could," he continued. "You can shoot like th' hammers of h—l, an' that makes it all th' funnier. Shoot again!" he invited, holding up his hat. A hole appeared in it, to his surprise, but he jeered again instantly. "Fine! *That's* shootin'. Shoot again!"

Johnny stroked Pepper's neck and then leaned over and looked down. "Not so deep," he muttered.

"Shore; look it over," shouted Lang. "That's what I'm aimin' to do. I'm aimin' to look it over, right to th' finish. I've allus wondered how a man would act in them sands, an' I'm goin' to find out now. Mebby if yo're polite I'll put you out of yore misery when yore chin gets wet. Then I'll ride over to th' Bar H an' tell 'em who kidnapped th' Doc, an' did for Squint. I've seen shows, but this here is goin' to be th' best of th' lot."

Johnny's eyes glinted and he fired twice in succession— then a third shot after an interval, endeavoring to force Lang to keep his head down while his other hand worked swiftly under his slicker roll. Emptying one gun, he slipped it back into its holster and used the other, still struggling with the slicker. At the last shot in the second weapon he worked Wolf's gun loose and slipped it into the holster on the far side from Lang. Standing up in his stirrups he gave vent to a burst of profanity and hurled his Colts, one after the other, at the hidden observer.

Lang looked up in time to see the first gun bounce from the ground and then the second fell close to it. He laughed nastily and ducked down again as Johnny drew the heavy Sharp's from its sheath and sent an ounce of lead smashing into the sand and pebbles close to his head. Another, another, and another struck the top of the ridge, the last striking a rock and screaming high into the air. Then Johnny gripped the heavy weapon at its muzzle with both hands, stood up in his stirrups, whirled it around his head and sent it through the air toward the hidden man. It struck loose sand and slid ten feet in a little cloud of dust. The Triangle puncher looked out again, chuckled, and slowly emerged from his place of refuge.

"I calls that kind," he laughed. "There *wasn't* no use of lettin' good weapons like them be lost. I can use 'em all—an' just for that I'm goin' to end yore misery like I said I might. First," he said, going over to the nearest Colt and picking it up, "I'm goin' to load this gun an' do somethin' for my hoss an' that cow." He walked unsteadily toward the edge of the sands, pulling half a dozen cartridges from his belt as he advanced. Reaching the danger zone, he tried each step before putting his weight into it and slowly advanced to the last tuft of grass, where he stood, swaying slightly as it moved gently under his weight. The sand at its outer edges moved a little and changed color as the water flooded and receded in it. "Reckon this is th' jumpin' off place," he said. "You'd be plumb tickled if I fell in, wouldn't you?" he jeered. "Well, I ain't aimin' to. I'm figgerin' on loadin' this gun—*this* way: Number One," he said, sliding a cartridge into the cylinder, "is for my hoss; Number Two is for th' cow; Number Three is for a hole through yore hat; *this* one is for yore hoss when only its head is out, or as soon as you jump off. I'm givin' you that chance to help it—an' to save my valuable time; these two are for yore head when yore chin gets under. One'll be enough, but two will be dead shore—I might miss th' first to hear you cuss."

Lang raised the Colt and put his horse out of its misery; then he did the same for the cow. "That's what I call fair shootin'," he said. "Of course, you might 'a' done it faster— but I'm in no hurry. Now, this next shot has got to be dead shore if I put it high enough in yore hat to miss yore head—an' I ain't aimin' to hit that *yet*. So if I takes plenty of time, don't you get jumpy."

He raised the gun above his head to increase the torment and there was a flash and roar at Johnny's hip. The Triangle puncher's hand opened and the gun dropped behind him as a look of great surprise flashed to his face, and remained there. Twisting sideways, he fell face down, sprawled full length upon the greedy sands.

"There, d—n you!" gritted Johnny. "Th' show's over, for *you!*" He brought the gun back on its mark, but did not release the hammer again. There was no doubt, this time, about Lang. He let the hammer down on an empty chamber and slid the weapon back in his holster.

Reassuring Pepper, he glanced down and saw that her legs were being pulled to the sides, which sprawled them out. "Slow," he said, and looked again to make sure. "Mighty slow. This stuff is different in places—but d—d sure," he added bitterly. "You take it easy, Pepper Girl. I won't let it last much longer—'though it's goin' to take a lot of nerve. Good little hoss—good little Pepper Girl."

He now knew there was no hope of riding out. He knew quicksands—he had seen them on other ranges, but never such a one as this, for the others had been small—the size of this bed was far beyond his experience. He studied it and watched the tremors running through it—the sand seemed to be moving and new surfaces to be forming. Wet spots appeared, became covered with water and then were uncovered again as it drained away. Hollows slowly formed here, slight bulges there, but with no stability. Undulations showed frequently near the bodies, which were slowly sinking. The cow was nearly under. This trap had no definite edges, for it met and merged with the honest sands around it in such a way as to show no lines; but he knew, by looking at the tracks of his horse, which, strangely enough, had not been quite obliterated, that he was too far from firm ground to have any hope of getting out in that direction. He cogitated upon the possibilities of escape in other directions, for it was possible that along some other course he might find firm earth closer to him. To his right was a grass tuft, not as far from him as was the place where Lang's body marked the other edge, but it lay too far away. Behind him the nature of the sands was evident for a like distance, and questionable for half as far again. To his left was the Triangle horse, which he could gain by leaping from his saddle; beyond that, half as far, was the cow, still useful if used soon enough and not rested on for too long. He believed that the cow could not have crossed much of the sands before becoming mired, and this gave him renewed hope. It was the only way worth trying with a chance of success. At the best it would be a gamble, but while those two bodies remained above the surface they would serve as stepping stones. From the body of the horse he would do the last kind act in his power for Pepper, and then, throwing away the gun to save its weight, jump to the cow. This would be easy; but from there on he would need all his strength and wits and will. Looking beyond the cow, he searched for something to put his rope on, and found nothing nearer than the fence posts, which were too far away. And then, while he looked, he saw water ooze up and cover the sand some distance beyond the cow, and he admitted that his case was hopeless; and as he admitted it the cow disappeared from sight.

Hopeless, but not to be submitted to without a struggle. He would neither sit apathetic nor frantic, nor turn the gun on himself. Hope had gone as a matter of reasoning; but something had taken its place which in power transcended hope—cold rage, and a savage, defiant hatred for that deadly, silent trap; a rage such as he seldom had felt before, which urged him to tear and rend the sands as though they were a sentient enemy. Hope, living in him, had been faint-hearted when he thought of how ghastly the thing was; how he, a man with all a man's strength of body and mind and will, mounted on the finest horse for hundreds of miles, armed with a weapon, the use of which no man knew better; how he could not do a thing to save his life. What is hope but a wish? But the dynamic rage which crept through him was a force of another kind—defiant, savage determination to cheat the workings of that mobile bed of horror, or go down to a death made glorious by the fight.

He shook his fist at it. His thin lips drew back over set teeth in a snarl primitive in its timbre and in the savage nature behind it. "D—n you! You may win; but I'll make that winnin' hard!"

Gripping the pommel he climbed up onto the saddle and poised for the leap. Could he believe his ears? Glancing around, he saw a woman tearing down the valley toward him, the drumming roll of her horse's pounding hoofs growing ever louder. What a sound! What music ever was so sweet? What sight had ever been so beautiful as that trim figure mounted astride a horse which seemed to spurn the grass in its arrowy flight? Hatless, her hair streaming behind her like a glorious battle flag of Hope, came Margaret, and her voice rang out like a trumpet.

"Wait!"

Hope returned again to bulwark Rage and give Determination a better footing and stronger lever.

"Pepper Girl," choked Johnny, "I'm glad I waited. There's mebby many a mile we'll do together, better friends than ever. I'm tellin' you that if there's any way outside of h—l to get you out of this, yo're goin'. Hear me, little hoss? An' that thoroughbred girl has brought us th' way. Cheer up—we're goin' out, you an' me. But we'll have bad dreams—plumb bad dreams—for many a night to come." He suddenly raised a warning hand. "Look out!" he shouted. "Don't come too close!"

"I know this grisly thing like a book," she replied. "What shall I do?"

"Don't come too close!"

"This is the edge; tell me what to do!" She looked at Lang's partly submerged body and shuddered.

"Hold your cayuse fast by th' reins an' get off, so I can put my rope around that pommel. But I'm afraid it's a little too far," he replied, swinging the braided lariat carefully around his head. She quickly obeyed, but led the horse to another point on the edge, and gained a few inches. The rope shot out and up, struck the saddle and then the sands. Jerking it back again, he coiled it carefully, and then looked up, and nodded. Margaret was holding to the pommel with one hand and leaning out over the sands, her other arm extended toward him. The second cast went over her wrist and she caught the rope, drew back to the saddle and made the loop fast around her pommel.

"Get up in th' saddle an' pull this rope tight—*tight*," he said, and at a word from him Pepper braced herself, as well as she could, as if a cow were at the other end. He slid from the saddle, touched the sand for an instant, and pulled himself at his best speed along the lariat, moving too rapidly to be caught, and soon stood at the side of the woman who had saved him.

"Can't we save that darling?" she asked, tears in her eyes.

"We're goin' to try mighty hard," he said. "Start ahead, *slow*— a little more. You watch yore cayuse an' stop instanter when I says th' word. I'm scared we'll break Pepper's laigs, 'though if it's done easy we may get along all right; it looks soft, right there. Ready? Then, *pull*. Come, Pepper! Come on, little hoss! Come on! Come on!" he cried, and then he whistled the well-known signal. "Come on! That's th' girl! That's th' girl! Keep a-churnin', tear it up! Come on! Come on, you black darlin'! That's th' way! Keep a-comin', keep a-comin'!"

Slowly Pepper went sideways, Margaret fearing that its legs would snap under the strain, but the struggling animal fell on its side, and then came the tug of war. Johnny added his strength to the rope and slowly, an inch at a time, they gained, and then had to rest for a moment because flesh and blood could not stand such a continued effort. Johnny breathed deeply and relaxed.

"Once more, Ma'am," he said, getting a fresh hold on the rope. "I'm glad that saddle is a rim-fire—I'd mistrust a center-fire, with its one cinch. An' I'm glad it was made by Ol' Hawkins—that pommel can stand twice th' strain. Now then—*pull!*" Again they rested, the blood pounding in his ears. "Yo're comin' fine, little hoss! We ain't handlin' you very gentle; but yo're *comin'*!" A few minutes later Pepper slid across sand that was dry and honest, and with the slackening of the rope she scrambled to her feet and trembled, weary but safe.

Johnny hung the lariat on his saddle and then rubbed the velvety muzzle which sought his cheek, and stroked the quivering shoulder. Impulsively he buried his face in the wet, sandy, roughened coat on her neck and flung an arm around it; and when he turned away his face was drawn and wet, and there were tears in his eyes despite all effort of will.

"Ma'am," he said, huskily, "Pepper an' me owe you a debt we never can pay; but we can try right hard to square up some of it. I'll never forget th' last half-hour, never."

"How did you come to get in it?" asked Margaret, glancing where she last had seen the body of Lang. It was gone, and so was the horse. The sands, still undulating, were slowly assuming their mask of innocence.

"Pepper got goin' so fast she couldn't stop quick enough, which was my fault. I didn't try to turn her in time."

"And that—that other—man. Who was he, and what happened to him?"

"I reckon he got tangled in th' wire, an' got his rope mixed up with it. An' somehow we got to shootin'. When th' excitement stopped he was there, an' I was where you found me."

"Who was he?" she demanded.

"He was a Triangle puncher, Ma'am; Lang was his name."

"He was one of the men whom I ordered to stay off our range—we couldn't keep the wire on those posts, and I suspected them strongly. Are you sure he was only tangled in the wire?"

"Well, I wouldn't just say nothin' about that. Mebby he was tryin' to help th' cow that was mired, an' got afoul of th' wire. But that don't make no difference, anyhow, now. Have you got any wire at th' ranch?"

"I think so," she answered.

"We'll put it up some day soon, so it'll take some time, an' more trouble, to get it loose."

She nodded and took a paper out of her waist. "Here are the figures for the year we took possession."

He looked them over. "Uh-huh," he said, "they're what I want."

"It is surprising that we have as many left as we have," she said. "We are about ready to give up, admit our failure, and go back East."

"Ma'am," said Johnny, with great earnestness, "don't you do it. Just sit tight an' see things come around yore way. Luck allus turns. Stick it out, an' see."

"Do you believe in luck?"

"I do; when somebody's behind it pushin' hard. Now, Ma'am, I reckon we hadn't ought to stay here no longer, where folks can see us. They might talk, an' there's no tellin' what harm it might do. Besides, this little Pepper hoss needs a bath an' I'm aimin' to take her into th' river as soon as she gets a little quieter—she looks like she mixed up with a tornado." He walked around collecting his guns, blowing sand from them, and cleaning them as well as he could. "There's shore some guns around here," he grinned, getting Lang's Colt and throwing it into the quicksand. "This here gun," he said, reloading Wolf's Colt and tying it under the slicker roll, "shore come in handy. Some folks would call that luck—mebby it was, as far as totin' it is concerned—but I'm tellin' you there wasn't no luck in th' way it was used. But as for totin' it, I reckon that was luck, even if I did carry it to fool somebody, sometime. Now, Ma'am, I'll be ridin' west. There's a regular bath tub near th' main trail, where th' river runs over solid rock: an' solid rock is th' only kind of river bottom I have any use for today. Pepper an' I won't forget what you did for us—an' I'm tellin' you to sit tight, an' watch th' luck swing yore way. I'll be leavin' now—good-by, Ma'am."

She spurred her horse and shot even with him. "Why are you doing this?" she demanded. "You can't fool me about that—that man's rope fouling the wire. I know what he was doing. Why are you running such risks for total strangers?"

"Ma'am," he replied, smiling quizzically, "I don't know, unless it's because I can't keep out of trouble. I'm allus gettin' mixed up with it, somehow, an' th' habit's set, I reckon. I'm gettin' so I like it. But we shouldn't be ridin' like this. You have no idea how much folks can talk, or figger from a little thing like this."

"Can't you stop them, as you did that Bar H foreman?"

"Reckon so; but I ain't ready to," he grinned. "There's a time for everythin', an' I'm not shore th' time has come for that. When it does I'll know it without no doubts. I'm askin' how you learned all th' things you said yesterday?"

"I suppose it is a natural curiosity, even in a man; but I prefer to say nothing about the matter." She drew rein and he took off his sombrero. "I'm tempted to see if the luck will turn," she smiled. "Good-by."

"I'm thankin' you again, Ma'am," he replied. "It shore will, an' you can bank on it," and he pressed Pepper's sides. The horse struck into a stride suggestive of a wish to put miles between her and the scene of her torture, but he pulled her down to a walk. "Yo're entirely too willin', little hoss of mine," he reproved, patting the roughened coat. "I was aimin' to do somethin' today, but it can wait, Wolf or no Wolf. If he horns in I won't waste no more time on him, none at all. There's a nice little wooded draw over there, an' we're goin' for it. You got to get rested up an' quieted a little—th' bath can wait a couple of hours. You got to keep in good shape, because th' time is comin' when I'll have to ride you like I had a *remuda* to draw on—an' I ain't worth a cuss unless yo're in good shape. Yo're my laigs, Pepper, an' no puncher is better'n his cayuse. An' mebby Two-Spot, th' tattle-tale, won't be surprised when he sees you!"

Margaret looked after him and smiled, and then turned and stared at the innocent patch of wet sand under whose hypocritical surface lay grisly death. Shuddering, she sent her pony into a sharp gallop and set out for home, a color in her face which might have been due to the exhilaration of horseback riding.

XII

♦

"Coming Events ——"

Johnny entered the draw, found a small clearing, and let Pepper wander, watching her closely, while he went over his guns again, cleaning them thoroughly. The afternoon had half gone when he whistled her to him and rode her down to the rocky pool he had mentioned. Stripping himself, he removed the saddle and its blanket and, mounting bareback, rode her into the stream, where he found a place deep enough to swim her. Crossing and recrossing this several times, he took her out and started to dress; and no sooner was she free than she trotted to a dry, warm patch of sand and rolled to her heart's content, grunting with pleasure.

"Now look at what you've done," he grinned. "After me gettin' you all washed up, you go an' blot yoreself just like a common cayuse. I've been wastin' sympathy on you—there ain't nothin' th' matter with you. An' there's somethin' I want to ask you, before I forget it: Was you ever in a quicksand just like that one? I bet you wasn't. I've crossed some rivers in my time, an' had cattle bogged in several—but this was different somehow. Mebby it's because it wasn't under water; but I don't know. I was scared we'd bust yore laigs; mebby we didn't because we pulled you sideways, an' you raised so much h—l when you felt th' rope tighten, an' heard me call you. Just th' same, I'm sayin' we had a close call. An' we mustn't forget it. Come here, now, an' let me throw this saddle on you. We're goin' to town, an' yore goin' to get rubbed till you shines. I'm as stuck-up about you as a gal is over her first beau."

In a few minutes they were on their way to Gunsight, but they did not reach the town without incident. They had ridden to Pine Mountain and Johnny, wishing to see if Squint's saddle had been discovered, hid Pepper in a clump of brush and scrub timber well back from the trail and, taking his rifle, crossed the beaten road at a rocky place and worked his way into the brush on the mountain side. When he had climbed about eighty feet he reached a little rock shelf and rested a moment. As he was about to go on he heard hoofbeats down the trail and he flattened himself behind a tuft of grass growing in a crack. Looking down the trail he saw a horseman round into sight from the arroyo leading from East Canyon.

"Smitty," he muttered. "I don't think much of him, an' I reckon he'll scare. An' mebby if he's scared near to death a few times he'll figger he ain't wanted around here, an' hit th' trail out. Mebby I'm wrong, but here's where Mr. Smitty gets a jolt he won't forget. It will be Number One. Whether or not he gets any more will depend on how he takes this one. I'm bettin' he don't stalk me for it— here he comes, ridin' lazy an' tryin' to sing. I ought to be able to come awful close at this distance, with a rifle layin' on a rock rest."

Mr. Smith, of the Bar H, rode at a walk, singing a song, the words of which should never appear in print. He had a message to deliver to the Doc and was in no hurry. His hat, a Mexican sombrero with ultra-fancy band, and a high crown, which appeared to be even higher because of the vertical dents which pushed the top into a peak, was tilted rakishly off-center and looked rather ludicrous to the man on the mountain, who noted that there appeared to be plenty of hat and horse, but very little man. When just across a short stretch of rocky trail there rang out over the rider's head a roar such as only black powder can make, and the tilted sombrero flew into the air and struck the ground. The horse and its rider heard the roar at the same instant and each acted as their instincts prompted. The horse shot forward, clearing a dozen feet in the jump, sprang back, wheeling in the air, and bolted for the arroyo it had just left, where it quickly recovered its poise and stopped to search out succulent grass tufts. Mr. Smith's instincts seemed to have come to him through genera-tions of acrobatic ancestors, although he was not aware that any of his family tree claimed any such accomplish-ments, at least since they had forsaken arboreal surroundings. Certainly he never boasted, even in his maddest sprees, of being in any way gifted in acrobatics. Nevertheless, he performed a creditable exhibition when the roar smashed against his ears. As the horse leaped, he grabbed at the pommel, missed it, and in his haste to jerk his head back from the screaming lead he lost his balance. His feet left the stirrups, and then came swiftly upward as he pivoted on the saddle. They swept up past the horse's neck, kept on and described a half-circle, the saddle as the center. As they went up Mr. Smith's head went down, and as the horse leaped back and whirled, he was jolted into a position rarely seen in horseback riding except in exhibitions. For a moment he stood on his shoulder against the cantle of the saddle and then turned a pretty, if unintentional, back flip onto the ground, landing squarely on his hat. The whole thing happened in a flash and the sound of the shot was still rumbling among the hills when, grabbing his sombrero, he started on a dead run for the horse and the ranch. When he reached the animal he leaped into the saddle without touching the stirrups, and urged a speedy departure, which his spurs obtained.

Johnny rolled over on his back and laughed heartily. Finally he sat up, put the empty shell in his pocket, reloaded the rifle and went up the mountain to hide Squint's saddle in a better place, for he now believed such a precaution necessary. It was more than probable that Pine Mountain would be searched as soon as the indignant puncher could lead his friends to the scene of his discomfiture. He found the saddle where he had left it and carried it to a narrow, shallow split in the mountain's rocky side and dropped it in, after which dead branches and grass and rocks covered it and hid it securely. Scrambling back to the trail he looked cautiously along it and then dashed across and made his way to his horse, stepping on rock whenever possible. Not long afterward he rode down the Juniper trail and went to the hotel shed, where he led Pepper inside and prepared to groom her. He hardly had begun work when Two-Spot sidled in, and there was wrath in his eyes.

"What you been doin' to that hoss?" he demanded, as his gaze swept over her. "She looks like she's been rolled in th' river."

"Mebby she has," replied Johnny, rubbing briskly. "She likes a swim as well as I do—an' we both had one, which is somethin' I can recommend to you."

"What did you do with them rifle ca'tridges of Pole-cat's you was goin' to give me?" asked Two-Spot, going to work on the other flank.

"I hid 'em," answered Johnny. "Look out she don't hand you a stomachful of hoof—she don't like strangers."

"Huh!" snorted Two-Spot, "what do *I* care about strangers? Where'd you hide 'em?"

"In them sweepin's, under th' manger," replied Johnny. "Wait till after dark."

"What you figger I'm goin' to do—show everybody that Two-Spot's startin' an arsenal?" He rubbed for a moment in silence, and then began to chuckle. "Ol' Chief Smell-Um-Strong had a plumb fine gun—I got a laugh comin'; you gave th' best one away."

"I'm satisfied," grunted Johnny.

"Dave was on th' prod this noon when I showed up," continued Two-Spot. "What did you say you was swim-min' in?" he demanded, curiously, examining one of Pepper's hocks.

"Water," answered Johnny. "What did he say?"

"Mebby it was," observed Two-Spot. "How'd you get out?"

"Swum."

"At th' end of a rope? Why, Dave, he wanted to know where th' this, that, an' th' other thing I was last night. Reckoned, mebby, I'd got full of berries an' hibernated. What was you doin' in th' SV valley?"

"What did you tell him?" asked Johnny, grinning.

"Told him that I was rustlin' a passel of cows an' that they went so fast I had to run to Juniper before I could head 'em off. You must 'a' had one h—l of a time gettin' out. Shore Pepper ain't hurt?"

"It ain't th' first bath she's had—she's a good swimmer, 'though for much of it I'd ruther have a cayuse with a bigger barrel. She won't shrink."

"Why in h—l don't Dave set out th' bottle, like he used to?" growled Two-Spot. "There ain't no sense in totin' it by th' glass to a crowd of blotters. They'll hold more liquor than a gopher hole—an' I've broke my back carryin' water to drown them fellers out when I was a kid. How long is your rope?"

"Dave's a friend of mine, that's why," answered Johnny. "My capacity is so limited that ol' Dailey could clean me out after my fourth drink. Them leather-bellies can drink me into a heap on th' floor, an' never know they'd been drinkin'."

"Shore," said Two-Spot, chuckling; "yo're a teethin' infant, a reg'lar suckin' calf—I've seen you put away a dozen an' not bat an eye. An' it's bad medicine; look at me. How long's that rope?"

"Eighty feet."

"Yo're another. There ain't a man livin' can throw such a rope an' ketch anythin'. I've seen some good uns, but I've never seen even a sixty-foot rope. Who fastened to you?"

"Yo're loco—plumb loco," said Johnny. "You want to forget them hallucernations—somebody might believe 'em."

" 'Hallerlucinations'—humph! I'll have to remember that an' throw it at Dave. Where was you today?"

"Mindin' my own business," retorted Johnny. "What ever put you hangin' 'round a saloon, emptyin' boxes?"

"Whiskey," said Two-Spot. "I was smart, like you, an' liked to hold up my end, drink for drink. Here's some more of that water you swum in—looks familiar."

"I'm goin' to drag you out to a ranch some of these days," threatened Johnny, "an' give you a job—an' whale th' skin from yore bones th' first time I see you takin' a drink. You got brains an' that ranch needs 'em."

"You can't learn an old dog new tricks," grunted Two-Spot, and then burst out laughing; "but you can change a wolf inter a skunk if you goes about it right. He! He! He!" In a few minutes he threw down the brush and went to the door. "Seein' as how yo're playin' fresh-water clam, do it yoreself!" he snorted and, dodging the other brush, he scurried around to Dave's.

Down on the Bar H, Smitty's arrival made a ripple of excitement. Big Tom was mending a shirt and cursing the clumsiness of his fingers and the sharpness of the needle, when there came the clatter of hoofs outside and he looked up to see Smitty leap from the saddle and jump through the doorway, holding a much-abused Mexican sombrero out at arm's length. It was trampled and soiled and there was a fuzzy-edged rip an inch long in the brim where a 550-grain bullet had ploughed before passing through. Eight years before Smitty had paid twenty-five dollars for the hat, perhaps entirely too much, and next to his saddle it was his most prized possession. It had seen hard service, but he fondly regarded it as being as good as new.

"Lookit my hat!" he cried, jabbing it under the foreman's nose, which caused the needle to find the finger again.

"D—n th' hat!" growled Big Tom. "Take it away from my nose!"

"Lookit it!" insisted Smitty. "Some coyote shot at me from up on Pine Mountain an' plumb ruined it! He came so close I could feel th' slug—cuss it, I *smelled* it! It fair grazed my nose. Lookit it!"

Big Tom threw the shirt away and took the hat, turning it over in his hands. "I'd say it was close—plumb close," he admitted. "How far off was he?"

"Right over my head—couple dozen feet," answered Smitty. "Here! Don't poke yore blasted finger in it like that! Cuss it, it's bad enough now! That's more like it. I could feel th' concussion an' smell th' smoke. I was ridin' along at a walk, when *whango!* It near stunned me, it was so close. An' lookit what he done to that hat! There ain't another hat like that on th' whole range!"

"Yo're right, they throw 'em away long before that," retorted Big Tom, an idea coming into his head. "Did you pick up his trail?"

"How could I?" indignantly demanded Smitty. "My cayuse fair went wild, an' before I could get him under control he was clean out of th' canyon—I tell you I did some highfalutin' ridin', stickin' to a crazy hoss among all them rocks."

"How'd you get yore hat? Didn't it go off yore head?"

"Shore it did! I scooped it up as my cayuse wheeled—an' talk about turnin' on a saddle blanket—that jack rabbit can wheel on a postage stamp if he's prodded enough. He just simply climbed up straight an' swapped ends."

"You should 'a' gone back an' stalked that feller," said Big Tom, using plenty of salt on what he heard. "Or at least rustled to Gunsight to see who might come ridin' in. Where did all this happen?"

"Right on them benches on th' east end of th'

mountain—at that rocky hump in th' trail. How he ever missed at such close range is more'n *I* can understand—why, a kid oughta be able to make a hit, every time, as close as that. An' it was a rifle; th' roar was deafenin'."

"He missed because he wanted to miss," said Big Tom. "One of th' boys is playin' a joke on you—you know what they've said about that tent. He come closer than he reckoned on—I'll bet you rocked forward in th' saddle as he shot."

"Yes, I reckon I did—you know what ridin' is over that hump," Smitty said. "I remember that when I jerked back as it passed my nose I went quite a ways—my neck is sore from th' jerk. But I'm tellin' you I ain't nowise shore it was any joke. An' I says, if it was, it was a cussed pore one. I'll nat'rally skin any fool *I* ketches playin' any more jokes like that on *me*. Cuss it, it skun my nose!"

"A skin fur a skin, huh?" chuckled the foreman. He handed the hat back to its owner. "There ain't no man on th' range that would miss yore head, hat or no hat, from them benches. It ain't more than seventy-five or eighty feet from up there. They aimed to miss you; an' they shaved it a little too fine, not allowin' for you bobbin' forward. I says it was one of th' boys. You lay low an' use yore eyes an' ears, an' if you find out who it was I'll give that fool a dressin' down he won't forget. A joke's a joke—we all play 'em; but there's such a thing as ridin' 'em too hard. Did you give th' Doc my message?"

"What message?"

The foreman stared at him and slowly raised his hands. "I'll be cussed—it was more of a joke than I thought. Didn't I tell you to ride up there an' tell th' Doc that we wanted to see him tonight? Didn't you leave here to tell him that, an' for nothin' else?" he demanded, his voice rising.

"Yeah, I reckon mebby you did," admitted the puncher, uneasily. "You want to see him tonight, shore."

"I do. Now you fork that cayuse an' get goin'. Good Lord! That bullet must 'a' hit yore mem'ry." He glanced at his puncher's thigh. "An' where's yore six-shooter? Did you forget that, somewhere?"

Smitty's hand went to the holster and he cursed heartily. "D—n these open sheaths! It must 'a' fell out when that jack rabbit did th' fancy swappin' of ends. Now I got to go get it, but I'm borrowin' a gun to wear, or I stays here. Somethin' tells me it's unhealthy to go ridin' around this God-forsaken country without no six-gun."

"Take that spare one of mine, hangin' up over my bunk," offered the foreman. "She's in good shape. Now, yo're plumb shore you didn't lose nothin' else, more valuable than earthly belongin's?" he grinned. "Yo're shore yo're goin' back for yore gun?"

"Shore I am; what you mean?" replied Smitty, suspiciously.

"Nothin' worth mentionin'," smiled Big Tom. "I reckoned mebby you'd take th' over-mountain trail, seein' as it's shorter."

"Then how could I get my gun?"

"That's what I was wonderin'."

"I'll get it," Smitty assured him. "I'll get it unless yore fool joker picked it up. Mebby he's a-settin' on it, waitin' to hand it to me, an' 'pologize for missin' me."

"He won't be within miles of here by this time," said Big Tom. "He dusted quick. If he was jokin' he'd get away *pronto,* an' if he wasn't, he'd do it quicker. I reckon you'd better climb up on that bench an' see what you can find—an empty shell might help us a lot. But don't forget to see th' Doc, this time. After that you can go to town an' find out what you can learn. Now get started. An' take good care of that hat—that ain't no way to treat it, nohow."

Smitty growled, took down the six-shooter, strode out to his horse and swung into the saddle. "Hope nobody picked it up," he said. "Twenty dollars is twenty dollars, an' I ain't got th' twenty. Anyway, it's a better gun than they're makin' nowadays."

"Don't lose that one while yo're pickin' up th' other," laughed the foreman.

When he was out of sight of the ranch Smitty wheeled sharply and rode eastward. "I got to get it," he muttered, "or I'll never hear th' last of it; but there ain't no reason for ridin' through th' canyon an' th' arroyo, along th' side of th' mountain for no four miles. It was too cussed close for a joke. An' mebby he aimed to spatter me all over th' trail. I just can't figger it, nohow. But I'm free to remark that any more of them jokes will send Smitty dustin' along th' trail, no matter what way he's pointin' at th' time, an' he won't never come back no more. Somehow, I just can't help thinkin' of pore Squint. Cuss it, I can feel it yet!"

Getting near the scene of his discomfiture, Smitty dismounted and went on a reconnaissance, viewing the benches from every angle, and after some time he located his gun lying in the grass near the trail. Returning to his horse he mounted and rode forward, striking into a dead run as he approached the rocky hump in the trail and, leaning down, he picked up the weapon as he swept past, no mean feat when the grass is considered. In a few minutes he pulled his mount to a lope and soon drew rein at the Doc's door, where he delivered the message, gossiped for a few minutes, and then went on to town.

The first person he saw was Two-Spot, leaning against the front of the Palace and who accepted, with alacrity,

Smitty's invitation to drink. Two-Spot saw the condition of the hat before its wearer had dismounted, and his curiosity burned strongly within him. The puncher engaged him and Dave in conversation but his efforts at these sources of information were futile. What knowledge he gained had no bearing on Johnny. Two-Spot casually remarked that Johnny had been loafing around most of the afternoon, pestering him and said that he was a nuisance. Buying another round Smitty sauntered into Dailey's, where he learned nothing at all. Having taken the census and found that everyone had been rooted in town all day, he began to accept his foreman's view of the mystery, and set out for home, burning for an opportunity to observe his bosom friends and listen to their careless conversation. But if he had not received any information, he had not given any, and Two-Spot's curiosity about the hole in the hat was still raging.

"Th' doin's on this here range are scandalous," observed Dave's factotum to Dave, himself. "They're gettin' worse an' worse, an' somebody's goin' to get hurt afore long. Now I wonder how th' devil Smitty's hat got abused like that?"

"What makes you think things is gettin' worse?" asked Dave.

"That Greaser tent never come by that hole from bein' used; an' Smitty was shore askin' a lot of questions; an' Nelson ain't swimmin' hisself an' that hoss for fun—I know *I* wouldn't."

"Which is an abidin' sorrer to all them as gets down wind of you," said Dave. "Was Nelson's saddle wet?"

"No-o; I reckon it was dry," grudgingly admitted the other.

"Was his clothes wet?" continued Dave.

"No-o-o," more reluctantly admitted Two-Spot.

"You got a head like a toad," contemptuously rejoined the proprietor. "Trouble with you is, yore imagination is on th' rampage. You got too much time on yore hands— suppose you 'tend to th' sand boxes? They ain't been touched in three days."

Two-Spot sighed and obeyed. "Huh!" he grunted, emptying a box into the road. "Mebby; but I saw somethin' about that hole that reminded me of some gosh-awful ca'tridges I seen lately. Cuss it—I'd *bet* on it!"

He chuckled, set down the box, slipped around the side of the saloon and poked his head in the hotel shed. "Don't she shine, though?" he remarked in congratulatory tones.

"She does," admitted Johnny, finishing the job.

"Say," said his visitor, "gimme an empty rifle shell."

"What for?"

"I want to keep matches in it. I'll get a cork from Dave an' have a waterproof matchbox."

"You need it," countered Johnny. "Aimin' to fall in th' crick? You need that, too."

Two-Spot ignored the insult, the second on that topic within five minutes. Evidently there must be some real or fancied foundation for it. "Got one?" he asked.

"I'll save you one," replied Johnny; "but mebby you'll have to wait quite a spell. I still got them I loaded," he said, truthfully.

"Well, there ain't no hurry," admitted Two-Spot. "Thought mebby you had one in yore clothes."

"I might go out an' shoot one off; but I reckon I won't, seein' that it ain't goin' to rain for a day or two."

"Don't shoot none for that," replied Two-Spot. "Smitty was in town a few minutes ago."

"Yes?"

"Uh-huh, he was. He was projectin' around tryin' to

find out who spoiled his twenty-year-old Mex. sunshade.
He was het up about it."

"Don't blame him. Was it spoiled bad?"

"Plumb sufficient. Looks like th' railroad thought it was
a tunnel. He acts like he's got hal—hallerlucerations,"
grinned Two-Spot.

"But you can't wear them on a hat," reproved Johnny.
"That is, not till after you open th' can, anyhow."

"Huh?" Two-Spot scratched his frowsy head, "mebby
not, but that's th' safest place to tote 'em—on th' outside,
leastawise. Did you think they was like a—a shirt?" he
demanded with great sarcasm.

"Mebby; they covers a lot of ignorance. Yo're not goin'
out, are you?" asked Johnny.

"I am," retorted his companion, shuffling toward the
door. "You think yo're d—d smart, don't you? You an'
yore hullercations? Well, you can go plumb to h—l!" and
Two-Spot made haste to get around in front of the saloon,
where he refilled the box and carried it inside.

"Cuss it, Dave," he complained, "nobody 'round here
treats me like I deserve!"

"An' it's d—d lucky for you that they don't," retorted
Dave. "You 'tend to them boxes, or I'll make a start at
treatin' you like you deserves. What's th' matter with
you, anyhow? You've been chucklin' all day like you've
lost what little sense you had. You ought to take somethin' for them spasms—they're too frequent to do you any
good."

Two-Spot sighed and carried out another box. He
dropped it and shook his head. "I don't care a cuss; I'm
still bettin' that hole was made by a Sharp's Special. But
what gets me is, how could he perforate th' brim while
that there pinched-up peak waves defiance, an' courts
destruction? You gimme a shot at it, and I'd blow th' hull

top off'n it. But I dassn't think about that, now that I've got a gun; it's so fascinatin' I'll be takin' a shot at it some of these days—an' I reckon I'd get more'n a hat. Shucks! that'd be all right; it's only Smitty." He leaned up against the building and laughed until Dave came out to see if he could get in one healthy kick, but Two-Spot avoided him and went back to the box. "Polecat is near Highbank now," he muttered. "I'd give his gun to read his thoughts! He! He! He!"

XIII

♦

Highbank Makes a Discovery

At the other end of the Highbank-Gunsight trail the warm afternoon was drawing to a close and the shadows of the buildings were reaching out across the dirt streets when a dust-covered, four-horse freight wagon rolled down the steep bank across the river to an accompaniment of rattling trace chains and grinding brakes, passed the end of the ford, followed the road along the river's edge and crept out onto the big, flat-bottomed ferry which awaited it.

"On time to a tick," smiled the ferryman, poling off and shifting the lengths of the trolley ropes leading to the block which ran on the great, sagging cable overhead. The current struck the side of the craft at the changed angle and sent it slowly across.

"I got an extra early start," explained Buffalo. "Got a fine load of hides."

"You young fellers are h—l on branchin' out," said the ferryman, grinning.

"Well," replied the freighter, "they was lyin' there; I only picked 'em up."

"Here we are; hold tight," laughed the boatman. He used his pole deftly and the ferry struck the bank squarely. Making it fast, he lowered the short gangplank. "All ashore, an' good luck!"

The quartet strained and the wagon rumbled up the bank and then up the road in the wide ravine, and in a few minutes struck the level at the top and entered the main street of the town.

"Brazos" Larkin, town marshal, pushed away from the Highbank bank and rolled out to the wagon, stepped on a hub and then up to the footboard, as was his custom.

"Judgin' from th' way those no-'count hosses was pullin' when they come over th' hill," he said, "I reckoned you got th' hides; but now I'm dead shore of it."

"Yep," chuckled Buffalo, "they smells good to me."

"Dodge th' Injuns all right?" asked Brazos, indulging in a time-honored jest.

"Dodged 'em ag'in," gravely nodded the driver. "Here comes th' postmaster. Hello, Jim!"

Jim Hands walked up to the wagon and alongside as it turned the corner and stopped before a frame building bearing in weather-bleached letters across its front: "Wheatley's Express." As it stopped, a tall, lean young man came out and smiled.

"Everythin' all right, Pop?" he asked.

"Right as a dollar. Can't you smell 'em?" chuckled the old man.

"Jerry," said Brazos, "I hears yo're quittin' th' office for a wagon next week?"

"I am; I wanted to swap jobs right along with Pop. Now that we're goin' to run two waggins I'll get a chance to bust out of this jail; an' Pop can still see his friends along th' trail, too. I start in a day or two."

A small group came up and joined them. In it was Rod Wilson, the liveryman; Reb Travers, the railroad freight agent; and Pete Wiggins, the owner of the hotel. They all were cronies of the same vintage as the driver and formed a closed circle into which, however, they had admitted Brazos.

"Bet you didn't git a load," said Rod.

"Bet you didn't git *half* a load," amended Reb.

"I'll show you scoffin' mossbacks what I got," retorted Buffalo, rising to the bait. He clambered down and went to the rear of the wagon, untied the knots and threw back the canvas. As he paused to wonder how the bale had become spread out, the top skin moved up and down, and he jerked back his hand. "There's some kind of a varmint in there!" he cried in pardonable amazement.

Brazos left the group with a leap and reached for the hide as his gun slanted down on it. Giving it a quick, hard jerk, he threw it behind him and then gazed in astonishment at a pair of boots which moved energetically, while strange, strangled gurgles were heard in the wagon box. "I'm d—d!" he muttered. "What th'—who th'—how th'—" He grabbed hold of a boot and pulled heartily. It resisted and tried to kick. Following his gun under the canvas, he moved another skin and then emerged and stared at Buffalo.

"What is it?" demanded the freighter. "*Who* is it? How'd he git there, hey?"

"It's Wolf Forbes, blind-folded, gagged, hog-tied, an' lashed to th' box," accused Brazos. "Was you aimin' to skin him when you had more time?"

"Skin him?" indignantly retorted Buffalo. "You can't

skin him; he's so tough a plough wouldn't scratch his hide. How'd he git in there, an' tie hisself up like that?"

"Mebby you can tell that to a jury," retorted Brazos, slying winking at the dumbfounded group. "However, unless we want to call on a coroner's jury first, we better git him out," and, slipping the gun into its holster, he plunged back under the canvas.

Pete Wiggins was the first of the group to recover. "After all these years we done found you out!" he exulted.

"What's wrong?" demanded Jerry, from the office.

"Yore Pop is bringin' in hide on th' hoof," declared Reb.

"Kidnappin' innercent punchers like Wolf Forbes," accused Pete.

"Cuss it!" snorted Buffalo. "What I want you fools to tell me is how he got there?"

"You can't slip out that way," asserted Rod.

They listened to what Brazos was saying under the canvas. "Tied up four ways from th' Jack," he announced. "Rolled up in a stinkin' hide, he was, all but his head an' arms. Cuss me! this is somethin' new to me; an' I reckoned I'd been up ag'in' everythin' in human cussedness. How fur did he come this way?"

"How in h—l do _I_ know!" blazed Buffalo, his thin chin whiskers bobbing pugnaciously. "I didn't even know he was _there!_"

"You can't never tell," said a voice back in the crowd. "Sometimes it comes out in a man when he's even older'n Buffalo. Reckon it's th' breed."

"I'll show you what's in my breed!" shouted the freighter, pushing into the press. "Let me git a-holt of th' skunk as said that an'—an'—an'—" he faltered.

Pete grabbed him and pulled him back again. "None of that!" he warned. "You stay right here till we find out more about this!"

"Startin' a passenger business, too, I reckon," said the same voice. "Bein' an old hand on th' cattle trail he knowed a herd will often foller if one cow crosses a river."

"He got so used to skinnin' buffalers that he's itchin' to try it on a human," said another. "I says he shows spunk, pickin' Wolf to try it on."

"There's tricks in all trades," said Jim Hands.

"'Cept freightin'," laughed Jerry.

"Somebody pass in a knife," requested Brazos. "Mines's in my other pants where it allus is when I wants it. My sacred cow! I'm near choked! Them hides must be full of maggots." Receiving the knife he soon backed out. "Phew! An' hot! Now, as I pull him out, some of you grab holt under him so he won't drop. Don't try to stand him up; he can't do that for all th' money in th' country. Here he comes; stand by!"

Ready hands went under the puncher as he appeared, and lowered him to the ground. Wolf could not speak; he could not even move his jaw; but there was nothing the matter with his eyes and they served as points of concentration for his rage. They almost sparked.

"Jerry, get a bottle of liquor," ordered Brazos. "Get it sudden, too. Reb, you an' some of th' others rub his arms an' laigs. He ain't nowhere near goin' to die, but he's in bad shape, temporary."

Jerry appeared with a bottle of brandy and Brazos poured a thin trickle of it into the open mouth. When a fourth of it was used he started to rub the jaw muscles, whereat the eyes sparked furiously and the gurgling became more emphatic.

"He says he likes that," chuckled the marshal, "but he likes this better," and he gave another dose of brandy. "You can't kill these fellers," he remarked, rubbing the jaws with rhythmic strokes. "They're steel, rubber, an' rawhide—

tough as hickory knots. In administerin' a stimulant"—he paused, liked the words, and repeated them: "In administerin' a stimulant, as I says before, you got to consider what effect it will have on a liquor-drinkin' patient. This here feller looks like he was used to it, so we'll give him all six chambers. There ain't no harm in gettin' a man drunk, not if it's good for him, an' if I was him I'd ruther be drunk than sober when th' blood starts a-flowin' ag'in. Dose Number Three—it's fetchin' him; an' he ain't coughed once. Didn't I tell you he was brought up on it?"

Buffalo, holding back his laughter with all his will, shook his fist at the prostrate puncher.

"Think yo're smart, hey?" he demanded fiercely. "But I want my pay! Nobody can steal a ride with me without payin'. I want five dollars. You hear me? *Five dollars!* These fools act like they think it's a joke, but I ain't swallerin' it; no, sir! How do *I* know you didn't plan this all out, an' get yore friends to help you beat an old man out of his fare? There you was, snug in my skins, like a tick in a cow's hair, layin' there for forty miles, snickerin' at me! You wouldn't pay, an' ride alongside me, up in th' dust an' th' heat; but you got poked away on them soft hides, out of' th' dust an' th' sun, takin' it easy while I was drivin' them four wild horses for forty miles! Dozin' off, mebby, while I was doin' all th' work. I don't see no joke." He choked, controlled himself, and shouted: "But you can't do it! I want my pay! An' what will folks say up in Gunsight when they hears about you?"

"Oh, Lord!" yelled Pete. "What *will* they say? It'll never be forgot!"

"Life must be pleasant," said Reb, "livin' with *that* outfit! There's allus somethin' to pass away th' time. I reckon they must 'a' saved up a long time for this feller."

"Can you imagine what he's been through today?"

asked Pete, his imagination becoming active. "It was plain, common h—l!"

Buffalo suddenly let out a whoop, draped himself on a wheel and burst into laughter, and when he could get control of himself he looked around at his audience. "Fellers," he groaned, "it wasn't *his* outfit! It was them Double X fellers. There was four of 'em in Gunsight last night, an' they was feelin' good. They've got th' nerve to tackle a joke like this, too; an' there ain't no love lost between them two ranches. When I was goin' into th' hotel after puttin' up my team, I heard a lot of laughin' in Dave's saloon, an' I remembers some of them Double X fellers howlin' 'bout a kidnappin'. That's it! They done it! An' I tell you it took nerve, tacklin' this two-gun man for a joke! It won't be no joke when he gits back—there'll be killin's over this. But, killin' or no killin', I can't help it—Oh! Ho! Ho! Oh! Ho! Ho! An' me settin' up there, drivin' like a dodderin' old fool, with this feller tied up in them odorous skins! Wolf Forbes, two-gun badman of th' Bar H! Oh! Ho! Ho! There'll be killin's; but I got to laugh—Oh, Lordy! Lordy! Lordy!"

"Forty mile! Forty mile!" senselessly repeated one man, weaving around, stepping on everyone in his path. "Forty mile! Forty mile!"

"Playin' mummy on a pile of stinkin' hides!" cried another.

"Tied up like a—like a—I dunno what!"

"Bouncin' an' jouncin' under that tarp on a day like this!"

"Forty mile" came around again, chanting his passwords, stumbled over Reb and flopped, still chanting.

Brazos held up the bottle, and put it down again, not daring to give the last dose for fear of spilling it, and rocked back and forth on his haunches: "Wrapped in a stinkin' hide—forty mile—mummy—oh, my sacred cow!"

"Forty mile" gasped and sat up. The bottle took his eye, and his hand took the bottle. Putting it back empty he slowly arose; and when last seen he was trying to walk on both sides of the street at once, still chanting his lay.

Wolf stirred, tried to get up and, falling, rolled over.

"'Oot 'ell out ah th'," he muttered. "No dah 'an." He desisted, since he could not pronounce labials, and tried his arms and legs. They responded somewhat, but there was a great uncertainty about them.

Brazos wiped his eyes, picked up the bottle, looked at it and then around at the crowd, and arose. "Come on, boys; give me a hand. In another hour he'll be petrified. After which, I'm takin' a drink—two of 'em—*three* of 'em! I needs it bad."

The cronies picked Buffalo off the wheel. "Give us a hand, ol' kidnapper," ordered Reb. "We'll lug him into Pete's. Come on—git a-holt, all as can find room."

A procession formed, with a line of dogs acting as skirmishers, and tramped to Pete Wiggins' Highbank hotel and bar, into which all but the small boys and dogs disappeared. Any stranger entering Highbank later that night would have carried away a very unfavorable impression about the sobriety of its citizens. And had he seen the innocent and unassuming cause of it all he would have marveled how a man could get so drunk, and live. And for a day or two Wolf did not draw a sober breath, but staggered, when he was able to walk, from place to place, muttering dire threats and drinking steadily while his money lasted. There is no telling where a periodical drinker will stop when once he gets started—and he had been started on more than a pint of brandy.

XIV

♦

Enough Is Sufficient

The following morning Johnny rode toward the northwest corner of the Bar H, the hilly, wooded section which had been presided over by Wolf Forbes. On his ride from the Bar H bunkhouse to the Triangle he had seen numerous unbranded cattle and wondered what he would find on the difficult section over which Wolf was wont to hold jealous guard. Riding to the west of the town he then turned and went south, passing behind the Doc's cabin, and parallel with the over-mountain trail. Reaching Clear River he followed it onto Double X range and then let Pepper pick her way over the mountain, and soon came to his objective, where he found large numbers of cattle, with an unusually high percentage of mavericks among them.

"Pepper," he said, alert for signs of Bar H riders, "th' SV has lost a lot of cows—an' folks can't make cows. So if it's goin' to make up its losses, it will have to do it with cows that are livin' this very minute. Now, it ain't reasonable to go on a ranch an' round up a lot of unbranded cattle, 'specially if it ain't willin' for 'em to be rounded up. On th' other hand, there ain't no harm in ridin' around an' sizin' things up. We want to find out where th' mavericks are, an' get some idea of how many there are of 'em.

"Mebby you don't know it, but a lot of mavericks means, generally, a lazy outfit, not to say nothin' worse. An' when a ranch reckons it's fenced off by natural barriers from other herds, that don't excuse 'em. A dishonest foreman or outfit, or a couple of dishonest men in it, can get rich with mavericks, if they know their business, an' don't work too hard. An' if th' whole outfit is dishonest an' workin' for its ranch, mavericks belongin' to surroundin' ranches are awful temptations.

"Now, th' SV don't earnotch its calves. They don't have no sleepers, at all; an' I know that calves will wander from their mothers after they are weaned, an' get notions of their own; an' they can be cut out an' drove to another range an' grow up to be big cows. On a ranch like th' SV, that ain't had no round-up in three years, all calves will be mavericks. There won't be a sign on none of 'em to tell where they belongs.

"Now then: We'll say th' Bar H is dishonest, but its foreman an' outfit is workin' for th' ranch an' not for their own pockets. If they drove SV calves to their own ranch, they'd put an iron on 'em as soon as they could, after which they wouldn't have to bother with 'em no more. They wouldn't have to be guarded jealous by th' best man of th' outfit, an' turned back when they tried to get off th' ranch. When I heard how Wolf almost lived out here, I got suspicious, Pepper; an' when I saw too many mavericks on this ranch, I got more suspicious; an' you've mebby heard that I was brought up in a plumb suspicious outfit. Of course, all ranches are goin' to have some mavericks, 'specially if it has a wild, rough range. Brush, timber, scrub, an' broken country hides cows that don't get combed out in a round-up; we had some, ourselves, down on th' old Bar-20, along our west line—but th' numbers out here are scandalous. I'm keepin' cases on these cattle, an' I says it's so scandalous that it just can't be true—but it *is* true, so far. There's folks down here that are careless an' lazy, or crooked an' I've got my suspicions about which it is.

"Now, we'll say that th' outfit is crooked, an' workin' for its own pockets. They wouldn't want to brand any mavericks, not with th' ranch mark. There's two ways of dividin' that conclusion. First: That they're doin' it for their own pockets, th' foreman not knowin' about it. But no foreman is so dumb that he'd overlook so many mavericks—he'd raise h—l, an' weed out his punchers an' get new men. There wouldn't be many cows unbranded if he was workin' for his ranch. Th' second is: Foreman an' outfit are workin' for themselves, dividin' up th' profits accordin' to some plan. Then nobody would care how many mavericks there was, for th' more th' merrier. They'd have a right smart herd to brand with th' mark of some friend's ranch, road brand, an' throw on th' trail for some shippin' point up north, near th' railroad. Or mebby they figger on stockin' a ranch of their own that they has in some other part of th' country. Rustlers plumb love mavericks—an' if I was one, an' wanted to get rich, I know where *I*'d start out. An' if it wasn't for th' Double X layin' between this ranch an' th' Snake Buttes country, them rustlers over there would give this outfit sleepless nights. Them Double X punchers bein' on th' job all th' time is all that saves these here mavericks from swappin' ranges. Th' Double X is workin' for this passel of thieves, an' don't know it.

"Now, then: These mavericks out here are mostly all three years old, or younger. There's some four-year-olds, an' others, of course. An' th' SV ain't had a calf round-up in three years. Ain't that remarkable? Th' Bar H owners get good reports every round-up. Th' new calves keep right up to th' factor of natural increase, an' there ain't nothin' to make anybody jump out here for a good look at things. An' when th' drive figgers go on, an' show five hundred cattle on th' beef trail, an' really there is a thousand, th' books balance just right; an' Big Tom gets a Christmas present from th' owners for bein' such a good, honest foreman. Where that extra five hundred head goes to nobody knows but th' outfit. I've heard that Wolf is th' *segundo* down here, an' is trail boss on every drive. Do you wonder he's jealous of his mavericks out here, an' watchin' day an night for some of them Snake Buttes rustlers to bust through th' Double X riders an' pay this section a visit? Him bein' so alert was another reason why I packed him off to Highbank for a day or two, where he can have excitement, an' there's things to do an' see. An' while he's enjoyin' th' hilarity of town, we'll have a good look around. *Pull up,* Pepper, there's hoss tracks—fresh, too. They was made while th' mornin's dew was heavy, which is told by th' little chunks of dirt his hoofs picked up an' turned over. You stay right here while I go ahead. *Lay down!*" He slapped the horse and gave a low, peculiar whistle. Pepper laid her ears back, but slowly obeyed the signal and went down, "playing dead" on her side. Taking his rifle, Johnny slipped into the brush, following a course parallel to but some distance from the tracks. For an hour he trailed, seeing numbers of mavericks and but few branded cattle, and twice he was in danger of being charged by crusty, old long-horned "outlaws" who, while having a due and well-founded respect for mounted men, evidently regarded a man on foot as being a different and less dangerous species of animal. These he eluded by taking to the brush and swiftly getting out of sight, detouring and picking up the trail again farther along. Suddenly he stopped and laughed silently. On the farther side of a clump of brush a conical, vertically dented Mexican sombrero loomed against the sky. Waiting a moment to be sure that he had not been heard, he raised the rifle and took long, deliberate aim. With the roar of the gun the peak of the hat flipped up and over, reversing itself as if on a hinge, and hung down on the side of the high crown like a cup. There was a yell of surprise, the hat dipped down below the shielding brush, and the sudden noise of pounding hoofs rolled toward East Canyon. Johnny reloaded and ran to a place from where he could see the fleeing horseman. It was Smitty, and he was mounted on his own horse, a long-legged, big-barreled roan, and it was fresh from a three day's rest. The speed it made awakened a surprised admiration in the laughing rifleman, who watched the departing horseman until he dashed into East Canyon.

"Thanks, Smitty," chuckled Johnny. "I'm glad you ain't headin' for th' bunkhouse. Now I won't be bothered by no curious outfit combin' these hills, lookin' for me. Reckon Smitty is goin' to town—or he never would 'a' rode for th' canyon. Just th' same, I'm leavin' for th' Double X. I've seen all I wants out here, an' now I'll try to fix up a round-up for th' SV, an' get the rest of th' figgers I needs." He returned to the horse and rode into the northwest, giving vent to occasional bursts of laughter.

"Pepper," he chuckled, as he rode down the other slope of the watershed, "we're havin' more fun down here than we had up around Twin Buttes, but th' show ain't hardly begun. However, we'll laugh while we can, an' meet trouble when it really comes."

Smitty pounded into and through East Canyon, busy with his crowded thoughts and harrowed feelings. His horse from habit chose the left-hand turn at the other end of East Arroyo, and swung around the bend toward Gunsight.

"Twice!" he soliloquized. "Twice in th' hat! He was close up, th' murderin' coyote—sneaked up on top of me when I was so far away from th' mountain I had plumb forgot him. Sneaked up to th' other side of that brush—couldn't 'a' been forty feet away—an' he missed *again*!

You can't tell me he didn't aim to miss, not *this* time. An' I'm dead shore he aimed to miss me that other time. Why? Because he didn't want to hit me, *yet*! It was a warnin', it was. He says plain: 'Smitty, you ain't wanted around here no more. I'm warnin' you th' second time. But, mebby, th' third time I won't miss.' I'm sayin' there won't be no third time. Practice makes perfect, an' *I* ain't no target. He won't score no bulls-eyes on *me*! Big Tom says it's a joke; all right; but if it is, it ain't goin' no further. An' th' reason is, *I* am. *I'm* goin' further, an' I ain't comin' back. I ain't even wastin' time to go back to th' house for my war bag, an' have to give em' an argument about quittin'. There ain't much pay a-comin' to me—none, when I pays up what I owe—an' I'm callin' everythin' square, all around. Pore Squint! Huh; I'd rather be able to say 'Pore Squint' than hang around here till somebody up an' says 'Pore Smitty.' This here country ain't fit for a dog no more an' I'm goin' to find one that is. Keep a-goin', you long-laigged rabbit!"

He whirled over the rock hump below the historic stone benches on Pine Mountain and streaked toward Gunsight, seeing the Doc come to the door of the shack and wave at him. The Doc was haggard and sallow, nervous and poorly nourished after an unfavorable bout with his worst enemy, and leaned weakly against the door casing as he watched the hard-riding puncher whirl toward him. He made up his mind that if Big Tom wanted to see him, Mahomet could come to the mountain, for he was in no condition to go afield. To his surprise and great relief, Smitty followed the bend in the trail and headed to ride past. Then it was that Doc waved again.

Smitty's hand went to his nose and he shouted a greeting and prophecy in three words. The Doc, unstrung and highly irritable, took enraged umbrage at the insulting greeting, jerked the Colt from its shoulder holster and took three erratic shots at the derisive rider, followed almost instantly by three more. Smitty's anger flared up and centered on this tangible escape valve. Shooting at him seemed to be the fashion these days, but it had to stop. There were five rapid reports and five puffs of smoke, spaced at regular intervals along the trail behind his horse. He was lucky in his off-hand shooting, for all of the bullets found a target. One smashed the Doc's window, already cracked; one drilled a hole through the edge of the door behind him; one turned his water bucket into a sprinkling can, and the other two screamed past him into the room and accounted for a dishpan and his lamp. The owner of the aforesaid articles waxed wrathy and indignant, and jumped up and down, making strange noises; then, running after the irritated puncher, tried in vain to find the chambers of his six-gun with the wrong ends of a handful of cartridges, at the same time indulging in a spirited monologue, which was jumpy and spasmodic from shortness of breath. Smitty turned in the saddle and let loose an insult which cannot be excelled in words, wig-wagged again, and flashed up the gentle slope toward town.

Gunsight heard him coming, and those inhabitants who suspected that strange things were likely to happen, made haste to look out and see what it was. Dailey chose his doorway, Dave an open window, while Two-Spot wished to be unhampered by walls and roof, and chose his favorite hang-out, the front of the saloon.

"Where you goin' so fast?" shouted Dailey, pleasantly curious. He became instantly indignant at the gesture which answered him, and the words which followed the action left no doubt in his mind that he had interpreted it correctly. He reached for his gun, thought better of it and, shaking a fist, shouted instead: "All right! But you'll be comin' back, cuss you!" and forthwith reached toward the gun again at the shouted answer he received.

Two-Spot saw the felt cup flapping up and down at the edge of the sombrero's peak and he let out a howl of pleasure at the sight, whereat Dave discreetly ducked back from the window, fearing Smitty's reply; but the puncher kept on ahead of his dust cloud and whirled over the trail toward Juniper.

Two-Spot shouted with laughter. "Did you see th' hat? Did you *see* it? Just what I was sayin'," he cried, delighted by the idea that his humorous conception had appealed to another. "Number Two, an' Smitty pulls his stakes. Hey, Dailey!" he shouted, "you says he'll be comin' back; *I'm* sayin' he won't. I'm bettin' we won't see Smitty no more. He's takin' what's left of his hat where it won't be spoiled no more. Did you notice th' hoss he's on? That ain't no Bar H critter; that's his *own*! I'm givin' you two to one he won't come back—two to one, you gapin' jackass!"

Dailey's open mouth closed suddenly, and he stepped forward, feeling for his gun again; but Two-Spot went around the corner of the saloon, kicking his heels together. "He won't come back! Squint, Polecat, an' Smitty! Wonder who else will be missin'? Three in a row—if Polecat stays away. But Polecat won't, cuss him. I know him too well for that. He won't—and I'll be glad of it, too, th' coyote. Who's next?"

XV

◆

A Diplomatic Mission

Riding northward after he had left the hills which lay along the line between the Double X and the Bar H, to find and follow the trail used by the Double X punchers when they rode to and from Gunsight, Johnny was nearing it when he saw a horseman far to the north, riding at speed down a hill and headed straight for him. Keeping on, Johnny turned into the trail in the direction of the Double X bunkhouse, whereupon the other changed his course and rode as if to head him off. From the way in which the other stuck up above the horse, Johnny thought him to be Slim Hawkes, and he pulled Pepper to a walk, rolling a cigarette while he loafed along. His surmise was correct, and soon Slim joined him, his look of suspicion having some time back given way to a smile.

"Hello, Nelson!" he cried. "Lost?"

"Not quite," answered Johnny, smiling in turn. "How are you?"

"Cheerful, if not handsome," grinned Slim. "Judgin' from th' way yo're headed, I reckon yo're headed my way. Wolf Forbes chase you away from his pet mavericks?"

"Didn't see him down there. What's he doin'—trainin' 'em?"

"Keepin' 'em from strayin' over on us," growled Slim. "If he'd 'a' seen you there he'd 'a' been plumb nasty."

"Then I'm glad he didn't," replied Johnny. "I don't like people to be nasty to me. It hurts my feelin's; I'm what you might call tender."

"Lookin' you over, I'd say you was," retorted Slim.

"I'm aimin' to pay you fellers a visit," said Johnny. "Bein' so tender, I won't stay long if I ain't treated nice, or if yore cook is worse than George."

"Yo're welcome if you has money with you," laughed Slim. "We make it a point to entertain visitors with plenty of poker. Which reminds me that this must be visitors' week on th' Double X. Larry Hallock's three brothers is visitin' him, an' Pete Wiggins' boy, Arch, dropped in last night. Arch quit th' Circle 4 an' was goin' to Highbank to see his dad, an' spend his month's wages. He's still able to go an' see his dad, but there ain't no danger of him spendin' any of them wages in town. He can't leave us, now. We got him interested in our entertainment an' he ain't got no money left. He aims to stay around an' get it back. We aim to get his hoss an' fixin's, an' then lend 'em to him so he can go down an' strike old Wiggins for enough to redeem 'em. Th' Hallock boys are doin' a little better, but we have hopes. Now that yo're headed for our web, I'm shore everythin' will be real cheerful. Anyhow, we'll make you welcome, little stranger, for we've got ideas about you that have kept grins on th' faces of our outfit. Th' boys are honin' to pump you. Has th' Doc been kidnapped again, or has Squint come back?"

"Neither of them calamities has happened," chuckled Johnny. "How much can th' Double X scrape up, in case I makes up my mind to stay a week?"

"Four dollars an' two bits. I'm aimin' to play 'em so that you'll have to put up that black wonder yo're ridin'. I shore can use her for my very own ridin' hoss."

"This cayuse won't never put no interest in gamblin'," said Johnny, stroking a glossy shoulder. "She's my pardner."

"I'd say she was northern raised," guessed Slim. "The, north ranges shore do make a difference in stock. I've heard of Texas ponies puttin' on a couple of hundred pounds, 'an' even growin' higher, up there. 'Tin-Cup,' " he read. "Where's that located? I never saw that brand before?"

"Up in Montanny," replied Johnny. "I worked for it, an' bought this cayuse while th' brand was still red. She's got *blood* in her, I'm tellin' you."

"I knowed that as fur as I could see her," replied Slim. "But you ain't no Northerner. Did you go up with a trail herd, an' stay over?"

"No, I went up by myself. Went up to help a friend spread th' gospel over his ranch, which was done proper. It's fine country, but it's gettin' crowded."

"See many Texas an' Greaser cattle up there?"

"Shore; we wasn't so far from th' Musselshell. They're on th' trail all th' time. An' they ain't loved a whole lot, neither. Th' northern punchers try to keep their herds from grazin' too close to th' trails. They're plumb scared about Texas fever. Sometimes a trail herd will pick up quite a lot of local cattle, an' when they're cut out they're mostly held on a range by themselves over a winter, until th' danger is reckoned to be past. You can't blame 'em, for th' fever raises th' very devil in northern herds. I know what I'm talkin' about, because some fever cattle was throwed over on th' Tin-Cup by some two-laigged skunks, an' we had one busy time, *I*'ll admit. It went through our cattle like fire through dead grass; an' if it hadn't been for an Englishman, with plenty of brains in his deceivin' head, it would 'a' been good-by Tin-Cup. It was a squeak for us. How's everythin' with you fellers?"

"Our troubles are periodics," replied Slim. "We'll have a long stretch of peace an' quiet, an' then things will happen in bunches, an' keep us crow-hoppin' all over th' range. We got our southeast section tamed, but our west section

boils over every once in a while. Even when it ain't boilin', or even simmerin', we have got to watch it close. An'
it's generally on th' simmer. If you go broke a-visitin' us,
which I hopes you do, you can earn quite some cash. All
you got to do is to go over in th' Snake Buttes country,
just west of us, an' get Nevada for us. We'll pay five hundred dollars for his body, an' a hundred apiece for each of
his men. I've heard tell about th' Hole in th' Wall, up north,
but I reckon we've got its first cousin down here, right
next door to us. We have to keep four men on our west
section day an' night. Don't you never ride out there for
fun—we shoots first, an' then finds out who it was."

"Nevada!" mused Johnny, "who is he?"

"Some say he's white, others, a half-breed," answered
Slim. "Nobody I ever met knew anythin' about him, except that he come from Nevada. While I never saw him, I
shore heard an' felt his lead one night; an' if he can shoot
that good in th' dark, by ear, I ain't honin' to meet him for
fun an' excitement in th' daytime when he can use his
eyes. He skinned my ear, put one through my arm, another
cut my shoulder, one went through my hat, th' fourth
grazed my side, an' th' fifth killed my cayuse. It sounded
like a loud *r-i-i-i-p!* Since then I don't make no noise at
night out there. I imitates a ghost when I move around, an'
I'm on full cock, with a hair trigger, every minute, which
is some strain."

"How'd it happen?" asked Johnny.

"We was roundin' up last fall, an' had a beef herd we
was holdin'. Th' night come on windy an' rainy, but there
wasn't no lightnin' or thunder. Four of us was ridin' th'
middle trick an' singin' plenty as we went around. Th' herd
had fed heavy an' was well watered, an' tired, an' we
wasn't worryin' much about it. Just after midnight we
heard a rumble from behind us, an' th' whole herd was on

its feet like one cow. It was a small bunch of stampeded cattle, an' when it hit our herd everythin' went that had hoofs. Th' cook, back in th' waggin', was awake because of a leak over his bed-roll, an' as soon as he heard th' rumble he let out a yell an' woke up th' off-shifts. They had their cayuses tied to th' waggin, or staked out close at hand, an' they forked 'em quick. Tom Wilkes saw my six-gun flashes an' he joins me. We lean against one end of th' front rank of our bunch, tryin' to turn 'em, an' get 'em to mill; but it wasn't no use. Th' herd had split up into bunches, an' our bunch run for half an hour southwest. When we finally got 'em millin', an' then busted that up, they figgered they had all th' runnin' they wanted an' behaved themselves. I rode back to take th' rear when I heard what sounded like another bunch runnin' west, quite a ways north of us. I sung out to Tom that I'd be back, an' streaked up to give a hand with th' other herd. When I got to it I rode right up front an' sung out that I was givin' a hand. My mouth wasn't hardly shut before I got in th' way of that stream of lead I told you about. I got my gun workin', but I was afoot an' had to hear th' herd leave me behind. Managin' to get my saddle off, I hoofed it for th' cook's fire, which was blazin' high when I got to where I could see it. By th' time I got there th' rain was comin' down in sheets, an' I was done up. They got away with over forty head, as near as we could figger it, an' th' rain had smoothed them sandy valleys over in th' Buttes so they didn't show a print. We wouldn't 'a' follered far, anyhow—Nevada likes ambushes, an' that country was made for 'em."

"I've been through it," growled Johnny. "There's th' fourth muley I've seen in ten minutes," he said, nodding to the right.

"He was made a muley by a saw," replied Slim. "That

feller was a bloody-minded terror. He's cost this ranch a dozen times what he was ever worth. We don't know what was th' matter with him—just born savage, I reckon. He killed an' ruined a lot of young steers before we got onto him. At first we was goin' to kill him; then we said he had been so all-fired mean that he ought to be punished. So we sawed off his horns an' turned him loose to play with th' rest of th' longhorns. He got some good lickin's before he learned that he wasn't dangerous no more. He got mauled so much before he quit his mean ways that we sort of felt sorry for him. Here comes Quantrell. He's our *segundo,* an' boss of our trail outfit. Good man, all around. Hey! Look at that old reprobate go for him! What do you think of that? Cimarron was th' man who sawed off his horns, an' cussed if he don't remember it!"

The approaching rider evaded the charge, fired close to the steer's nose as the animal went past, which turned its chain of thought, and rode up laughing.

"Did you see th' old boy?" he chuckled.

"Reg'lar friend of yourn," laughed Slim. "Here, shake han's with Nelson. He's comin' out to show us how to play draw—an' his pockets are full of money."

"Yo're welcome," said Cimarron, grinning, his hand-clasp solid and sincere. "Better put yore rope on him, Slim, in case he gets scared off."

Laughing and chatting they rode westward until about mid-afternoon when, hungry as wolves, they arrived at the bunkhouse, where Cimarron dared the sanctity of the cook shack to rustle warm, if rather dried-out food, from the back of the stove; and they ate to the frank and personal comments of several loafing onlookers. The rest of the afternoon was passed in discussions and reminiscences of things concerning range activities and in telling stories about men they had known. It was not long before other men began to come in from the range and the cook showed signs of activity. When he was ready he let out a yell: "Are you all a-comin'?" They were, and ate hungrily, for the most part in silence, listening to the three who had enjoyed a late dinner and who could take time to talk. Four men soon arose and exchanged banter as they looked to tobacco, guns, and other things requiring their attention and, saying good-by, went out to the corral. They had the first night shift on the west section and soon were riding away. Hardly two hours later another four-man group came in, fell upon the second meal the cook had prepared in less than three hours, and then loafed, joining in the conversation.

"How's things over Gunsight way?" Cimarron asked Johnny.

"Just th' same, I reckon," came the answer. "Everythin' is all right, a cussed sight better than they are further east. It's a shame, too; a cussed shame."

"Meanin'?" queried Lin Sherwood, the foreman, a tall, wiry man of about forty years, whose broad, sloping shoulders suggested great strength. His face was frank and kindly, and his steel-blue eyes twinkled from their frames of wrinkles in a manner to win Johnny the moment he had looked into them.

"I'm meanin' that old man with th' busted laig, over on the SV," answered Johnny; "an' that kid, an' that helpless girl. Do you know they ain't had no round-up in three years, neither calf nor beef?"

"What's that?" exclaimed Cimarron in surprise. "That ain't no way to run a ranch. Ain't they done no brandin' at all?"

"Ain't had an iron hot in three years," replied Johnny.

"What's th' matter with 'em?" demanded Matt Webb.

"They can't keep an outfit," answered Johnny. "Every

time they hired a man he was either scared off or bribed to quit. After a while they gave it up. Three of their men are workin' on th' Triangle, or th' Bar H right now."

"Then they didn't lose a whole lot," snorted Art French.

"If they don't round up, how do they know where they are?" asked Bud Norris. "How do they know how many cows they got, or if they're runnin' at a profit or a loss?"

"They don't," answered Johnny. "But there ain't no round-up necessary to tell 'em about profit an' loss. They can see th' herds skrinkin', it's so plain; an' when they has to sell off a few head every time they needs chuck, I reckon they know about th' profit an' loss. They want to have a round-up just to get a tally of th' cattle now on th' ranch. Knowing how many there was from th' tally th' year they took possession, they could tell what their losses are. But how can they hold one, without punchers?"

"They ought to know," said Slim. "But that wouldn't help 'em much, at that. It would only make 'em feel worse, I reckon."

"Their herds ain't got no business to shrink, not on a range like theirs," said Bud. "If they ain't throwed many on th' trail they ought to have more now than they had three years ago. Cattle don't stop multiplyin' just because they ain't rounded up once in a while!"

"Mebby their cattle are different, then," said Johnny. "An' there's one thing shore: I never saw so few mavericks on any ranch as there are on th' SV; nor so d——d many as I saw on th' Bar H. Why, when I was on th' Bar-20, down in th' Pecos Valley, we wouldn't 'a' let no ranch close to us hold so many unbranded cows."

"Where did you say?" quickly demanded Bill Dusenberry, who answered to the name of "Deuce."

"Bar-20," replied Johnny, "down in th' Pecos."

"Did you ever hear of Lacey?" excitedly asked Deuce.

"Lacey? Why, he run a saloon, over in Perry's Bend; an' he was a white man clean through."

"Holy mackerel!" cried Deuce. "Was you one of Peter's outfit?"

"I was near since I was old enough to throw a rope," answered Johnny, a pleased grin coming to his face. "Did you know Lacey, or Buck?"

"Lacey is my cousin," exclaimed Deuce. He turned to his friends. "We ain't goin' to have no poker tonight. This feller is goin' to entertain us with th' doin's of th' cussed-est he-man outfit that ever lived under one roof. Lacey has told me just enough to get me on th' prod—an' here's a man who was one of that outfit. You can begin with that cow-skinner you fellers went to Perry's Bend after. I'm tellin' you that if you can show us that you belonged to that hair-trigger outfit there ain't nothin' Bill Dusenberry an' his friends won't do for you. What was that cow-skinner's name, an' where did he die?"

"I'm glad to meet a relative of Lacey's," replied Johnny, smiling. "Lacey turned a buffalo gun loose on that gang of rustlers when they had me in Jackson's store after they had killed Edwards. As to Jerry Brown, he died in some sort of a church, or mission, or somethin' like that. He shot me in Harlan's saloon, shootin' through his coat pocket, th' skunk. Speakin' of mavericks, you fellers all know that if th' natural increase ain't branded yo're goin' to have a fine crop of unbranded cattle; an if there ain't no calves branded for three years, yo're shore goin' to have one slashin' big herd of mavericks. Now, if them mavericks wander off th' ranch there ain't no tellin' what'll happen to 'em. An' if they ain't allowed to git back again, or ain't kept off some other ranch, somebody's goin' to have a fine lot of cattle that can be marked with any brand they feels like puttin' on 'em. They won't even have to be vent branded: they can be sold, an' th' first an' only brand they start with can be th' sign of th' man that buys 'em. With a road brand to take 'em over th' trail, there ain't nobody can question 'em, is there? At least not down in this country, where there ain't no laws to question 'em."

"Yo're right!" exclaimed Slim, his eyes glowing with a sudden inspiration. "Where have our brains been, all this time? Reckon we was too busy out on our west line to do much thinkin' about other things."

"Yes, an' none of 'em will be much more than three years old," said Cimarron, looking around the room, where various expressions met his eye. "A plumb fine lot of unbranded cattle, runnin' up to three-year-olds, ready for any iron. I've been as dumb as a locoed dogie!"

"Lin," said Gus Thompson, turning to the foreman, "I'm tellin' you that when folks get th' maverick habit, an' ain't bothered, they get so, after a while, that they don't care a whole lot *where* them mavericks come from; an' you know that there are *some* parts of our ranch that are plumb heavy with scrub timber, brush, an' rough ground."

"Tell us about Perry's Bend," impatiently demanded Deuce.

"Tell us about yore gran'mother's cat!" snorted Bill Sage. "That can wait: Nelson's goin' to stay here a couple of nights, anyhow." He looked around. "I'm beginnin' to see through th' holes in th' ladder; an' I'm honin' to listen to why th' SV don't show no mavericks, when it ain't had a spring round-up for three years. Does it sleeper?"

"Not an earnotch," interjected Tom Wilkes. "You ought to know that, you flathead; you've seen enough SV cattle, anyhow."

"Mebby Nelson can explain it," suggested the foreman.

"I'm willin' to talk it over, anyhow," said Johnny. "In th' first place, there's natural enemies."

"Then you can leave 'em in th' first place," laughed Slim. "There ain't none, that I knows of, down here."

"Well, then, there's them quicksands," continued Johnny, gravely. "Cattle are plumb fascinated by quicksands—"

"Huh!" snorted Cimarron, "you ain't figgerin' them sands are takin' th' increase of three whole years, are you?"

"Or pickin' mavericks, as a choice?" grunted Matt Webb.

"They'd be so full of bones if they got three years' calves," said Bud, "that you could build a shack on 'em, an' never feel a quiver."

"Well, then, there's th' freezin' cold an' th' ice on th' grass," suggested Johnny, grinning. "We all know that cattle ain't got sense enough to paw through ice to get at th' grass under it."

"Shore!" snorted Slim. "Did we have a freeze-up last winter?" he asked the crowd.

"Not so no cows was killed," replied Cimarron. "An' I didn't see no driftin' herds at all."

"What's th' matter with you fellers?" indignantly demanded Johnny. "Here I'm tryin' to explain a mystery, an' you keep pullin' me out of th' saddle as fast as I climb up. That ain't fair. Then how about this one: Th' SV wasn't no good for winter range, bein' all et off?"

"Yo're down again," laughed Art French. "Th' SV is good winter range, an' summer, too."

"An' spring an' fall, an' th' Fourth of July, as well as Christmas," supplemented Bud.

"You fellers are shore ornery," complained Johnny. "Then mebby th' mavericks, bein' different than marked animals, all got th' travel itch an' left that arid valley for th' thick, green grass down south of 'em, or for th' juicy scrub an' clean rocks north of 'em."

"'Arid valley' is purty near as good as 'thick, green grass south of 'em,'" chuckled Cimarron. "Was you ever over on that luxuriant south range?" he asked, ironically.

"I wasn't, but Ol' Buffalo was," answered Johnny.

"Shore, but he don't eat grass," retorted Cimarron; "an' what's more, he don't stop on it at all."

"Well, I'll try once more," said Johnny, in simulated desperation. "Mebby cow-hawks flew away with 'em seein' that there wasn't no brands to prove nothin'."

After the laughter quieted down, Cimarron jammed his fist into an open palm with a resounding smash. "I'm thinkin' we got more interest in th' way them SV cows are handled than we ever thought. I'm gettin' interested in seein' that th' SV runs itself some better than it has. There's ideas millin' around in my head that some folks might say are scandalous an' unpolite. You all heard *me*—lemme hear somethin'."

"An' I'm wantin' to know," said Johnny, "what kind of barb wire is sold down in these parts?"

"Mean, cussed mean," replied Slim.

"Then mebby that's why it won't stay up," muttered Johnny. "It keeps a-comin' down from off them posts around th' quicksands, pullin' out double staples, an' draggin' itself all over th' valley. A couple of them posts set fire to themselves, too, an' burned till they busted themselves off, close to th' ground. I'm shore doin' a lot of guessin'."

"Lacey told me—" began Deuce.

"—to rope yourself," interrupted Cimarron. "We got lots of time, later, to hear about what Lacey told you."

"I believe in bein' neighborly," said Matt, "an' givin' folks a hand when they deserve it."

"Is th' Doc a friend of you fellers?" asked Johnny.

"We ain't weepin' none over his kidnappin', if that's what you mean," chuckled Matt. "He mebby will be kidnapped ag'in, sometime—an' hoof it back home. Why?"

"Well, I didn't want to hurt you fellers' feelin's," replied Johnny.

"What you mean?" asked Cimarron. "You'll have to be plumb rough to hurt any feelin's out here."

"Matt was sayin' he believes in bein' neighborly," explained Johnny, "an' I happened to think of somethin' about th' Doc, what stirred me a-plenty. That's why I asked."

"What was that?" asked Slim.

"Why, that Arnold girl was took sick about a year ago, an' they sent for th' Doc. He said he would doctor cows an' horses, but he wouldn't sling a laig across a saddle if th' whole SV was dyin', an' he refused to go. That kid had to ride to Highbank for that drunken doctor down there."

"Th' h—l you say!" snapped Thompson. "Is that right?"

"It is," answered Johnny. "An' it made me wonder what kind of country I'd got into. I maintains that no doctor like that measures up to th' standards of cow-country men; an' when th' old man busted his laig I says it was plumb proper that th' coyote was kidnapped an' made to do his plain duty."

"I'm admirin' that kidnappin' more every day," exclaimed Slim. "Th' dog wouldn't have to be kidnapped if he was needed on th' Bar H."

"Huh!" snorted Cimarron. "If Big Tom had a sore toe th' Doc would bust his neck an' kill a hoss gettin' there."

"Will somebody tell me what's th' matter with that coyote?" asked Larry Hallock. "One day he's as bright as a new dollar an' witty as blazes; th' next, he looks like somebody had dragged him by th' heels through th' hottest parts of h—l. Talk about quick changes! He's a wonder. What's he drinkin', anyhow?"

"I reckon it ain't drink," said the foreman, reflectively.

"I once knowed a gambler, up in Dodge, that could play longer than anybody in town—hours longer—but when he went to pieces he shore hit hard. An' he'd rather lie than tell th' truth. However, th' devil with th' Doc; I'm wonderin' about somethin' else."

"Lacey knowed a man like that," said Deuce, but got no further, for Cimarron balanced a gun in his hand and seemed to be considering.

"I'm itchin' for to shoot Lacey," Cimarron remarked, "but as he ain't on hand any of his tribe will do. You shut up about Lacey till th' time's ripe to talk about him!"

"It'd look too set, too plain, an' sort of hintin'," soliloquized the foreman, "to send a Double X bunch over there. If we could make it universal, sort of free-for-all, with others joinin' in, it would be better. It would look like a surprise party an' not point too strong in one direction. They should have a round-up an' get a tally. Even a little iron heatin' wouldn't be out of place, as long as it was done by them as didn't belong to th' SV. Nobody could hardly blame th' SV for brandin' mavericks, an' say they was stealin' cows that didn't belong to 'em, if punchers from other ranches did th' brandin'. How many men do you reckon we'd need, Nelson?"

"More than you could spare if you kept a good watch on that west section," answered Johnny, seeing the drift of the foreman's thoughts. "Quite some few more. An' you got to count me out of it, 'though I'd be glad to stay here an' take some man's place while he's gone. I don't aim to be hobbled in th' future by comin' out strong an' plain. That may sound funny, but I got things to answer for if they're found out an' laid to me—which I ain't aimin' to have found out, positive. It ain't that I'm gun-shy, or tryin' to slip out of trouble, but I just ain't ready to smoke up, right now. It's shore a puzzle."

Arch Wiggins slapped his thigh with stinging emphasis. "I'm seein' th' drift of this here conversation, an' I ain't declarin' myself in because th' wool is bein' pulled over my eyes at all; but I *am* declarin' myself in, clean up to my hat, because I'm a cowman, through an' through, first an' last; an' because I'm a human bein'. If any round-up gang needs a first-class hoss wrangler for a few days, or a week, without pay, an' willin' to feed hisself, I'm speakin' for th' job. An' I ain't too lazy to keep irons hot, neither. Do I hear anythin'?"

Jim Hallock leaped to his feet. "I come down here to visit, an' get a rest," he declared, grinning. "I've had all th' visitin' I wants with a bunch of cold-deckers; an' I ain't had no rest since I arrove. My fingers ache from dealin' an' cuttin' an' drawin'; an' I can see deuces an' treys in my sleep, when I get any. Speakin' for myself, I'd enjoy seein' that lazy Wiggins wranglin' cayuses for me every mornin' before sunup. I'll do my cussedest to wear him to a frazzle. How about you, boys?" he asked, turning to his brothers.

"I ain't got no love for Arch Wiggins," announced Wood, "but I'm swallerin' my pride. If he wants an assistant wrangler that knows more about th' job than he ever will, I'm ready to take orders, an' sacrifice my independence an' self-respect."

"Where you find one Hallock," chuckled George, "you finds more. We was brought up like that. I can use an iron with any man on th' range, no matter who says I'm lyin'."

Larry burst out laughing. "I never let my cub brothers put on no airs," he declared; "an' some older member of th' family ought to go along to keep 'em from gettin' into trouble. I'm signin' this pay-yoreself-pay-roll, with Lin's permission."

"I can't give no permission to anybody in my outfit to

brand mavericks, or run another man's ranch for him," said Sherwood, "but I reckon I can give some of you boys a few days off, in case you want to go fishin' over in Green Valley, or chase them cow-hawks Nelson was tellin' about. Do you chase 'em, or trap 'em, Nelson?"

"You put a hunk of maverick meat on th' end of a rope, an' tie knots in it," said Johnny. "Th' cow-hawk swallers th' whole thing, an' th' knots get caught in his innards. Then you shoot him through th' epizootic with a hunk of lead. Didn't you ever go huntin' 'em?"

"No, but I've heard all about it," replied Sherwood, apologetically. "Now, lemme see: some of you fellers have got to stay here. There's twelve, not countin' me, which nobody ever does, anyhow. Twelve, thanks to them Snake Buttes coyotes, on a ranch that shouldn't have more'n eight. Well, after all, sizin' up th' twelve an' lumpin' 'em, an' dividin' it by one real, shore-enough puncher, they only come to eight, after all. I figger I can do without four of th' laziest—five, if Nelson stays to show somebody how his job ought to be done. Now, that makes nine goin' to Gunsight to spend their time an' money. Somebody ought to remember about a cook, for I'm sayin' right out loud an' flat, that our cook ain't gettin' no time off."

"You can't make me sore," chuckled Lem Curtis, culinary artist of the ranch." It'd only be out of th' fryin' pan an' into th' fire for me. Thanks, Lin."

"I can cook good enough for any bow-laigged coyote that ever set foot on this ranch," declared Art French. "An' besides, I got some scores to settle up. I'll cook."

"Well," said Sherwood, "I promised Cimarron sometime ago that he could have a few days off, to rest up from them poker parties. He's a good foreman an' round-up boss, only he ought to do some work hisself. But I'm bettin' our wrangler ain't got enough saddle stock within a day's ride to give you fellers a *remuda* apiece—say about five to a man."

"If you wasn't th' foreman an' keeper of th' payroll," retorted Rich Morgan, "I'd say you was a cross-eyed fabricator. Cuss yore nerve! I'm th' best hoss wrangler, barrin' Arch, of course, that ever took a cussin' from a fool outfit. What th' devil is a little matter like a herd of forty-five saddle hosses to a man like *me*?"

The foreman leaned back and laughed contentedly. "You would think we was wantin' 'em to go to a dance," he said to Johnny, his eyes twinkling, "instead of goin' out of their way to do some hard work. I'm bettin' th' SV has a proper round-up. Who's goin' to be tally man?"

"That takes a good man away from work, when anybody can count knots or make a pencil mark," growled Cimarron. "We ought to have somebody that can't do nothin' else like that Two-Spot over in Gunsight."

"That's th' tally man!" shouted Arch.

"He's ourn, if we has to do some kidnappin' ourselves," exulted Larry. "We won't let him have a smell of liquor till we drop him off at Gunsight on th' way back. An' then we'll pickle him so he'll keep for a week."

"He won't do," asserted Slim. "He can't keep a tally straight."

"I'm sayin' he can," contradicted Johnny, smiling. "Seems to me I've seen him do little things that showed me he was a-punchin' once—an' punchin' for a long time. I'll bet he can keep tally as good as any man in this outfit, an' count 'em as they pass, too. Mebby he wouldn't suit a buyer, or a seller, but he's good enough for me. Anyhow, you can call th' figgers when yo're countin' herd. There won't be a new brand get away from him if you let him alone. It's time he was put to work."

"Mebby he won't work on th' SV?" suggested Arch.

"Th' Doc didn't want to, neither, did he?" demanded Slim; "but he did. What's th' use of kidnappin' anybody that wants to be took? He'll work, all right—or he won't eat."

"Hey," said Cimarron, turning to Johnny. "We got a lot of gall runnin' a round-up on another man's ranch. What'll we say to 'em? We got to say *somethin'*!"

"Tell 'em it's a neighborly act," replied Johnny. "Say you'd 'a' done it before if you'd 'a' knowed about things."

"They got any wire?" asked Wood. "I'm aimin' to run a fence around them posts that'll make some thief cuss some dark an' stormy night, as th' books say. Staplin' is fine, but takin' a couple of turns around th' posts an' staplin' all around is better."

"I reckon so," answered Johnny. "If they ain't tell Dailey to give you a spool an' charge it to me."

"Not bein' in on this personal I'll pervide a spool," offered the foreman. "I'd like to see this crew at work over there—a man allus works harder for somebody as a favor than he does for th' man that pays him. It would give me a line on how hard I could crowd you fellers. Wood, if you throw about three half-hitches over them posts before you staple 'em, you'll bother anybody that tries to unwind it from a hoss. Try it an' see."

"Yo're talkin' gospel," said Wood, grinning. "It'll just wind up th' other way, an' before he knows what he's doin' he'll have one plumb, fine job on his hands."

"I'll give two bits, purty near," chuckled the foreman, "to see some faces in this country when th' news gets out about this here high-speed round-up. But I don't reckon there'll be no trouble about it. I'm sayin', however, if you'll listen to me, don't nobody start none. Yore job is takin' care of SV cows, an' not gun-fightin', 'though I know there ain't no danger of anybody chasin' you off th' range."

"There won't be no trouble, Lin," assured Cimarron, "not if I has to shoot up th' whole blasted country. An' I'm aimin' to have some of them Triangle riders join hands with us: we're roundin' up wide an' regardless, an' it stands to reason that we'll have to cross their boundary line. But we'll be polite an' fair; we'll tell 'em three times, smiling. After that it'll be their own bull-headed fault."

"There's one man on th' Triangle I hope is hard of hearin'," chuckled Tom Wilkes; "that's Gurley. Can *I* ask him, Cimarron?"

"You'll stay right here," replied the *segundo*. "We'll have trouble enough, mebby, takin' things as they come, without luggin' along no canned grudges."

"You watch me stay here!" retorted Wilkes.

"I'll do that very thing," chuckled the foreman. "Yo're goin' to show Nelson over our west range tomorrow night, an' cover more ground out there on account of there bein' fewer of you. Nelson," he said, turning, "have you any choice of men for this here party that's goin' to celebrate their freedom over in Gunsight?"

"I ain't sayin' a word—not one word."

"All right, then," continued the foreman. "Now, boys, them that are goin' to have a few days off are: Cimarron, Larry, Art, Slim, an' Bud. I ain't lendin' no cayuses, wire, or no chuck waggin, for they ain't needed goin' to Gunsight on a spree; but, I'm sayin' that I don't expect to go in th' storeroom, nor th' waggin shed, nor have no time to bother about my hoss wrangler's job. If he wants to keep a lot of saddle hosses away off somewhere where they can't be seen, that's his business. He's doin' th' wranglin' for this ranch, an' nobody else is. An'," he grinned, turning toward the cook, "Lem, here, has a pore mem'ry an' never would miss no pots an' pans."

"I has; likewise I'm blind," said Lem. "But lemme make a prophecy: If there are any cookin' utensils that gets misplaced an' can't be found for near a week, an' they ain't as clean when they're found again as they was when they got lost, there'll be some h—l-roarin', excitin' times on this here packet. You all here me chirp?"

"Now, then, Nelson," said Deuce, "tell us about Lacey an'—" he broke off his request as he dodged Cimarron's boot, for the *segundo* was a man of set ideas, and he was going to turn in.

"If I hears any more about that cousin of yourn, to-night," quoth Cimarron, pulling off a second boot and balancing it, "there is goin' to be weepin' in th' Deusenberry family. I'm turnin' in, an' I only turns in when I want to go to sleep. I got plenty of work ahead of me for a few days. An' I'm sayin', further, that if there's any poker playin' tonight, it's goin' to be held in th' kitchen, an' played by a lot of dumb men."

"An' if I ketches any poker parties in my kitchen," announced Lem, arising and flexing his muscles, "I'll heave 'em out again. I ain't goin' to clean up after no pack of bums. You hear me real plain?"

"Couple of grouches," growled Slim, looking around. "Get th' cards an' beans, Tom. We'll pull th' waggin out of th' shed, an' play in there, out of th' wind. Somebody else get th' lanterns."

"An' what are *you* goin' to get?" demanded Rich, pausing as he started to take a lantern down from its peg.

"I wasn't goin' to say nothin' about that," answered Slim, grinning; "but as long as you asked, I'll tell you. I'm goin' to get th' money. Come on, Nelson; we'll move th' waggin for them suckers."

"I don't mind lookin' like a sucker," retorted Rich, getting the other lantern, "as long as I don't play like one. Who'll buy Slim's watch from me tomorrow?" he asked from the doorway.

"Yo're blockin' th' door, an' talkin' foolish," said

Thompson, shoving him aside. "Anybody wants that watch'll have to come an' see *me.* Don't forget them beans," he called over his shoulder.

"He ain't got time to get 'em," muttered Tom, "but he'll have to wait for *me, if I* get 'em. Can you figger him?"

XVI

♦

A Neighborly Call

At daylight there was hubbub, horseplay, and banter on the Double X. Art French climbed up into the chuck wagon (the cook's supply list in his pocket), banged on a huge pot, and announced that the race was on. Arch Wiggins, on this part of the journey, at least, had plenty of assistant horse wranglers, for the eight riders, Cimarron with the rest, herded the horses and started for the SV, happy as schoolboys on a lark.

Reaching Gunsight, they caused quite some commotion, and fired into the air to give zest to the occasion. Dave mopped his beaded brow several times before his share in the festivities slackened, and Two-Spot, burning with a fever of curiosity, shuffled from the chuck wagon being loaded in front of Dailey's to the saloon, asking shrewd questions and making pertinent observations.

"An' why th' waggin?" he asked Slim.

"To put Juniper in," answered that cheerful disciple of George Washington. "We reckoned we'd like to have a town closer to th' ranch, an' Gunsight ain't good enough."

Two-Spot wandered around and put the question to Cimarron.

The *segundo* regarded him with level gaze. "It's for th' widder's mite," he answered. "We're on th' rustle, which ain't to be told."

"Huh!" snorted Two-Spot, "you might be aimin' for some widder, at that; but I'm sayin' that if she sees you first, you'll need more'n eight men an' a waggin to take her away from her home an' fambly. What are you aimin' to rustle?"

"Every cow on a certain ranch between here an' Juniper," whispered Cimarron, looking stealthily around.

"Then don't you waste no time hangin' around here," warned Two-Spot, also looking stealthily around. "Big Tom's gettin' up early these mornin's, I bets."

Cimarron gravely shook his head, whereat Two-Spot remarked carelessly, apropos of nothing, "Smitty has left th' range for good. He had two holes in his hat, th' upper hole like a coffeepot with th' lid back. He rode his own hoss, an' was goin' strong when he passed here. But nobody was chasin' him, then."

"Hey, fellers!" shouted the *segundo,* joyously, "Smitty has follered Squint, with a couple of gun-shot wounds in his Mex. hat!"

Laughter and cheerful remarks greeted the news, and Dave had to verify it.

"Bar H: mark *two*!" cried Norris. "Bring 'em up, you ropers—th' irons are hot!"

Two-Spot, despairing of gaining any real information in Dave's, shuffled out and went to Dailey's where Art French was putting the last of the provisions on the wagon.

"Hello, French!" greeted Two-Spot, putting a foot on the spokes of a wheel. "Where are you fellers headin' for?"

"Up th' Juniper trail," answered Art. "Want to come along? Have you got th' nerve to take a chance with somebody else's cattle?"

Two-Spot looked at him intently. "What are you aimin' to do with 'em?" he asked.

"What do folks usually do with cows that don't belong to 'em?" countered Art.

"Holy mavericks!" muttered Two-Spot. "These here ijuts ain't carin' a whole lot who knows about it! What you got th' waggin for? Aimin' to squat out there an' steal 'em as fast as they grows up?"

"That's for th' hides of them that gets killed. We're goin' to round up every hoof, clean and prompt."

"You didn't stop at th' Doc's on yore way up, did you?" asked Two-Spot, paying no attention to the noise made by several men who had mounted and were riding toward the wagon at a walk.

"Why?"

"Oh, nothin', only I reckon'd mebby you'd got some of them little white pills he shoots into hisself."

"Can you keep a tally?" asked Art, carelessly.

"I can; but I won't."

Art waved a hand at him. "He can tally; but he won't."

Three ropes dropped over the surprised ex-tally man and were drawn not unpleasantly tight. He thought it might be a joke, so he grinned; it would not do to let anyone think he took it seriously, because it might cause them to take it that way. "Takes three men on hosses to rope me," he jeered, chuckling. "Better get th' rest of th' gang before I gets rough an' boisterous."

"Can you set a horse?" asked Slim.

"I shore can't," regretted Two-Spot. "It's one of th' sorrers of my life."

"Then we'll have to tie him on," said Wood. "Chuck us out a couple of hobbles, Art."

"I can ride any hoss you can," boasted Two-Spot. "I was bustin' 'em before you was borned."

"Then we'll hobble th' hoss," laughed Wiggins.

"Loosen 'em up; I hears Dave a-callin'!" exclaimed Two-Spot, suspiciously eager to answer duty's call.

"Where you aimin' to have him swing?" demanded Art. "Squint has got to be revenged."

"Th' first tree," growled Slim. "We gives you one chance to save yoreself an' help rid this range of lawbreakers. Who got Squint?"

"You go to h—l!" blazed Two-Spot as the ropes tightened. "Take 'em off me!"

"Who got Squint?" repeated Slim, threateningly.

"If I tells, will you let me out of these cussed ropes?" asked the shivering victim.

"We will!"

"Smitty got him," chuckled the captive. "Ask him if you don't believe me. Take 'em off, now!" As soon as he was freed he danced away, wary and anxious, and bumped into Cimarron, whose muscular arms held him as in a vice. "*Now,* what's th' matter?" blazed Two-Spot, wriggling in vain. "What you reckon yo're goin' to do?"

"We need a tally man on this rustlin' expedition," said Cimarron, "an' we like yore looks. Bring up a cayuse, an' he can go bareback; either that or ride with Art."

"I'm ridin' with Art if I goes, which I ain't aimin' to!" snorted Two-Spot. "I can't count up to more'n ten," he protested.

"You won't have to count at all," Cimarron assured him. "All you got to do is make little pencil marks like a picket fence on a piece of paper, or drop a pebble in yore hat for every cow. You can drop pebbles, can't you?"

"Not very good," deprecated Two-Spot. "I'm too oncertain."

"Well, when yo're oncertain," chuckled Slim, "yore chuck will be oncertain. Th' oncertainer you are, th' less you'll eat."

Cimarron picked Two-Spot up and put him in the

wagon, whereupon Slim and Wood rode up close to it, ropes in hand. "There ain't nothin' oncertain about Slim's ropin', or Wood's, neither," warned Cimarron. "You better stay right in that wagon." He turned to go to his horse. "Come on, boys! We're startin' *now*!"

Dave went to a window to see them off, caught sight of Two-Spot's appealing face in the wagon, and hastened to the door and out toward the vehicle.

"Hi!" shrilled Larry, his rope darting from his hand.

"Hi! Hi! Hi!" yelled the others, their ropes going to the mark.

"What'n h—l!" shouted Dave, struggling, and glaring around. He was the center from which four rope radii pointed to the cardinal points of the compass. "Leggo me! Loosen 'em up, you coyotes! Loosen up!"

"Does Two-Spot go with us?" asked Larry.

"Can we borrow him for a few days, to keep tally for us on th' SV, Mr. Green?" politely inquired Bud, tightening the rope.

"You can; an' go to blazes, for all I cares!" snorted Dave. He loosened the ropes and lost no time in getting back to his window. "Cuss 'em! All right; *take* him!" he yelled at the noisy cavalcade. "But if anythin' happens to him, you'll settle with Dave Green! You hear me?"

They did not.

Margaret, responding to her brother's excited summons, went to the door and her hands flew to her breast. A wagon, loaded with packages, pulled up at the dilapidated corral and eight rough-looking men, driving a herd of horses, stopped near it. One of them kept on at a walk and approached her. Removing his sombrero, he pulled up and bowed.

"Ma'am," he said, slowly and kindly, a smile wreathing

his weather-beaten face, from which genial gray eyes twinkled at her; "Ma'am, we have come out to round up for you. We understand that this ranch ain't' been combed for three years—an' it shore is time it was. I saw a wire fence north of th' trail: how far does it run?"

"Why, why—I didn't know—we were not expecting any round-up. Isn't there some mistake?" she faltered.

"I don't reckon there is, Ma'am," Cimarron assured her. "Mr. Nelson was tellin' us about th' SV, an' we all reckoned it was time there was a round-up run over here. You ought to know how many cows you got; an' mebby there's some as should be branded."

"I hardly know what to say—how to thank you," Margaret replied. "Won't you come in and speak to father? He doesn't want to leave his bed for a few days more."

"Shore, Ma'am," said Cimarron, dismounting and throwing the reins over the head of his horse, and following her into the house.

"Father, this is Mr.—Mr.—?" she looked at Cimarron inquiringly.

"Quantrell—Cimarron Quantrell," he smiled. "I was born on th' banks of th' Cimarron when they wasn't exactly safe for bein' born on, but our fambly was lucky."

"This is my father, Mr. Quantrell," smiled Margaret. "I'll leave you men to talk by yourselves. If you want me, please call."

"Arnold," said Cimarron, with simple directness, "we've come out here, nine of us, from th' Double X, to round up for you. Nelson said you hadn't held none in three years, an' we reckoned it was time we was payin' you a neighborly call. When you get an outfit of yore own some day you can give us a hand. By helpin' each other we'll both be helpin' ourselves. How far does that wire fence run, up north of th' house?"

"Mr. Quantrell, I don't know how to thank you," replied Arnold. "I was growing to think there were no human beings in this country, but I'm beginning to change my mind. Even Doctor Reed has had a change of heart."

"Don't you bank on th' Doc changin' his ideas," warned Cimarron. "He come out here because he was made to come. He shore was plain kidnapped that night."

"You amaze me! Surely you are mistaken. Who would force him to come here?"

"That ain't known," answered Cimarron, "but everybody knows he was forced, all right. Th' fool says so, hisself."

"This is astonishing!"

"How long did you say that wire was?"

"Oh, yes; I forgot. It's nearly a mile; why?"

"I'm aimin' to hold a herd ag'in' it; it'll save men. Now, we're aimin' to start on th' west end first, before anybody knows what's up," and the *segundo* sketched the operations as he had planned them. Leaving as soon as he could, he was crossing the kitchen when Margaret stopped him.

"You told father about Doctor Reed coming against his will?" she asked.

"Why, yes, Ma'am; did I trample on anythin'?"

"It doesn't matter—only I hoped to keep that from him. It pleased him so to think the hostility was dying out."

"Ma'am, I'm shore sorry, but I didn't know that. An' it's all right, too, for th' hostility *is* dying out."

"It's perfectly all right. Where do you expect to cook; and what are you doing with Two-Spot?"

"We aim to cook on th' range, Ma'am; an' Two-Spot is goin' to be our tally man. He was plumb tickled at th' chance to help."

"Can't you cook here? Or, better yet, can't I cook for you? I would like to do something."

"Well, at first we'll not be near enough to th' house for th' boys to have time to ride in for meals," Cimarron replied. "You see, as we move over th' range, our cook moves with us, which saves time. Mebby when we work close at hand you can cook a meal for us—but I'm sayin' that you don't know what yo're tryin' to get into. I'll be leavin' now, Ma'am. If you hears anythin', or sees anythin' that you don't understand, don't you worry none. I'm goin' out to start th' boys. Good afternoon, Ma'am."

She watched him join the riders and saw them, with chuck wagon and horse herd, drive down toward Green Valley, noisy with cheerful laughter and shouted jests. They passed around a hill and became lost to her sight, and soon the voices could be heard no more.

"Margaret!" came an excited, impatient call from the front room.

"Yes, Father; I'm coming," she answered, turning and entering the house.

"It begins to look like people are getting friendly," he exclaimed, smiles playing on his drawn face. "Perhaps things will change, and we can make the ranch a success!"

" 'Luck always turns,' " she smiled.

"Are you getting to believe in luck?" he demanded.

" 'I do; when somebody's behind it pushing hard,' " she replied, turning her face away.

"Are you crying my dear?" he exclaimed, but she had left the room.

While events were moving smoothly and swiftly on the SV, a new freight wagon rumbled north over the Highbank-Gunsight trail; and about the time that a circle of tired but happy punchers sat around a roaring fire on the west end of the SV ranch, the great wagon rolled around the corner of the hotel in Gunsight and the weary driver got down stiffly to put up and attend to his four-horse team. After becoming acquainted with George, and eating a hasty supper in the hotel, Jerry Wheatley went around to Dave's to make the acquaintance of that person and whoever else might be in the saloon, and to tell about Wolf Forbes and his trip to Highbank. He found the place quiet, but he left it full of hysterical laughter, wet eyes, sore sides, and some hiccups. And before he had gone to sleep, Dave's patrons were emulating some of the substantial citizens of Highbank in the avidity with which they sought strength from Dave's merchandise. An occasional burst of uproarious laughter brought the freighter back from the shadowy boundaries of sleep and set his bed shaking as he silently joined in. Realizing that Wolf's miseries were going to do more for him in the matter of getting acquainted along the way than a dozen ordinary trips up the trail would accomplish, he smiled contentedly and fell asleep.

XVII

♦

News All Around

At daylight Jerry went on his way rejoicing; the round-up started again in full swing on the SV, crossing the line onto Triangle range, to the later astonishment and vexation of Frank Gurley, Triangle rider on that section, whose hasty visit to his bunkhouse aroused a lively discussion, fortified him with Sam Gardner and Jim Lefferts to protect the interests of their ranch, and upon their return to the scene of activity, fortified Cimarron's

smiling, but firm outfit, with three more men. In Highbank, Wolf Forbes, penniless now, was beginning to go
without liquor and drift toward soberness, and the lambent
flame of his reawakened anger burned constantly stronger;
while out on the Double X, Johnny and the sleeping members of that outfit awoke to a new day's work, and to a
firmer and warmer bond between them. The Bar H awakened to a new puzzle; the mysterious disappearance of
Smitty and the discussion which followed his inexplicable
absence resulted in Dahlgren being dispatched to Gunsight
to see if the erring puncher had yielded to his well-known
thirst and might be found snoring in that vicinity. Also, he
was to keep an eye out for Wolf, and to make cautious inquiry concerning him.

Dahlgren was most successful in his mission, accumulating a fund of information staggering in its total and
barren of reason. His first accretion of wisdom came
when he left East Canyon and descried numerous punchers zealously bent upon an operation well known to him,
and he rode up for what information he might be able to
obtain. Hoping for a full loaf, expecting a half, he left
with a few crumbs which only increased his appetite for
more. In Gunsight his appearance caused unnecessary
hilarity, and his questions as to Smitty's location were
received with impolite guffaws, followed by an explicit
description of Smitty's riding, looks, words, and actions,
coupled to various prophesies, variously stated. When he
mentioned Wolf, a veritable gale of laughter deafened and
confused him, and the roundabout, cryptic, and fragmen-
tary references to Wolf taxed his brain. He gathered the
information that Wolf was wrapped in hides as his preference in perfumes; that Wolf was in the skin business,
without competitors; that he had descended in the social
scale to the point where he traveled as freight; that he took

an arduous, unnecessary, and uncomfortable journey and
was to be known, henceforth and hereafter, as Polecat, a
name being better suited to his habits and preferences. It
was explained that he was not expected back, which accounted for the half-masted flags and the black bands on
the hats. He learned that Smitty was on the trail of Squint
and would catch him if he went far enough in the right direction, and that Polecat was on the trail of Smitty, but
would have to ride hard; and a further suggestion postu-
lated the belief that Squint was on the trail of Wolf. Gunsight was as generous in its liquor as it was in its
explanations; it was open-handed and lavish, and insisted
that the distinguished Bar H ambassador imbibe freely,
which he did; and when he was helped into his saddle and
started for home, he tried to repeat what he had heard so
that he would not forget it; and by the time he reached the
bunkhouse he had not forgotten anything but the relations
between the various parts of each thing to be remembered,
and his account was verbal hash. Big Tom learned, among
other things equally lucid and valuable, that Polecate Forbes
went after Squint hunting Smitty's holy hat rounding up
SV cows on the Double X part of the Triangle journey and
would not be back until forty miles of hides went up toward Juniper with Two-Spot keeping tally on Cimarron's
wagon.

In the presence of such loquacity, Big Tom lost the power
of speech, choked with feelings of a murderous kind, and
used the flat of his foot as a propulsive agent, which Dahlgren found helped him in getting to his bunk, where he
sprawled out on his back and snored through a cloud of
flies foregathered for their share of what had dribbled.

The foreman strode to the horse corral, swearing at every step, caught, saddled, and mounted his best horse and
rode off to see and hear for himself. The first man he met
was Cimarron, who was expecting visitors after Dahl-

gren's departure, and had placed himself where he would be seen easily. The *segundo* had been thinking things over and had about come to the conclusion that it would be foolish to try to deny the part the Double X was taking in the round-up; and when he caught sight of Big Tom riding toward him a feeling of contempt swept over him and decided the question.

"There's more excitement on this ranch than I've seen in some time," smiled the Bar H foreman. "Makin' a clean sweep of everythin' that's got hoofs?"

"Clean is th' word," answered Cimarron, his smile as friendly as the visitor's. "I reckon Lin is mebby thinkin' more about beef, though."

"Aimin' to start a herd up th' trail?"

"I don't just know what dickerin' there may come out of this," answered the round-up boss. "He says for me to take some of th' boys an' round up over here. There's no tellin' what he may do. I know that I can report that there's quite some four-year-olds, an' a few three-year-olds. Where th' devil th' cattle under four years old are keepin' themselves I don't know. But if he's aimin' to throw in a herd for Arnold an' send 'em up th' trail with some of ours they'll be numerous enough to make a showin'. He may be gettin' sweet on this ranch, because of them Snake Buttes thieves. If he is, I reckon Arnold wouldn't turn down a fair cash offer for grazin' a couple of herds over here through th' fall an' winter. He's got room for three times th' number feedin' here now."

"There ain't no doubt about that," answered Big Tom. "When are you aimin' to round up for strays on our north end?"

"Why, there can't be many over there," replied Cimarron. "Th' natural barriers would keep 'em back. Have you noticed any?"

"Nary a one; but if you want to make shore, I'll lend

you a couple of th' boys, 'though I'm shore gettin' short of men."

"If you say you ain't seen none, that's good enough for me until th' spring round-up, anyhow; an' then we can start combin' at the same time, if we do th' work for th' SV, of course."

"What's Arnold askin' for th' SV, lock, stock, an' barrel?" bluntly asked Big Tom.

"Don't know," answered Cimarron, surprised. "I don't reckon Lin would consider buyin' it, 'less, mebby, he could sell th' Double X. But what's th' use of you an' me talkin' about that? I don't know, nothin' except orders, an' th' only orders I got was to run this round-up an' get back as soon as I can. I'll be leavin' you now, for I'm workin' harder than any man here, which shore is sayin' somethin'."

"An' I got to be ridin' on," said the Bar H foreman, and he made the words good. Reaching the Doc's shack, he dismounted and went inside, where he remained for nearly an hour, came out, glanced at the bullet holes and then went on to town, where he found the saloon deserted except for the proprietor.

Dave looked up and let his hand rest on the cap-and-ball under the bar, said cap-and-ball being .44 caliber, with the annoying habit of often sending one through the barrel, and igniting the caps on the nearest chambers and sending their contents along each side of the barrel with roving commissions.

"Well, Dave!" smiled Big Tom, motioning for a drink that he did not want, "I'm lookin' for strays—two-laigged strays."

"What you wants is another outfit to ride herd on this one," sympathized Dave. "Lookin' for Smitty?"

"He's one of 'em. Have you seen him?"

"I have. He didn't stop here, so I don't know where he got it," said the proprietor, grinning; "but from th' way he acted, insultin' folks, I reckon he must 'a' been bit by a passel of snakes, an' took too much cure."

"That's th' worst of them sponges," regretted Big Tom, a scowl going over his face. "I don't mind a periodic if there's plenty of time in between; but Smitty's periodics are like th' days in th' week durin' a round-up—they come too close together. Have you seen any others?"

"I ain't—not since Wolf was in here one afternoon last week," answered Dave. "Let's see: that was th' day Ol' Buffalo come down from Sherman, which would make it on a Friday. But," he said sorrowfully, "I has had distressin' news about Wolf. Young Jerry Wheatley, who's freightin' now, stopped in here only last night an' says Wolf was down in Highbank drinkin' 'em out of everything but water. He says yore puncher was on th' worst bender he's seen in months, which I says means somethin', comin' from a town like Highbank."

Big Tom's fist crashed on the bar. "Cuss it!" he exclaimed wrathfully, "that's th' worst of them periodics! You can't never tell when they'll start, an' nobody knows when they'll stop!"

"You lose, both ways," nodded Dave. "Jerry says he didn't have no hoss, saddle, or guns; an' a man can travel rapid on what they'd sell for."

"They wouldn't buy th' cayuse," reflected Big Tom, "seein' as he ain't supposed to own no Bar H animal. But I reckon it might 'a' strayed th' Lord only knows how far. We ain't noticed no cayuse missin', so far, but that don't mean nothin'. All right! He can come back when he goes broke an' sobers up an' he can walk, d—n him! Was Lang with him?"

"Lang? Is he missin', too?" Dave's astonishment was genuine.

"Disappeared like th' earth swallowed him," growled Big Tom. "They've hunted all over for him, an' can't find nothin' at all. I'm sayin' this country is goin' *loco;* an' I'll give a hundred dollars cash to find out what's at th' bottom of it all. Why, cuss it! Sherwood is roundin' up for the SV—what's th' matter with *him*? Is he *loco,* too?"

"Mebby he figgers on makin' them idle punchers of his'n bring in somethin' besides appetites," guessed Dave. "I don't blame him at all."

"Mebby; but they acts like they was havin' a picnic out there. Have you heard anythin' about th' Double X startin' a herd of their own up on th' trail?"

"Not a word; but ain't they throwin' their cattle into McCullough's this year?"

"They're supposed to; but you can't never tell," answered the foreman. He glanced around and then looked fixedly at his companion. "Yo're not forgettin' what I said about a hundred dollars' cash, are you?" he asked.

"That's somethin' I ain't likely to forget," replied Dave ambiguously, "if you mean it, shore."

"I'm meanin' it 'though I ain't wantin' you to have no rivals," replied Big Tom, significantly. "You hears an' sees a lot in here an' there ain't no use of lettin' anybody else in on it, an' splittin' up with you."

"There ain't nobody else goin' to get in on it," truthfully assured Dave.

"Nelson got over his grouch ag'in' wimmin?" laughed the foreman.

"Don't reckon so; but he ain't seen her yet, I guess," replied Dave, grinning. "When he does, there ain't no tellin' what's goin' to happen to him. Don't it beat all? You better look out, Tom; he may edge you out of th' game."

"Me!" demanded the foreman. He let out a roar of laughter. "I ain't got no interest thataway at all. I passed, cold." He turned away. "Don't forget Dave."

"Goin' so soon?"

"Yes; I'm ridin' back. *Adios.*"

Dave stared out of the window for a few minutes, his face slowly getting redder. "Yo're lyin', Big Tom," he muttered. "Yo're aimin' to get that girl more'n ever you was. An', d—n yore shriveled soul! Do I look like a Judas?"

Down on the SV, Cimarron was weighing something in his mind. Perhaps he had said too much to the Bar H foreman. Coming to a sudden decision he rode over to Bud Norris.

"Hello, Boss!" said Bud, grinning from ear to ear. "Big Tom's visit ridin' you?"

"Bud, we've got enough men here for this toy roundup," replied Cimarron. "There ain't no use of robbin' th' ranch of a man that ain't really needed here, an' I'm wishin' to send word to Lin by somebody who won't shuffle it. Now, you listen close," and the round-up boss gave him the facts of Big Tom's visit. "Tell him that, an' what I said. He ought to know my leads in case that big coyote rides out to th' house an' gets curious. Now you tell me what I've just told you." Bud complied, and when he had finished, his companion nodded. "Big Tom ain't seen you. You go north, foller th' Juniper trail back, an' don't pass within sight of th' Doc's place. Tell Lin to keep you with th' outfit—I don't need you here, an' he's too short handed. Get a-goin'."

Bud obeyed and in due time he came within sight of Gunsight, where a growing thirst lured him to ride in for a visit at Dave's. The proprietor still was smarting under the sting of Big Tom's attempt to bribe him and was glad to see someone who would help him get his mind on pleasant subjects. Dave regarded the story of the kidnapping of Wolf as being in that category, and when Bud left he was howling with laughter, and drove his horse toward home at a speed which awakened a resentful surprise in that animal.

"Th' locoed sons-of-guns!" repeated the delighted rider at intervals. "I knowed we had some locoed sage hens under our roof, but I thought they had limits! Why th' devil wasn't *I* in on that? *I*'m stickin' too close to home nights; but not no more. Any future Double X parties goin' to Gunsight will shore have little Buddie right in their midst! Th' nervy coyotes! Th' stem-windin' fools! Ha! Ha! Ha!

Farther on he gave vent to another burst of laughter as a new thought struck him. "It's all Nelson's fault. Cuss it! *now* I know why there has been so much hilarity about th' kidnappin' of th' Doc! They was plannin' to go it one better—an' I'm sayin' that they shore succeeded. They aimed purty high, but they done it, an' without even a scratch. I wonder who put th' sand burr under Smitty's saddle? Cuss that west section! I'm goin' to change an' ride our southeast line!"

When he pulled up at the bunkhouse door he found Lin and two other men who had ridden the last trick on the west section and he delivered Cimarron's message as soon as he dismounted. Answering the foreman's few questions, he let out a whoop and unburdened his news about Wolf and Smitty, painting the word pictures in a way which did him credit, and he felt the thrill of pride of an artist in the responses he obtained. After the greater pressure of their hilarity had escaped they began the puzzle of trying to name the jokers, and their foreman did that for them.

"Friday night," mused Lin. "Huh! Th' last that went to town was Slim, Tom, Gus, an' Bill. An' it was Friday night, too, because they said somethin' about hearin' Buffalo rumblin' in. That *makes* it Friday night, an' puts 'em in town when th' wagon was there. Well, I'm d—d! I can believe it of Slim and Tom, purty near, but not Bill an' Gus; still, there ain't no tellin' what any man of this fool outfit will do after he's been in Dave's all evenin'. I'm sayin' that mebby they got a tail holt on a mean varmint; that's their business, 'though, an' they ain't helpless kids."

"Mebby Wolf don't know who done it, but blames us all," suggested Rich Morgan, unconsciously resting his hand on the butt of his gun. "In which case I'm all eyes an' ears from now on."

"He knows who was in town that night," replied the foreman. "But if he goes shootin' promiscuously like, I'll have to take my rifle an' go get him, an' any way will do." He thought for a moment. "He knows who to look for. Well, they started it, an' nobody's got any right to help 'em out, not if he goes about it open an' aboveboard. Now, if Big Tom Huff comes a-visitin', you don't know nothin' at all. Cimarron sort of declared us in an' I'll play our cards, myself. You better fix that horse corral. There's five posts loose near th' northeast corner. Set 'em tight an' bind around th' corner with a couple strands of wire. Keep it outside as much as you can so th' barbs won't do no damage. Th' locoed fools—kidnappin' a man like Wolf!"

"Wait till Nelson comes in tonight," exulted Deuce, who by this time had learned quite a lot about the old Bar-20 outfit. "We got somethin' that beats th' kidnappin' of th' Doc every way!"

"Huh!" muttered the foreman thoughtfully. "That was th' night Dailey played in such hard luck, wasn't it? Shore it was. Then Nelson was there, too." He paused and looked out of the window for a moment. "Well, go out an' wrestle with them posts. Bud, you go on day shift with Tom an' Nelson. I'm takin' th' second night shift with Bill an' Gus."

Darkness had fallen when Johnny and Tom Wilkes rode in from the day shift after being relieved by the first night shift. They had heard the bare outlines of the joke, and now got it as completely as the foreman could give it to them while they ate their supper. Johnny looked serious and did not laugh as much as they had expected he would.

"What's th' matter, Nelson?" bantered Matt. "Jealous?"

Johnny pushed back. "Boys, you've forced my hand. I wasn't goin' to say nothin' to nobody about some few things till I had made all th' plays I was aimin' to make. But this here joke on Wolf, gettin' out like it did, shore forces me to lay down my cards, face up. An' I want th' whole range to see 'em—to spread th' news before it's too late. It ain't my way to sneak out of anythin' I've started an' let some innocent party take th' comeback. I freighted Wolf away; I shot th' holes in Smitty's hat; I drove Squint out of th' country; I kidnapped th' Doc, an' I killed Lang in a fair fight, his wits ag'in' mine, in fair sight of each other, when I was mired in them cussed quicksands. I can prove what I say by showin' where Squint's things are hid, by Wolf's six-gun, that I kept to remember him by, an' by describin' what them holes in Smitty's hat looked like. I was savin' Wolf's gun to show it to him, sometime, an' ask him if he couldn't take a joke. Now I ain't apologizin' to nobody for nothin' I've done. I claim I was justified—an' I'll leave it to you if th' joke on Wolf wasn't a hummer? Wasn't it a three-ringer with a side show? I says it was; an', further, I says I'll do it over again if I feel like it. No cussed man can spy on me without riskin' a comeback. An' I says there wasn't nothin' I could do to him that would 'a' been as good a joke as what I did do. Now, Sherwood, I better be ridin' to tell Cimarron's boys about it, so they won't be caught off their guard in case Wolf gets to them before he looks anywhere else. I'm wantin' to warn Slim 'specially—he was in town that night. Then I'll rustle to town an' stay there. I reckon he'll come to Gunsight, an' I'm aimin' to be there when he does, to ask him if I ain't the cussedest practical joker he ever knowed. If he's gone an' got on th' prod about a little joke like that, then I'll have to look out for myself. I'm startin' now."

"No use goin' now," said the foreman quickly. "That's a bad trail for a stranger to tackle at night, an' that cayuse of yourn is too good to risk bustin' her laigs. If you leave here before daylight—say half an hour before—tomorrow mornin', you'll be in plenty of time. Them boys ain't kids. I'm honin' to hear about these jokes, an' so are th' boys. You stay here, with us, tonight."

"Lin's dead right," earnestly endorsed Tom Wilkes, the others unanimously backing him up. "You ain't goin' till we hears about 'em—that is, of course, if you feels like tellin' us."

Johnny looked from one to another and then sat down again, and for the rest of the evening he had an audience which expressed its appreciation of what it heard, and in unrestrained enthusiasm. When he had finished and started to turn in, the foreman strode over to him and held out his hand.

"Nelson, I'm proud to know you. Put it there!"

The others shook his hand with an enthusiastic sincerity which warmed Johnny's heart, and he fell asleep with a smile on his face.

XVIII

◆

Whom the Gods Would Destroy

In gunsight, Dailey rubbed his eyes and cursed the slowness of his breakfast fire, and then padded in his stocking feet to the window and looked out in time to see a black horse go past with a reach and swinging smoothness which brought an appreciative glow into his blinking eyes. The rider sat his saddle with a supple grace and erectness which harmonized with the beautiful leg action of his mount.

"He ain't stoppin'," muttered Dailey. "Must 'a' been up to Juniper. I'm sayin' again that if that pack of coyotes lets him start ahead of 'em out of rifle range, there ain't nobody from down here as will ever get close enough to see him again. There's mebby purtier things on earth than a hoss like that, but I'm admittin' I never saw 'em. Cuss that fire—it's smokin' again!"

The Doc heard the rhythmic beat pass his shack, muttered drowsily, and turned over to go to sleep again. "Hope it's that Smitty, blast him!" and his snores grew steadily louder.

Leaving the Double X quite some time before daylight, Pepper had been sent over the upper trail, which joined the Juniper trail north of town. Now she spurned the Highbank-Gunsight road beneath her flying hoofs with an eagerness and power that belittled the twenty-five miles she already had put behind her.

Johnny stroked the satin skin under which the powerful muscles of her sloping shoulders rippled and bunched, and pride surged through him.

"I used to think Hoppy's Red Eagle, an' Red's Ginger was th' real thing in hossflesh," he told her, "but they was cows compared to you, Pepper Girl. There ain't nothin' on four laigs has any right to look at you—an' some few on two laigs, too." Swinging around the hill where Green Valley met the trail he patted her again. "There they are, little hoss, ridin' off to comb th' range. See that tied-in pinto Slim's a-ridin'? Show it what runnin' is—I want to talk to him."

Slim glanced around, drew rein and had a brief argument with the pinto, which did not like Slim, or his habit of stopping suddenly. "Changed yore mind?" he asked, smiling.

"In quite some ways," replied Johnny, forthwith explaining the situation in terse sentences. Slim's mouth opened and forgot to close until his groping mind at last mastered what his ears fed to it, when the mouth opened wider and gave vent to loud, sustaining laughter. Finally subsiding, he demanded the story in detail, but Johnny wheeled around.

"I'm warnin' you, not amusin' you, you human rope," retorted Johnny. "If Wolf comes back he'll mebby come a-shootin'—pass th' word along."

Slim shoved his hat well back on his head and jammed his gloved hands against his sides. "Th' h—l he will!" he rejoined. "Let him, then. He ain't th' only man out here as packs a gun; I mebby got one, myself. Havin' been kindly warned, now I'm all ready to be amused. Tell it slow. If you can't talk it, sing it. Wait! Here comes Cimarron."

The round-up boss rode up wearing a grin, in sympathy with Slim's far-reaching guffaws. "What's th' scandal?" he demanded.

"Th' cussedest thing you ever heard," laughed Slim, putting his hand on Pepper's bridle. "Nelson is in a hurry to go somewhere, but he's got to give us all of it now that he's whetted my appetite with th' mustard."

"I want to get to town an' give Wolf his chance," objected Johnny.

"If he's achin' to smoke up he'll come here, won't he?" demanded Slim. "This is th' place to wait for him—right here."

"All of which I admits is interestin'," said Cimarron; "but what is it all about?"

"Slow now," prompted Slim. He looked around. "Would you listen to that dickey bird up on th' hill?" he asked.

The dickey bird was Larry Hallock, whose voice barely reached them. "What do you reckon yo're doin'?" demanded Larry, but in far different language. "Gettin' married?" Further inquiries not receiving the attention he felt they were entitled to, he suspected trouble and made haste to get where he could hear about it. "Hello, Nelson!" he smiled as he joined them. "Lookin' for Two-Spot?"

"No; where is he?" demanded Johnny.

"I reckon he's downin' liquor in Dave's about now," answered Cimarron. "He's been raisin' th' devil for a drink which he didn't get. Slim, th' fool, owns up that he gave him a dollar last night—an' when we woke up this mornin' our tally man had disappeared. But that ain't tellin' me what Slim was hee-hawin' about, or about Wolf."

"Slow, an' deliberate, with everythin' in," chuckled Slim. "Go ahead."

Johnny complied, to their hilarious enjoyment, and when the tale was ended, Slim wiped his eyes, pointed out over the range, and said: "You can stay right here an' do somethin' worth while. Not one man in a thousand would come back with that pinned on his shirt tail—an' I'm sayin' Wolf ain't that man. He blames th' Double X—an' there's *only* twelve of us. He's shore about four bein' in town that night, but I ain't lettin' my modesty stop me from sayin' that, barrin' Cimarron here, he knows that th' four who was there are th' best six-gun men on our ranch; an' that we ain't takin' lessons from nobody when it comes to throwin' lead. He might get one of us, mebby two, an' I'll stretch h—l out of that word probability an' say he might get three; but he won't get us all, an' he knows it. But worse than shootin' it out is what he'll have to face; an' he hates ridicule worse than a rattler hates a king snake. You ain't goin' to set in Dave's, takin' it easy, while we're sweatin' out here—I got a nice little place where you'll fit in an' stop th' gaps that Larry is allus leavin' open."

"Gaps!" snorted Larry, indignantly. "Trouble is, you drive 'em so hard they gets stubborn an' go on th' prod. Anybody'd think you never saw a cow before, th' way you acts. You ought to know you can't crowd 'em too hard."

Cimarron cogitated. "If yo're aimin' to meet with Wolf, Nelson," he said, judicially, "I reckon you'd do better to stay here. He ain't got no reason to want anybody in town—nobody there has done anythin' to him. An' he knows none of us boys hang out there, except once in a while. What's more, he ain't likely to want to face Gunsight till he's squared up for his kidnappin'. As to him comin' back, I ain't nowise shore he won't. Some fellers are so full of th' idea of revenge that everythin' else plays second fiddle when they go on th' prod. They go fair mad an' don't care about nothin' else. Wolf's bad—bad as a mad rattler. I figger this is th' place for you. I'm sayin' this, too: If Slim had worked that razzle on him I wouldn't take a hand; but, knowin' Slim didn't, if that venomous reptile comes tearin' around here with his guns cocked, I'll just nat'rally puncture him at long range with my Remington. I ain't sympathizin' with no man that shoots till he knows why he's doin' it."

"Stay here till this afternoon, anyhow," said Slim. "We'll be needin' our tally man before night, an' you can ride to town, look around, an' bring Two-Spot back with you. I'm sayin' Wolf won't come back—I'm cussed shore *I* wouldn't in his place."

"Shore," endorsed Larry. "Turn yore cayuse loose an' get one from Arch—take that bay gelding—he's near human at this kind of work. Anyhow, he's got more sense than Slim."

Dawn in Highbank found a sobered Wolf, unarmed, penniless, and hectic, with a steadily growing rage. He went to place after place in search of a horse, finally borrowing one from a saloon-keeper who knew the foreman of the Bar H. Promising to use the animal only as far as the ranch, and to send it back behind the freight wagon, he threw the saddle on it and then rode around in search of a gun. Knowing about the joke, and feeling the man's murderous rage, no one would lend him a weapon. He had about decided to leave without one when he chanced to pass the small horse corral and shed behind Pete Wiggins' hotel, and espied a sodden figure asleep against the palings. Stealing the puncher's gun he rode away and in a few minutes was cursing the ford, of which a few yards was swimming water. Emerging on the other bank he pushed up the bluff trail at a walk and then, reaching level ground, set off for his ranch at a pace which might have killed a poorer horse.

As he rode, his mind became clearer and clearer, and he began to unravel the tangled skein of his abduction. Like his kind who, accustomed to hours of solitude, often talked their thoughts, he did his thinking aloud.

"Double X, says Buffalo. Mebby. First we'll accuse everybody else in town. Dave?" he laughed sneeringly at the thought. "Dailey? Fanning? Jerry? George? Why them? They ain't th' kind to stack up ag'in' such a risk for th' fun of it; an' they ain't none of 'em got any other reason. Dailey an' Fanning was in Dave's all evenin'—they never left th' table. Jerry was snoring in his shop when I went around th' buildin's, an' he wouldn't dare try to kidnap a blind pup. George is another without nerve, an' he was snorin' worse than Jerry. Nelson? He was with th' others. Mebby he did it, but I'm thinkin' there was more'n one man mixed up in that. If my senses hadn't been knocked out of me I'd know more about it. We'll put him aside as a possibility.

"Them Double X coyotes ain't lovin' me, 'specially since I've been ridin' sign along their line. There was four of 'em, an' they was all primed for a good time; an' from what I heard 'em say about th' Doc an' Squint an' me an' th' rest of our outfit, they wasn't needin' much urgin' to tackle a job like that. But they was in Dave's too; still, they left before I did.

"That leaves my own gang of practical jokers. They knowed that I was in town, but they didn't know I was goin' to ride home that night because I didn't know it myself. They might 'a done it, but I'll find that out cussed quick when I get back.

"Who else was there? Dailey, Fanning, Jerry, Dave, Nelson—*Two-Spot!* He wasn't in sight at all. Dave was raisin' th' roof about him not bein' around. But h—l! Twenty Two-Spots wouldn't 'a tackled a play like that; an' he couldn't sling a rope, nor carry a man as heavy as me *that* distance. Slim can rope—he's the best down here. I don't remember much about it till I was put down near th' waggin; but I'm shore that th' man that throwed that rope was an expert.

"Two-Spot? I don't see how he could fit in—*cuss him! I* got it! Somebody must 'a' seen me movin' 'round or else nobody would 'a' knowed I was in town. None of them fellers could 'a' seen me; but Two-Spot could have. Whoever did that job had to be told I was there; an' I'm sayin' they *was* told. That bum hates me; he'll never forget my kickin' him off'n th' tie-rail an' makin' him dance th' tenderfoot's fandango. I'm goin' to see Two-Spot after I stop at th' ranch—an' if he don't talk fast and straight, he'll dance to h—l this time!"

It was not yet noon when Wolf swept up to his bunkhouse and rode in through the door leaning forward in the saddle to clear the rafters, his gun freezing Big Tom and Dick Carson as stiff as statues.

"Don't you move till I says so!" he snarled. "Who was in town th' night Buffalo stopped there on his way home? Think quick; an' talk straight!"

"What are you doin'? Goin' *loco*?" demanded the foreman. He stopped in his tracks when he saw the look on his puncher's face.

"I'm askin' th' questions!" snapped Wolf, his rage climbing anew. "You answer 'em, an' *pronto*! Who was there that night?"

"Don't know; but none of our boys was."

"Nobody left here at all that night?" demanded Wolf.

"Not one."

"How do you know? That was near a week ago. How do you know they was all here?"

"That was th' first night you went on Nelson's trail," answered the foreman somewhat angrily. "I told them to stay home, an' give you plenty of room. They did it."

"I reckon they was glad to do it," sneered Wolf. "Coyotes don't go cougar huntin', less'n th' pack is big."

"They might as well stay home as go on a drunk in Highbank," retorted Big Tom, coldly.

For a moment Wolf was balanced on a narrow edge, but controlled himself because of genuine liking for his foreman. "Don't you ever come that close again," he said, almost in a whisper. "Do you know *why* I went to Highbank? You ought to, for I reckon everybody does by *this* time," he grated.

"I'm listenin' to you," answered Big Tom. "I don't know *why* you went."

Wolf dismounted, drove the horse out of the house, and paced up and down the long room in a frenzy of energy.

"I was roped off my cayuse ridin' home that night. I must 'a' fell on my head, for I don't know nothin' about it till I got to town. When I came to my senses I was bound, blindfolded, an' gagged, an' my head was spinnin' an' near bustin' with pain. I was dumped into Buffalo's wagon, pushed in among a load of hides, an' staked out so I couldn't move. All that day I lay here under that tarp, joltin' over that long trail, near faintin' with th' pain of th' lashin's an' th' gag, swelterin' in th' heat an' stink, sick with th' pain in my head, parched an' burnin' with thirst, ragin' with my thoughts, mile after mile. There was times I must 'a' lost consciousness; but I can remember a-plenty!

"Down in Highbank I was hauled out by a gang of cacklin' sage hens who thought it was a joke. If I'd had a gun, an' could 'a' used it, I'd 'a' showed 'em what kind of a joke it was!" He flew into a burst of rage which awed his companions, and he nearly wrecked the room before he subsided, his words one quivering stream of profanity. "An' what have I got to face?" he shouted. "What have I got to live down? I'll be th' laughin' stock of this whole country till I die, an' after! But I can show 'em that it costs somethin' to make a fool of Wolf Forbes; an' I will, if I dies for it! I want a six-gun, an' a rifle, an' yore pet hoss. I'm ridin' to town to see th' one man who can tell me where to start, an' I'm ridin' alone."

"Think it was Nelson?" asked Carson.

"Mebby; but I'm not sayin' till I know," snapped Wolf, pacing again. "I'm askin' you: Do you figger ropin' an' kidnappin' Wolf Forbes was any one-man job? Is there any man in this country that would tackle that job, alone, for th' fun of it? Yo're right. I says not, too. An' if he didn't do it for th' fun of it, would he 'a' dared tackle it, at all? What I mean is, if he did it to get rid of me, wouldn't he 'a' killed me from that ambush. I'm tellin' you he'd 'a' figgered it would be a lot safer to shoot me, for there wouldn't be th' risk at th' time, an' th' dead shore danger of th' comeback. One man, alone, would 'a' shot; three or four might 'a' took a chance with th' rope. I'm ridin' to town to learn for shore; an' I'm ridin' now. Carson, saddle me that hoss, while I get th' guns I want. Gimme a drink of yore flask, Tom."

"You shore you want it?"

"Gimme a drink. I know what I want."

In a few minutes he rode north at a dead run, headed for the over-mountain trail, and it was not until he was gone that the foreman realized that he had not told his puncher a word about the events which had taken place during his absence.

Wolf crossed the mountain, turned to the left, and went around Gunsight on the west, heading back toward town to approach it on its blind side. He rode up behind the hotel shed, dismounted and crept along it, and as he passed a crack in the warped boards his eye caught a movement, and he stopped to peer through the crack. Two-Spot was crawling out from under the saloon. Arising to his feet, the tramp looked carefully around for signs of any of Cimarron's outfit who might have come after him, and then slipped through Dave's rear door.

The watcher stiffened, and a sudden thought sent his

rage up to the border line of madness. Two-Spot's mysterious sleeping quarters were no longer a mystery to him. His eyes swept the side of the saloon, and the narrow space between its foundation sills and the ground. This open space ran along three sides of the building and he knew that a man under the floor could see the feet and ankles of anyone who passed along the building. Returning to his horse he mounted and rode off the way he had come, careful to keep the shed between him and Dave's rear wall. Reaching an arroyo, he dropped into it and followed it until far enough from town, and then, keeping under the cover of hills and brush, he emerged upon the trail and loped along it into Gunsight. Dismounting in front of Dailey's, he walked swiftly and quietly toward Dave's, bending low to keep under the two front windows, and paused at the door to listen.

"He! He! He!" shrilled Two-Spot, warming to the liquor he had taken. "I'd 'a' liked to died when Jerry told about him. I could smell them hides before they turned th' corner of th' hotel that night. They was so odorous they near made me sick. An' if he went into 'em a Wolf, I'm sayin' he come out a Polecat; this range never will forget it. He can't never live it down—never! An' Jerry's tellin' it all along th' way, too. I'm wonderin' if he'll come back."

Dailey laughed sarcastically. "I'm bettin' he won't. *No* man would."

"I'm shore *I* wouldn't," chuckled Fanning. "I'd ship off to South Americky, *pronto*—an' I wouldn't care what happened to th' ship while I was on it, neither."

"I'll take three to one he *does* come back," said Dave.

"Is twenty dollars too much?" asked Dailey.

"Twenty to my seven suits me," replied Dave. "I'll take th' same from Jim, too."

"Yo're on," chuckled Dailey.

"Me, too," replied Fanning.

A man slipped through the door, a gun in each hand. "Dave wins!" he snarled. "Keep 'em both on th' bar!" he snapped at Dave, who forthwith forgot, for the moment, all about the cap-and-ball. The little group in front of the bar stiffened into whatever postures they had been caught in, their eyes on the muzzles of the steady guns. Death hung poised on Wolf's thumbs like a hawk balanced in the blue, ready to strike. The only sounds in the room were the hushed breathing of four men facing destruction for the slightest slip, the insistent buzzing of a bee cruising across the ceiling and the soft *slip! slip!* of the gunman's feet as he slid them forward a few inches at a time. His face was ghastly and working with rage, his power concentrated in his dull, threatening weapons. He jabbed one of them at Two-Spot.

"Step over there, on th' end!" he snapped. "I'll shoot at th' first move," he warned them all, feeling the hostility which he faced. Three of them were armed and needed only an instant's carelessness or indecision on his part to prove that their courage was only held in leash by calculating reason. "Not a move, cuss you!" he warned, his eyes not for a moment leaving the three armed men. Dailey's face was tense, but his body had slouched into a relaxation, the danger of which was well known to Wolf. Fanning's eyes were glinting and his lips were hard and thin, while enmity leered out of his eyes as though it were a living thing. Dave, his face paling after the redness of his first flush of anger, stood as a cat stands in the presence of a foe. Not for a fleeting instant did Wolf dare to take his eyes from this crouched danger.

"You'd 'a' done better if you hadn't come back," said

Dave, quietly, but the timbre of his voice sent a chill up Two-Spot's spine.

"Don't move yore paws," snarled Wolf. "Two-Spot, come over here, by th' bar."

Two-Spot obeyed, sullen and fearful, taking a place which shortened the arc of danger for Wolf.

"Where was you that night?" demanded the gunman.

Two-Spot stared at him and tried to moisten his throat.

"Where was you?" snapped Wolf, venomously. "Talk fast!"

"I don't remember," answered Two-Spot.

"You was in yore hang-out under this floor," accused Wolf. "Did you see me?"

"It was too dark," answered the tramp, flashing an appealing look at Dave, whose face was growing red again.

"Not with th' light streamin' out of them side windows! Who did you tell?"

"I didn't see you."

"Who did you tell? Th' Double X?"

"No; it was too dark."

Warned by a premonition of impending disaster, and feeling that they were unawed, and restrained only by reason, Wolf ordered the three armed men to turn their backs to him, which they did with a slowness which in itself was an insult. He took the guns of Dailey and Fanning and ordered Dave to come out and join them. Dave took time enough to keep his dignity unsmirched. Free from the necessity of keeping a high-tension vigilance, Wolf walked up to Two-Spot and struck him on the face with the heel of his hand.

"Did you tell th' Double X?" he demanded. "D—n you, answer me!"

"No," whispered Two-Spot, and in his bleared eyes there smouldered the sparks of a fire long dormant.

"Did you tell Nelson? Quick!"

Dailey and Fanning hung on the slow answer, for they remembered that little incident with startling clearness.

"No!" snarled Two-Spot.

Wolf kicked him on the shins and, dropping one gun into its sheath, grabbed the skinny throat, gripping it cruelly. "Who did you tell?" he growled, shaking his victim, and quivering with rage at such resistance where he had expected to encounter none.

Some ghost of a former stalwart courage, shaken awake by desperation and rage, came back to its forsaken habitation and spoke through a mouthpiece for too long a stranger to it. Two-Spot tried to speak and Wolf, a gleam of triumph burning through the madness in his eyes, loosened his grip and stepped back.

The voice which answered him was not Two-Spot's, although it came through his lips. It was level, cold, self-possessed, and biting. "You ask somebody who's a-scared of you, you three-card flush. An' keep yore paws off'n me—they stink of hides an' maggots."

The crashing roar sounded like a thunderbolt and the acrid cloud of smoke swept forward and shrouded the falling man. Wolf leaped back, out of it, and stopped the instinctive advance of the horrified and enraged onlookers, who had turned at the shot, his two guns barely sufficient for the task. Dave's expression took his instant attention and he snapped a warning, venomous as the jet from a copperhead's fangs: "Don't you try it, Green!" He flashed a look at the other two, and nearly fired in instinctive answer to the malevolent looks in their eyes.

"Anybody that itches to take this up will get their chance: I'll be back!" he promised, and retreated swiftly to the door. Shoving his guns forward in a silent, final warning, he slipped from their sight and dashed for his horse, firing several shots behind him past the windows and door. Leaping into the saddle, he wheeled around the store and rode at a dead run for the cover of an arroyo several hundred yards beyond.

Dave started toward his bedroom for the rifle hanging on the wall, reconsidered and looked at the huddled heap on the floor. "We'll take care of th' best man first," he said, picking up the limp figure and carrying it to the base of the front wall. Getting a blanket, he went back again, and as he stood up he drew a deep breath and faced his companions, a look almost reverent coming to his face and softening the malignancy of its expression.

"He died like a man—I hope I do as good. Let's liquor."

The afternoon shadows were beginning to lengthen when the low voices in the saloon ceased to allow the speakers to catch the sounds of a horse coming up the trail. Dave, moving with surprising celerity for one of his build and habits, grabbed a rifle and hastened to the front window, where he peered out cautiously, and then, walking to the bar, he reached over it, stood the weapon behind it, and replied to the unspoken inquiries of his companions.

"It's Nelson," he said, quietly.

The hoofbeats ceased abruptly and Johnny's voice was heard promising the horse some sugar. He entered and strode straight for the bar, nodding cheerily at the three, and then smiled quizzically.

"You shore look glum," he remarked, "glum as a funeral. Come up an' take somethin' for it. Well, th' SV is bein' cleaned neat an' proper. Cimarron knows his business, an' that crew of his is goin' at full speed. I come in to get Two-Spot. They're needin' a tally man, an' he ought to go through with it. Seen him around, or is he hidin' out, layin' low?"

"He's layin' low," replied Dave.

Johnny looked at him curiously, puzzled by the proprietor's manner. "Meanin'?"

"He's dead," said Dailey, bluntly, staring fixedly at the front wall.

Johnny flashed him a glance and looked back at Dave, who nodded significantly at the front of the room. Johnny turned quickly and followed the other's stare. He straightened and walked slowly to the blanket, drew it back a little and then replaced it with reverent care. Arising to his full height, he turned and looked at them. The silence was oppressive, crowded with potentials. They could feel a tension which fairly crackled, and which made them shrink, guiltless though they were. The erect figure radiated a ferocity which numbed them and caused Fanning to lick his dry lips. Overhead the bee, which had buzzed monotonously for so long a time, increased its buzzing and bounced from point to point, its wings striking the ceiling with a dry whirring not greatly unlike the angry whir of a rattler. From an unrinsed glass on the bar came a buzzing from drunken flies renewing their efforts to escape from it. The measured breathing of four men sounded loud and unnatural, and from Dailey's forehead rolled a bead of sweat. They stared at the cold, motionless puncher, fascinated by what emanated from him, unable to look away from the glinting eyes which peered out between narrowed lids at each in turn, and back again. Outside a horse pawed restlessly and the intermittent sound of striking metal reminded them of the slow pealing of a bell. A board cracked suddenly as it contracted from the encroachment of a cooling shadow and sent a shiver up their backs. Fanning's nerves were on edge and seemed about to snap, and his clenching fingers cut into his palms. He suddenly slumped down into his chair.

"It was *Wolf*!" he shouted. "Two-Spot wouldn't tell!"

The others sat rigid, not heeding the words.

Slowly the puncher's hand went to his sombrero and slowly readjusted it with deliberate care and precision. He turned slowly, and slowly departed, the sound of the diminishing hoofbeats echoing in their brains long after the sound had ceased. The unrinsed glass became quiet, the bee blundered out through an open window, and a great peace, soothing and enfolding, stole over them. Fanning stirred, arose to his feet, and stumbled toward the door.

"Christ!" he whispered.

"Amen," said Dave. "Death's flyin' low."

The Bar H outfit, loafing near the bunkhouse, were deep in discussion when they heard a horse. Looking up, they saw Johnny Nelson coming toward them at an amble. He nodded gravely and soon stopped near them. Carelessly throwing the reins over Pepper's head, he lazily swung down, pushed his hat back on his head, and sauntered up to them, stopping when only an arm's length away, Wolf stirring restlessly and not taking his eyes from the visitor's face.

"Two-Spot was my friend," said Johnny in a matter-of-fact voice.

Wolf's slouching frame shifted slightly and froze.

"He never went heeled," continued Johnny's even, dispassionate voice. The open palm of his right hand struck Wolf's face with vicious force. There came two roars which sounded almost as one, and Johnny, leaping pantherishly aside out of the rolling smoke, held two guns on the paralyzed group.

"Wolf shot him," he explained, backing away behind his ominous guns. He whistled softly, and Pepper, despite the dangling reins, lifted her head high and came to him.

Big Tom recovered himself first and took his eyes from the figure sprawled on the ground. He was beginning to believe them. He glanced at Johnny and back to the prostrate figure. It was incredible that a man with Wolf's courage, and ability with weapons, should shoot down an old, helpless tramp, whose greatest offense could hardly be more than a verbal one, especially against a two-gun killer. Bad as he was, and hardened, the foreman could not stomach such a murder, and, snapping a warning to his companions, who still stared at what had been Wolf Forbes, he looked at Johnny, who was preparing to mount, and he called out in a voice ringing with sincerity: "Put 'em up, Nelson; an' ride off. I'll knock th' man down that pulls a gun!"

Johnny slipped the guns into their sheaths, swung up into the saddle, wheeled, and pushed Pepper at a lope over the trail toward town without a single backward glance.

Big Tom watched him for a moment and then wheeled and glanced down at the ground. "*Wolf,* huh? All right." He turned to the thoughtful group. "Dig a hole somewhere out on th' range an' dump that into it," he said contemptuously, and strode toward the ranchhouse.

XIX

♦

"Give Eternal Rest ——"

The deaths of Two-Spot and Wolf created a mild sensation over the range, particularly the manner in which each had occurred. The respect which Johnny had enjoyed in Gunsight and on the Double X was increased and the range enjoyed his other exploits. Dave was open in his sympathy for the SV and his growing contempt for the Bar H. Dailey said that he had a gun and could use it any time Johnny needed help, adding with a grin that he hardly expected to be called upon. The Double X was hilarious and brutally frank in everything concerning their neighbor on the southeast. On the Triangle, Frank Gurley became moody and silent, Sam Gardner and Reilly noisy and assertive. The latter, with Lefferts, took over the north end of their ranch and worked nearly as hard for the SV as they did for the Triangle.

Two-Spot's funeral was a holiday by tacit consent, and Gunsight was the Mecca for the surrounding country. Fanning offered the hotel, but Dave's eyes grew red and he declared that the saloon had been Two-Spot's home and that he would be buried from it, even if the cap-and-ball had to cast the deciding votes. Slim rode to Juniper half an hour after he had heard the news and brought a minister back with him. Cimarron sent Larry Hallock to the ranch with the news, George Hallock to the SV, and went down to notify the Triangle himself.

The day dawned clear and reasonably cool, and at an early hour the riders began to come in. The saloon was as clean as Dave, Johnny, and George could make it, and the rude box which had kept Dailey and Fanning up most of the night with hammer and saw, was covered by green boughs and a few wild flowers. As each newcomer rode up to the door he was quietly informed by Dave that the bar was closed and would remain so until after the funeral. There would be no instrumental music, for Arch Wiggins' offer to ride to the Double X for his fiddle was politely but firmly declined after he had been questioned about his repertoire; Jerry's harmonica was overruled, and Reilly's accordion was declined for the same reason which had barred the violin.

When Margaret Arnold rode up alone with a huge bouquet of old-fashioned flowers, Gunsight became tremendously interested and there was a great amount of surreptitious grooming going on in out-of-the-way places. Lin Sherwood regretted that he had not been more neighborly, and that he had decided against his new boots, tight though they were. He accused himself of being a poor sort of a grown-up man not to risk a corn or two under such circumstances. He frowned down Slim's sheepish remark about seeing Miss Arnold home after the ceremony as being unwarranted and too forward; and he kept Slim in sight thereafter. Dailey cursed Big Tom's warning about selling supplies to the SV and was gloomy because of the handicap it put him under, but it became him well in such an atmosphere and nearly gave him the place of chief mourner. Several of the rejected suitors formed a consolation circle and deeply reflected the sorrow expected at funerals, grumbling because the universal remedy for grief would not be obtainable until the return from the grave. There was a suggestion concerning a concerted rush on the bar, but the tender flower of hope was frostbitten by a glance at the cap-and-ball protruding from Dave's waistband. The proprietor had no consideration for the sacredness of the occasion to hang around the walnut armed like a highwayman, and the amount of pugnacious confidence he exhaled and exuded was entirely out of place.

"He acts like a cow with its first calf," growled Sam Gardner.

"He acts like it was *his* funeral, which I'm sorry it ain't," snorted Pete Wiggins' young hopeful, still raw about the matter concerning his fiddle.

The minister walking around from the hotel was the signal for the groups to fall in behind him and file into the Palace. This sky pilot was a stalwart member of his cloth and acted as though saloons were not strangers to him. He looked about and nodded his appreciation of Dave's efforts and at once became the friend of every man there.

"Friends," he said, looking slowly around, "a good friend of the deceased, and one who knew him well and who cherishes his memory with gratitude and affection, will sing. Miss Arnold, if you please."

Margaret, tears in her voice and eyes, arose and began her favorite hymn, her rich contralto voice playing upon the heartstrings of the rough men until they dared not look around. Cimarron coughed, and received Slim's elbow in his side with unnecessary force. Dave developed a sudden cold and reddened with self-consciousness, wishing he had chosen a seat in the rear of the room instead of standing at the end of the bar, which was an altogether too suggestive place for one in his line of business.

The singer's voice grew slowly lower and lower and it was only by exercising all her will-power that she managed to finish the last verse. Her own emotion and faith throbbed in the beautiful words and gave them a power which brought tears to nearly every eye. Finishing, she sank down in her chair and sobbed softly.

The minister, arising, looked over the room.

" 'Nearer to Thee,' " he repeated softly, and then paused, and when he resumed, his voice struck through to the hearts of his hearers as a hand plucking the strings of a harp. " 'Greater love hath no man than this, that a man lay down his life for his friends.' Two-Spot. The name was lowly, and with thoughtless cruelty was given to Henry Travers, who once was under foreman for Simon Verrier, the former owner of the SV ranch. We have no knowledge of the interval between the days of his responsibility and strength, and that cold winter evening when Margaret Arnold found him, weak from hunger and exposure, freezing in a snowdrift not far from her home. Of the man's weakness we will not speak, except in charity and to show that the character which won for him the confidence and trust of old Simon persisted in spite of that weakness and blazed out gloriously, to win for him an honorable death. It would have been easy to betray the confidence of another, especially when he knew the ability of that other to protect himself. He could have saved his life by telling the truth, and I say to you that there are some untruths more glorious than those truths which mean danger, or perhaps death, to a friend. And if he had yielded to fear to save his life he would have found that life to be a thing without value. He would have lost to himself all that remained worth while. Two-Spot, weak with a weakness perhaps passed on to him by the thoughtless and vicious lives of those others who had preceded him, was, nevertheless, a man, and will live in your memories as a man, a man who at the threat of death, rallied the best within him and died to protect a fellow-man who had been kind to him. He was a lowly card, but even a two-spot has a value, as every man in this room can testify. A two-spot, at the right time and in the right combination, makes a winning hand; and I have it on the authority of two people here that he was given one spot too many. Hardly an ace of diamonds, but surely an ace of hearts, for in his breast beat a heart as true and sympathetic as that of any man in this room.

"There was not a thing coming to his knowledge which affected the welfare of a struggling, defenseless family on this range, that he did not tell them; and when I say that for a man of his age and weakness to walk nine miles to warn them, and nine miles back again, in any weather, at the only time he could do so without being seen and arousing suspicion, required such a heart, and a fine quality of courage, I know that you all will agree with me. Many nights when the range was wrapped in sleep, Two-Spot made that journey. And I say that he was a man, and I pay him the respect which such a heart and courage merits. And no matter what his weaknesses were, no matter how unworthy you may have thought him to be, I say that this man whom you knew as Two-Spot was as good as any who sneered at him, as much a man in his last moment on earth as a material being as any man in this room! And I say that if we all, every one of us, can die as fearlessly and as honorably as this man died, we need not fear the Judgment Day. There may be some of you who do not give much thought to that Judgment Day, or to that Merciful Judge. There may be some of you who do not believe in God—but I say, that, no matter Who or What waits beyond the Open Door, He or It will deal gently with Henry Travers. And I say for those who do not believe in any divine faith, and say it aside from any viewpoint of religion, but purely as a question of ethics, of effort and reward, of right living or wrong, that every man in this room can find something in the strength of this weak man, something in the way he faced death, that

can be taken with profit to himself and serve as an inspiration. Under all his fleshly weakness, with all his yielding to a dominant craving, there blazed the white flames
of sympathy, affection, and loyalty. And I cannot find this
occasion to be one for sorrow, or for grief. Rather, I should
say it is one for congratulation: Two-spot, shorn of his
weaknesses, saved from jeers and cruelty and injustice,
and the misery coming with old age, which cannot but be
tragic to such a one as he, found himself at the last moment, and died the man which circumstances would have
refused to have let him live. Let us pray."

If his auditors had been impressed by his address, the
prayer reached down and gripped their very heartstrings,
stirring into groping life the vague fear and awe of the
supernatural, by heritage firmly implanted in each consciousness. Death, with its mystery and threat, brought its
awesome fear like a wave, with an impetus acquired from
rolling down past generations, to minds prepared to quail
before it in momentary surrender. From the distant and
impersonal, it suddenly loomed out of the fog of the mysterious unknown real, and made real by a mind trained to
present truth as it is, and became close and personal. And
at the conclusion of the gripping words, only the fresher,
newer momentum of the carelessness and indifference of
their everyday lives could offset the fear which spread
like ripples over their superstitions and set their religious
instincts aquiver. But like concentric ripples, it grew weaker
even as it reached farther out; yet the reacting ripples enduring for days, showing intermittently and intermittently
arousing vague unrest in their minds.

He glanced at Margaret and walked quickly to her,
placing his hand on her shoulder. "I would not attempt it,
my dear. Two-Spot would not allow another hymn, at such
a cost to you."

Dailey, Johnny, Dave, and Fanning moved slowly forward, feeling as they never had felt before, reverently and carefully picked up the box and led the way out of the building and across the street to a grassy knoll not far from the road, where the warmth and brightness of the sun rested from dawn to dark. The ceremony at the grave over, they returned to Dave's, where they shook hands with a parson who had jolted their ideas regarding men of his calling.

"Friends," he protested, raising his hands at the coins in the hat held out to him, "this is too much. I cannot take so much for doing my duty. It is not reasonable."

"Parson," said Dave, a grin coming to his face, "we ain't had no gunplay today, but if you don't take that money, I can't promise that there won't be none. Some of us leather-backs has been eddicated today, an' they say eddication costs money. I reckon a parson livin' in such a hole of iniquity as Juniper can find use for our offerin's. If you can't take it for yoreself, take it for yore church—it'll help you to build one all th' quicker. An' I'm sayin' that we'll allus be glad to see you in Gunsight, as a parson or as a man. Shake."

Margaret came forward and thanked him, and turned to Dave.

"Did you know that he slept under your floor?" she asked. "He was always wondering if you did."

"Ma'am," smiled Dave, feeling to see if his tie had slipped, "I knowed it th' very first time he snored, which was th' second night he was here. An' I've had many a laugh at him th' way he wiggled out of little slips he made. He heard a lot under here, an' sometimes he let things out that made him dig frantic to explain away. I reckon I'm goin' to be lonesome, 'specially this winter. Here comes Lin Sherwood—Miss Arnold, meet Mr. Sherwood, th' bashfullest man in this country. He don't mind a little thing like an extra eighteen miles in th' saddle—an' I'm admittin' that nobody will steal yore cayuse while he's along. Now that I've broke th' ice an' pushed him in where he was afraid to go hisself, I'll take th' parson around an' make him better acquainted with th' boys."

As they moved away, the minister noticed the restraint and restlessness visible around him and he turned a smiling face to the proprietor. "As soon as Miss Arnold leaves, open the bar. I'll take a cigar with the boys and then say good-by."

Dave stopped in his tracks, his jaw dropped, and then he beamed upon his clerical companion. "I'm repeatin' what I said about bein' glad to see you any time," he exclaimed, slapping the broadcloth shoulder. "Parson, I'm proud to know you! Put it there!"

Johnny, going over to say good-by to Margaret, and concealing to the best of his ability any sign of jealousy, received a distinct shock and one which made him wrestle hard to keep his dignity.

"Oh, here's Mr. Nelson, now," smiled Margaret. "I just told Mr. Sherwood that he was too late; but perhaps he will beat you the next time. I think we would better be riding, for these men feel a restraint while I'm here; and I'm getting anxious about father. So if you will excuse me, Mr. Sherwood, I'll say good-by to the men and ride on."

Sherwood stood on his foot and did foolish things to his hat, but was spared any further embarrassment by Johnny, who gripped his arm in a friendly way and escorted Margaret on her round of the room. And as the pair rode away Sherwood turned from the door, kicked Cimarron, and tramped to the bar.

The *segundo* stared after him. "Well, I'm cussed!" he

muttered. "So *that's* it, huh? Well, you'd 'a' done better if you'd 'a' kicked Nelson."

The minister having left, Dave became very busy, and Dailey found a pack of cards and dragged out a table. "Havin' been generous to th' church, now I aims to get back some of it," he remarked. "He is a fine man—an' what he said is true; an' if I can get four little two-spots I'll show you all an inspiration that's stem-windin'. One at a time; don't push!"

"Yo're shore hard-boiled," reproved Slim, slightly vexed. "You ain't got enough reverence in yore saturated carcass to start a prairie dog out in life like he ought to go—an' G—d knows that ain't much."

"Which same I says is true as h—l," endorsed Cimarron, scowling. "Let th' old mosshead herd by hisself. I'm goin' back an' pick up that round-up where we dropped it. We got to get that over with as soon as we can, for we'll be roundin' up for McCullough purty soon—an' he ought to be along next week."

Sherwood heard him and turned from the bar. "He ain't getting many from us," he said. "We'll send our own herd up th' trail next spring, an' take a gamble on gettin' more for 'em. I'm sayin' th' SV has got plenty of friends from now on, too. I'm ridin' home; who's comin' with me?"

Plans and Preparations

On the last day of the round-up Johnny rode out to the SV and found a herd held against the wire fence. A branding fire was burning off to one side and Larry Hallock had just thrown a calf, its pitiful bawl turning its mother into a charging fury. The mother, being unbranded, was thrown instead of being diverted and received the same treatment being accorded to her sturdy offspring. Larry's helpers arose, let the calf up and grinned at its eagerness for maternal protection. They wiped their foreheads with wet sleeves and welcomed the visitor.

"There's some calves at that," said Larry, "but they're this year's crop. An' that's th' last brandin', I reckon, for here. Cimarron an' three of th' boys are startin' a cleanup north of th' east end in that grassy valley. I reckon today will finish it."

Slim nodded. "It wouldn't hurt to keep a few men ridin' well back, for a few days, pickin' up strays; but I'm sayin' this ranch has been combed to a T. We've cussed near branded even th' shadows. You'll never have no trouble tellin' them that Larry has branded. He paints wide an' free like he was paintin' a house. Just look at that yearlin' over there; an' them two weaners—they're cussed near all brand."

Larry grinned. "Shore; it saves a lot of ridin' when you can read 'em far off. I'm in favor of histin' flags on 'em an' ridin' sign with a telescope hangin' from th' saddle."

Johnny laughed at the grinning pair, dust and sweat from head to feet. "This ranch will have stampin' irons as soon as it can get 'em, 'though Larry must hate 'em like poison. I'm comin' out here, some of these days, an' put that horse corral at th' house in better shape; an' anybody that offers to help won't get insulted. Now I'm ridin' to th' house. I got an idea an' want to see how it sets with th' Ol' Man. See you later."

"I been scratchin' all day for an idea like that," chuckled Slim. "All I could think of was a drink of water; an' Larry goes an' shoves out his canteen to me!"

"If I didn't," said Larry, "everybody would 'a' got thirsty, 'an' then who would 'a' held this herd?"

Johnny laughed and rode off, his friends watching him for a few moments. Then Larry went toward his horse, Slim following him.

"Well," said Slim, "Nelson knows where he can find a parson ten miles closer than Highbank, anyhow. After he got her on her hoss th' other day in Gunsight an' went off to get his own, she looked after him—an' I ain't no fool. I'm in favor of holdin' it in town. An' I says this here busted-down ranch needs a good man to take hold of it an' run it. I reckon an outfit of four would swing it handsome. Yes, three good men could do it."

Larry swung into the saddle. "I got three brothers that shore do love singin' since Two-Spot was planted. I'm leanin' strong to th' melodious myself. An' I'm admittin' that I never knowed what singin' was before. Well, you maverick, let's go an' help 'em count that herd. You an' me aim to stop in town tonight on our way home, don't we? Then come on."

Johnny dismounted at the kitchen door and knocked. Charley came running and acted as host.

"Gee!" he exclaimed, his eyes sweeping to the six-guns and resting on them. "Come on in! Peggy's readin' to dad. He's gettin' plumb ornery an' says he's goin' to get up tomorrow, anyhow, come h—l or high water. Here she is now: Hey, Sis! Here's Mr. Nelson—bet yo're plumb glad to see him. Is dad still on th' prod?"

"Charley! What language! How you do pick things up! How-do-you-do, Mr. Nelson?" she smiled, holding out her hand. "I am so glad to see someone who may have a good influence on father. Come in. Father, here is our friend, Mr. Nelson."

"Which gun got Wolf?" demanded Charley.

"Glad to see you, sir!" exclaimed Arnold. "You have been entirely too much a stranger to this house. Sit down, and tell me what is going on. That Cimarron may know how to talk, but he doesn't seem very anxious to prove it. When I ask him how he finds the ranch he tells me about everything else that he can in one minute, pleads work, and leaves."

"I think a whole lot of Cimarron," replied Johnny. "He and his boys have worked like slaves out here—they've done an amazin' lot. They expect to have everything cleaned up an' counted by tonight, or by tomorrow, without fail. Then we can do some figgerin' ourselves, an' see how many cows are comin' to you. What I called for was to make a proposition to you, an' I think it's a good one."

"Go ahead; I'm sayin' yes to it right now," smiled Arnold.

"I reckoned mebby you would say that after you heard it," said Johnny. "McCullough, trail boss for Twitchell an' Carpenter, is comin' up from th' south with two thousand head of mixed cattle. His deliveries call for four thousand head, an' he is countin' on gettin' th' second two thousand right up here around Gunsight. Th' Bar H is throwin' a thousand over to him an' th' Triangle has promised him five hundred. Th' other five hundred was to come from th' Double X, but Sherwood has got other ideas. He's got a good outfit an' hankers on gamblin' a little. He's made up his mind to sell McCullough only a hundred head of older cattle an' keep th' other four hundred for his own trail herd next year. He says Dodge, but I reckon he's fishin' for a government contract up north; an' if he is, an' lands it, he'll make a lot of money."

"I wish somebody would show me how to make some," replied Arnold, gloomily. "We are headed for some poorhouse, I'm afraid."

"Father!" exclaimed Margaret, reprovingly. "You should not say or think such things. Everything will come out all right. Our luck is turning."

Johnny glanced at her and smiled.

"Perhaps it is, but I can't see its face, yet," retorted Arnold. "We'll know how many head we have, and how many we have lost, but that knowledge won't keep us, will it?"

"Perhaps Mr. Nelson has something to say concerning that."

"I have, Ma'am," smiled Johnny, his eyes for an instant resting full on hers. "I'm goin' to suggest that th' SV sells McCullough that missin' four hundred head. That will be th' best way to turn some of yore cattle into money, an' it will bring you as much as you can hope to get without startin' an outfit up th' trail. If you put a herd on th' trail, it would have to be a small one this year, an' there ain't no profit in drivin' four hundred cows up to Dodge, 'specially th' kind you'd have to take. You'd have th' risk an' th' worry, an th' spendin' of quite some money. This other way you'll get yore money, an' McCullough will have th' wrestlin' to do. Now, I suggests that you let Cimarron drive four hundred head home with him tomorrow, an' keep 'em handy on th' Double X for th' drive herd. They'll road brand 'em an' hold 'em with their own, and when Sherwood gets th' money, he'll send yourn to you, an' you'll have something to work on."

"And we will be four hundred head nearer bankruptcy," growled Arnold, more to give vent to his pessimism, which had become nearly chronic by this time.

"There will be more than that many turned over to you before winter," said Johnny. "Cattle stealin' don't go very long down here, even. Now, don't ask me nothin' about it; but I'm wishin' you'd give me authority to act for you in any little thing that might come up—I might not have time to ride out here for it, then."

"Why, certainly; and I'll be glad to have somebody act for me who knows what to do," replied Arnold.

"All right. I'm advisin' you to tell Cimarron to go ahead with that little trail herd. I'm goin' out that way now, an' I'll speak to him about it if you want me to."

"I think that is a splendid idea," enthused Margaret. "If we did not sell them, they will be a year older next year, and we will have to sell them then, anyhow."

"All right!" grunted Arnold. "Sell them. I don't care what is done, if only I can get out of this cursed bed. And I'll be out of it tomorrow or know the reason why!"

"We'd better have th' Doc come out an' look at it," said Johnny. "I'll be ridin' to town purty soon an' I'll drop in an' tell him. He shore ought to finish what he started."

Margaret's hand went to his arm. "Please!" she pleaded. "Don't—don't have any trouble—we—father can wait a little longer, I'm sure."

"I certainly can, Nelson," quickly spoke up the quasi-invalid, "if it will save you from any trouble. I don't know just how much I would do for you."

"There won't be no trouble, at all," Johnny gravely assured them. "Doc an' I know each other real well. You've got no idea how well we get along together. You'd be surprised if you only knowed how prompt he'll start for here. Why, trouble with me over a little thing like this is th' last thing he'd think of. You just stay where you are till he sees you an' says you can get up."

"That's the least I can do," replied Arnold. "D—n it, man! If I only were up and about, and could get a few good, honest men to work for me, I'd *make* something out of the SV!"

"You'll be up an' around before you know it," Johnny assured him. "An' you won't have no trouble gettin' three honest men to ride for you. That parson must 'a' had a good influence on this range, even before he come down to Gunsight. Did I hear Sam Gardner tell him he was tired of workin' for th' Triangle?" he asked Margaret. "Why, of course you didn't. Well, I'll have to ask Sam if I heard right. I'm going to ask you to send to Highbank for three SV stampin' irons—Arch Wiggins is ridin' down there tomorrow. They're real handy—an' chute brandin' shore saves a lot of time. They'll be needed in a month or so. Arch knows a blacksmith that can turn 'em out alike as three cartridges."

"You get anything you think we need," said Arnold. "How about some wire for those quicksands?"

"They're fixed to stay fixed," answered Johnny. "Arch an' that Wood Hallock are great boys when it comes to wire, an' I'm gamblin' on that wire stayin' up till it rusts, which won't be soon. There's six strands, an' they set quite some few more posts. Arch does things right. I reckon he'll be lookin' for a job when he gets through visitin' Highbank. He says as how he's quittin' th' Circle 4. An' from what I've seen of Arch, I like him a lot."

"Tell him to see me before he leaves the ranch," exclaimed Arnold. "Why, we're sailing along at a great clip.

Look here, Nelson, there's a spare-room here—you come and use it until you ride south. You're better than a tonic. Quit that hotel—God save the word—and come out here."

"Well, I hardly think I can do that," smiled Johnny, "'though I'm thankin' you, just th' same. I've got business close to Gunsight that'll keep me there for quite a spell, but afterward, I'll mebby spend a couple of days with you."

"Well, come when you can," replied Arnold. "If you think of anything else this ranch needs to get from Highbank, order it. You can tell that Arch that there's a job here if he wants it. I'll leave the question of wages to you."

"All right, but I'll send him in, anyhow," said Johnny, arising. "I'll be goin' now. You better stay where you are till th' Doc comes an' looks you over," and he followed Margaret out.

"You are sure that you will have no trouble with Doctor Reed?" she asked, as he stepped onto the porch.

"Why, no, Ma'am; th' Doc is seein' th' error of his sinful ways, an' I reckons he'll do purty near anythin' I tell him to if I tell him right. An' of course, I wouldn't tell him no other way."

"You are a puzzle to me," confessed Margaret, smiling. "I'm never quite sure about you."

"Puzzle?" He turned his hat over and looked into it as if to find something puzzling. "Why, Ma'am," he said, grinning, daring another deep look into her eyes, "I'm as simple an' easy to read as a—as a—Injun. Now if it was you I'd say there was a puzzle—but, pshaw! I never was no good, at all, figgerin' puzzles. I remember once I was watchin' some tenderfeet playin' billiards, when I was in Kansas City, after leavin' some cattle at th' yards across th' river. They did things to them balls that I never thought could be done, an' they did them easylike. Billiards is mebby an easy game, Ma'am, for them that knows how. It looked plumb easy to me, an' awful temptin'. I got me a table over in a corner an' took off my coat. I ain't never tried it since. Th' proprietor come a-runnin' an tells me that th' blacksmith-shop is down th' street a couple of blocks. That's me, Ma'am—my touch ain't gentle—I can't help smashin'. An' when somebody gives me a puzzle to figger out I allus look to see if I can smash through it. But puzzles ain't made that way I reckon."

Margaret stepped back into the kitchen, half closed the door and said, quickly, quietly, although somewhat breathlessly: "There is no puzzle worth the solving that the right man can't solve—if he tries hard enough."

Johnny started forward, but the door closed in his face and he heard the bar drop, and then the front door slammed. He tensed himself and then relaxed, a smile lighting up his face like a sunrise bathing a granite mountain. "This weather is bound to change," he said, loudly. "I can feel cyclones in th' air—an' I ain't th' only one that had better look to their tent pegs!" He reached Pepper in two leaps, the second of which put him in the saddle, and he dashed off to find Cimarron as though it were a matter of life or death.

The *segundo* looked up, a covetous expression on his face. The black whirlwind slid to a stop at his feet, a cloud of dust enveloping him and drifting slowly south with the wind.

"I'm solvin' puzzles with an axe," came the astonishing statement from the heart of the cloud. "I mean, have you got a match?"

The round-up boss put his fingers in a vest pocket and produced the desired article. "I got one; but mebby you ought to roll somethin' to smoke before you lights it."

Johnny scratched his head and burst into a roar of laughter, Cimarron joining him purely because it was infectious.

"Seein' where you come from, I'd say you was *loco*," chuckled Cimarron. "What's on yore mind besides matches an' axes?"

"Why, I was just wonderin' if you could take four hundred head of these cows over to th' Double X, road brand 'em with th' Question Mark, an' throw 'em in with Lin's hundred. McCullough shore is countin' on gettin' five hundred from you fellers, and he shouldn't be disappointed."

"I can do it unless I lose my health an' strength," answered the boss. "We ain't got 'em here—but on yore way to town stop an' tell Slim an' Larry to pick out as many as they can from that herd they're holdin'. If we're still short we can get th' rest easy enough. Where you goin' now?"

"To see Arch. I reckon he's got a new job if he wants it."

"That so?" replied the round-up boss. "He is a good man. You aimin' to be in Dave's tonight?"

"I am."

"Slim an' Larry will stop there with th' tally figgers on their way home. Are you reckonin' there'll be any blast tonight? They ain't in no hurry—an' I'd just as soon come with 'em."

"There won't be no blast—that'll come later," replied Johnny, smiling. "I only aim to light th' fuse tonight. Mebby it's a long one, an' mebby it's busted somewhere."

"You move cautious just th' same after tonight," warned Cimarron. "Some fuses hang fire; others get crossed, which cuts out some of th' waitin'. You've been packin' in quite some giant, off an' on. I'd say it's overcharged, with

Squint, Smitty, Wolf, Lang, an' th' Doc all packed in together. Don't you get slack, son."

"I'll be hummin' like a fiddle string," replied Johnny quietly. "There's Arch, over there. See you later, mebby."

Arch tested an iron and put it back in the fire, and looked up. "Well," he said, smiling cheerfully, "We're near through."

"Glad to hear it," replied Johnny. "Are you aimin' to bum around Highbank, or get yoreself a new job an' keep out of mischief?"

"I knowed that parson wouldn't have no good effect on you," growled Arch, "seein' how strong he affected me with my strong mind. What you want to know for? Found somethin' for my idle hands to do?"

"Arnold needs a good man out here steady; two of 'em to start with, an' mebby another later on. I told him that you wasn't worth a cuss; but bein' stubborn he says mebby you'll do."

"I ain't heard no offer yet," grinned Arch, impudently.

"You ought to be glad that folks will let you hang around," retorted Johnny. "What were you gettin' on th' Circle 4?"

"Forty-five," answered Arch. "I ain't no kid, an' I asks for fifty. They couldn't see it; so here I am."

"Fifty is yours; but you better see Arnold first. Are you goin' down to Highbank tomorrow?"

"I am, an' I'm shore set on it," answered Arch, firmly, "An' when I'm set, I'm set solid. I'm goin'; why?"

"I'm glad of it," chuckled Johnny. "You bring back three stampin' irons for this ranch; an' be shore that you can get both ends of 'em on a cow at th' same time."

"If I'm totin' 'em with me on my hoss, you can gamble they won't be no pets of Larry's," laughed Arch. "Anybody goin' to be in town tonight?"

"I reckon so. I'm dead shore that Fraser will be there. He's got a plumb affectionate disposition. He's been follerin' me around steady since Wolf cashed in. He's over there in that patch of scrub right now—don't look!"

"I ain't lookin', you ignoramus!" retorted Arch, indignantly. "I'm comin' in to have a little of Dave's fire water tonight, an' sleep in a bed once more. It looks like rain," he observed, scanning the cloudless sky, "an' I shore hate a blanket an' slicker roll when it rains."

"So I see," gravley rejoined Johnny. "I don't care where you go, of course, if you don't crowd me. I like plenty of elbowroom when I'm millin' around indoors keepin' out of th' rain. But I don't figger there'll be any trouble tonight."

"You'll have plenty of room," promised Arch. "In case you ain't got enough, sing out an' we'll bust th' front out of th' Palace." He considered a moment. "Mebby it'll be just as well to have a couple of friends hangin' 'round outside in th' dark watchin' th' weather. Dave hardly ever pulls down his curtains."

"It won't be needed—not tonight, anyhow," smiled Johnny, his heart warming to the cocky youngster. "I'm thankin' you just th' same, you flathead. Well, so-long!" and Johnny rode toward town. After he had spoken to Slim about the herd to be collected he sent Pepper into a pace that defied any horse on that range to equal. There was to be no third man present when he visited the Doc.

Arch looked carelessly over the range, stretched the kinks out of his back and let his gaze rest idly for a moment on the distant clump of scrub timber. "You pore jackass," he muttered. "You'll mebby be another one of them fellers that didn't know it was loaded."

* * *

The Doc glanced idly out of the door and resumed his packing. Big Tom had promised to send the chuck wagon for his effects on the morrow and to give him the extra room in the ranchhouse. The offer had been accepted with reluctance, for the Doc did not like to live in the same house with another, especially if the other was the boss of the house. Visiting was all very well, but he yarned for privacy, and there was good reason for it besides a natural inclination. He had little in common with the minds about him on the range, for he was a student and a reader, and his book shelves held a literature far above the understanding of those around him. He had no choice, however, for the time had come to get out of an impending storm. Being energetic, and impatient to finish a disagreeable task, he had kept at it and there now remained only a few odds and ends to be collected. He drew the corners of an old blanket over the bundle of clothing, extra bedding, and miscellaneous linen, pulled them tightly together and knelt on the bundle, straining at the rope. He had just finished the knot when a moving shadow on the east wall caught his attention and made him reach instinctively for the gun in its shoulder holster; but he checked his hand in mid-air, and just in time. There was only one man whom he had reason to fear, and that man had killed Wolf Forbes under the noses of his own outfit and in an even break; and what chance had he, a novice, against such gunplay? He let his hand drop to his side and slowly looked around.

"That was shore close, Doc," remarked a quiet but not unfriendly voice. "You don't never need to reach for no gun for me if you acts square. I ain't on th' warpath, at all; I'm peaceful, I am; an' I come down to ask you somethin' that nobody but you can tell me."

The Doc arose, anger glinting in his eyes from the

memory of a former indignity. "Well, what do you want?" he growled. "Framing up another kidnapping?"

"There you go," accused Johnny in great disgust. "You shore hop on th' prod as quick as any man I ever knowed. I only come down to ask you how soon Arnold can get out of bed an' get some use of that laig of his'n."

"I don't know," replied the Doc. "Not knowing, I wouldn't care to say. I've not been out there since."

"He's all ribbed to get up," continued Johnny. "An' there's this about things: Folks that act square with me allus find that I act square with them. An' I'm tellin' you that them fellers will mebby be plumb lucky durin' th' next few weeks. I've been foolin' a lot down here—holdin' back, sort of; but I quit foolin' th' day I went down an' dug Wolf out of his outfit. I'm aimin' to be serious these days. You said you don't know about Arnold—but it ain't much of a job to make shore, is it? You only got to take th' rough goin' dead east of this shack for a little ways until you get into Green Valley—an' from there on th' ridin' is easy. There's too much confusion along th' reg'lar trail with them touchy Double X punchers ridin' around up there. An' if you left right away you could get back in plenty of time for yore supper. Looks like yo're movin'?"

"I am," replied the other. "I might go down to High-bank, and start practicing."

"You might," admitted Johnny; "but I'm sayin' that you don't have to go to th' Bar H ranchhouse to keep out of trouble. I've passed you my word—you play square with me an' you'll mebby find this shack is safer for you than that ranchhouse ever will be if you don't play square. I'm meanin' this, Doc."

"I don't see where the question of safety comes in at all. I've found this place pretty lonely, sometimes, and

I'm getting tired of it. What's more, I'm squatting on the SV range."

"I'm glad to hear you say that last, an' I reckon mebby it is lonely," replied Johnny, "'though it shouldn't be. Yo're only a couple of miles from town, an' you got a good cayuse. There's some good boys up in town, too. You ought to ride in more often an' get friendly 'stead of holin' up like a bear dodgin' th' winter. An' as for squattin', why I'll say th' SV won't say nothin' at all to you about that, 'specially after you tells some of th' boys in town that you are only squattin' down here an' don't lay no claim to this land. Doc, th' time is shore comin' when nearly everybody on this range will be choosin' sides or settin' on th' fence—an' them as takes to th' fence should set awful tight an' still. But gettin' back to my reason for visitin' you: I reckon Arnold is plumb sick of layin' abed; I'm shore *I*'d be. You can't say when he should get up?"

The Doc was looking at him intently and his frown had slowly disappeared. He was no fool, had no real affection for Big Tom, and he was beginning to see a great light. He turned deliberately, yanked the knot loose and let the blanket open and spread out over the floor. Picking up his bag, he considered a moment. "Hazarding a guess, I'd say that he has another week in bed. Did you notice any fever, any flush, or anything else that seemed abnormal to you?" he asked.

"Nothin' but stubbornness an' a grouch like a she bear with cubs," answered Johnny. "I reckon he stays on th' prod purty much when there ain't no strangers around. He must make life excitin' for his family. Now that he's gettin' ambitious, he'll be worse."

"Well, I'll go prepared for anything, anyhow. If you are riding down this way tonight drop in and I'll tell you how

I found him. It was a clean break and everything was in his favor."

"I reckon I'll be too busy in town tonight," replied Johnny. "I got a job to do. If you ain't got nothin' special to keep you here an' feel like seein' th' boys, ride up an' spend th' evenin' with us. We'll be glad to see you."

The Doc listened intently. "Who's that riding up the trail?" he asked.

Johnny looked deep into his eyes, smiled cynically, banished his suspicions, and glanced out of the window. "I reckoned so," he muttered. "That's Fraser, goin' back to look for somethin' he's lost. He'll mebby find it tonight up in Dave's, if he looks hard enough. Times are shore changin' down here."

The Doc stepped forward and passed out. "When you leave, close the door behind you. The dust gets on my nerves and there will be plenty of it flying with this wind," and he walked briskly to the little corral.

Johnny watched him bridle and saddle the horse, mount, and canter away straight for the rough going east of the trail. Pulling the door shut behind him, he walked to the brush-filled hollow where he had left his horse, mounted, and set off at a lope for Gunsight.

"Mebby he means it," he soliloquized. "If he does, all right. I gave him a chance to go for that shoulder holster when I looked out to see who was ridin' up th' trail, but that don't mean much, for he might have figgered it was too risky. Mebby he's aimin' to set on th' fence waitin' to see how things'll settle down. That's all right, too—it's his natural play—but I'm keepin' cases on him just th' same. He's had his warnin' "—he shrugged his shoulders expressively and looked up the trail where he thought he could distinguish Fraser's horse in front of the Palace. "An' *that's* all right, too," he growled, "he's where he'll be handy." After a moment he slapped Pepper's shoulder.

"Sorry, little hoss," he growled, "but mebby you'll have to play pack animal for a while if I'm goin' to watch them mavericks until after McCullough gets that Bar H herd. Didn't I tell you we'd likely be popular, an' unpopular? Well, it's shore comin' true."

XXI

♦

The Message

Dailey, seated at a table, the everlasting pack of cards in front of him, beamed upon Fanning and Johnny as they entered. "Thought mebby nobody was goin' to show up tonight," he said. "Dave's scared of me."

"I never did care much for wild animals," retorted Dave. "An' I says that you shore go wild when you sees a deck of cards. If you'd only win somethin' once in a while, I wouldn't have a word to say."

"That's what makes him wild," chuckled Fanning. "Ben, how much has Nelson taken away from you?"

"Not very much, an' I more than got it back from th' others," retorted Dailey. "If I only had his luck with my skill—but what's th' use?" he asked, shrugging his shoulders.

"You shore has got to have plenty of luck with *yore* skill," jibed Dave, "or you wouldn't even have a shirt left."

"Lemme ask you somethin', seein' that you know so much about poker," said Fanning. "How far should a man back two pairs?"

"Them assassins? You get up to this table, you scoffin' innocent, an' I'll show you when you ought to let loose of two pair," chuckled Dailey. "Who's this comin'? Fraser! Come over here, Bill, an' help me rope a couple of tender-feet into a little game of draw. They're shy tonight."

"Who's th' other, besides me?" inquired Fraser, leaning against the bar.

"Huh!" snorted Dailey. "All right, then; help me rope in th' other two."

"If I'm goin' to be yore come-on, what do I get out of it?" laughed Fraser.

"Every cussed thing you can get an' hold onto, but you'd better sand yore hands. Here's another sheep: Hello, Gurley! Yo're just in time to get a seat—I allus did like a five-handed game. Come on! Come on! Don't be afraid of th' iron!"

"Make it four-handed for a little while," said Johnny. "That'll give Dailey a chance to stack it up in front of him all ready for me. I ain't as good at draw as some down here, but I can allus take it away from Ben, somehow. How's things on th' Triangle, Gurley?"

"Slowin' fast since them Double X fellers moved off. They made me wear out four cayuses a day. When will they finish up?"

"Purty soon, I reckon," answered Johnny, turning to Fraser. "You fellers are lucky. You don't get many strays over th' mountain, or through that canyon, I reckon."

"Not any that I've noticed," replied Fraser. "But we've been plumb lazy in our round-ups. We got an awful sight of brandin' to do next time."

"That so?" asked Johnny. "Been takin' life easy an' lettin' 'em go?"

"Shore; that northwest section is so rough an' full of brush that it's near impossible to get 'em out. There must be an awful lot of unmarked animals over there. We're goin' to have our hands full with 'em."

"Aimin' to tackle it this fall?" asked Johnny, carelessly.

"Mebby; mebby not. McCullough will save us from goin' up th' trail this year, so we might run a special combin' up out there."

"I'm runnin' one right here!" exclaimed Dailey, banging his fist on the table. "I'll run a brand on you fellers that'll smart so you can't sleep. Come on, let's get a-goin'. Hot iron! Hot iron! Ropers up!"

"I'll just take a bite out of you," said Fraser. "Anybody else hungry?"

"I just ain't never had enough to eat," chuckled Fanning, dragging up a chair, "not since I was a growin' kid—an' I ain't nowise shore that I had enough then."

"Which I says is frank, comin' from th' keeper of a hotel," laughed Gurley. "I've often felt th' same way when I ate in town. Turn it loose. I'm on."

"Let me see," pondered Dailey, "we deals five cards, don't we?"

"We do; but only one at a time," replied Fanning patiently. "Don't turn no trump."

"It's sorta comin' back to me," smiled Dailey, spreading out the cards to be cut to see who dealt. "It's sorta comin' back," he repeated.

"Then I'm sayin' it's due to be laig weary, for it's goin' to have a long journey," remarked Dave. He looked up. "Cuss it! Here's th' Doc! Hello, stranger! Shore, this is Gunsight. Hey, Dailey! he's got a whole satchel full; ring him into th' game."

"Bet he's got a wad of wool soaked with that there chloryfoam. Somebody ride herd on him," laughed Fraser, but he was tense. It was the first time anyone had seen the Doc and Johnny together since the kidnapping had been explained, and anything was possible.

"I'm not collecting buttons," retorted the Doc, smiling.

"Hello, boys! Hello, Dave! Say, Fraser, I wish you would tell Big Tom not to send in the wagon for me; I've changed my mind. I got a hurt leg, and it won't be right for nearly a week. Set out a round on me, Dave; I'll drink mine and hurry along. I just rode up to get word to Tom. Dave, you should use something milder when you load this whiskey— ever try nitric?"

"Don't you do it, Dave!" expostulated Dailey in alarm. "I can't hardly taste it now."

The Doc looked at him, shook his head sadly, said good night, and went out.

"He didn't act like his laig was hurt," remarked Fraser wonderingly. "But you can't never tell nothin' about him; he's a queer bird. An' changeable? There ain't no cussed word for it."

"I've often wondered how he made a livin'," said Johnny curiously.

"Well, I'll be cussed!" snorted Dailey incredulously. "You have been here all this time an' don't know that? Huh! Th' Doc is a sort of self-actin' remittance man. He's got a wad banked back East, an' once a month I cash a check for him."

"Two pairs," muttered Fanning, scratching his head, and telling the truth to mislead his opponents. "That was what I was askin' about. Well, I'll see it an' add a blue."

"Any time *you* raise a blue, you got two pairs, all right!" snorted Dailey. "Two pairs, deuces up!" He held up a finger warningly. "I hears hosses' feets," he chuckled. "Move over, Gurley, an' give th' visitors a chance to edge in."

The sounds grew louder and soon stopped outside, and a laughing voice said, "There's Dailey, th' hoss thief, try-in' to learn th' game. He's a persistent dummy, for he's allus tryin'."

"He don't know one card from another," laughed a second voice.

"Hey!" shouted Dailey. "Come in here, you fellers, an' I'll show you how much I know!"

Slim appeared, followed closely by Larry and Arch.

"They ought to make you roll up yore sleeves, you mosshead," said Larry, grinning.

"Sit down there!" ordered Dailey, "an' I'll have *you* rollin' up th' bottoms of yore pockets!"

"Wimmin' an children first," quoth Fanning. "Come on, Larry."

"Did you hear that?" snorted Larry, staring at him. "I shore will, *now!*"

"This is goin' to be pay-day for me," said Dailey in great content. "Where th' devil are we at, anyhow?"

Over at the bar Johnny and Slim were carrying on a low-voiced conversation and figuring on a piece of paper, while Arch and Dave entertained each other at the other end of the counter. After a few minutes Johnny nodded his head in quiet satisfaction, put the paper in his pocket and, going up for a few words with Arch and Dave, wandered over to the table and sat down close to it, leaning back to enjoy the fight. He always found keen enjoyment in watching the storekeeper play, for Dailey's red-brown face was suffused with wrinkles of good nature, quite independent of how his fortune tended; his high, shining forehead and the bald spot above and behind it reflected the light and glistened. The eternal cigar he chewed on, cold, stale, and odorous, bobbed animatedly and his shrewd black eyes peered out from under bushy eyebrows, glittering, glinting, and alive with his emotions, like twin mirrors on which were reflected the subtle complexities of a nature enriched by a life crowded with experiences. He had no poker face, but knowing the sad fact, he had made an adept liar out of the one to which Nature had given so much expression.

He glanced at Johnny, his eyes dancing. "Yo're comin' nearer th' candle all th' time, little moth," he laughed. "I'll singe them wings of yourn—you see! My flush takes *this* game. Deal 'em up, Dailey," he grunted, raking in chips and cards.

"Come on, Nelson," said Fanning. "Better get in this. Th' old hoss thief is stackin' 'em up for you."

"Huh!" Johnny remarked. "It ain't as big a pile as I was hopin'. Oh, well," he sighed, "I'm like th' SV round-up: I take 'em as they come."

"How'd they come to start that so early?" asked Fanning. "It's plumb warm for workin' hard."

"Wanted to know how many head they had," answered Johnny. "An' what do you know about workin' hard?"

"He's seen me lots of times," cut in Dailey. "Did they find out?"

"Shore. They've got twelve hundred an' twenty, which would be fourteen hundred an' fifty-five, if Arnold hadn't sold two hundred an' thirty-five head."

"That's good, considerin' how things has been let slide over there," remarked Fraser.

"Th' old figgers of three years ago," said Johnny, "when Arnold took possession, were sixteen hundred an' eighty-five, in th' fall. Now, lemme see—do I need two or three?" he mused. "Reckon there ain't no use of throwin' away a nice, high card, so I'll take two. I'm plumb fond of holdin' up a sider." He glanced at the two cards, slipped them into his hand and looked around. "Now, I was askin' th' Double X what factor they used to figger natural increase—an' they says one to five. That right?"

"That's allus been sort of gospel down here," said Fanning. "For th' Lord's sake!" he snorted, in playful pretense. "You takin' eight cards again?"

"You ain't got no right to ask nobody but th' dealer how many cards he takes," retorted Dailey. "As a matter of fact, I only took seven. I'm h—l-bent to get me a pair."

"You *are* dealing," declared Gurley. "How many did you take?"

"Three jacks," answered Dailey. "If I only had th' other three mebby I'd *have* a pair."

"Which same I calls enlightenin' an' 'lucidatin'," muttered Gurley. "I demands a count of th' deck. But, speakin' of factors, I'd say one to nine was nearer right, over on th' SV."

"Let him count th' deck," growled Fanning, "before he gets worse. One to nine! I'm sayin' one to five is close whittlin' down on this range. It'll come right eight out of ten. Well! well!" he chuckled, as he looked at his card. "Welcome, welcome, little stranger; how I wondered what you was! But I'm not pressin' my luck too hard. I sees, an' trails."

"I'm passin'," sighed Johnny. "Now I says that th' natural increase of them sixteen hundred an' eighty-five cows th' next year would be three hundred an' thirty-nine, usin' that gospel factor. Th' herd would finish th' second year with two thousand an' twenty-four. Usin' that gospel factor again, it would increase four hundred an' five, an' finish th' third year with twenty-four hundred an' twenty-nine. This is the summer of that third year, an' that twenty-four hundred an' twenty-nine ain't there. There's only twelve hundred an' twenty, which added to them that Arnold sold, makes fourteen hundred an' fifty-five. Now I figgers that fourteen hundred an' fifty-five from twenty-four hundred an' twenty-nine leaves nine hundred an' seventy-four head. That's what is missin'—nine hundred an' seventy-four head. Call it nine hundred seventy. Cimarron O.K.'s th' last tally figgers. Everybody but th' Bar H allows one to five is right. Where did them cattle go to?"

"I call," growled Gurley. "Kings up!"

"You can't never trust assassins," chuckled Dailey, laying down three tens.

"An' three tens ain't no good tonight," said Fanning, revealing an eight-full. "Two pair ain't no good to bet on hard, but they're plumb fine to draw to. What you got, Fraser?" he demanded.

"A headache," grunted Fraser, throwing down his hand.

"Deal 'em up, Fanning," said Dailey. "Where *did* they go to?" he asked Johnny.

"I've gone over everythin' I can think of," replied Johnny, leaning back. "I've figgered hard winters, wolves, fever—there wasn't none of them. Strayed off? Where to? Would they leave Clear River for an arid stretch forty miles wide—an' *stay* away? They have to drink, don't they? Quicksands? Those that wandered in wouldn't be many, an' them that was drove in we'll count part of that nine seventy. Where did they go?"

"Mebby they heard them angel voices callin'," said Fanning, grinning.

"I'm sayin' somethin' is plumb wrong down here," replied Johnny. "Somebody has been ridin' th' line careless, an' a lot of mavericks has got across. Fraser, how many riders has Big Tom kept on his northwest lines?"

Fraser looked serious and pretended to ponder deeply. "Only one—Wolf. An' he was allus payin' more attention to th' west line, facin' th' Snake Buttes country than he was to th' north line, though. All he could think of was rustlers. Cussed if he didn't near sleep with 'em, he had 'em in his mind so strong." He did not see Slim's sneering smile or the look he exchanged with Arch. Slim was beginning to regard that outfit very much in that light.

"That's what I thought," replied Johnny, triumphantly. "He wasn't ridin' sign at all—he was only lookin' for rustlers. An' while he was prancin' along that west line lookin' for Nevada, them mavericks was driftin' off th' SV to get in that brush where th' flies wouldn't bother 'em so much. That accounts for a lot of them unmarked cows you was speakin' about."

"Does look like mebby there's somethin' in that," cogitated Fraser. "As I said, we never paid much attention to th' cattle out there; but it don't sound reasonable that all them SV mavericks would drift over onto us. An' why only mavericks?" He thought for a moment. "I'm sayin' nothin', but there's somethin' plumb wrong, somewhere. Want me to ask Big Tom about it? Mebby it was rustlers— they're plumb active."

Johnny considered. "Well, you might," he said, slowly, leaning slightly forward in his chair. "Tell you what, Fraser; I'm dead shore about them nine hundred seventy. Suppose you tell him to brand that many mavericks, takin' 'em as they come, with th' SV mark, an' throw 'em over to Arnold when he holds his fall roundup? Th' SV will provide stampin' irons, an' a couple of men to help. As to rustlers, they'd have to drive across th' Bar H an' th' Double X to get to Arnold's ranch—any rustlin' that was done would be done on th' fringes of th' Double X. Why, you fellers ain't never been raided; an' to get to th' SV would be worse than gettin' to th' Bar H. That's what we'll do; we'll have him throw over nine hundred an' seventy head this fall, an' that'll make things right."

Fraser boiled inwardly, but controlled himself. There had been no accusation, nothing to call for defense, and to take it angrily or as an accusation he felt would be to play into Johnny's hands. Being guilty of the very thing which the other had gone so carefully around, made him find the hidden meaning in the heavy circumlocution, and keep quiet about it for fear of revealing the real meaning of the words to the others in the room. He knew how Big Tom would take it, for he knew that his foreman was smouldering like a volcano, charged with the cumulative anger caused by recent events; and he felt sure that the news he would take back to the ranch that night would cause an eruption, and a great one. This was another reason for remaining calm: not knowing what Big Tom might decide to do, it would be well to give Johnny no cause to exercise any unusual caution, or to strike hard and suddenly. So he growled a little as he resumed the play.

"That's shore a whole lot of cattle to throw over to anybody, free, but, h—l!" he said, "it ain't no funeral of mine. It's Big Tom's business, 'though I reckon it'll sort of take his breath. Did Arnold say that?"

"He's sayin' it through me," answered Johnny quietly. "I'm workin' for him, an' actin' for him, an' I'm usin' my own judgment."

Slim lounged into an easier position against the bar and grunted. "Well," he drawled, "we're comin' to th' conclusion that th' round-ups down here has got to be general, spring an' fall. This here maverick business allus is a bad proposition, an' it's worse in th' kind of country that's plentiful on parts of this range. Sherwood is standin' out, set for a general drive. He says for all th' ranches to join hands, sweep th' whole range, do our brandin' an' divide up an' brand th' mavericks accordin' to some fair plan. I suggests dividin' 'em in proportion to th' number of cattle on each ranch, but that's only *my* idea. He goes even further, an' says that th' runnin' iron an' this brush brandin' we all have been doin' down here has got to be done away with, on th' Double X an' every other ranch in this section. Anybody knows that chutin' 'em, an' stampin' on th' brand is easier, an' that there ain't no honest reason for th' straight iron no more. Texas threw it into th' discard ten years ago or more. We're discardin' it, an' we're goin' to raise th' devil with any outfit that don't foller suit. That's flat, an' goes as it lays, regardless, to th' SV, th' Triangle, an' th' Bar H, with Sherwood's compliments."

"What about that nine hundred an' seventy, then?" asked Gurley.

"We've got nothin' to say about them, but if they are throwed over, th' rest will be divided," answered Slim. "Bein' th' biggest ranch out here, we stand to lose more than any other by throwin' over them cows to th' SV; but we admits its title to 'em. Tell Big Tom to think it over, an' see us about it before fall."

"One to five is figgerin' too strong," remarked Gurley, thoughtfully. "One to nine is nearer th' real figgers."

"There ain't no reason that I can see to change figgers that have proved themselves, time an' time again, down here," replied Slim.

"Havin' been talked plumb weak," growled Dailey, "suppose we rest ourselves with a nice, quiet game? It's yore deal, Fraser. Comin' in, Slim?"

"No, I ain't; I'm goin' out," answered Slim. "I got more than twenty miles an' I'm tired. Comin', you fellers?" he asked Larry and Arch.

"Shore," said Larry, arising. "Glad to escape. Better come along, Arch—what's a few more miles?"

"I'd like to," replied Arch. "Cuss it, I will! I can go to town th' next day. Good night, fellers."

They made a noisy exit and soon their banter and laughter grew silent down the trail. Fraser stretched, and yawned prodigiously, and his friend Gurley became restless.

Dailey, sensing the break-up of his beloved pastime, made an effort to save it. "Don't bust up th' game, boys," he begged. "I got a feelin' comin' over me that I can clean up th' whole pack of you. Let's see if I'm right."

"Try it on th' rest of th' boys," growled Fraser. "I'm cashin' in what's left, an' dustin' up th' trail for my little bunk. Comin', Gurley?"

"As far as th' partin' of th' ways," smiled the Triangle puncher, "unless you aim's to ride home by way of our house, so I won't be lonesome. It's only a few miles out of yore way."

"I'm likely to," retorted Fraser. "So-long, fellers," and he preceded his friend to the horse rail.

The remaining four smoked and talked for a little while and then Johnny arose. "Put them supplies in th' shed, Dailey?" he asked.

"Shore; in a strong sack, like you said," replied the storekeeper. "I put in a few more cans of tomatoes, seein' as they're handy when there ain't no drinkin' water near."

"Yo're usin' yore head," commended Johnny, and turned to Dave. "I'm goin' to th' SV to let Cimarron's boys know that there's trouble comin', shore. You don't know when I'll be back or where I'm goin'; but I reckon mebby th' whole town will *hear* me, when I do come back. Somethin's goin' to bust loose tomorrow. I ain't no blind fool. Good night."

XXII

◆

The Ultimatum

There was movement on the Gunsight trail at an early morning hour. Five men rode to within half a mile of the town and then halted for a final consultation, which was soon over. Three rode westward at a walk, another went on, bearing slightly to the east, while the fifth, dismounting, led his horse from the trail, picketed it in a steep-walled ravine and went north on foot.

The eastern sky paled, grew silvery, and then became tinted with red and gold. A man crouched behind the hotel shed, swearing softly because he heard no sounds of a horse within it. He snuggled close to a knothole, peering at the hotel wall not far from him, and the rifle in his hand was full cocked. Behind the saloon shed another man had thrust his rifle through a crack and as the light increased, he cuddled his cheek against the stock and peered along the sights into an open window in the rear wall of the hotel. Lying in a clump of weeds north of the saloon and near the trail was another rifleman, who could see Dave's north wall and the front of the saloon as well. A fourth had settled down in the end of a shallow gully across the trail from Dailey's store, his Winchester needing but to move over a short arc to cover the door of the saloon. It was point-blank range for him, and in this matter he was no better off than his three friends. The fifth, the angry and determined foreman of the Bar H, not finding cover as close as he would have liked, was forced to ensconce himself over two hundred yards from the front of the hotel, and a little to the right of Jerry's shop, where he kept turning problems over in his mind. Desperate ailments called for desperate cures, and if Gunsight objected as to methods, then it would have to object in the persons of the three easy-going inhabitants who were likely to be offended. The actions of the Double X were far more serious, but had to be risked if life were to be worth living for the outfit of the Bar H. With the coming of dawn Big Tom pondered less and looked more, his rifle at his shoulder, ready for instant use.

Back on the trail there was silent movement as an indistinct and bootless figure crossed it and paused, waiting for light. The darkness thinned and the figure moved forward again, bent over close to the boot marks on the ground, which it followed with slow sureness. The stockinged feet made no sound, avoiding twigs and dead leaves, and not an out-thrust branch whipped or scraped as the man worked forward. He carried a heavy Sharp's, the heel of his hand over the cocked hammer, his fingers covering the trigger guard as an extra precaution against accidental discharge.

The few buildings in Gunsight appeared as though a curtain were slowly rising and finally stood revealed in their entirety. The sun rose and threw soft, delicate shadows from the bases of all standing objects, too weak to mark their patterns far, melting into oblivion. A door slammed, sounding irreverent and out of place, and from the hotel chimney curled a timid wisp of smoke, this way and that, finally climbing straight up and losing its identity against the gray-blue of the sky, while its supporting column twisted and turned and danced as it hurried to self-effacement. Dailey's chimney sent up a skirmishing film, which died out; and then, as if in stalwart support of the fainting advance, there came a darker, thicker column, telling all who cared to read that

Dailey put his trust in kerosene. The hotel door opened, causing a quick movement of Big Tom's rifle, and George, sleepy and unpleasant in looks and disposition, glanced idly around and went back again. From far off in the west the quavering, long-drawn wail of a coyote, mercifully tempered by distance, arose to greet the rising sun. Birds sang with delirious abandon and the soft noises in grass and sand and brush told of a waking world. In the vague grayness of the hotel, framed by the open door, something moved, steadily growing plainer and soon took the form of a towel in the hands of George, who drove winged pests before him and, with a final, frenzied waving, took hold of the door and slammed it shut. As it closed Big Tom relaxed, eased his hold on the rifle and reached back to remove a stone which was beginning to assert its presence under him to his growing discomfort. Turning his head, he looked back, and froze, his groping fingers rigid. Ten feet behind him and to his right was the black muzzle of a heavy rifle, and behind that a pair of gray-blue eyes regarded him malevolently through narrow slits in the bronzed face. For a tense, appreciable interval eyes looked into eyes, and then the foreman squirmed.

"Don't move, only as I tell you, an' slow," said Johnny's clear, low voice. "I got you just th' way I want you—ambushin'! Don't touch that gun, an' don't make no noise. First, put yore hands up even with yore armpits, palms down, on th' ground. Now inch back, away from that gun. Keep on—more—more—all right—stop! Slide 'em forward, straight out ahead of you, an' then lay still. You can admire Fannin's front door, an' imagine me in it, careless an' easy prey for a pot-shooter, if it'll do you any good. Don't look around till I tell you to, an' don't make a sound, blast you!"

Not being able to do anything else, Big Tom obeyed and soon felt his Colt leave its holster. A hand felt up under his coat, to see if the back-strap of his trousers held a gun. Being right-handed, the foreman would hardly choose to carry a six-gun there under ordinary circumstances, but this situation was not in that category. The back-strap was guiltless.

"Roll over on yore back," came the next command, and when it had been obeyed the same inquiring hand passed lightly and quickly over waist-band and shirt bosom, the left hand holding a six-gun now instead of the rifle. "All right, wiggle down in that gully, and then head for where you left yore cayuse, keepin' low down, like yore nature, an' out of sight of town."

"What do you think yo're doin'?" wrathfully inquired Big Tom, but obeying as he protested.

"Huntin' for an excuse to blow you apart, you ambushin' dog," came the metallic reply. "Shut yore mouth, an' keep on goin'. I'll give you a chance to talk later. Any harm that comes to you will be of yore own makin'. Keep on!"

They reached the brush at the edge of the trail, waited a moment, and then crossed swiftly, and when they stopped again it was at Pepper's side. Johnny quickly mounted and urged his captive on again. Coming to a picketed Bar H horse he ordered the foreman to mount it, and as the helpless man obeyed Johnny revealed their objective.

"Head for yore ranchhouse," he said. "Ride on my right side, yore stirrup even with my pommel, where my Colt will have a fair view of you from under my coat. If we meet anybody, pass 'em on yore side, an' don't make no remarks that ain't needed. We go at a lope; hit it up!"

And so they rode, except at a few places in the canyon, where the narrowness of the twisting trail made Big Tom go ahead. Arriving at the ranchhouse they rode around on its farther side, tied the horses to a stake, and went indoors.

"Sit down," commanded Johnny, indicating a chair in the middle of the room. "Here, look at this," and he handed the foreman a piece of paper which was covered with sprawled figures. "I don't know what Fraser forgot, or what he got tangled up, so I'll go over it again. Them top figgers are based on th' tally sheets of th' SV in th' fall of th' year that Arnold took possession. They ain't like th' figgers Ol' Simon could 'a' showed, for th' ranch had been on th' slide for some years, an' plenty of its cows went on th' drive trail to give money to th' heirs. Th' lowest figgers are based on th' tally Cimarron finished yesterday. Natural increase, figgered as one to five, shows what they ought to be, minus them that Arnold had to sell to get grub. It's all there."

"Th' h—l with 'em!" blazed the foreman, crushing the sheet in his hand and hurling it from him. "What do *I* care about any figgers belongin' to th' SV? Take yore figgers an' get out—I'm advisin' you to leave this part of th' country, an' cussed quick. I ain't playin' godfather to th' SV, an' I'm runnin' this ranch without no help from you, Sherwood, or anybody else."

"When I leave this range I'll go of my own accord, an' there won't be no pushin'," retorted Johnny. "Sherwood can 'tend to his own business; I'll 'tend to mine; but I've got time to look after a little of yourn. If you ain't godfather to th' SV, yo're shore goin' to act like one. There's nine hundred an' seventy head clean missin' from it, an' there's plenty of big ranches down Texas way that would yell for th' rangers, an' holler calamity if they had lost that

many. For a little ranch to lose 'em it is shore enough calamity. If anybody would put that many cows on th' trail
for me I'd show 'em a lot of money at th' other end."

"SV calamities don't mean nothin' to me," rejoined Big
Tom. "It was allowed to run itself, an' it run itself into th'
ground. Why wouldn't it lose a lot of cattle?"

"It shore might do just that," conceded Johnny, "if it
wasn't for one thing. Yo're an old hand in th' cattle business, an' you know that a bunch of cattle can run wild an'
grow amazin'. An' they'd shore do it on a range like th'
SV with that valley an' them brush-filled draws for winter
shelter. There ain't no natural enemies to cut down th'
calves—an' that ranch is good grazin' all year 'round.
There wasn't cows enough to eat it down."

"There's them quicksands, an' there was a lot of gray
wolves runnin' down here th' last couple of years!" shouted
Big Tom, red with anger. "They never even kept up th'
wire fence around th' quicksands. Why wouldn't they
lose cows?"

"The quicksands would get a few," rejoined Johnny.
"They would get more if th' cows was drove into 'em like
I caught Lang doin'—an' them will be figgered in th'
herd to be throwed back. I've asked about wolves an' everythin' else—there wasn't nothin' to keep 'em down.
An' as for that fence, th' less you, or any of yore gang
have to say about that, th' better it'll be for you."

"Then yo're callin' me a liar," blazed the foreman.
"There *was* wolves down here! An' I never touched that
fence, neither."

"Mebby you didn't personal; an' I ain't callin' you a
liar while you ain't got a gun," retorted Johnny. "But I am
admittin' that yo're plumb mistaken. Comin' down to
cases, pleasant an' friendly, I'm sayin' that th' Bar H owes
the SV nine hundred an' seventy head of cattle, as they

come in a round-up, all kinds an' conditions. When do you aim to start deliverin'?"

The foreman sprang to his feet. "When do I aim to start deliverin'?" he shouted, staring into the calm, gray eyes of the man whose Colt covered him. "When do I aim to start deliverin'?" he repeated, his neck swelling. "I ain't aimin' to at all! Nine hundred an' seventy! That would plumb ruin us!"

"It ain't ruined th' SV," replied Johnny evenly. "Not quite, anyhow," he added. "An' it won't ruin you, because they can all be figgered as extras. We all know they ain't never been put on th' tally sheets with th' other cattle, for th' owners to know about. They're strays, you might say, that have been eatin' up yore grazin' scandalous. They've wandered over on you an' are likely to eat you into some kind of ruin. You ought to be able to do better without 'em, an' you shore ought to be glad to get rid of such a hungry bunch of cattle that you can't prove title to."

"I've got all th' title *I* need—they're on my ranch, an' that's good enough," shouted Big Tom. "It's good enough for me, an' it's good enough for everybody else, you included."

"Not for nobody else," corrected Johnny, "me least of all. That title is questioned now by more than a dozen men. You can't keep 'em, nohow, for th' general roundup will cut 'em four ways. Th' times are changin' down here like they changed some years back on th' older ranges. Th' runnin' iron is dyin' fast, an' for good reasons. Maverickin' is goin' out of style—an' nothin' can stop it. An' with it goes that title you was mentionin'. Why not get ahead of 'em, an' throw them cows over onto th' SV before anybody gets insultin' you?"

"I'll have somethin' to say about any styles changin'

down here," retorted the foreman. "Mebby more than some folks think."

"You ain't got a chance, not a chance," Johnny assured him. "You'll be like th' Injun that tried to push back th' first, an' last, engine he ever saw. It was goin' strong when he tried it."

"An' I ain't got th' authority to give away a cow, not even a single dogie—not to mention a herd. I'm not ownin' this ranch; I'm workin' for it. How can I straighten out my tally sheets to cover th' loss of a herd like that? They don't belong to me—they belong to th' ranch, to th' owners." He was wasting as much time in argument as he knew how in the hope that his outfit would return.

"Pshaw!" laughed Johnny. "They can all be accounted for. Didn't I just say that they never got on th' tally sheets at all? You shore found you had been feedin' a hull passel of cows that didn't belong to th' ranch in case they did get on th' tally sheets. You found it out, an' it was so plumb careless of yore line riders that you up an' fired them that was responsible. That won't bother you, because you got three names off yore pay-roll right now. There ain't nothin' we can't get around if we pull together."

"But th' title to 'em wouldn't stick," objected the baited foreman. "Every one of them cows could be took away from Arnold. I ain't got th' authority to make it stick. An' th' only reason I'm wastin' time talkin' to you over a fool thing like this is because you got a gun on me, an' I can't help myself." His brain seized upon and rejected scheme after scheme for getting out of the situation, one of which he recalled and examined anew. It was not a bad one, if bad came to worse, and he nursed it, sorry that so much time would have to elapse before he could carry it out.

"I just said we could get around anythin'," replied Johnny, pleasantly. "There's an awful lot of mavericks runnin' around on this ranch, most of 'em under four years old. They wouldn't show any Bar H brand. They'd only have a SV. There wouldn't even be a vent brand to single 'em out; an' cattle ain't tellin' where they come from, or we'd 'a' heard a lot of scandals long ago."

"Nine hundred an' seventy mavericks!" snorted Big Tom. "A fine chance I'd have of roundin' up that many! Yo're plumb loco."

"That is a lot, I'll admit," conceded Johnny, apparently balked. "Of course, if you owned this ranch, you could make it up with Bar H brands. But you don't. You can't give away nothin' that you don't own. I can see where that would put you. Anythin' that was yours you could give away; but not no Bar H belongin's. That yore idea?"

"Yo're gettin' th' drift, slow but shore," sarcastically rejoined the foreman. "Anythin' I own I can give away; but not nothin' I don't own. A kid can understand that. An' there ain't that many mavericks on this ranch."

"I still say we can get around anythin' an' I ain't no kid," muttered Johnny. "Lemme see: First, we'll consider cash. Got any?"

"Nothin' but my wages," answered the foreman, a sarcastic smile playing around his lips.

"Too bad," mused Johnny, "wages ain't a patch. If we could have you ownin' a nice pile of money—but you can get money!"

"Look here!" snapped Big Tom, aggressively. "I can't sign no checks over a certain amount a year—th' bank wouldn't cash 'em. An' they've all been signed for this year, all but th' pay-roll. An' I don't own that money, neither. That belongs to th' ranch."

"Well, failin' in cash," said Johnny, crisply, "I'll take a note. Will you gimme one?"

"I will; you can have it," nodded Big Tom, his pet scheme coming more vividly into his mind. "I'll make it out right here, an' now."

"I don't want yore note," objected Johnny. "What good is it? Now, if it was endorsed by somebody that could make it good, why that would be different. You said you'd gimme a note; then gimme that one for three thousand dollars, of Arnold's, that *is* endorsed by somebody that can make it good. An' also a receipt for it. That'll cut down that nine hundred an' seventy an amazin' lot. Th' difference won't be too many to get right here on th' Bar H, an' all of 'em mavericks."

Big Tom was staring at him as if doubting his senses. His face flushed and the veins on his neck and forehead stood out like serpents. He stepped forward involuntarily, but the gun stopped him. He was incapable of speech for the moment and could only make inarticulate sounds.

"That'll help a lot," said Johnny, lightly balanced and leaning slightly forward. "We'll let th' Double X say how many cattle, takin' 'em as they come, they would sell for three thousand dollars. Then we'll take that many away from that nine seventy. You can easy round-up what are needed to make up th' difference, brand 'em with th' SV stampin' irons, an' throw 'em over where they belong. I'll take th' note *now*."

'You'll take h—l!" yelled the foreman. "You'll take h—l!"

"You'll *get* h—l!" snapped Johnny, his eyes narrowing; "an' you'll get it *pronto*! Hunt up that note, an' without no more cussed nonsense. It's yore play, an' you shore want to play fast!"

"You won't get no note!" shouted Big Tom, his face twitching with rage. He seemed about to spring.

"Don't!" ordered Johnny, softly, but with a cold ferocity in his voice that carried conviction. "I'll shoot you like I would a coyote, you pot-shooter, for you are a coyote! Get that note!"

Big Tom, seething with rage, swayed in agonizing hesitation. He had courage, plenty of it; but he also had common sense. Unarmed, he could do nothing against the gun which had killed his two-gun man in an even break; and his common sense came to his rescue, and barely in time. Glancing out of the window, he detected no signs of his outfit on the trail, and craftily attempted to begin the argument all over again.

"That'll do," said Johnny. "We've finished that. My time is valuable, even if I ain't lookin' for company; an' if they come, you'll be th' first to go under. Get—that—note!"

Shrugging his shoulders, the foreman stepped forward, but Johnny slipped aside and snarled a warning, so venomous and tense that Big Tom gave up the desperate idea, and slowly turned, a beaten man. He walked toward a metal-bound box in a corner of the room, Johnny close at his heels, the gun against the foreman's back. Unlocking it, he slowly raised the lid, and felt Johnny's breath on his neck, the gun pressing solidly against his spine. As the cover went up it revealed a derringer lying on top of a few papers, and the foreman's hand slowly passed by it and fumbled among the contents, reluctantly withdrawing with an unsealed envelope. Shutting down the lid he turned the key, and arose to his feet as his captor, alert as a cat, stepped aside.

Johnny took the envelope, backed off a little farther, opened it, glanced at the note and nodded. He looked around the room and then ordered Big Tom to the table. Taking the pen and ink from a shelf, he placed them before the foreman and then handed him the envelope, telling him what to write. When the pen ceased scratching he took the receipt, read it, and held it out a moment for it to dry.

"This saves you a lot of brandin'," he remarked. "Somewhere around two-thirds, I reckon, 'though th' Double X will set its value in cattle. Now, you listen close. There ain't goin' to be any round-up or brandin' on th' northwest section of this ranch till th' SV gets its herd. When we know how many will be needed you will have till th' general round-up to use th' SV irons. Send for 'em when you get ready, an' an SV puncher will come with 'em. I'm warnin' you fair: A Sharp's will talk to anybody runnin' a brand or round-up out there unless a SV man is on th' spot. An' there's goin' to be some SV men right soon— good ones—an' they'll be plumb touchy about wire fences comin' down. Now I'm takin' you for a little ride with me, so you won't be tempted to smoke up out of a window while I'm ridin' off. Come on; I'm shore in a hurry."

In a few moments they rode westward, Big Tom leading the way, and it was not until more than an hour had passed that he was free to ride back again, or to Gunsight for his outfit, as his fancy dictated.

He chose to return to the ranch and while he rode he elaborated the plan which had come to him, and rubbed his hands as its details unfolded. Since Nelson had admitted being the man who was responsible for the mysterious events which had puzzled the country, Big Tom had remembered Lang's report about having seen Margaret and Johnny riding together. The foreman had not given her up, although pretending to have no interest in her. Having lost the note he had to change his plans, and go about it in a different way. Now his rage and jealousy fanned the flame of his impatience, gave a keener edge to his schem-

ing wits, and added zest to what he purposed to do; and
before he knew it he arrived at the house. Entering, he
saw the crumpled piece of paper and, kicking it across
the room, laughed sneeringly.

"You've been proddin' th' wrong man, Mr. Nelson," he
growled. "I'm slow to start; but when I *do*, there ain't nothin'
that'll stop me."

XXIII

♦

Range Activities

On the day following Johnny's message to Big Tom,
Gunsight had awakened expectant, and had remained so all the morning, but to no end. Not a Bar H
man had come in, so far as they knew, and the trio in
Dave's changed from the belief each had retired with and
discussed the situation from a different point of view.

"Big Tom is a wise ol' owl," said Dailey. "He'll move
when he gets ready. Just now he's on a nest, hatchin' out
somethin' that is mebby tender, bein' so young. He ain't
layin' down so easy. I know him."

"He reckons, mebby, that th' man that dealt th' hands
has got an ace in a hole," replied Fanning. "It's an old
sayin' that you never want to buck another man's game. I
don't know that Nelson has got an ace laid away, but he
don't have to have any; Big Tom figgers he has, mebby,
because them Double X *hombres* are so friendly with
him; an' it's what Big Tom thinks that counts with him.
Mebby somethin' will happen today, an' mebby it won't;
but it's goin' to happen, just th' same, some time."

"I'm favorin' th' ace idea," said Dave, thoughtfully. "If I was Big Tom I'd be plumb suspicious of any man that made th' suggestion that Nelson made when he knew there was an outfit ag'in' him. I'd figger he was either a cussed fool or knowed just exactly what he was doin', an' all th' time. Nobody down here believes that he is a fool, not now, anyhow; an' I'm dead shore he wasn't bluffin'. He's got an ace, all right—an' I'm admirin' Big Tom's waitin' game. When he thinks he's figgered out how far th' Double X will go we'll hear his answer. Besides, th' Bar H has got to round up an' brand that herd for McCullough. That may be holdin' him back some."

"Slim's remarks slid in like they was made to fit," commented Dailey. "An' *he* wasn't bluffin', neither. If th' Double X is backin' Nelson all th' way, he'll win; if they ain't, he won't. But I'm shore waitin' to see, an' hear."

Down on the Bar H dinner was over before the foreman had much to say, and he was careful not to reveal his personal experiences of the morning. He counseled patience, and gave good reasons for it. They had until fall to start on the SV herd, and many things could, and would, occur before then. The first thing to do was to get ready for the round-up of the trail herd, and in order to lull suspicions they would not work on the tabooed section. There was to be no branding done out there, and in order to show their fairness in not too noticeable a way, they would help the Triangle with its five hundred head. This over with, the Triangle punchers would have to hold the herd together until McCullough came along and, not being able to call on them for aid, the Bar H would have to appeal to the Double X for the loan of some of its men, who thus would be on the ground and see what cattle were to be cut out for the trail. Nelson was to be ignored until the herd was sold and the money put in the bank at Sherman, after which he would be taken care of.

"Nelson is a good man," Big Tom assured them; "but he ain't good enough not to never make mistakes, an' no man can take every trick. He's goin' to miss one, th' last he'll ever miss, or win, for that matter, but there ain't no use of any of us gettin' killed unless we have to. We can get him without it, an' without gettin' any of his sudden new friends on th' prod. I promise that. I know how we're goin' to play it—an' it's so easy it makes me laugh. He's a good man; but there are older heads than his'n. You foller my orders an' set tight. I'll handle this when th' time comes, an' it ain't here yet. Stay out of Gunsight unless you can go in peaceful, keep yore mouths tight shut, an' stay sober. I've said enough about him.

"Now, we got work ahead of us, an' we start at it on th' Triangle day after tomorrow. I'm goin' over to see Hank Lewis now. There'll be somebody from Twitchell an' Carpenter comin' up any day now to select th' cattle an' stay with 'em till McCullough counts 'em into his herd. After I see Hank I'm ridin' to town to leave word at Dave's for Sherwood to see if I can borrow some of his boys when we start our own round-up. Look over yore gear an' be ready for workin'."

His prophecy regarding the representatives of Twitchell and Carpenter was fulfilled at mid-afternoon, when two strangers rode up to the bunkhouse and inquired for him and, being told that he could very likely be found in town, they explained who they were and rode on to Gunsight, accompanied by Fraser. To the saddle of each were fastened three stamping irons bearing their road brand.

Big Tom was in Dave's when they arrived and after a few rounds of drinks they settled down to discuss the herds and range topics in general.

"Th' T an' C sendin' many over th' trails this year?" Dave asked during a lull in the talk.

"Shore," replied the older and taller visitor, who answered to the name of Ridley. "We've been busy since winter. We looked over a big herd of beeves south of th' Grande for th' first herd. There was over thirty-five hundred head and they was three- an' four-year-olds. They went up north of th' Yellowstone, on government contract. Another herd of three thousand two- an' three-year-olds went past th' Platte, bound west for new ranges. There was two more big herds went up to Dodge—one of 'em bein' sold without th' new owners even seein' 'em. This bunch is goin' to new range north of here, some of 'em. I don't reckon there'll be many more this year. There ain't an animal in them that McCullough's bringin' up that's more than two years old, an' those are th' ones goin' to range. We took 'em from four different ranches to get 'em choice, an' they're all long-laigged longhorns an' a purty sight to a cowman. I'm bettin' Mac won't lose a single head neither. He's a trail boss that *is* a trail boss. He knows every river an' ford, water hole an' dry section from here to Montanny. He took that first herd north this spring, an' here he is back in time to swing this drive. He has a knack of pickin' good men for his trail outfits, an' he's daddy to 'em all from th' jump, without nobody knowin' it."

Big Tom arose. "Well, friends," he said, shaking hands, "yo're welcome to stay at either ranch while yo're here; but I reckon Fanning can make you more comfortable. We start on th' Triangle day after tomorrow—come down when you get ready. I told you how to get to th' Double X. If you go over there before any of 'em come to town, let 'em know that I'm countin' on usin' three of their men when I start my own round-up. See you later."

Dawn found activity on the range. The Double X, having rounded up its hundred head the day before, with a few additional to make up for possible rejections, held them apart from the SV herd, which also had extra cattle to offset any not up to the required standard. The majority of them, those which were certain to be accepted, had already been branded. The C and T inspectors watched the cutting out and indicated their choices as the cattle left the round-up herd, those rejected being turned aside and allowed to go back to freedom on the range, while those accepted were driven to the beef cut, which grew rapidly. A hundred and five finally were accepted, the odd five to make up for possible losses on the trail. Then the SV herd went through the same proceeding until four hundred and ten had been thrown into the beef cut. Because of Cimarron's discriminating judgment in making up the herd there were but few rejections; and, besides, the standard was not high, for, broadly, a cow was a cow. The remaining SV cattle were not returned to their ranch, but were set free to wander where they would. The general round-up would find them later and throw them back then if Arnold wished, although with the coming of the new round-up conditions there would be no great reason to throw them over—the brand would protect his interests, no matter where it was found. There was some talk about the SV cattle, but Johnny was credited as representing Arnold, and the matter was settled by agreeing that the T and C should pay Arnold, direct. Then the road branding began, and when it was over the consolidated herd was held to await the arrival of McCullough. It was then that Sherwood turned to three of his men.

"Th' Triangle ain't asked for no help, but you boys go down an' give 'em a hand," he said. "We're introducin' th' comin' of th' general round-up out in this country, an' we're doin' it gradual. There won't be no thought of us watchin' out for Arnold's interests over there, because these inspectors will do that anyhow. Go down an' show that we're friendly; an' from there go to th' Bar H."

On the Triangle the following morning things were running in full blast. After a breakfast eaten by firelight, the outfit was in the saddle at the first flush of dawn, and rode far out on the range. At an agreed-upon point it spread out in a thin line, the riders spaced at irregular intervals, depending upon the nature of the ground, and as they turned and moved back in the direction of Rock Creek they were joined by the Bar H contingent, which took up its position on one end of the line.

Draws, brush, and coulees shed cattle before the advance. A cow with a big, husky, and friskily independent calf arose to its feet and looked wonderingly at the disturbance. Gardner espied her and galloped forward, shouting and waving his hat as he rode. "G'wan, you! Get goin'!"

The cow stood irresolute, debating between the lessons of experience and her own wishes, and the pugnacious counseling of her indignant offspring. Deciding in favor of the former, she wheeled and moved away, the rebellious calf protesting by kicking up its heels and by the defiant erectness of its tail.

"Th' devil you say!" grinned Gardner, watching them depart. "Yo're big enough to be weaned, you overgrown baby—an' yo're shore goin' to be, for yore ma's goin' north."

Out of a clump of brush popped a group of two-year-olds, heads up, curious and mildly frightened. They stood defiant until Gardner was nearly upon them, and then his sudden whoop sent them whirling and off toward Rock Creek, discretion overbalancing valor. He gave them no further thought, for they would continue to travel unless crowded too much, and he was too old a hand to do that. A cow with a dogie he let slip through, pity joining hands with common sense in their behalf. It was not his purpose to bother with sickly, stunted youngsters, nor to take from them the maternal care so necessary to their sense of security.

By this time the outpouring of cattle had put a respectable number in front of him, and as others were routed out they more willingly went forward, for the gregarious spirit urged them to join the little herd. Occasionally one having more spirit than the others would wheel around and attempt to escape, but in all instances, except one, the speedy dash of the trained cow-horse headed them off and sent them on the about-face. The exception was a five-year-old steer, crusty and sullen, his hide bearing mute witness to his combativeness. He planted himself on rigid legs, lowered his sweeping horns and without even a grunt of warning charged straight for the watchful horseman.

"Blasted mosshead," muttered Sam, avoiding the rush, and watching some of the cattle which had turned to see how the affair came out before making up their minds to duplicate it. Too old for the drive, Sam would have let him go, except for the bad effect it might have on the rest of the cattle, and except for his own aroused spirit. He swung his rope and it darted up and out, and caught a hind leg of the "mosshead" as the pony settled back. There was a blur of overturning steer, a bellow of rage, injury, and surprise, and a resounding thump. Riding forward and taking up the slack as he went, Sam suddenly took two quick turns of the rope around his pommel, checked the horse, and grinned. Down went the mosshead again with another thump, and before the animal could get on its feet the rope was slipped off his leg, and when he arose he found himself alone. Gardener had seen the waverers start back to freedom and had to leave the craggy fighter to check a catastrophe. Hard riding won out for him and again he went forward. Several weaners shot out of a draw and took great credit to themselves for outwitting the puncher; but Sam saw no use of collecting infants only to have them turned loose at the cut-out. One cow arose, spread its feet apart and moved its low-held head slowly from side to side. He gave it a pitying glance and let it alone. "Locoed," he muttered, and as he spoke it shied at a weed swaying in the wind and went cautiously around it. There came a sudden bellowing ahead and he dashed forward at the pair of bulls who were pawing streams of dirt into the air as they met in the dust cloud, head on, and locked for the fight, their great, muscular backs bowed under the power of straining legs. This was no time for masculine duels and he broke it up with quirt and hat, driving the testy combatants apart and sending them on their ways. Dust arose over the moving herd, under which was turmoil, confusion, the lowing of cows, and the bawling of calves; but it rolled steadily westward, slowly but surely. A rattler coiled swiftly and launched its venomous, dart-shaped head at the horse, which reared up with a snort of terror. Sam, stirred to sudden anger and recklessness, spurned a gun, and leaned over as the horse dropped to all four feet. His quirt whizzed viciously and a headless, splotched body writhed in the dust.

"I'm purty bad, myself, when I'm riled," he told it, and rode on. Shortly afterward a gray streak flashed from a heavy bit of brush, and Sam's Colt leaped into action, but in vain. The coyote punched a hole in the air and disappeared almost as though it had shrunk into nothing. He grinned: "That slug will catch you when you stop, less'n you turns out," he said.

Rock Creek coming into view, the long line of horsemen became a crescent, the ends moving forward as the center slowed, and soon a circle of riders held the herd on all sides. It slowed, grew compact, and stopped, shifting like a kaleidoscope, the different colors weaving in and out like patches of some animated, changing crazy-quilt. There was good grass here, plenty of water, and no more urging riders. Calves went bawling their panicky ways in frantic search for lost mothers, butting and worrying through the herd, receiving rebuffs and impersonal chastisements as they disturbed their elders. One stood outside the press and bawled like a spoiled child, its defiant tail as high as its sinewy neck and more erect. There came an answering call from the herd and a frantic mother shot out, nosed the squaller, and then both grew instantly silent, contented, and at peace with the turbulent world.

"G'wan back!" ordered Lefferts, grinning from ear to ear. "I'm sayin' that it's a great thing to have a ma, you bellerin' cry-baby."

The round-up had taken less time than had been expected and it was decided to go ahead with the cutting out. The riders took turns in going to the horse wrangler's flimsy rope corral, made by lariats strung from the wheels of the chuck wagon to the pommels of saddles on the backs of old, docile, and well-trained horses. Selecting from their best cutting-out animals, saddles were hastily changed, a quick meal eaten, and then the men rode back to the herd to relieve others, who duplicated the performance. The herd was gently made more compact so as to cover less ground and need fewer riders to loaf in their saddles and hold it, the inspectors rode out in front of it and the cutters-out went to work, trying to pick from the outer fringe of cattle. Cows and steers lumbered from the press and went either to the beef cut, or to freedom, according to the signal of the inspector. Quickly the round-up herd shrunk and the beef cut grew. At first there was some trouble to get the chosen cattle to leave the herd—they tried to rejoin it; but as the beef cut grew it drew more and more until it was hardly more than necessary to start the individual cattle for it. When night fell the original herd had disappeared, its more fortunate units ranging free upon the ranch. The beef cut, allowed to graze and not bothered more than necessary, was headed for a rise, where in due time it bedded down and prepared to spend a quiet, peaceful night.

A passer-by would have come upon a picturesque scene on the banks of Rock Creek that night. The cook's fire, blazing high, was surrounded by the men off watch, squatted, seated, or reclining as they swapped stories and told jokes. The chuck wagon was magnified and made grotesque by the firelight and shadows, saddled horses tied to it or picketed a short distance away, and the flimsy rope corral running from wagon wheels to stakes driven in the ground, was ready to hold a change of mounts in case of a sudden need. In the distance was the bedded herd, lying on the top of a rise where it could catch any passing breeze, the cattle chewing their cuds and blowing and grunting contentedly.

A yearling bummed among them, filled with the mischievous deviltry of youth, making life miserable for its elders as it stumbled and butted its erratic way. It left a fight or two in its wake and finally fled, abandoning all dignity when a crusty steer arose to chastise it. But the chip on its shoulder remained there until it tried to butt a calf from its warm bed, whereupon the indignant mother scrambled to all fours and sent the disturber on the run for safety. The calf was there because it bore no brand, which would be taken care of on the morrow. The bummer had no excuse to create any trouble over a warmed bed because the night was warm. Finally, the edge gone from its exuberant deviltry, it began to look for a place to sleep—and after barely escaping several thrashings it worked out of the herd and sought a place by itself, doubtless to ruminate upon the cruelties and indignities endured by yearlings.

The four night riders of the first shift went slowly, lazily around the herd, keeping a score or more yards from it, singing and carrying on chanted conversations as they met and passed each other. Gone was the dust and turmoil of the day and in its place had come rest and quiet. Over all the crescent moon, nightly to grow fuller, worked its alchemy on earth and cattle, shedding its soft silvery light. The distant camp fire grew steadily lower and finally glowed like the end of a great cigar, winking as gentle breezes fanned its embers and passed on. Somewhere out on the silvery range a lonely coyote poured a burbling plaint to the moon and passed on like a shadow in search of food to stop the clamoring ache of an empty stomach, gradually approaching the winking fire, where choice titbits might perhaps be found.

"I want a big chew of tobacco," chanted Gardner, as he drew nearer to Reilly, "An' I want it bad, for mine's all gone."

"It allus is," sang Reilly. "Don't bother that spotted yearlin' over by them bushes. He's finally quit his bummin' an' has bedded down all by hisself outside th' herd. You'll know where he is even if you went blind. He's real friendly an' lonesome, an' likes to converse with everythin' that passes."

'I know th' scamp," sang Gardner, returning the plug. "He's had one gosh-awful time today keepin' out of a lickin'. I'm sayin' he earned a dozen." Soon he made out Lefferts' song, who mourned a long-lost love.

Her hair was th' color of 'lasses,
*   As soft as a bundle of wire;*
An' birds made their nests in its fastness:
*   If they didn't I shore am a liar.*

Gardner was stirred by the melody and burst into song out of sympathy:

Her eyes was as bright as old saddles,
*   An' crossed on th' end of her nose;*
Her hands was as shapely as paddles
*   An' hung down almost to her toes.*

Lefferts retaliated promptly:

Her cheeks was as smooth as th' cactus,
*   An' pink as a big hunk of mud;*
At primpin' she was allus in practice,
*   An' she was daintily shaped, like a tub.*

From across the herd came Reilly's natural tenor, a little ragged, but still a tenor:

Her voice was as sweet as a longhorn's,
*   It sounded as soft as a scream;*
I'm scared to roll up in my blankets
*   For fear that of her I will dream.*

The song was too much for the coyote, and he paused to yield to the craving for harmony reawakened in him.

"He's imitatin' you, Jim," chanted Gardner as he passed Lefferts. "Which same I says is well done."

"Go to th' devil, an' join yore tribe," sang Jim in delicate repartee, and forthwith began the mournful lay of Clementine:

> In a hut a-mong th' bushes, all a'long th' foamin'
>   brine,
> Lived a min-er, 'forty nin-er, an' his daugh-ter, Clem-
>   entine.
> She was fair-er than th' ros-es, an' her for-m-m, it was
>   di-vine;
> Two dry-goods box-es, without their top-ses, made
>   gaiters for-r my Clementine.

At half-past eleven Gardner rode in to the wagon, aroused the next shift, sought his blankets and was sound asleep before his three shift companions reached the camp. At three o'clock the second shift was relieved by the third, and last, which would stay with the herd until it was taken over by all the others, after breakfast.

The new day brought further developments. Several fires burned not far from the herd, irons projecting from them. The cattle were again cut out and driven away to a new herd, one by one, but this time they were taken close to the fires, and because of their weight and strength two ropers joined in the efforts of branding each animal. The glowing iron bit deeply through hair and into the skin on the left flank, filling the air with bellowing anguish, surprise, and indignation, and the odors of burning hair and flesh. There were fights, balkings, charges, but the hard-working, hard-riding punchers, the deftly cast ropes, and the trained horses, together with waving hats and an occasional revolver shot close to the nose of refractory, pugnacious bulls, and an occasional waved slicker or coat, won out, and the work proceeded at a good pace in spite of the general and apparent confusion. But whatever aspect of confusion there was, very little really existed except among the victims themselves, for the men proceeded along well-established lines, and the work went on as though it were running in a groove. Horses were changed every hour or two, depending upon the rider's judgment, and the inspectors, with the Triangle foreman, checked off the branded animals as they joined the road-branded herd. This herd grew rapidly and its guards were increased as needed from the ropers and iron men as they became too tired to hold the pace set. All day long the busy scene continued in the dust and the heat of the sun, with a bedlam of noise, an endless weaving and shifting, with lathered horses, sweat-and-dust-grimed riders, shouts of "Hot iron! Hot iron!" "Tally one!" "Ropers up!" and cries of warning and bursts of laughter. It were well that the Double X had sent three men to help; ten would not have been too many. Even with their help there was only one pair of ropers working at the fires and only three cutters-out, the rest being used to hold the two herds of restless cattle; and when night finally put an end to the operations less than half of the trail herd had been branded.

"Two more days," growled an inspector. "It's time you fellers throwed this worn-out, ancient way aside, an' got up even with th' times. You can build a chute that'll hold eight head an' by usin' stampin' irons you can turn out from sixty to eighty, yes, sometimes even a hundred, an hour, after you get th' hang of it. This handful should 'a' been done by noon. If I was you, Huff," he said, turning to the Bar H foreman, "I'd get on th' jump an' make a couple of them chutes, an' lay in half a dozen irons. One iron will do two or three with one heatin'; sometimes, if th' iron handlers work fast, two irons will stamp th' whole eight. You'll laugh when you see 'em comin 'out, all branded, eight to a clip; an' th' work ain't near so hard. There ain't no holdin', nor ropin', nor throwin'. Here we've toted half a dozen Question Mark irons up here, an' they ain't hardly saved us any time. You've got plenty of time to put up a chute before we start on yore thousand—if you don't, we'll be a week on 'em, an' a week's too long."

His companion nodded emphatically, and offered to superintend the work. "Ridley can handle th' tallyin' for us out here. They've all been selected, an' comin' as slow as they do, it ain't no two-man job. Mebby th' Double X will lend a couple more men to help—they're finishin' a pair of chutes up there, an' know what's wanted. What you say about it?"

Big Tom considered, and grudgingly gave his consent. Gus Thompson, tired as he was, volunteered to go to his ranch with the request, and started as soon as he had eaten. And by the night of the second day following, when the road-branded Triangle herd was being held to await the coming of McCullough, two eight-cow chutes were ready on the Bar H for the handling of its thousand head.

The round-up on the Bar H went forward with a swing and when it came time for the road branding the chutes proved their worth. The cattle, driven up in groups of eight, were forced into the long, narrow boxes as fast as the branded group went out at the other end. A bar dropped past the nose of the leader, and another bar dropped behind the last one in. Two men standing on a platform running along the side of the chute, each was handed a freshly heated iron and hurried from animal to animal, stamping the brand on each in turn. All morning the long chutes filled and emptied, the men changing places as they tired, the iron handlers so bothered by the stinging odor of burning hair that none of them worked longer than two or three hours without being relieved.

"I'm backin' this here magazine-action brandin' with a hundred an' fifty pounds of fightin' Irish," declared Reilly, chuckling at the almost automatic working of the chutes. "Eight in, stamped an' out again while we'd be workin' on one slippery cuss. Seventy th' last hour for Sam's chute, an' Fraser crowdin' him close; an' us tenderfeet at it—I'm bettin' th' last hour does ninety to th' chute. We're gettin' th' hang of it, an' gettin' it fast."

"Slippin' along like water down hill," laughed Slim, borrowed from his bed and board to help the Bar H. "Hey, Ridley!" he called to the busy inspector, "got any new-fangled improvements that'll make these chutes do it themselves, so th' hard-workin' punchers won't have to loaf in their saddles, but can set around an' gamble? Holy Maverick! Look at him tallyin'! He's shore workin' harder than he was yesterday."

"Who's loafin', you fool?" snorted Sam, taking breath while the chute was being refilled. "I've stamped close to eight thousand since I climbed up here. An'—*Hot iron! Hot Iron!*" he yelled as the front bar dropped. "Wake up, you tramp!"

"You've got a lot to say, you has!" snapped Lefferts, running up with the irons. "All *you* got to do is push 'em ag'in' their hides—I'm near wore out!"

"Why use any bars at all?" queried Reilly, grinning at the hard-working Sam. "Just let 'em filter through, stamping 'em on th' run. We're wastin' time, this way."

"You've got near as much sense as Sam has!" retorted Lefferts, stirring his fire. "Which ain't payin' neither of you no compliments," he grunted.

Big Tom could not deny the advantage of chute and stamping irons, and the ocular demonstration took from him his last reasonable objection to them, although he found fault with them because the herd had to be driven to the same place each round-up, and because he did not believe them to be suitable for calf branding; but when it was pointed out that the cattle had to be driven somewhere before the herd would be worth bothering with, and might as well be driven to the chutes, and that it would be a saving of time to do that, or to build more chutes on the ranch rather than to revert to the old methods, he could not deny it. Regarding the branding of calves there was a division of opinion; but calf branding was not nearly as hard or slow as the branding of grown animals. He knew, however, that the styles were changing, and changing under his eyes, and that for him to become stubborn and set against the change would be to appear ridiculous, and to become a source from which much levity would spring.

The branding done and the tallies compared, the visiting punchers departed for their ranches, the inspectors accepting Big Tom's invitation to spend the night with him, and rode to the ranchhouse; and the herd, restless, sore, and in sullen mood, was watered well at the muddy pond and thrown upon the high bed ground, and would remain a herd until delivered to McCullough, and for some weeks thereafter.

XXIV

◆

On the Trail

After breakfast the following morning Ridley and his companion saddled their horses to ride back to Highbank, where they would wait for the trail boss. As they finished cinching up, Big Tom strolled into the corral and smilingly watched them.

"I suppose you want Mac to bring you a check, as usual?" queried Ridley, swinging into the saddle.

"This is th' one time I'd rather have cash," replied the foreman. "With cash, in th' next week, I can make a quick turnover."

"Cash it is," said Ridley. "Gold or bills?"

"Make it bills," answered Big Tom. "I'm glad I met you boys—come up again next year. If yo're lookin' for good cattle then I'll have plenty."

"Then I reckon we'll be here. So-long."

"So-long," replied the foreman, watching them ride away. As they dropped from sight over a rise he smiled cynically and went back to the ranchhouse. Pausing at the door, he looked out over the range in the direction of the northwest section and the Double X, and slowly turned his head, his gaze passing along the horizon, behind which lay Gunsight, Green Valley, and the SV ranchhouse.

"I said it was easy," he growled. "*Me* throw over a couple of hundred head of mavericks to Arnold, an' split up th' rest four ways? It makes me laugh! An' when I hit Nelson he'll wonder what kind of brains he really *has* got. There's a jolt comin' to this section, an' it'll be Big Tom that springs it. About one week more an' *I* play *my* hand!"

Four days passed and then, in the afternoon of the fifth, a great dust cloud appeared far down the Highbank trail. Fraser discovered it and called Big Tom from the ranch-house. The foreman glanced south, told the puncher to ride off and get the herd started, and then hurried to his horse, sprang into the saddle, and rode toward McCullough's sign. He had hardly more than gained the regular trail when he saw seven men riding toward him at a good pace, and no second glance was needed to identify the one who rode in the middle and slightly ahead.

The trail boss was a character to demand attention wherever he might be. Over the medium height, he was so heavily and solidly built that he appeared to be well under it when standing alone; he had the barrel-like chest that stands for strength, and his sloping shoulders were a little rounded from a careless saddle seat of many years. His rugged face was brown, the skin tough as parchment, and the faded blue eyes peered out in a direct, unwavering gaze between lids narrowed by the suns and winds, rains and dusts of a life spent in the open. His head was massive and the iron-gray hair, falling almost to his shoulders, gave it a leonine appearance. He wore no chaps, for his riding took him into few thickets and there was no reason for him to bear their discomforts. His clothing was simple and loose: black, heavy, woolen trousers thrust into soft, high boots with moderate heels, and bearing no spurs, for he depended on his quirt; a black, woolen vest, buttoned at the bottom, from an upper pocket of which protruded the well-chewed stem of a pipe; a heavy, faded, blue flannel shirt, open over the bronzed, hairy chest and throat; a faded blue kerchief, knotted loosely about his neck; a heavy, gray sombrero, moderate in height of crown, but with a wide brim. He rode a Cheyenne saddle, devoid of ornamentation, its housings covering the horse from rump to withers, and the reins of the bridle, contrary to the prevailing fashion of that southern range at that time, were short. A .44 Winchester lay in its sheath under his right leg; a braided hair lariat was coiled at the pommel; a heavy, plain six-shooter rested in an open holster; and behind him was rolled the everlasting yellow slicker. He rode a magnificent bay horse whose spirit was shown in every movement, and which would follow him about like a dog. Over all was dust, gray, thick, impalpable dust.

"Hello, Huff!" he bellowed. "Come down to see if I got lost? Join up with us; I'm figgerin' that Triangle herd may be up at this end of th' crick, an' if it is, it's got to move. Them long-laigged cattle of mine ain't had a drink since yesterday mornin', an' they'll shore rush that crick. We'll have some cuttin' out to do if th' other herd is in their path. How 'bout it?"

"You can pull up, then," replied Big Tom. "They're well to th' south of th' bunkhouse—you got plenty of room for ten times that little bunch yo're so peart about. I heard they are th' leavin's of four Greaser ranches."

"Glad to learn they ain't there," said McCullough.

"They're such leavin's an' scourin's," smiled one of his companions, "that I'm advisin' Mac to double th' night guard while he's within' forty miles of this bunch of ranches."

"We'll count that Triangle bunch right away," said the trail boss. "Where's yourn?"

"It's on its way," answered Big Tom. "It'll be on hand soon enough. Goin' to count that, too, tonight?"

"Shore. An' throw 'em together, an' bed down on Clear River, so we can get a two-hour jump-off in th' mornin'. Is th' Double X holdin' its bunch in th' same old place?"

"I reckon so," replied Big Tom, and soon they passed

the Triangle ranchhouse, where Hank Lewis rode forth to join them.

"Get yore boys, Lewis," shouted the trail boss. "We'll count that herd right away."

"They're with it now," replied Lewis, as he drew nearer. "Glad you brought some of yore boys along—I'm short-handed for quick work."

It was not long before they reached the herd and it was slowly crowded into a more compact mass, and became wedge-shaped. McCullough, one of his men, and the two foremen stopped before the point, the trail boss and Huff on one side, the others not far away and facing them. The herd started slowly forward, narrowing to an animated ribbon which flowed between the two pairs of counters and kept them busy. McCullough and Lewis counted on knotted strings fastened to their pommels, Huff used his fingers to check off the tally, fifty head to each digit, while the fourth man threw a coil of his rope over the pommel of his saddle at each hundred. The counting was finished well under ten minutes and the results compared. Lewis said five hundred and five, the other three announcing five hundred and six.

The Triangle foreman laughed. "Here is where I get paid for a missin' cow."

"Three to one bein' good enough for me," replied the trail boss, grinning, "I says you do. It's worth that to see you again; an' what's a cow between friends?" He turned in his saddle. "You might move 'em up closer to th' trail, boys," he shouted, and added with a chuckle, "they'll disappear when my long-laigs come along."

His prediction was justified, for the long-legs, having run the last mile or two with the scent of water in their red nostrils, poured into the creek and soaked themselves inside and out. By the time McCullough and his group reached the scene, the Bar H herd was crossing the trail. The counting was gone over again, the tallies agreeing to a single cow, and the Bar H herd was allowed to join the strangers along the creek. In due time the enlarged herd was thrown back on the trail, and when the Triangle five hundred joined it they were, indeed, swallowed up.

The trail boss and Big Tom rode off to the Triangle ranchhouse, figured for a moment and then exchanged cash for a receipt. The foreman shoved the bills into his pockets and went with McCullough back to the herd, picked up the squad, and had the Double X contingent counted before the trail herd reached the river.

As the herd came along it made a fine sight for a cowman to look upon, the cattle strung out for three-quarters of a mile in length and spread well out on both sides of the trail, well watered and fed, and making under these conditions four miles an hour. The chuck wagon, drawn by four mules, rolled far ahead of it, the caviya of a hundred and thirty saddle horses to one side and also ahead. Each of the two point men was followed by four swing men, five to a side, and they had nothing to do now but look out for stragglers and to keep local cattle from joining the invading host. The bed ground was well chosen and the night promised to be a good one, notwithstanding that clouds were forming and the moon would be more or less obscured.

After the Double X contingent had joined their trail mates for the long journey and the great herd had bedded down, half of the trail outfit, together with the punchers from the ranchers, headed for town, McCullough electing to remain with the herd. Big Tom and Lewis shook hands with him and returned to their ranchhouses, riding together part of the way.

Just before they separated Lewis looked up. "I heard

that Arnold was ridin' today—one of th' Double X boys met him at th' trail. I reckon it must feel good to be in th' saddle again after such a long siege in bed."

"I'm bettin' it does," smiled Big Tom. "I had a dose of it when I was a young man, an' once is shore a-plenty."

"He must think so, for he's aimin' to ride to town every day, an' spend some of his time gettin' acquainted with Dave an' his friends. Well, I'm leavin' you here. Good night."

"Good night," replied Big Tom, riding on with a sinister smile on his face.

The following morning was cloudy, which suited the Bar H foreman, who had a long ride ahead of him. He opened the south door of the ranchhouse, looked out and caught sight of a movement near the right-hand corner. A full-grown rattler was crawling slowly across a sand patch, and the foreman watched it idly. Then he grinned.

"Wonder how good my gunplay is these days?" he muttered, and his Colt leaped from its holster and roared. The snake writhed swiftly into an agonized coil, its flat head moving back and forth, its tongue darting angrily, and its rattles buzzing steadily. Huff growled at himself and fired again. The flattened, venomous head sank down, twisting and turning on the writhing coils.

"H—l!" growled the marksman, walking slowly forward for a closer look, which showed him that his last shot had cut through the vertebra and half of one side of the neck. It was good enough, and he turned and walked along the side of the house. Passing a window, he suddenly stopped and looked closely at the ground just under its sill, where boot prints were plainly visible. Before doing anything else he reloaded his gun, and then followed the prints with his eyes until the corner of the house cut them from sight. He stepped back until he could see the bunkhouse door to learn if anyone was coming up to investigate the shots, and his gaze followed the prints straight toward it until they became lost on harder ground. No one being curious about the shooting, he went back to the window and peered in. He could see nothing because of the curtain, and had about decided that he had enjoyed secrecy the night before, when a sudden thought struck him. The interior, being dark now, was not right for a test, and he went around to the door, opened it, threw up the other shades, and hastily returned to the window, where he smothered a curse as a small hole in the curtain let him see quite plainly. Again returning to the house, he closed the door and slipped his extra Colt into the waist-band of his trousers, where one side of his open vest covered it, put on his coat and, going out the rear door, sauntered toward the bunkhouse, his eyes finding and losing the boot marks as the trail passed over varying ground. Before he reached the house his four men emerged from it and began the regular, humorous, morning wrangle as to preference in the use of wash basin and towel. They grinned at his approach and he smiled in return, his eyes missing nothing in their expressions, and it was Fraser at whom he looked longest when he spoke.

"Throw my saddle on th' big bay, Bill," he smiled, pleasantly. "I'm goin' up to Sherman to fatten th' balance at th' bank. I may be back tomorrow night, but if I hear of any cattle that can be got cheap I may go on an' look 'em over. You boys have plenty of supplies, but if you run short go up to Dailey. If he's got any cigars, get a box—I reckon we can afford that much of a celebration, in view of that herd. But don't drink too much. You know why."

Fraser got the saddle from the storeroom and went out to put it on the foreman's best horse. As he came out of the door he nodded toward the north. "There's Mac's sign already; he must 'a' passed around Gunsight. He's well on his way."

The others looked at the faint thickening in the air beyond the town and past the east end of Pine Mountain, where the dust from four thousand cattle rose heavenward.

"He's a wise bird, gettin' to th' crick last night," commented Carson. "He's been movin' since dawn; an' I bet he's glad it's cloudy, with that dry stretch ahead of him."

"Shucks!" snorted Dahlgren. "Thirty mile of dry trail ain't nothin'."

"Not much," admitted Carson; "but, still, it's better cloudy than boilin' under th' sun."

"I reckon Mac ain't thinkin' as much about it bein' cloudy as I am," smiled the foreman, turning to take the horse Fraser was leading to him. He had asked Fraser to get and saddle his horse in the hope that the puncher would stand on his dignity and, perhaps, provoke a quarrel, out of which anything might come; but Fraser paid no attention to the request, unusual as it was, and grinned as he stepped back.

"It's fifty miles to Sherman, an' I'd ruther have it cloudy, all th' way," smiled Big Tom, mounting. "Well, so-long, boys!" and he was off.

He chose the trail over Pine Mountain, not so much for its saving in miles, but because it gave him a high, distant point from which to look back over his trail, and it avoided the Doc's shack and Gunsight as well. Reaching the top of the mountain, he turned and closely scrutinized the trail, finding nothing to bother him; but he was bothered, nevertheless, and he determined to pay as much attention to the trail he covered as to that which lay before him. Setting out again, he went well to the west of Gunsight and struck the Sherman trail ten miles beyond the town.

* * *

Back on the Bar H, Fraser was thinking. He had been do-ing a lot of it the last week, and he had not been alone in it. When his foreman had ridden off he leaned against the door and watched him until he was lost to sight. Dahlgren and Carney passed out, joked with him and went to the corral, soon riding off to the south. Dick Carson passed out a little later, paused, retraced his steps and leaned against the other door jamb.

"Wonder if yo're thinkin' th' same as me?" he quietly asked.

Fraser looked at him closely. "I don't know; *I'm* thinkin' of a gamble," he replied, hooking a thumb in an armhole of his vest.

"Shore; so am I," nodded Carson, carelessly. "This here range is shot full of holes, for us."

"It is," admitted Fraser. "We been driftin' them mav-ericks for three years—an' now they're goin' to be throwed back, branded, an' th' rest cut four ways. How are we goin' to stop it?"

"I'm figgerin' on driftin' myself; but I hate to drift alone, an' empty-handed," growled Carson. "I come down here to work for Huff, for fifty a month, an' pickin's. I've been gettin' th' fifty—but there won't be no pickin's, less'n I run some off with me. I'm tired of this blasted country, anyhow. Why, I'd ruther take chances, like Ne-vada, than go on this way down here. H—l!" he snorted in angry disgust. "I'm sayin' I fair itches to gamble," he added.

Fraser shifted to a more comfortable position.

"What do you think th' boss has got in his pockets right now?" he asked, cynically.

"A big, fat check, that won't do him nor us any good," replied Carson.

"Check!" Fraser laughed sarcastically. "Check? He allus used to have a check, after delivery; but he ain't got one now. He's got bills, wads an' wads of bills. Quite some over six thousand, I reckon, in bills. I saw his pockets bulgin', an' I wondered why he didn't take a check, same as usual. I wanted to make shore, so I did some scoutin' up around th' ranchhouse last night—I *saw* 'em. Wads, an' wads. I was shore tempted."

Carson was looking off toward Pine Mountain, an evil expression on his face, and he moved restlessly. "There's only one reason for that," he muttered, and turned to his companion. "Are you still thinkin' of a gamble?" he demanded, all thought of cattle out of his mind. "Th' herd money is shore worth while—what you say about it?"

"I was sort of turnin' it over in my head," Fraser admitted. "It's a lot of money; a powerful lot of money for one man to tote."

"It'll still be a lot of money if it's split in two," suggested Carson. "Do you figger he's goin' to bank it? All that cash? Why didn't he take a check? Why did he change, just when things was gettin' worse down here all th' time?"

"I don't know; but he's allus been purty white to me."

"Has he been three thousand dollars' worth?" asked Carson, smiling evilly. "I'm figgerin' he's lettin' us hold th' sack, that's what *I'm* figgerin'. An' if he don't come back, who's goin' to sign checks for our pay? We're losin' our share of all them mavericks. There won't be no nice bunch of cattle goin' up th' trail for us fellers, not now. But there's one whoppin' big bunch of *cash* goin' up a trail for us, if we go after it. How's yore nerve? What's th' use of playin' for buttons, when there's *bills* to be had?"

"If I reckoned he was goin' to bank that money I

wouldn't touch it, not if I was shore he was comin' back to stick with th' ranch," muttered Fraser. "But I reckon he's throwed us down. I reckon we're holdin' th' sack, all right. An' if he aims to keep it, then we has as much right to it as he has. Cuss him! he's chicken-livered! Come on: I'm with you," and he led the way into the house to get some of his personal belongings.

"He's got a start on us, an' a cussed good hoss," growled Carson as they hastened to the corral. "We can't save nothin' by cuttin' across, neither."

"No, we can't; but we can take a lead hoss apiece," said his companion, "an' ride without carin' what happens to th' ones we start on. He won't be pushin' hard—he don't like hard ridin', he thinks too much of his hoss, an' he ain't got no reason to be in any great hurry. He's serene as a snake full of birds, chucklin' at how easy it is."

Down on the southern part of the ranch, in a draw, there was another conference, where Dahlgren and Carney also were mourning the deplorable state of affairs on the range.

"Three years' work gone to blazes," grumbled Little Tom, resentfully. "I'm near on th' prod."

"Gettin' near on th' prod ain't worth nothin'," replied Dahlgren. "It's gettin' on one, a good one, an' stayin' with it, that counts. I figgers we still got a lot of interest in them mavericks, an' I'm dead shore there ain't nobody watchin' 'em this side of th' Double X line."

"There's a lot of 'em away south of there," said Carney. "There's a couple of herds hang out closer to th' water hole in West Arroyo. I've seen 'em often when I rode that way. We could round up near three hundred, hold 'em in that blind canyon till evenin', an' then run th' whole bunch over th' Double X southwest corner an' get 'em well away tonight. It's cloudy, an' there won't be much moon showin'—just enough light to see what we're doin', an' not enough to show us up for any distance. Th' four of us can swing that herd in bang-up style—an' Big Tom won't never catch us, once we get into th' Snake Buttes country. An' what's more, I know where unmarked cattle can be sold, with no questions an' at a fair price. Th' game's up for us, down here, anyhow."

"You aimin' to let them two in on this?"

"I'd ruther let 'em in on it, an' swing more cattle, than have 'em trailin' us tomorrow. An' four ain't too many for drivin' through th' Buttes."

"I don't like splittin' 'em four ways," growled Dahlgren, but he grudgingly gave his consent. "All right. Go up an' feel 'em out, while I start roundin' up. Don't give nothin' away before you know how they feel about it."

"I'm off. They wasn't goin' to ride out till late, an' mebby I'll catch 'em at th' house," and Carney was off like a shot. He was not gone long, and when he returned he spread out his hands expressively.

"They've pulled their stakes, I reckon," he reported. "Their blankets an' 'most everythin' they owned, of any account, was gone. My extra gun is missin', an' our stuff is spread all over th' place. I rustled some supplies, an' found they had been there, too. Let 'em go!"

"Cussed glad of it; now it's halves, instead of fourths," replied Dahlgren, cheerfully. "Come on; let's push this work. Don't get any more branded cattle than you can help; but we ain't goin' to waste no time cuttin' any out."

Up on the Sherman trail Big Tom was swinging along within ten miles of town when, passing a particularly high, abrupt hill, he turned out, rode along it and, dismounting, went up on foot until he could peer across the top of it. He did not have long to wait, for soon two horsemen appeared far back on the trail, where it crossed a wide, open space.

Going back to his horse, he led it into a thicket and tied it to a bush, took his rifle and returned to the hill top, where he chose cover close to the bank at the trail's edge, and settled down comfortably to wait.

As the two riders drew nearer he recognized them by their ensemble, and by the way they sat their saddles, and it was not long before he could make out details. They were riding hard, both keenly alert, peering along the trail ahead of them. Nearer and nearer they came, pushing ahead at a fast, hard pace, eager to overtake him before he reached the town. Sweeping past the steep bank, they shot around a bend and went on.

Big Tom watched them until they had passed from sight, and then arose and nodded. "It's a good thing for you that you missed me!" he growled. "I hate to lose th' pay-roll money; but what's got to be done has got to be done. My interest in Sherman has plumb faded. Now for a smash at Nelson that'll hurt him to his dyin' day, d—n him!"

Darkness had fallen on the range and the night riders of the west section of the Double X were Slim Hawkes, Tom Wilkes, and Cimarron, who had the first shift. They were back on the old three-shift plan and would be off duty at half-past eleven. Cimarron had ridden south and had reached the end of his beat, the north side of a shallow arroyo. He softly gave the night's signal and, receiving no reply, decided to wait for a while, for Slim was due to reach and stop at the other side of the arroyo at any minute. He could faintly discern the outlines of objects at quite a respectable distance and wondered how soon the moon would break through the filmy clouds. Suddenly he listened closely and thought he detected the noise made by a herd. Slim's signal came faintly to him and he replied to it with a double one. In a few minutes Slim loomed up out of the dark.

"Are you hearin' that, too?" asked Slim in a whisper.

"I am," replied Cimarron. "That's a herd, an' there's work for me an' you. It's comin' up from th' south, bearin' a little west, I reckon. How do you figger it?"

"West, bearin' a little north," answered Slim. "But it's shore comin' *from* our range, which is enough for us. I'm askin' no questions tonight. Th' last time I sung out Nevada shot me up. I'm doin' my talkin' tonight with my gun. An' I'm hopin' it's Nevada, personal: I *owe* him somethin'."

"Don't separate, or we'll mebby shoot each other," growled Cimarron. "If we hit 'em from this side we'll mebby turn th' herd so it'll stampede back where it belongs; an' if it does, th' fellers on th' other side will have plenty to do for a couple of minutes, an' give us a chance to get to 'em. It's closer. Are you ready?"

Slim loosened his left foot from the stirrup and then lay forward along the neck of his horse, Cimarron doing likewise; and then the two animals moved forward at a walk, innocent of any silhouetted figures sticking up in the saddles. Louder and louder grew the sound and soon the two clinging riders could plainly distinguish the rattle of horns from the hoofbeats. A few minutes more, and then a mounted figure became vaguely outlined. The herd was being moved at a walk, possibly to avoid greater noise until it was well across the Double X line, and now its bulk could be guessed at.

The herder leaned forward suddenly to scrutinize two moving blots he barely could make out against a rise of ground behind them, and the movement was the beginning of the end, for him. A sudden stream of fire poured from the left-hand blot and he slid from his saddle without a sound. The blots let out yells and dashed for the front ranks of the herd, which wheeled like a flash and thundered across the range over a course at right angles to the one which they had been following. The two night guards spurred toward the place where they hoped to come in contact with other rustlers, but found no one to oppose them, and they then set out to follow the herd. Far ahead of them they saw two flashes, followed at certain, agreed-upon intervals by another and then a fourth. Cimarron fired once, counted twelve and then sent two more shots into the air as close together as he could make them, which left nothing to be desired on that score. When he and Slim neared the herd again the moon shone down faintly and let them see what they were doing.

"Where'd you get 'em?" yelled Matt Webb. "There ain't a brand on 'em, that I can see; an' I can see plain enough for that."

"Where do you suppose we got 'em?" retorted Cimarron, "from Europe?" He rode at one end of the front rank and had the satisfaction of seeing it falter.

"I see a Bar H mark!" shouted Rich Morgan. "An' they're stoppin', thank th' Lord!"

In another ten minutes the herd started milling and soon afterward became sensible.

"I say we have been made a present of some of Huff's pets," chuckled Rich. "He says mavericks take title from th' ranch they're on; an' I'm gamblin' these are on th' Double X!"

"If they was ours I'd say to let 'em wander," spoke up Cimarron. "Seein' as they ain't, I reckon it'll save a lot of work if we beds 'em down an' keeps 'em together. I'll go on in an' let Lin know, so he can turn out th' off shift. We shot somebody out near that dividin' arroyo between Slim's section an' mine; you might take a look out that way. Slim's hopin' it was Nevada; but I'm sayin' mebby he'll be surprised when he finds out who it is."

"I'm guessin' right about th' outfit he belongs to, anyhow," replied Slim. "An' I'm not goin' in till I sees which one he is. Comin', Matt? I'll ride out with you."

Leaving Cimarron to go to the bunkhouse for the off shift, Slim and Matt rode rapidly toward the scene of the fight, and when they reached it they saw a figure on the ground. Dismounting they bent over it, and then looked at each other.

"Dahlgren!" breathed Slim.

Matt nodded. "They wasn't waitin' for their mavericks to be split four ways," he said, covering the upturned face with the dead man's sombrero. "They was stealin' a march on Big Tom while he is up in Sherman. Well, anyhow, he was on th' rustle—an' there ain't no harm done. Go on in, an' get yore sleep. As to th' herd, I reckon Arnold has got th' best title to it—but that's for Lin to say. If he does throw 'em over to th' SV it'll save Big Tom th' shame of doin' it hisself. Good night."

XXV

◆

Still a-Rollin'

Arnold finished his breakfast and, telling Margaret that he was going to Gunsight to see Johnny and Dave, the hiring of another puncher being uppermost in his mind, went to the corral and soon was riding along the trail, gratified by the entire absence of pain in his leg and with the stimulation which came from the easy motion, the sun, and the crisp morning air. When Margaret turned back into the house her brother had slipped out of the front door and had gone, eager to shirk his few duties and play scout. Since he had found an old, broken rifle in the deserted and disused bunkhouse it formed the foundation upon which he based his play. As she called to him, vexation in her voice, he was wriggling through a clump of brush not far away, his part of his scouting being earnest and real. Wiping dishes was woman's work, as he firmly believed, and he detested and scorned it. His pony had been saddled and picketed in a draw south of the house before breakfast, and when the opportunity offered he intended to get to it and ride off over the ranch until hunger forced him to return. Lying quietly in his cover he kept a keen watch until, the beds made, his sister should begin the kitchen work and give him a chance to cross the open space between him and the pony. He was growing more and more impatient when he caught sight of a horseman riding down the slope of a hill north of the house, and his anger and curiosity flared up when he saw that it was Big Tom.

The Bar H foreman rode leisurely past the corral, noting the absence of Arnold's horse and the pony, and stopped before the door. Swinging from the saddle he sauntered up to the kitchen door and knocked. Margaret wondered who it could be, a sudden thought of injury to her father coming to her, and she hastened to answer it. When she saw who the visitor was she stopped and recoiled a little.

"How-do-you-do?" she said coldly.

"Glad to see you, Ma'am," came the answer. "I rode over to see yore father about some mavericks of his that are eatin' up my grass."

"You have just missed him," replied Margaret. "If you return by the way of Gunsight you can see him there."

"Now, ain't that just my luck?" regretted the foreman, stepping inside. "Might I have a drink of water, Ma'am? I wasn't aimin' to ride back that way. Of course there ain't no chance at all of his comin' back soon?"

"Why, no," answered Margaret, handing him the dipper. "He may not return until evening. But you can leave a message for him with me."

"It's somethin' we has to talk over," Big Tom replied, giving her the empty dipper. As her hand touched it he grabbed her to him, her screams muffled by his hand. Struggle as she would she was helpless against his bear-like strength and soon was limp with exhaustion and partially suffocated. Holding her with one arm and hand he took a clothesline from a peg on the wall and quickly trussed her with it until she was powerless to move. Gagging her with a towel he carried her to the corral, caught her horse, and threw her on it and cinched up the saddle which lay at the gate. Hurrying back to the house he collected provisions and ran out again, and in another minute he rode rapidly for the brush and rough ground west of the house, leading her horse. Bound, gagged, and tied to the saddle she could do nothing, every beat of the horses' hoofs increasing her terror.

Back at the house Charley wriggled around the corner, his curiosity overcoming caution, and he stared in amazement as he saw them crossing the open, his sister bound with rope. Suddenly cursing the useless rifle in a burst of rage, he dashed for his horse, mounted and rode for town to tell his father, keeping to the low levels until the hills and brush formed a screen behind him. The little pony ran at top speed, shrewdly guided over the rough trail, and the nine miles did not take long. Dashing up to Dave's,

Charley shouted at the top of his lungs and pulled up at the door.

"Peggy's kidnapped! Dad! Peggy's kidnapped!"

A chair crashed in Dave's and three men jammed in the doorway, Johnny forcing his two companions back as he fought his way past them. "What's that?" he demanded.

"Big Tom's stole Peggy, d—n him!" shrilled the boy, tears of helpless rage in his eyes.

Johnny needed no further proof than the words and Charley's earnestness. "Where was it? Which way did he go?" he snapped, leaping to the black horse standing at the tie rail.

"At th' ranch—they went west. Oh, Peggy!" he sobbed. "Oh, Peggy!"

"Come a-runnin'!" shouted Johnny over his shoulder, wheeling his horse. He spoke to the black thoroughbred and she struck into a gait she could hold for hours, and one which was deceptive in its smoothness. As he rocked down the trail three Double X punchers rode in from the south.

"Keep a-goin'!" Dave yelled to them, apoplectic with his emotions. "Foller *him*! Big Tom's run off with th' Arnold gal!"

Slim's brief remark is better left unrecorded. Three sets of hoofs rolled out of the town and sent the dust swirling high along the trail. The punchers overtook and passed Arnold, who cursed the slowness of his mount, shouted profane reassurance at him and left him their dust. Dailey led Fanning around the corner of the saloon and aroused surprised resentment in his horse, which heretofore had regarded him as a sane being. Fanning's gray felt a touch of its youthful spirits return; if it had to race, all right; it wasn't much for speed, but it expected to be better than last at the finish.

Big Tom, having passed the boundaries of the ranch, pulled up long enough to remove the gag. "If you behave yourself I'll untie you," he said. "You can't get away—if you try it you'll learn what a rope feels like."

Margaret managed to nod and the rope came off of her.

"'Twon't do no good to yell," he told her, "nor to hold back. You won't be missed till supper time, an' then nobody will do much worryin' till dark. They'll search th' range first—an' by th' time they finish that we'll be so far away that they'll never find us. Yo're thinkin' they'll trail us? Huh! Let 'em, then. Once we get into *my* country they can trail an' be d—d! You might as well make th' best of it. I got th' herd money in my pockets, an' we can have a nice little ranch an' live like th' story books say—happy ever after. Yo're goin' to live there with me. If yo're sensible you can do it as my wife. I'm going to give you that chance. But, yo're goin' to live there with me, just the same."

"You are even more of a beast than I thought," she retorted. "You'll never reach that ranch; and if you do, I'll kill you while you sleep."

"I'm chancin' th' last," he retorted. "Yo're thinkin' of that Nelson, huh?" he grinned. "When Big Tom *does* play his cards it takes more'n a fool like *him* to win th' pot. An' I'm sayin' I stacked this deck. I've been stackin' it for a long time, figgerin' everythin'. He's cold-decked, Ma'am; beat clean when he'd reckoned he'd won. Thinkin' they'll trail us, an' get us because we're not pushin' hard?" He laughed ironically. "Didn't I say I've been plannin' this a long time? There ain't no use of wearin' horses out when it ain't needed. With twenty hours, or more, start, ours will be fresh when we need speed—which we won't. You'd do better to begin practicin' callin' yoreself Missus Huff—it'll come easy before you know it. I'm givin' you that chance, an' I'll not bother you till a parson is handy. Then it will be yore move. You've got three days." Receiving no reply he looked around the range and thenceforth ignored her.

A black thoroughbred swept across the little SV valley, passed the corral, and rocked westward along a plain trail. The rider, his sombrero jammed tightly down on his head to baffle the pull of the whistling wind, cold with a rage which had turned him into the personification of vengeance, felt an exultant thrill as the double trail sped past him, for his quarry had but eighteen miles start, and he felt sure that it had been cut down by the speed at which half of it had been covered. There was nothing on hoofs on all that range that could keep an even lead against Pepper. She flashed past mesquite, around chaparrals, her great heart beating with a gameness which excelled even her love for the race; her trim legs swinging rhythmically, the reaching of her free, beautiful stride eating up the range and sending it past like the speeding surface of some great rapids. A Gila monster moved from her course barely in time, and a rattler coiled and struck too late. Off in the brush a startled coyote changed its mind about crossing the open and slunk back into cover, following the black with suspicious gaze. The great muscles writhed and bunched, rippled and bulged under the satiny skin, the barrel-like chest rising and falling with a rhythm and smoothness which graphically told that it was a perfect part of a perfect running machine. Down the slopes at top speed, up them at a lope, the undulating range slipped swiftly past. Brush and scattered mesquite, chaparrals and lone, sentinel cacti; hollows, coulees, draws, and arroyos went behind in swift procession. Still the double trail lay ahead, now lost as it crossed hard ground, now plain with small, shallow basins where the sand had slid back and hidden the outlines of the roofs, and then clear and sharp and fresh in soils possessing claylike cohesion.

The rider gave no thought to ambush. There was a time for everything, but hesitation or caution would not claim its turn until the ride was done. If an ambush lay ahead, what mattered it? Others were coming along that trail, and only one need survive. The picture which he carried in his brain was not one from which counselings of safety could arise. Its message was to ride, ride, ride; and kill, kill, kill; and it turned the thin-lipped, narrow-lidded rider into an agent of Death, merciless and untiring. The ages rolled back from around his soul and stripped it of the last, pulsating film of civilization's veneer. No gray wolf ever ran a trail, no wolverine hunted in its northern fastness that was more coldly savage or cruel than this man whose grim confidence gave no thought of failure. Mile after mile he rode, motionless in the saddle save for the rhythmic rise and swing of a saddle poise superb. Neither to right nor left he looked, nor back where the billowing dust swirled suddenly high to roll spreading over the drab earth, slowly settling. Straight ahead he set his gaze, to the fartherest new-made mark on the winding, twisting trail, a trail which twisted and wound as though vainly seeking a place to hide until that flying Death were past. A high ridge of limestone poured into view and the swinging black was pulled to a walk, for a breathing spell wise in its length, and canny in its shortness. Then up slowly and off again on her far-reaching stride, the noonday sun blazing down unheeded.

To the west the ribbon-like trail was widening. Behind Johnny it was bigger by one more strand; behind Slim, a furnace of rage, was another strand; Tom Wilkes, grimly determined, made another; half a mile behind him rocked Cimarron, vengeful and silent, and added the sixth. Certain memories, returning to the *segundo,* caused him to ride off and make a trail of his own, confident that it would be a chord in a great arc and lead him past his two ranch mates. There was a certain pass far to the northeast which he vaguely coupled to the Bar H foreman, and with three men ahead of him to follow the certainty of the tell-tale trail, he could afford to gamble. Two hours later Slim became indignant and wondered if Cimarron's black-and-white had grown wings, for his *segundo*'s dust did not suit his mouth and eyes.

"He can do it with me," muttered Slim, "but that Pepper hoss won't be seen by any of us till she stops. I hope Nelson ain't killin' her."

The Pepper horse was neither stopping nor being killed. She skimmed along with no faltering in her stride as though she remembered a day in a quicksand. There was a debt to be paid, and if heart held out and the heaving sides did not prove false to her thoroughbred courage, the lengthening shadows would see it canceled before they became lost in the day's deepening twilight. Down a narrow valley she sped, the hills rolling the tattoo of her drumming hoofs as though they liked the sound and were reluctant to let it die. Taking a brook at a bound and scorning her rising thirst, she swirled around a sharp bend, and twitched her ears suddenly forward, the quick pressure of her rider's knees telling her that he had seen.

Johnny slipped his Sharp's from its long sheath and, holding it at the ready, stood up in his stirrups, his horse somewhere finding a reserve power that fairly hurled her forward, the trim black legs whirring under her like flashing spokes of jet. The rider's lids narrowed to thin slits and the tight-pressed lips pressed tighter. Yard after yard he gained, second after second. The half mile became a quarter, steadily lessened and then, Pepper pounding over a stretch of rocky ground where the hammering of her hoofs rang out loudly, there was a quick turning in the saddles ahead, and a roar from the saddle behind, a ragged cloud of acrid smoke tearing itself to filmy bits and blending with the suddenly tenuous dust cloud in the rear.

Big Tom cursed in sudden rage and whirled his horse behind Margaret's, his rifle spitting past her shoulder. His shelter bolted from in front of him as a Sharp's Special stung the SV horse, its rider barely able to keep her seat during the convulsive lunge. Big Tom leaped down behind his mount and rested the gun across the saddle. Before he could pull the trigger another Special passed through the animal's abdomen and, its force spent, struck his belt and doubled him up, gasping for breath as the agonized animal leaped forward. The cantle of the saddle, striking the barrel of the Winchester, tore the weapon from its owner's hands and left him, slowly straightening up, with a Colt for his only defense.

Coming at him like a skimming swallow sped Pepper, her rider, having slipped the rifle back into its long sheath, standing erect in the stirrups, each hand holding a Colt. For a moment they were held aloft and then as the Bar H foreman drew his six-gun they chopped down and poured jets of flame and puffs of smoke over Pepper's head. The foreman twisted, fired aimlessly, lurched, fired again, and plunged forward, face down on the sand. Johnny slid his guns back into their holsters and raced for Margaret, who was fighting a pain-crazed horse.

Slim and Cimarron, neck and neck now, jumped the brook, sped along the little valley, keyed to fighting pitch by the sound of distant shots, and flashed around the bend, where they pulled up sharply and looked across the level pasture.

"H—l!" growled Cimarron. "I thought we was ridin' to

a lynchin'! This here looks more like a weddin'. Get back, around that bend, you fool!"

"It shore does," said Slim, grinning. "A weddin', huh? Well, then, I says he's still a-rollin'."